The FINAL COUNTRY

The FINAL COUNTRY

JAMES CRUMLEY

Published by Warner Books

An AOL Time Warner Company

Copyright © 2001 by James Crumley
All rights reserved.

 Mysterious Press books are published by Warner Books, Inc., 1271 Avenue of the Americas, New York, NY 10020.

Visit our Web site at www.twbookmark.com.

For information on Time Warner Trade Publishing's online program, visit www.ipublish.com.

 An AOL Time Warner Company

The Mysterious Press name and logo are registered trademarks of Warner Books, Inc.

Printed in the United States of America

First Printing: October 2001

10   9   8   7   6   5   4   3   2   1

Library of Congress Cataloging-in-Publication Data
   Crumley, James
      The final country / James Crumley.
         p. cm.
      ISBN 0-89296-666-1
      1. Milodragovitch, Milo (Fictitious character)—Fiction. 2. Private Investigators—Fiction.
3. Texas—Fiction. I. Title.

PS3553.R78 F56 2001
813'.54—dc21   2001030640

For Martha Elizabeth, again.

Author's note:

There is no Gatlin County in Texas.

The country is most barbarously large and final. It is too much country—boondock country—alternately drab and dazzling, spectral and remote. It is so wrongfully muddled and various that it is difficult to conceive of it as all of a piece. Though it begins simply enough, as part of the other.

It begins, very much like the other, in an ancient backwash of old dead seas and lambent estuaries . . .

Billy Lee Brammer
The Gay Place

Montana seems to me to be what a small boy would think Texas is like from hearing Texans.

John Steinbeck
Travels with Charley

CHAPTER ONE

I T WAS LATE NOVEMBER on the edge of the Hill Country, but
I had learned very quickly that down here nothing was ever quite
what it seemed. As I drove through northwest Austin that day, it
might as well have been spring. The thin leaves of the pecan trees
hadn't turned. People still mowed their lawns in T-shirts and shorts.
Or in this upscale neighborhood, watched various illegal aliens hustle like dung beetles back and forth across the thick St. Augustine
lawns through scattershot swarms of gnats. Overhead a brilliant afternoon sun floated in the rich blue sky polished cloudless by the
soft southeastern breezes. A single buzzard overhead seemed to be
keeping a weathered eye on things. Winter seemed a distant
promise, bound to be broken.

Back home in Montana fall already would be hard upon the
land, a thick mantle of snow draped across the peaks and high ridges
around the Meriwether Valley, the cottonwood branches fingerbone
bare, the western larch golden among the dark pines, and the willow
aflame along the frost-limned creeks. Of course, back home I would
be working my ass off, laying in ten cords of firewood for the win-

ter coming, falling and bucking and splitting pine and fir and alder until my hands bled and my back ached like a heart attack.

This was my fifth fall in Texas, and I had to admit my aging bones hadn't completely forgotten how to dread Montana winters, although the memories seemed as dim as sunlight dazed by a late spring snowstorm. But when the Caddy's automatic air conditioner kicked on, I was reminded that nothing was free in this world. The winter price had to be paid in one way or the other. The vents still carried the stench of a bad weekend with my woman down at her uncle's ornate beach house north of Port Aransas. The air was still thick with the stink of the coastal marshes and mud flats, the spoil banks and tidal pools, the place where everything begins—or ends—where the land rises slowly from the shallow sea like the flesh of a drowned corpse oozing through watery skin. A chase after money and revenge had brought me to Texas, and a woman, Betty Porterfield, had kept me here. But as our love failed, I found myself homesick for Montana more often than now and again.

I was on the job this afternoon, though, so I pushed Montana out of my mind as I cruised toward the southern border of Gatlin County where it nestled like a sluggish political afterthought into the rich, fat software back of northwestern Travis County. Even though I owned a bar the southwestern side of the county, I'd never been in this unincorporated part tucked along the breaks of the Balcones Escarpment. Surrounded by the urban sprawl, this area didn't even have a name. Lalo Herrera, whose sons managed my bar, had told me that the locals sometimes called it *el Rincón Malo*, "the Bad Corner." Whatever the place might be called, though, it was just another un-zoned trashy suburban slum. The limestone slopes were spotted with dusty cedar shrubs, and the narrow potholed street sported two convenience stores on opposite corners wrestling for the beer, bait, and overpriced gasoline concession, and one locker–cum–butcher shop where the local hunters converted their little whitetail deer into dry-smoked sausage or stinky hamburger threaded with hair. Several flashy but cheaply built apartment complexes littered the steep hillsides, surrounding a mobile home park that looked neither mobile nor homey.

Not even the great weather could hide the disorder and deep sorrow here, as the pastoral degenerated into unplanned urban sprawl. I could almost smell the bitter energies of change and failure. And not just the Bad Corner's. I seemed to be in some sort of downhill tumble myself, going from bad to worse as I stumbled through the transition from a semiemployed private eye to a solid citizen and back down again. A few years before, I had recovered my father's stolen inheritance, plus a considerable sum of unlaundered drug funds stashed in an offshore bank, and I had real money for the first time in my life. Lots of it.

But it didn't change my life all that much. Bored and looking for a way to get out of Betty's ranch house, and perhaps, too, hoping to wash a bit of the drug money, I had gone into business with her uncle, Travis Lee Wallingford, investing in the final stages of an upscale motel, the Blue Hollow Lodge, on the southeastern border of Gatlin County.

I also signed on to own and run the bar in the western corner of the Lodge, the Low Water Crossing Bar and Grill. But my enterprising businessman act had worn thin very quickly. So I drifted back into what I knew best, shuffling through the emotional debris of other people's lives, telling myself that going back into private investigation was just a harmless hobby—like building sailing ships in whiskey bottles or collecting beer cans—a silly diversion of late middle age. I picked up a Texas license, put up my own bond, and had taken to spending my free afternoons piddling around at detective work. Mostly pissant jobs no self-respecting private investigator would take.

One of these jobs had brought me to the Bad Corner and a flagstone-and-barnwood beer joint called Over the Line, even though the faded sign painted on the sideboards still clearly stated that it had originally been called Duval's Place. A shy, middle-aged high school teacher up in Burnet County had offered me five hundred dollars to find his young wife, Carol Jean, although I suspected that

Joe Warren didn't want his young wife back as much as he wanted something to show for the retirement fund money he had squandered on her orthodontics and breast implants. At least that was the impression I had gotten when he showed me her picture. Carol Jean had one of those narrow but pretty country faces—large, over-painted eyes and full red lips smiling bravely around an overbite only slightly restrained behind a field of barbed wire—all of it tucked like a child's Easter egg into the tangled nest of her big, blond hair. The half-moons of her new breasts peeked shyly over the neckline of her blouse, and her sly, metallic smile suggested that these new babies had changed her from a skinny high school girl into a woman with whom to be reckoned. In the six years since Carol Jean had graduated from high school and married Joe Warren, instead of looking pretty, canning peaches, and popping kids for Baby Joe, she had worked as a hairdresser, cocktail waitress, legal secretary, and a kick-boxing instructor at a health club. But the only thing that her heart really fancied was hustling pool in afternoon beer joints. Sometimes at Over the Line. Information that six margaritas and a line of bullshit had bought me from Carol Jean's hairdresser mom.

As I pulled the El Dorado into the parking lot beside three pickups and a battered Suburban, I tossed my sunglasses into the glove box with my S&W Airweight .38, then locked it. I had taken a spent .25 round in the guts some years before, lost eighteen inches of intestine and much of my fondness for sidearms. I hadn't carried a piece very often since then. If Carol Jean was here today, I could only hope she wouldn't shoot me. Or bite me. Or hit me with her new tits.

But before I could ease out of the sour mood and the El Dorado, a black Lincoln Town Car with Oklahoma dealer tags slid into the lot with locked brakes, raising a veil of dust that almost obscured the fine afternoon. The black guy who stepped out of the Town Car wasn't any larger than a church or any more incongruous than a nun with a beard. Six nine or ten and an iron-hard two-ninety. Above his dark shades, his shaved head gleamed coppery and metallic like the jacket on a high-powered rifle round. His black leather pants rippled like a second skin and his bloused red shirt announced itself like a matador's cape. And the way he walked across the lot shouted "yard boss," as if he had survived a ton of hard time somewhere and was damn sure ready to do it all over again.

When the big guy slammed through the swinging doors of the beer joint, the hinges squealed and the doors flapped like sheets in a rising wind. I thought about postponing my quest for Carol Jean. But, as usual, once I had started looking for somebody, I made the mistake of feeling vaguely responsible for them. So I climbed out and headed for the joint. Before I got there, though, I heard a nasal drawl, shouting, "Watch out, you fuckin' nigger!" And moments later a large Chicano kid streaming blood from a pancaked nose tumbled out of the joint, staggered to his feet, then ran for the safety of his pickup truck. When I reached for the doors, Carol Jean crashed into my arms, her salty new tits as hard as the custom cue clutched in her hands. Dressed in skintight jeans and a tank top that could have been painted on her torso, I assumed her opponents spent more time watching Carol Jean than the table. She was taller than she looked in her photograph, and without braces, prettier, too, but I had been right on about the attitude. She turned, raised the cue like an axe, and headed back into the beer joint.

"I wouldn't do that if I were you," I said.

"And why the hell not?"

"There won't be enough of you left to fuck, sugar," I suggested. "Besides, you're holding it all wrong."

But Carol Jean wasn't having any of it. Where reason fails, try money. I slipped a twenty off my money clip, handed it to her.

"Just wait over there by that Cadillac, and I'll give you another one when I come out."

Still Carol Jean hesitated, her head cocked like a fairly bright chicken, until a redneck kid flew out of the front window and landed like a sack of shit in a pile of broken glass.

"Hi, Vernon," she said calmly, but the kid wasn't up to answering. "Okay, man," she added to me, "I don't know what you're doing, but if you don't come back, I'll take the other one off your dead body." Then she laughed, a sound as shrill as worn brake pads.

"Thanks for the vote of confidence," I said, hitched up my jeans, arranged my mouth into my most beguiling smile, and sauntered into the shadows like a dumb tourist.

The bar had been built into the slope, giving it two levels: pool tables and booths on the lower level in front, a short bar and half a dozen tables about four feet higher in the back. The large black gentleman hadn't quite made it to the upper level yet. Another sizable black guy in a Dallas Cowboys jersey leaned over a pool table, leaking blood and broken teeth onto the felt—the big guy seemed to be an equal opportunity disaster area—and a rat-faced beer-joint cowboy had a cue raised over his head, his narrow mouth curled in contempt, but when he brought the cue down, the big guy casually blocked it with a muscular forearm. The cue snapped briskly, and the handle weight spun out to slam the already damaged Cowboys fan in the forehead with a sound like an egg dropped on a sidewalk. He disappeared behind the pool table as if shot. The cowboy grinned apologetically, then dashed past me as fast as his tight jeans and high-heeled boots would let him.

"Next time use it like a bayonet," I suggested as the cowboy stumbled past, "not a club."

"You must not be from around here," the big guy said softly. "Most of these Texas assholes are dumber than hammered dogshit."

"Nobody ever accused me of being from around here," I said as I stepped up to stand beside the big guy, who loomed over me like an unstable rock outcropping.

"Whatever," he said, slapping me on the shoulder hard enough to make my knees flex. But the huge hand on my shoulder was polite instead of insistent. "Let's you and me have a drink, old man."

It's the hair, I thought. Several white streaks had appeared after a bad session with a bunch of *contrabandistas* a few years before. *I'm not as old as I look*, I started to say. But I could tell that the big guy wasn't interested. So I followed him up the short stairway, where we leaned against the bar.

"I don't mind a little whip-ass, when it's deserved," the chubby bartender said as he leaned on the bar, "and that Meskin kid was way outa line." He was a soft, round-faced man with a fat, bald head. "I don't want to have to call the law," he maintained stoutly. But I suspected he had delivered this line a few times before without success.

"Just shut the fuck up," the big guy said as he set his shades on the bar, "and pour us a drink. I ain't had time for a peaceful drink since I left Tulsa this morning. How about a couple of handfuls of that Crown Royal over a little ice."

The bartender found two water glasses and filled them with ice and whiskey. The big guy nuzzled his drink for a second, then poured it down his throat. I nibbled around the edges of mine.

"Goddamn that was good, man," the big guy said, then he noticed my drink. "Come on," he said, laughing and dropping his hand like a grubbing-hoe handle on my shoulder. If he wasn't careful, the big son of a bitch was going to kill me with affection. With his shades off, his eyes were an oddly gray shade of light blue, shining like tiny bulbs on either side of his hooked nose. "When you drink with Enos Walker, man, we don't allow no sipping."

You might as well argue with an avalanche, so I dumped mine down my throat, too, though I didn't enjoy it nearly as much as Enos Walker had.

"Set us up again, bartender," he said, "then I want to have a word with somebody who knew that fuckin' Duval."

The bartender's hand shook a little this time as he poured, then he rubbed his sweaty head as if it had suddenly sprouted hair. "Ah, Mr. Duval ain't been here for some time . . ."

"I just been in jail, motherfucker," the big guy said as he held up his second bundle of whiskey, "not on the moon. Who the hell's in charge these days? Either Duval's buddies or that fuckin' silver-haired bitch—"

"Mandy Rae?" the bartender interrupted, then snapped his mouth shut as if the name hurt his teeth.

"—one of 'em owes me big-time, chubby."

"I don't rightly know nothin' 'bout that," the bartender said.

"Well, who the hell you reckon might know," Walker said, leaning easily over the bar and burying his index finger to the first joint in the bartender's pudgy chest, "Mr. Fucking Pillsbury Doughboy?"

"Ah, maybe Mr. Long knows," he answered with a tortured sigh.

"Billy Long? I remember that redneck piece of shit. Where is he?"

"He's in the office," the bartender said, thumbing over his shoulder, "but I don't think he wants to be bothered right now."

"No bother," Enos Walker said, then gunned his drink and headed around the bar.

The bartender mopped his head with a bar towel, chugged a bubbling drink straight from the bottle, then sighed deeply as his right hand drifted under the counter. I reached over to pinch his snotty upper lip. Hard.

"What have you got under there?"

"Sawed-off double twelve," the bartender whimpered as the whiskey courage squirted out of him like puppy piss.

"Better let me have it," I said, "before somebody gets hurt. Stock first, if you don't mind."

The bartender handed me the shotgun, and got his upper lip back in return. I broke the piece open, ejected both shells, and handed it back to him just as we heard loud voices from the office. The shouting ended with an even louder gunshot.

"Oh my God," the bartender moaned and shoved the sawed-off deeply into the ice.

Enos Walker came back to the bar, not hurrying, a huge semi-automatic pistol dangling from his hand. Probably one of those Desert Eagle .50 cannons, I thought. "Is everybody in this fucking place stupid?" he asked, waving arms like small logs, but I didn't think he wanted an answer. Walker shoved the pistol under his belt, slipped on his shades, and said, "You ain't finished your drink, old man."

"I think I've had enough," I said. Unfortunately, getting older had not made me any smarter.

"Don't push your luck."

"Fuck it," I said and left the drink on the bar.

"Maybe you ain't as smart as I thought you were, old man," he said.

"I expect that wasn't your first mistake today."

That nearly kicked it into the cesspool. But suddenly Enos Walker grinned and placed his hands gently on my shoulders, smiled, then said, "You got balls, old man." Then he laughed his bitter, hopeless, hard-timer breath right into my face, breath as rank as the winter den of a grizzly. He picked up my drink, slowly poured it down his throat, grabbed the remains of the bottle from the bartender, then left without a backward glance. As he hit the door, the bartender let out his breath, then leaned against the back bar while he guzzled another drink. I headed to the back to check the damage, which was, as I suspected, extensive.

Long had been a tall man with long gray hair, perhaps even good-looking before the muzzle blast had burned off his face and the heavy round had scattered the back half of his head all over the whorehouse wallpaper and a Troy Aikman poster behind him. A clot of hairy gray matter hung from the quarterback's upper lip like an incipient mustache. I thought the kid looked better with some hair on his face.

The bartender peeked around the edge of the office door, then hit the floor in a dead faint. I checked his pulse and made sure that he hadn't swallowed his tongue, then pulled him over to the side and propped up his feet on a chair. As I did, a meaty fart fizzled out of his backside.

I went back to the office. From the look of the desk— cluttered with scales, folded and unfolded Snowseal bindles, milk sugar, and a Jack Daniel's bar mirror—Long had been cutting cocaine and breaking it down into grams, but there was no sign of the source, an ounce bag at least, which was probably riding away in Enos Walker's leather pocket. The right-hand drawer of the desk was partially open; an empty cash box, a Rolodex, and a partial box of .50 Magnum pistol rounds were visible.

"Stupid bastard," I said, but wasn't sure who I was talking to.

Because I used the nail of my little finger to flip through the Rolodex to the Ds and wrote down the telephone and address of the only Duval listed, somebody named Sissy. But that wasn't the real stupid part. I wrote it down on the back of the largest bindle, the one that had "mine" scrawled on it. Maybe it's a clue, I thought, as I shoved the bindle into my shirt pocket.

The battered black guy in the Cowboys jersey had disappeared when I went back through the empty joint. I picked up the only purse I saw and a custom cue case with CJW embossed on it. Outside, Carol Jean leaned against the fender of the El Dorado, looking sweetly befuddled, the tip of her tongue sticking out of the corner of her mouth as she concentrated, twirling her cue like a demented majorette.

"Took you long enough," she said, not looking at me. "I would have gone with that big black dude. But he didn't ask."

"A piece of luck, sugar."

"What the hell happened in there, anyway?" she asked. "Sounded like a bomb or something."

"Something," I said. "You got wheels?"

"Nope. I came with Vernon, but he jumped in his pickup and took off like a spotted-ass ape."

"How about money?"

"Baby Joe sent you, huh?" Carol Jean said as she dangled the twenty from her crimson nails.

I nodded as I dug out another one, then handed it to her. "Listen, kid, carry your ass over to that telephone booth across the street," I said, "and call a cab."

"Shit, man, I can get a ride."

"I'll just bet your sweet ass you can," I said, "and that's probably a better idea anyway. Go home to the hubby, lie like a Navajo rug . . ."

"A Navajo rug?"

"Complex but serene, simple but beautiful," I explained.

"Are you on drugs, man?"

"Just high on life," I said, "and happy to be alive."

"At your age you should be."

"Listen," I said, slightly miffed, "just keep your head down for a couple of months. I'll tell the cops I missed you, and you tell them you were at home watching soap operas."

"That bad, huh," she said, then finally stopped twirling to look at me.

"Let's just say that Mr. Long lost his head," I said.

"Jeez," she whispered. "Anybody get hurt?"

"Hey, next time you want to take off, at least talk to Baby Joe first. He's a little miffed about the teeth and the tits."

"Things change," she said as she broke down and packed her cue. "But never quite enough," she added sadly, then just as quickly grinned brightly, as lively as a baby chick. "Is that what you do for a living? Find people?"

"Hard times, people, lost dogs," I said as I lit a cigarette.

"Want to see these puppies, old man?" she asked, smiling as she cupped her new breasts.

"Not right now, sugar," I said, "I've got a headache."

Carol Jean squealed with laughter. It sparkled like a wire behind my eyes. She pranced out of the parking lot, then across the highway, where she stuck out her thumb. The first passing pickup smoked its tires stopping to give her a ride.

Truth is, I would have liked nothing better than to rest my weary head on her firm young chest. Maybe it would wash the image of the dead man out of my head. But I knew better. Nothing ever really washed the images of the dead away, not tears, or time, or whiskey. At eleven, I'd seen my father on the floor of his den, the top half of his head demolished by a Purdey double-barrel. Some years later, but not long enough to suit me, when I was stuck in a muddy front-line trench in Korea near the end of the war, everywhere I looked, everybody looked dead. Except the dead don't blink. So I finished the cigarette, ground the butt into the settling dust, walked across the road to the dirtier convenience store, stashed the bindle behind the toilet tank, bought a couple of beers, then went back to the empty joint to call the cops, preparing myself for their serene complexity.

Of course, it wasn't that simple. Absolutely nothing in Texas had been simple yet. The bartender had revived and disappeared, and I didn't want to be in the office, so I dialed 911 from the pay telephone in the parking lot. When the dispatcher answered, I told her that there had been a shooting at a place called Over the Line. "Again," she immediately said as if she were a regular, then asked for my name and the details.

I thought about lying, wiping my prints and heading for Montana—but elk season was probably over and it was too late to catch the brown trout run on the Upper Yellowstone—so I decided against running. I had too much invested in Texas now.

After several hours of the usual cop rigmarole, most of it done by rote because everybody knew Billy Long was headed to no good end, I wound up in a small gray office filled with the inevitable paperwork clutter of a cop's life in the limestone fortress of the Gatlin County courthouse across a messy desk from a large, paunchy man with tired gray eyes and an even more exhausted suit.

"Mr. Milodragovitch, I'm Captain James Gannon, chief of detectives for the Gatlin County Sheriff's Department," he said in some sort of gravelly East Coast accent, "and I've got some good news for you. We found the bartender at home—one Leonard Wilbur—and when we sobered him up a little bit, he verified your story."

"I can go home?"

"They're typing up your statement right now," he said, ignoring me. It was clear Gannon was a street cop disguised as a deputy sheriff and that he wasn't ever going to answer a question. "There's a couple of things bothering me. Maybe you can set me straight."

"I feel a little more cooperative now," I said. "Your deputies pushed me pretty hard."

"They're just kids and they've covered a lot of confused and bad calls at Billy Long's place," Gannon said, but it didn't even border on an apology. Then he rubbed his worn face. "Well, sir, I'm a bit concerned about the fact that we couldn't find the bulk cocaine that Long was cutting. Not even with the dogs. We found the cut stuff. But not the other."

"I wouldn't know anything about that, Captain."

"And then you wouldn't let my boys go through your vehicle without a search warrant . . ."

"Which they got very quickly."

"Well, things move pretty quickly in a small county down here, and in spite of urban sprawl, this is a very *small* county," he said, sighing, "but you know what your refusal says to me?"

"No."

"Well, sir, to me it says 'ex-con' or 'ex-cop.'"

Gannon knew exactly who I was, but it was easier to play his game. "I was a deputy sheriff a long time ago," I said, "up in Meriwether County, Montana. And I held a private investigator's license up there for a long time and I'm duly licensed and bonded in the state of Texas."

"Oh shit," Gannon said, shaking his head in mock surprise. "You're the guy who owns the bar at the Blue Hollow Lodge? How the hell did you ever get a liquor license with your record? Hell, the Gov did it for you, didn't he?"

"Mr. Wallingford and I are partners in the motel," I said, calmly, "but I own the bar outright." Travis Lee Wallingford had served half a dozen terms in the state legislature from Gatlin County, both the House and the Senate, both as a Democrat and a Republican, but he was always more interested in inflammatory oratory than detail, and his favorite speech involved an empty threat to run for governor, a position that in the morass of Texas government was usually reserved for a figurehead, rich men or unsuccessful politicians at the end of their careers. So lots of people referred to him as the Gov, and not always in a flattering way. "And in spite of any rumors you may

have heard, I don't have a record of any kind. Down here or anywhere," I said.

"Whatever," Gannon groaned dramatically, "you've got too
much local clout for me, Mr. Milodragovitch. Just sign your statement and be on your merry way." Then Gannon paused to rub his
face again. "Goddammit," he said as he jerked his tie open, "sometimes I wonder why the hell I ever took this job . . ." Then he buried
his face in his hands again.

"You playing on my sympathy, Captain? Good cop and bad cop
at the same time?"

Gannon peeked like a child through his thick fingers, then lifted
his smiling face. "Hey, it's a small department, everybody's got to
cover two or three jobs."

"What the hell are you doing down here?"

"My son-in-law teaches at UT," he said. "I came down here to
be close to the grandkids and . . ."

"Where from?"

"Bayonne, New Jersey," Gannon said. "What the hell are you
doing down here?" he asked as if he really wanted to know.

Even the dumbest cop had to be an actor occasionally, and I
suspected that Gannon was far from dumb. "A woman," I answered
honestly.

"Ain't it the shits," he said. "Truth is my ex-wife moved down
here after the divorce. She followed the grandkids down here, and I
tagged along like a piece of dogshit stuck to her shoe. Damn woman
took off after twenty-six years of marital bliss . . ."

"Hell, I've been married five times, and all of them don't add up
to half that."

"Look," Gannon said suddenly, taking my revolver and license
out of a drawer, then leaned over the desk, clasping his meaty hands
together, "can I put it to you straight?"

"Nobody wants to be fucked without a kiss." I had never gotten
along all that well with cops even when I was one, so I braced myself for whatever bullshit Gannon had in mind.

"Walker stepped out of McAlester this morning. Served a long jolt for possession with intent to sell and some other shit. Stopped at a bank, probably for a stash of money nobody could ever find, a Lincoln dealership, then drove straight down here, and killed Billy Long. Probably revenge for a coke deal gone bad."

"I didn't see it that way," I said.

"Doesn't matter," Gannon said. "Billy Long's a known slimebag, but Walker's a dead man down here, no matter what. Hell, there's more handguns than cows in this state, and since the governor signed that new carry law, almost everybody's got one concealed on their person. If some hotshot rookie or dipshit civilian doesn't get him, the needle will. And a guy that size, he won't be all that hard to find. He's probably gone to ground down in Travis County. He's got family in Austin. That's his old stomping ground, where he first went into the cocaine business big-time," Gannon said, "and Austin or Travis County, well, they don't give a rat's ass about me. Or my job."

"Your job?"

"The sheriff who decided he needed a big-city cop to prepare for big-city crime and hired me to organize his detective division . . . Well, he died last year," Gannon said, "and this new guy, Benson, he sure enough hates my Yankee ass. He's not about to let me make it to retirement, if he can help it. I may be the most unpopular peace officer in the state of Texas. Hell, if I don't end up in the slam, I'll end up shaking doorknobs until I'm sixty-five, and eating dog food till I die. But if I could put my hands on this Enos Walker skell, I'd be locked until my time is in.

"Because you're freelance and because of your connections, Mr. Milodragovitch, you've got resources I can't touch," he continued, "and you can go places I can't go."

"You didn't see this big bastard in action," I said. "I'm looking forward to spending my twilight years in one piece."

"Which is why you're chasing this nickel-and-dime shit? Run-away wives? Give me a break," he said, waving his stubby arms. "What's next? Lost dogs?"

"Man likes to keep his hand in," I said. "And, what the hell,

once I made ten grand dognapping a stolen Labrador retriever from
a bunch of Japanese bird hunters in Alberta."

"Whatever," Gannon interrupted, not interested. "You're not
exactly at the height of your career right now, are you?"

"Hey, fuck it, man," I said, trying to smile. "I'm good at what I
do. I'm just about the only son of bitch in the world ever repossessed
a combine in a wheat field. Drove the pig all the way to Hardin at
three miles an hour. Made more money that day than you make in
a year. So don't run that career shit at me."

"Right," Gannon said, shrugging. "Look at it this way. Your
bar's in my county, not too far down the road. Maybe I'll stop in for
a drink someday."

"I hope that's not a threat, Captain," I said, no longer smiling
but trying to be polite. I was in the process of laundering the stolen
drug money through the bar, and I didn't need even the smallest bit
of heat.

Gannon stood up quickly, opened his arms, and grinned. "Jeez,
I sure as hell hope it didn't sound that way," he said, moving around
the desk. "I sure as hell didn't mean it like that. Just thought that
both of us being strangers down here, you might hear something I
can use."

"As far as I can tell, Captain, everybody down here is either a
stranger or strange." *And getting stranger by the minute,* I might have
added.

"Hell, listen, we'll have that drink anyway. And there's no reason for you to wait around to sign your statement. I'll have one of
my boys run it over to you tomorrow."

"Maybe I'll just wait."

"You know, I'm like that. Favors from strangers make me nervous, too," Gannon said. "But we'll tip a few and maybe we won't
be strangers anymore."

Then he reached out his broad, thick hand. I shook it as well as
I could with my fingers crossed. I still had Walker's hard-timer's
breath in my mouth, the dingy stench of prison in my nose, and
could still feel the friendly grip of his huge hands on my shoulders.

At the end of summer before my senior year in high school, during that brief period between the time my job pulling the green chain at the mill ended and two-a-day football practices started, I had a free weekend. My football buddies and I had filled the backs of our rigs with ice and cases of Great Falls Select, then driven up a jeep trail deep in the Diablo Mountains to my grandfather's land so we could celebrate our brief release by getting shit-faced in the wilderness, a hoary Montana tradition.

We built a huge fire and drank ourselves stupid as we danced half-naked around it, as innocently savage as any beasts that ever lived. Until the bear showed up. About midnight, a curious black bear cub, drawn by the noise or the smell of the burned elk burgers, nosed into the circle of firelight, sniffing as if he wanted to join the dance.

Once when my father and I were fly fishing up Six Mile, a black bear had come up to the bluff across the creek. I must have been four or five, old enough to be curious and young enough to be nervous. He told me that if I wanted the bear to move on to bark like a dog. I barked as loud and long as I could. The sow scrambled up the nearest tree. "Sometimes, they'll do that," my Dad said.

So when I saw the cub, I started barking. Within moments, my buddies had joined me, and the little devil scooted up a bull pine, where he swung precariously from a thick branch, hissing and spitting like a tomcat.

We laughed like madmen at the frightened cub, swept by gales of drunken mirth, until I spun and fell on my back at the base of the pine, my mouth wide open. The cub spit straight down into my mouth, a skunky stream of saliva, more solid than liquid, which I swallowed before I could stop. An electric moment. Suddenly I was sober and sorry for the cub. But I couldn't stop my friends from laughing and barking. I punched and shoved and wrestled them, but they thought I was crazy and wouldn't stop. I fought them to a standstill. Or until they got tired of beating on me. Nobody re-

members which came first. Then they decided what they really
needed was a road trip to the whorehouses in Wallace, Idaho, another hoary Montana tradition, so they drove down the mountain,
leaving me with a couple of six-packs and a very sore head. I sat by
the dying fire until dawn, the stink of the bear in my mouth, my
nose, and seeping through my guts. The raspy sound of the bear's
breath echoed in my head. When the sun cleared the saddle below
Hammerhead Peak, we both went home. I never looked at a bear the
same way again—or my friends, for that matter—and never got that
wild taste out of my mouth. *Leave me alone, fool*, it seemed to say,
we're in this shit together.

Something else had changed that night, too, but I didn't know
what until much later. Turned out that it was the end of my childhood. After football season, after a shouting match with my crazy,
drunken mother—she had accused me of only going hunting in
eastern Montana so I could go whoring in Livingston like my
worthless, dead father, which was only half-true—I said I was leaving for good, and she said "good riddance to bad rubbish." Three
days later she signed the papers lying about my age, and I was in the
Army, where I learned a bitter lesson about fear. But I never lost the
taste of that bear. We were brothers, somehow, in this life and death
together.

I shook Gannon's hand, reluctantly. Whatever had happened in
Long's office, and whatever Enos Walker had done, he was a man
like me. If he lived long enough to make it to court, chances were,
with the testimony of the bartender and me, Walker could cop a
self-defense or involuntary manslaughter plea and wouldn't have to
die at the hands of a state I found much too fond of the needle. I
knew the sweet taste of revenge, but living in a place that killed people with such casual aplomb made me a little jumpy. In the long run
the death penalty had nothing to do with revenge or deterrence. It
was just a way for the fools to get elected.

CHAPTER TWO

I T TOOK LONGER to find the bartender than it did for me to find out that he wouldn't give me the time of day. For a man who seemed without much backbone, he suddenly bowed up his neck and stayed grimly silent. Either he was more frightened of somebody else than me, or he had some sort of protection that I couldn't find out about.

So Sissy Duval was my only lead. She lived in a fancy ground-floor condo on the south side of Town Lake, which she owned outright, as she did her fairly new BMW 7 series, but except for a small trust fund from her father and several modest alimony checks, she didn't seem to have any visible means of support. And Sissy was her real name. All of which Carver de Longchampe discovered in a quick Internet search. Carver D had retired from the underground newspaper business when he sold *The Dark Coast* to an alternative chain but that hadn't stopped him from being nosy; he was connected to every information database known to be legal and some I suspected weren't.

When I rang Sissy Duval's bell late the next afternoon, the door was half-opened by a well-dressed black woman with light dusky skin, fine features, and frosted streaks in her straight hair.

"Mrs. Duval?" I said, and the black woman looked at me as if I had cowshit on my boots.

"It doesn't matter who I am," she growled, "whatever you're selling, we've got at least two. Now if you'll excuse me, sir, I'm on my way out."

Before I could step back, though, a sleepy voice came from beyond the half-open door. "Who is it, Eldora?"

"Well, it ain't your date, honey," the black woman said as she opened the door all the way. Some decorator had gone through the living room in his beige-beach period—driftwood, glass, and sketches of sandy tan, wall to wall.

"Bobby Mitchell ain't coming, honey," said a tall, lanky white woman with tousled hair as she drifted into the room.

"Old bastard's seventy-five if he's a day, and he still wants to be called Bobby," the black woman muttered. But I didn't think she was talking to me.

"Bobby says his colon's acting up again," Sissy Duval said as she stepped up to the door. Except for skin color, the two women could have been sisters.

"Well, this gentleman might be full of shit, honey, but he doesn't look like he has a problem with a lower bowel blockage. Maybe he'll take you to the benefit," the black woman said, "after he scatters his bullshit around and sells you another set of aluminum cookware. Or maybe one of those vacuum cleaners that'll suck the dust mites out of your mattress."

"I'm not selling anything," I said as the black woman brushed past.

"Not to me, you aren't," she said.

"See you tomorrow, Eldora," Mrs. Duval said, but she was looking directly at me. And smiling as she estimated my value within five thousand dollars and my age within ten days. She'd never see forty again, and nobody would ever know which one of the myriad shades of her hair might be real, and she'd never actually worked a day in her life, but she had good bones and the Texas sun hadn't turned her skin into a roast duck hide yet. She cocked her hip, rested her diamond-studded hand on it, and smiled innocently. "And how can I help you, sir?" she asked. A question, I suspected, many men had rushed to answer.

I introduced myself, showed her my license, and told her that I would like to talk about her former husband. That seemed a good place to start her talking, since I knew she had several.

"I ain't got nothin' but exes, honey," she said, "and Jesus, they all live in Texas." Then she sighed deeply. "It's five o'clock somewhere," she said. "I'm gonna have a vodka. Can I get you something?"

"Maybe a beer," I said. It seemed that I could still feel my guts burning from the four ounces of Canadian whiskey Enos Walker had made me drink the day before. But the beach atmosphere in the room called for something liquid.

"So which one of the bastards are you looking for?" she asked over her straight vodka after she had lodged me on a raw cotton couch and handed me a Shiner and a frosted glass.

"The one that owned a joint up in Gatlin County."

"Oh, Dwayne, the only one that doesn't live in Texas. He's dead," she said, which I didn't know. She walked over to lean on the mantel of the gas fireplace. "Dwayne had a great ass. So I kept his name and his ashes right here to remind me to stay away from honky-tonk cowboys." She patted a ceramic pot on the mantel, then knuckled a tear from the corner of her eye. "That boy sure could dance," she said fondly.

"I'm sorry, Mrs. Duval," I said. "How long were you married?"

"As long as I had a hundred thousand dollars a year to shovel up his nose and keep his tight little buns out of jail," she answered, and finished her vodka, surely not the first of the afternoon, then poured another without freshening the ice. Then she began to rummage through the drawers of the small wet bar in the corner of the living room. "You got a cigarette?" she said as she leaned on the bar.

"Sure," I said, then walked over to lean on the bar across from her. Not a bad place for an aimless interrogation.

"Goddammit," she said once we were smoking. She reached back into the top drawer, where she found a small mirror, a single-edged razor blade, and a short silver straw. "Every time I think about that son of a bitch, it makes me want to smoke and snort cocaine like some East Austin street whore," she said. "I know I had some blow in here somewhere . . ." But she wasn't talking to me anymore. After a few minutes of clattering about, she stood up to dump more vodka in her glass and looked at me as if I had just appeared, saying, "You wouldn't have any, would you?" Then she said, "Oh, shit, you're not a cop or something, are you?"

"I think I fit into the 'or something' category. But I've got a taste." I had retrieved Long's personal bindle from the convenience store rest room that morning, and broken it down into smaller bindles, managing to do just a couple of tiny lines of the uncut coke. Cocaine, like alcohol, was a fucking snake, and I'd had troubles with both. And not that long ago, either. I poured a tidy sparkling pile on the mirror and chopped two short but shapely lines.

"You first," she said suspiciously when I offered her the straw. She looked ten years older, the fine bones almost visible through the clear skin.

I did my line, then offered her the straw again. She leaned over the mirror, sighed so hard she almost blew the coke away, then went through the line like one of those vacuum cleaners Eldora had ac-cused me of peddling.

Sissy Duval licked her finger, wiped up the residue, and rubbed it on her gums. "Oh fuck," she murmured, "where'd you get this shit?" Then her senses came back to her with the rush. "Sorry," she said softly, "none of my business. Jesus, I don't even remember your name. And why the hell are you looking for that sweet-cheeked dead bastard?"

"Just call me Milo," I said. "Actually, I'm looking for an old friend of his, Enos Walker."

"Jesus, don't be looking for Enos," she said, grabbing her arms as if cold. "He's not looking for me, is he? He's a bad one . . . and it seems to me that Enos is in prison up in Oklahoma."

"Not anymore."

"What the hell you want with him?"

"He was involved in a shooting yesterday, and my life would be a lot simpler if I could find him."

"Not for long," she said. "Enos used to be the kind of old boy didn't mind hurting people. And I don't expect prison did much for his attitude."

"I noticed," I said. "He was looking for your former husband. And somebody named Mandy Rae."

"Amanda Rae. That little bitch," she said, looking dreamily into the past. "She was the worst of that bunch. A fair to middling country singer but a wildass redneck girl. Hell, she was the only one of us who always carried a gun. But I haven't run with that crowd in years. Last I heard about her must have been ten, twelve years ago. Or more."

"What was she doing then?"

"I saw something in the paper," she said, "or maybe on the news. She whipped out a pistol and took a shot at some old boy in a beer joint out on the Bastrop highway. Didn't hit him, as I remember. She was a hell of a shot with a rifle, though. Christ, out at the ranch one afternoon—back when we still had a ranch—I watched her knock down a running buck at two hundred steps with an open sighted .30-.30. Cut his strings with a neck shot. Little bitch could shoot a single hair off a frog's ass."

"You mind if I ask why you call her a little bitch?" I asked.

"Why you think, cowboy?" She spat, then smiled. "You wouldn't have another line of that fine shit, would you?"

"You wouldn't have a picture of this Mandy Rae?"

"I think I'm gonna like you," she said, her phony smile nearly knocking ten years off her face. "You be chopping, I be looking." Then she pranced drunkenly around the bar and up the stairs.

Since I had already done enough, I chopped a single line for Sissy, finished my beer, slipped the bindle under the ashtray—I didn't think she'd be cleaning off the bar this afternoon—then got another beer out of the small refrigerator behind the bar. As she started down the stairs, I picked up the straw and made snorting sounds.

"Couldn't wait for me, huh?" she said, then handed me a publicity still of a sleek blond woman with a photo credit, Albert Homer, and a local address stamped on the back. I shrugged like a cokehead, a gesture I knew all too well. "This is all I could find," she added, her eyes darting to the long line shining on the mirror.

"And why was she a little bitch?" I asked, still holding the straw.

"She was fucking Dwayne," she sighed. "Hell, everybody was fucking everybody back in those days—before AIDS—but I caught them one Sunday afternoon up at the ranch. She was on all fours with his skinny dick up her ass, and the little bitch just grinned over the teddy bear tattoo on her shoulder blade at me. Like she knew I wasn't into that shit, like she could lead the bastard off by his dick any time she wanted." Sissy glanced at the straw again, then fixed herself another vodka.

"This Mandy Rae have a last name?" I wondered.

"Not that anybody knew," she said. "She just showed up one day with Enos Walker and twenty keys of pink Peruvian flake. They paid cash for a place up in Gatlin County and set up a network of college kid dealers. They had a steady supply and obviously some protection, so she was everybody's favorite lady for a while."

"You sure you never heard a last name?" I asked, still holding on to the straw.

Sissy thought for a moment, her eyes on the shining straw. "Quarrels," she said finally. "Seems like I remember somebody making a joke 'bout that—Amanda Rae Quarrels with herself . . ."

I held out the straw. "How did your husband die?"

"Sucker-punched the wrong kid outside the bar," she said, taking it with shaking hands. "That was always Dwayne's style. Fuckin' kid grabbed a sweet sixteen double-barrel out of his pickup, and let Dewey have two loads of quail shot—one in the guts and one in the face. Took him a long, bad week to die." Then Sissy sighed again, snorted the line, and smiled at me. "You got a suit and tie, cowboy?"

"Sure," I lied. If it was important, I could find a tie.

"Pick me up about eight? A fund-raiser for some political turd."

"Be my pleasure," I lied again, finished the beer, and headed for the door, listening to the rattle of ice in a heavy crystal glass across the empty desert of the living room. But I didn't shut the door all the way and I waited at the edge of the parking lot. I gave her a minute, then went back. But a tall, older gentleman in a tailored suit and a fifteen-hundred-dollar toupee beat me to the door. Bobby, I assumed. The old man had his finger on the doorbell as I walked up behind him.

"Can I help you, sir?" the old gentleman drawled.

"I forgot to leave Mrs. Duval my card," I said.

She came to the door with a cordless phone in her hand, confused to see both of us standing there. "I'll call you right back, honey," she said. "I promise."

"I'll just leave my card on the bar, Mrs. Duval," I said, then hustled around Bobby as she clicked the telephone off. I left one of the cards with just my name and cell phone number, grabbed the bindle from under the ashtray, and heard her whimper, "Wait."

"See you later, ma'am," I tossed over my shoulder.

"Please," she hissed.

"Who was that?" Bobby said as I hurried past them.

"Bobby, what the hell are you doing here?" I heard her say as I stepped slowly down the steps. I also heard her punch a button on the telephone and the beeping as it redialed. "Go get a drink or a suppository or something," she said, then, into the telephone, "Oh, not you, honey. It's that damned Bobby Mitchell littering my front porch again." Then Sissy's drunken laughter echoed through the cedar shrubs and the river willows that screened her condo from the street noise.

Something about Sissy's voice when she said "honey" into the telephone bothered me all the way out to Blue Hollow, bothered me all through my shift behind the bar, distracted me even when Betty

Porterfield stopped in for a cup of coffee on her way to the emergency vet clinic where she handled the night shift.

"Not much of a vacation," Betty said as she lifted her coffee cup. Her blue eyes were softly smudged as if she hadn't slept well that day, and wisps of her light red hair mixed with strands of gray drifted aimlessly across her freckled forehead. She brushed it back tiredly.

"Not much," I agreed. "We never seem to have much fun when we try to talk about things. Or get much talking done either."

"Is that my fault?"

Our silences had been louder than the constant wind or the slap of the shallow waves on the beach.

"Is that my fault?" she repeated.

"I don't know," I had to admit, then changed the subject. "You heard what happened yesterday?"

"I told you this PI stuff was going to get you in trouble," she said.

"You don't happen to know a Sissy Duval, do you?" I asked, ignoring her gibe.

"Sissy Duval? Jesus, I never ran with that crowd. Not much anyway," she said quickly. "They were too wild for me. But I knew them. Why?"

"She's about my only connection to Enos Walker," I said lamely.

"Who's he?" she asked, then looked away.

"He's the guy who tussled with Billy Long when he got shot," I said. "If I could find him before the cops do, it might save his life. And me a lot of official grief."

"You know, Milo," she said, the corner of her mouth lifted in a wry smile, "you don't owe this Walker guy anything. And we had a better life when you were retired."

"Maybe you did," I said, "but I didn't. I'm too young to be that old."

"Why don't you drive out to the ranch after you close? I'll fix breakfast when I get home," she said softly. "I'd like to work this out, honey."

It flashed through my mind that women called men "honey" in

a different tone of voice than they did women. But I was thinking about the photo credit on the back of Mandy's picture, so once again I begged off the late night drive out to the ranch. "I've got one more lead to follow in the morning."

"I wish you could hear how silly that sounds," she said, suddenly flushed with anger, her lower lip trembling. "Why don't you just admit you hate this place and carry your sorry ass back to Montana?"

"Thanks," I said. "Since I moved my sorry ass down here to be near you."

"That's too much responsibility for me to bear," she said, then left her coffee, and walked slowly out of the bar. The sad stiff stick of her back told me that once again conversation had failed us. We had moved farther away from each other with each word. Just as we had down at her uncle's beach house.

We had drifted into a fight that night, as effortlessly it seemed as we had drifted into bed when we were first together. After the usual silence, then the apologies, I had begun to rub her shoulders.

"I just don't know . . ." she murmured as we started to make love.

"What? What don't you know?"

"I don't know what we're doing anymore," she said softly, her voice barely audible above the sounds of the Gulf breeze and the soft slaps of the waves. "I don't know where this is going, don't even know if we're making love or just fucking . . . or if this is some sort of stupid contest to see who can come last . . ."

I didn't know what to say, so I didn't say anything, just eased out of her and into my sweats, then out of the house, across the glass-enclosed upper deck, then the long, shallow ramp down to the hard-packed sand of the beach. As I walked along the dark verge of the water, the low waves slipped across the sand, dying with a foaming hiss that sounded like a nest of baby snakes. Out in the Gulf, the lights of the oil platforms and derricks glowed like the false fires of ship wreckers, and the oily tar balls glistened in the scummy surf like the eggs of monsters. Texas, Jesus. What had been in my mind?

When I went back to her uncle's beach house, perched like a giant spider on concrete legs above the sand, she seemed to be asleep, so I crashed on a lounge chair on the upper deck out of the wind. The next morning we drove back to Austin without speaking.

After Betty left the bar, I was more than glad to listen to the aimless problems of my customers. I could think of possible solutions to their problems, solutions that were sometimes as simple as a free drink and a friendly ear. So it wasn't until after I had cleaned up, stocked, washed some illegal cash, and checked out that I had a chance to see if Albert Homer was still at the same place. There he was in the Austin telephone book, still on North Loop, and still in business.

Homer's studio sat on a weedy lot behind a ratty pool hall off North Loop within shouting distance of I-35 North. He might still be in business, but business didn't look all that lively at noon the next day when I pushed the buzzer beside the front door. Four long separate times. Finally, I heard a door slam and a distant voice from the second floor promising that it was on its way. Darkroom, I assumed, until the young man opened the door wearing a ratty robe over rumpled pajamas. He'd seen better days himself. The long fringe of hair hanging around his thin face hadn't been washed or combed in several days. Something gray clung to the corners of his scraggly mustache, much as the odor of the early morning joint clung to his night clothes, and the stink of stale beer wafted on his breath.

"We ain't open," he mumbled. I showed him a fifty-dollar bill, remembering the good old days when a twenty would have done the trick. "But we could be, man, if you had a cold six-pack, too."

"Don't go away," I said, then headed for the glowing beer signs of a pool hall just down the street.

During the years I had lived in Texas, I'd had almost no cocaine, not many tokes of marijuana, and damn few hangovers. But in the two days since I had the misfortune to run into Enos Walker, it seemed I had been servicing other people's addictions with my own shaky character: Sissy Duval's Hooverized nose, Capt. Gannon's lust for an easy retirement, and now Albert Homer's hangover. Anything for justice, I thought as I crossed the unmown lot, and the faint chance that I might be able to extend Enos Walker's wasted life. They say a lawyer who represents himself has a fool for a client. But there is no folk wisdom covering a PI who is his own client. Perhaps because it doesn't happen often enough to rate a cliché to cover it.

Five minutes later, I watched Homer suck down the first can of Lone Star and crack another one. From the photographs framed on his studio wall, the rack of Frederick's of Hollywood plus-sized lingerie, and the fake satin bedspread covering the round bed, I assumed that Homer specialized in sexy photos of fat women. It was sort of creepy, but I had to admit he wasn't a bad photographer, and I couldn't think of any good reason why fat women couldn't have as much fun as emaciated models with artificial breasts.

"I'm just guessing here," I said as I pulled the publicity photo out of a manila envelope, "but you probably didn't take this picture."

"Looks like one of my Daddy's," Homer said, barely glancing up from his beer. "He passed over seven years ago."

"You didn't keep his files, did you?"

"They're in a storage locker out in Pflugerville," he mumbled. "About the only thing besides this shithole that survived the divorce. But that fifty won't buy you shit."

"What would?"

"Maybe a hundred," he said, smiling broadly enough to crack the gray matter at the corners of his mouth. "Make it two, if I help."

"That's pretty stiff," I suggested.

But Homer just smiled.

Three hours later I understood why. We had been through another six-pack of beer and dozens of boxes of the ugliest pornography I had ever seen. The storage unit was as steamy as a sauna. The only good news was that Junior had showered and dressed in clean clothes before we drove out. The bad news was that the sleek blond was a woman named Sharon Timmons. Who had done unspeakable things with snakes when her singing career had gone south. And Amanda Rae Quarrels had no folder at all.

"Who buys this shit?" I wondered.

"You'd be surprised," Homer said. "Mostly people who find the new stuff too buffed and tidy for their tastes."

"This is it, right? Your ex-wife didn't take anything?"

"Shit, man," he moaned. "She took everything. House, both cars, and all the money my Daddy brought back from Vegas."

"Vegas?"

"Yeah, he hit one of those hundred-thousand-dollar slots at the Nugget," Junior said, "and got home with it before he blew it. First time for that."

"He gambled?"

"Does the Pope wear red shoes when he shits in the woods?"

"I don't know, I'm not Catholic."

Junior just looked at me.

"You don't remember a woman named Mandy Rae Quarrels?" I asked.

"Not offhand," Homer said, shrugging. "But you know how it is. You remember the tits longer than the names."

"What happened to your father?" I asked, just to be polite.

"Ah, shit," he said, "he was fishing up at Lake Travis a couple of years ago, got drunk, and fell out of the boat."

Somehow I couldn't imagine Homer's father fishing, not after seeing the sort of pictures he liked to snap. "What happened to your marriage?" That was the only thing I could think to ask as I handed Homer the rest of his money.

"Weight Watchers," he said sadly.

On the way back to Austin, I kicked myself several times. I couldn't believe I had let anyone as drunk and high as Sissy Duval lie to me. But clearly she had, and if I went back, I didn't think I had enough cocaine to whip the truth out of her. Maybe I should turn my license in, go back to being a retired gentleman as Betty suggested. But that seemed too easy. I called Carver D on the cell phone, but nobody answered, so I stopped by his unlocked, rambling house in Travis Heights before I headed back out to relieve the daytime bartender. Diabetes and liberal doses of Tennessee whiskey had limited Carver D's mobility. He was alone, which was unusual, in an antique wheelchair on the screened back porch. Petey, my silent partner in the washing of my bad cash, usually took care of Carver D when he wasn't pursuing his degree in computer science and accounting at UT. When he was in class, Carver D's driver, a tough ex-marine master sergeant named Hangas, took over the chores.

"Where the hell is everybody?" I asked.

"They've abandoned me, Milo," Carver D said, then tipped the bottle. Then he laughed, his rolling fat jiggling like a bad Jell-O salad, his tiny black eyes shining like watermelon seeds. "Petey ran to the store," he said, still choking with laughter. "Although Quarrels is not an uncommon name in this part of the world, I can promise you that your Amanda Rae Quarrels doesn't exist as any sort of person, singer, songwriter, or actress. No record of birth, marriage, death, taxes, telephone, or utilities. Nothing under that name. Enos Walker, on the other hand, his life is an open book. Born December 7th, 1960, in Hominy, Oklahoma. His mother was a registered member of the Osage tribe; his father a staff sergeant at Fort Sill who shows up on various records as either black, white, or Seminole and who was listed MIA in Vietnam, presumed dead. Walker's criminal record is longer than my dick, but mostly minor stuff—misdemeanor possession, disturbing the peace in bar fights—that sort of shit. Lots of rumors but no official interest in his dealing down here. Until that last bust. Smuggling cocaine. Got popped with two other guys outside of Tulsa. A sweet setup but they had some bad luck."

"Bad luck?"

"The private plane would file a flight plan out of Jamaica to Tulsa," he said, "and when they dropped down for the airport approach—Christ, who'd suspect Tulsa—they'd kick the coke out into a pasture. Great pilot, too. Hit the fucking mark. Dropped twenty keys wrapped inside an inflated tractor tire tube right on the pickup's hood. Fucking near killed them. Did kill the pickup and the driver. Made it hard to run away when the cops showed up."

"What happened to the two other guys?"

"Both died in the joint. One killed with a shovel," he said, "the other died of AIDS. Bad luck all around. Except for Walker. There was a rumor that somebody dropped a dime on him and some strong but inadmissible evidence that this wasn't the first time they had pulled this number. He was lucky to only do state time and only twelve years at that. Hell, it took five years to finally convict and sentence him. And it was another piece of bad luck when he jumped bail and got swept up in a random check at the Miami Airport. He was not exactly a model prisoner, but still he managed to stay out of serious trouble."

"No probation officer, huh?"

"Nope. Walker did the full jolt," Carver D said. "For the moment, he's a free man. Until they catch him again. Or perhaps you make the collar."

"It feels a little bit like a lost cause. I just don't know enough criminals down here," I complained.

"Hell, this is Texas, man, you don't know nothin' but criminals down here," Carver D said. "All great fortunes start with a small crime."

"Who said that?" I said.

"As far as you know, buddy, I did."

"Maybe I'll just have to take the heat."

"Well, you got a good lawyer in Phil Thursby," Carver D said, "and don't forget that your girlfriend's uncle is the Gov." Then he laughed so hard his tiny dark eyes disappeared. "You can surely pick 'em, partner."

"Guess I'd better handle the fucking mess myself."

"Your ex-partner always said that your favorite problems were your bullheaded refusal to ask for help and your obviously odious choices of womenfolk to lie down among."

"He should talk," I said. "He had to be gutshot and nailed into a hospital bed before Whitney could get him to date her."

"And speaking of the love birds. How's he handling law school?" he added, asking about my ex-partner and his wife.

"He's okay," I said. "You know, I saw him back in September when they inducted me as an honorary member of the Benewah tribe. Hard to believe that it took more than fifteen years for them to acknowledge the gift of my grandfather's land. The new bunch running the tribal council seems to have forgiven my family. Of course, they had to fight the government for the land."

"Fucking government," he said.

"Fucking government lawyers."

"Redundant," he said. "How's the madman doing?"

"She made law review," I said. "But I think he took a semester off to work on a case before he goes back to school."

"Crazy bastard," Carver D said, then hit the bottle again. "Must be the oldest fucker there."

"Almost. The oldest student is a little old postmistress from some pothole in eastern Montana. They closed her post office, so she enrolled in law school thinking she could sue the bastards. She's at least twenty years older than he is."

"What's he thinking about?"

"Finding a way to do the right thing. That's the only thing he said."

"Jesus." Carver D sighed, then stared into the giant live oak in his backyard until he slumped toward a liquid nap. "Stop by Sunday, man," he murmured. "I'm having people over."

"Working," I said. Carver D looked bored even in his sleep. I promised myself to stop by more often. He was about my only sane friend down here in this crazy place.

CHAPTER THREE

EVERYTHING STAYED CALM, even the beautiful weather—it might have been called Indian summer, but Texas had destroyed, displaced, or deported almost all of its native tribes—so it was calm and busy until Sunday night. I had a bar to run, woman troubles I didn't understand, and boredom to battle. I just didn't have the time or the energy to track down Enos Walker or brace Sissy Duval. But it wasn't all bad.

Since I wasn't exactly in the bar business to be in business, and it was my money, sort of, I had done it my way when I built the place. The gently arching bar had been constructed from pegged oak planks and faced with a black leather pad that matched the ten high-backed stools. Plenty of room to stand at the bar, and a real brass rail whereupon the drinkers could rest their feet. Comfortable black leather chairs circled the nine round tables set on three levels so everybody could have a view of the Hill Country sunsets above the rim of Blue Hollow. Even the three tables in the nonsmoking area, which was shielded by half-wood half-glass walls and provided with a separate ventilation system, had a view. Everything behind the bar was within two easy steps on the hard rubber duckboards.

Just as important were the things the bar didn't have: no beer signs and no sports paraphernalia—they attracted the wrong sort of drinker—no jukebox or canned music but a CD system with a collection of classical music and jazz; and no television, except for the small color set above the closed end of the bar where only the bartender and the bar drinkers had a view. For the occasional day drinker and my lonely nights. A small grill in a room behind the bar served only nachos, taquitos, tacos, red and green chili, and cold sandwiches. It was as close to a bartender's heaven as stolen money could buy. In addition, Petey had inserted a program in the computer system that showed random drink and food orders paid for with cash. All I had to do was match the overage with cash from the floor safe in the kitchen, and suddenly clean money appeared. When I first met Petey, he was a skateboard punk with spiked hair and lots of metal in his face. Now he was my silent yuppie partner. He was worth it. I could even turn the program off if one of us wasn't going to be there to close out the register.

Most of the people who worked the bar and grill were members of the Herrera family, and Sunday was their day to howl with the *familia*, so I worked most Sunday nights, but no two were ever the same. Some Sunday nights the bar resembled a fraternity party gone bad. The technocrats and software salesmen visiting the nearby computer companies sometimes drank like spoiled, nervous children, slobbering from rubbery lips onto their pocket computers or loosened silk ties. Then sometimes they didn't drink at all. The crowd was occasionally leavened by a clot of Japanese, who after their first burst of fun would droop politely like fragile flowers over their martini glasses, or demand karaoke until they passed out. Occasionally the evening would be punctuated by smart professional women hiding their disgust behind brittle smiles. On other Sunday nights, though, the bar resembled an elegant morgue.

Like that Sunday night. Three nicely buffed executive wives without husbands, down from the large stone houses in the hills to the west, idled over glasses of chardonnay in the nonsmoking section. A large, burly, but aging fellow with a gray crew cut—known as Paper Jack—in a wrinkled suit and a stained tie steadily downed Wild Turkeys on the rocks in the middle of the bar. At the far end a remote and beautiful young woman with a deep tan sipped a Macallan Scotch neat with an Evian back. Everybody left everybody else peacefully alone. The wind softly buffeted the glass walls as dusk rode gently into star-spangled darkness over the Hill Country.

Two of the grass widows drifted out, seeking either more excitement or the pharmaceutical solace in the medicine cabinets of their large, empty houses. The third one, a tall blond named Sherry, stopped at the bar, as she often did, for an Absolut on the rocks, three of my Dunhill cigarettes, and a gently bored pass at me. I ignored her offer as politely as possible, knowing, of course, that some cold Sunday night I might need the warmth of her bed.

Once Sherry ambled out, her slim hips as elegant as a glass harp, I watched, smiling sadly, then bought Paper Jack and the lovely young woman a drink, told the cocktail waitress to call it a night, went into the grill to send the cook home early, poured myself a large glass of red wine—Betty had been fairly successful weaning me from double handfuls of single malt Scotch whisky to red wine—and settled in to wait out the evening, leaning against the back bar as I polished glasses and watched Jimmy Stewart tremble and stutter through *Bend of the River*. So I didn't exactly notice when Paper Jack started forcing his mumbled attentions on the young lady at the end of the bar.

Paper Jack, with his seemingly unending supply of hundred-dollar bills, had always been long on cash and short on charm, but he was an old drinking buddy of Travis Lee Wallingford's and one of Jack's nephews managed the Blue Hollow Lodge, so I had always cut Jack a large length of slack when he stayed at the Lodge on one of his business trips–cum–binges. But his first clear words got my attention.

"Hey pretty lady," Jack said loudly, "where the hell I know you from? I know you from some place?"

"I beg your pardon," the young woman said quietly, the arch of a perfect eyebrow raised. "I don't think so," she added. She had elegant cheekbones and a generous mouth, and her makeup seemed professionally blended across the smooth planes of her face.

"I fuckin' know you, lady," Jack continued, a crooked smile elastic on his face. "I'll remember evenschually—"

"Believe me, sir," the young woman interrupted calmly, "I've never seen you before in my life." She took a long drink of her whisky and turned as if to leave.

Then Jack's drunken face suddenly brightened. "Does this fuckin' help?" he said, then cast a sheaf of Franklins in front of him and hammered his huge fist on the bar. "That's what it cost me last time, honey."

"Okay, Jack," I said as I stepped in front of him, "that's it." I dumped his drink in the sink, stuffed the bills in his shirt pocket, and told him to get the hell out of my place.

"She's a fuckin' whore, Milo," he said, "you dumb shit. And gimme my drink back, you cheap bastard." Then he stood up and reached across the bar to grab my shirt.

I had seen this act once before and knew that even in his late sixties Jack still had hands like ham hocks, hardened by years in the oil patch, and he was too big, too drunk, and too stubborn for me to handle without hurting him. So it had to be quick and quiet. I waved my hands in front of Jack's bleary eyes, grabbed his tie with my left hand, then popped him smartly on the forehead with the heel of my right palm. Not hard enough to knock him out. Just hard enough to slosh his whiskey-soaked brain back and forth against his skull bones. Stunned, Jack's eyes rolled up in his head. I caught him before his nose smashed on the bar, then laid his pudgy cheek gently on the padded front.

"Excuse me," I said to the young woman as I went around. "Would you watch the bar for a second, please? I'll be right back."

I hooked the half-conscious bulk of the old man under the arm, grabbed his room key out of his pocket, then steered him out the door and down the hall to his usual room, where I dumped him on the bed. Jack was snoring before I could prop him on his side with pillows so he wouldn't drown in his own vomit. I loosened his tie and shoelaces, then hurried back to the bar. The young woman was still there.

"Sorry for the trouble," I said as I went back behind the bar. "And thanks for watching the bar."

"Not the first one I've ever watched," she said. "Thanks, but I wouldn't come into strange bars if I couldn't handle drunks," she added.

"I didn't want you to hurt ol' Jack," I said, "and it's my job to keep the peace."

"And a thankless job, I'm sure," she said, smiling. "May I buy you a drink?"

What the hell, I could catch Jimmy Stewart in *The Naked Spur* tomorrow night, and this was a truly beautiful woman. Thick dark hair cascaded in soft waves off a warm, dusky face dominated by eyes as darkly blue as a false dawn. A small crescent-shaped scar at the corner of her broad mouth and a slight knot at the bridge of her arched nose kept her face from being perfect. But perfect would have been wrong. Beneath her dark blue pin-striped suit and light blue mock turtleneck blouse, her body looked long and lean, softly dangerous. Except for tiny gold hoops in her ears and a large pendant, a round black stone set in an irregularly shaped gold band, she wore no jewelry. The stone rested heavily between her full, fine breasts.

"What the hell," I said. "It's my place—why not?"

"And I'll have another, please," she said. "I'm not going anywhere." Then she smiled as if she had enjoyed the pleasure I was taking in the presence of such loveliness.

I hadn't spoken to Betty since the night she left the bar—that wasn't unusual these days—but we sort of had a standing date for breakfast at the ranch on Monday mornings, the beginning of her nights off, but damned if I was going to be the first to break the silence, so I poured the lady and myself large Macallans over ice.

"Absent friends," I said as I raised my glass.

"New friends," she said, smiling. "Molly McBride," she added, handing me her card, "lawyer."

"Milo Milodragovitch," I said as I glanced at the Houston address and slipped the card into my shirt pocket, and handed her one of my own. "Bartender," it said.

Then we shook hands like civilized people, her hand softly moist in mine, her blue eyes shining.

"Nice move you put on that old man, Mr. Milodragovitch," she said, not stumbling over the name. "But you didn't learn that move in a bar."

"I'm sorry?"

"Listen, my father, after he got hurt, ran a place over in Lake Charles, so I grew up in a bar," she said, a Cajun lilt coming into her voice, "and I tended bar all the way through my undergraduate degree and then law school, so I know something about violence in bars. You popped that old man as if you were cutting a diamond. Any harder, you might have killed him. Any easier, he would have been fighting mad." She raised her glass again. We drank deeply. I loved the warm burn of the whisky. Molly McBride reached across the bar to take the cigarettes and matches out of my shirt pocket. Her blood-red fingernails seemed to sparkle against my chest. "You're a pro," she added, lighting our cigarettes.

"Thanks," I said, my burning cheeks bunched around a kid's grin. "I spent some time in law enforcement," I explained, "and I've been a private investigator for years, but the real truth is that most of what I know about violence I learned in bars."

"Me, too," she said, laughing through a cloud of smoke, then filling her mouth with Scotch, smiling with pleasure.

"Not too many young women drink single malt whisky," I mentioned.

"Learned it from my Daddy, God rest his soul," she said. "He always said that the only people who drank white whiskey were sissies or drunks, and the only people who drank bourbon were white trash chicken fuckers, con men, and counterfeit Confederate gentlemen, and—"

But before we could continue the conversation, a string of rental cars and the motel van deposited a gaggle of traveling men who had come in on the last flight and who always needed a drink or two after the inevitable rough landing at the Austin airport. I found myself wishing that they would go away, hoping that they would not drive Molly McBride back to her room, but she stayed at the bar, smoking my cigarettes and sipping Scotch until the nervous fliers cleared out, and I offered her a last drink since I usually closed at ten on Sunday nights.

"I've got a bottle of single cask Lagavulin in my room," she said as she signed her check. "Two-fifteen," she added, "if you're interested."

"I've got to check out, make the drop, and stock," I apologized, "and I'm kind of involved."

"Who isn't?" she said, then smiled. "Let the day man stock. I don't have to be in court until one o'clock, so let's have a drink or two. And by the way, the ice machine on the second floor is on the blink." Then she walked toward the door, her long legs elegant above high heels. At the doorway she paused to smile over her shoulder, saying, "Give me ten minutes . . ." Then disappeared down the hallway.

I quickly totaled the register, then covered the phony overage with unwashed cash from the safe in the kitchen, wrote Mike Herrera a note of apology for neither cleaning nor stocking, locked up the liquor, washed my hands, did two quick lines of the dead man's coke, then went out the door with a bucket of ice under my arm, following Molly McBride quickly enough to catch the faint trace of lilac she trailed behind her.

Over the five marriages I'd never been particularly faithful. Or unfaithful, either. The whole question seemed theoretical and had nothing to do with the actual moment. Or the fact that marriage and the notion of fidelity had been invented when women could be bought for horses, cows, or in certain places sheep. The lies and the betrayal—that was the important part, the part that hurt forever.

Besides, maybe this woman just wanted a drink, some legal conversation, maybe even a soft and sad good night kiss to relieve the loneliness, but as I raised my fist to knock on her door, my guts shivered as if I were fourteen again, drinking whiskey downstairs at Sally's in Livingston while the dark, nameless beast of love waited between the stubby legs of a half-breed Canadian whore up those long carpeted stairs, a night already paid for by my dead father, the girl not much older than me just waiting to sing "Happy Birthday." Of course, by the time I got up the stairs, I was whiskey-drunk and scared stupid. But she fixed all that.

On my fourteenth birthday, the family lawyer gave me an envelope my Dad had left with him. Inside, the title and keys to the Dodge Power Wagon moldering in the three-car garage, a savings account passbook, and a note. "Hey, sprout," it read, "if I'm not around to watch you turn fourteen, Happy Birthday. There's a prepaid night at Sally's. It's hard enough being a teenager without confusing sex with love. They are both fine, son, but they're different." Then a P.S.: "Don't tell your mother about the savings account. She knows about the pickup. I'm sorry about the will." My mother had forced my old man to bind his estate in a trust that I couldn't touch until I was fifty-three.

That next morning, draped over the toilet as the girl giggled from the bed, "I hope this isn't your first time, kid," I first began to have a notion that my father's death had not exactly been an accident, but it took me another twenty years to figure out his suicide.

"Jesus," I whispered, waiting in front of Molly McBride's door, "get a fucking grip, old man." But still my knock was as hesitant as a teenager's.

Molly McBride had opened the sliding glass door to her balcony, and the room was full of moonlight. She still wore her prim suit, as if we were to have a legal conversation over drinks, but she had removed her blouse and bra, I realized as I held out the bucket of bar ice like a cheap gift. I noticed because her suit coat swung open as she plunged her hands into the ice, then rubbed her neck and without a word reached inside her coat to hold her cold hands under the weight of her dark-tipped breasts. In her heels she looked me straight in the eye, and in the hard moonlight her eyes glittered madly, her smile seemed grim rather than seductive, and the black stone hanging over her heart glistened like an obsidian blade.

"I'm glad you came," she purred. "I was afraid you wouldn't." Then she touched my neck with her cold fingers. Which was too much for me. I must have stiffened and turned.

"I'm sorry," I said, shoving the ice bucket against her naked chest. "Maybe this wasn't such a good idea. Maybe I should go."

And I might have. But she shoved the bucket back to me, burst into tears, then ran to the closed bathroom door, where she paused to glance over her shoulder, her face twisted with pain and grief, before she quickly slammed it. Leaving me holding the damn ice bucket, half in the room, half in the hallway.

After the first drink, I calmed down. And after the second, I was ready for anything. It was one of those crazy nights when anything seemed possible. The west wind had scoured the star-studded sky, and the slice of moon seemed white-hot and as sharp as a skinning knife against the night as I waited, leaning into the soft breeze on the balcony rail of Molly's room. I had found glasses and the Scotch on the small table outside, and convinced myself that a little Scotch couldn't make things any crazier. In spite of the traffic murmurs from all sides of the hollow, I imagined I could hear Blue Creek rushing over the low water crossing below, could even hear the artesian gush of the huge spring that joined the creek at the dark base of the hollow cupped in the limestone bluff that glistened, unfortunately, like the bits of Billy Long's skull bones on the flocked wallpaper. Surely it was the drugs and some sort of delayed midlife madness, I hoped, not something permanently engraved on my nights.

The bathroom door creaked quietly behind me, followed by a snuffle and the rattle of toenails as an awkward white dog drifted out of the bathroom and across the moon-bright carpet. Molly came out a moment afterward, barefoot, her hair pulled back and her face scrubbed, wearing an oversized Tulane football jersey, number 69, and sweat pants. The dog curled in the near corner of the room, snoring almost immediately. Molly fixed a drink, then leaned on the rail beside him.

"Pretty stupid, huh?" she said.

"Pretty effective. I nearly fainted."

"Please forgive me," Molly giggled, then apologized again. "I'm sorry," she said. "I'm supposed to be a tough, grown-up lady lawyer, and I should have simply approached you directly, instead of coming to your bar to check you out, then making that stupid pass. I feel like such an idiot."

"Please don't," I said. "Try to remember that I'm the fool it nearly worked on. And I'm beginning to feel like an idiot because I don't know what the hell this is about."

She paused long enough to freshen our drinks, then proceeded calmly. "The last time I was in town I was running with a lawyer friend of mine on the trail along the creek in the park," she said, "and we passed you, and he said he had heard some ugly rumors about you . . . and the trouble a few years ago, when you and your partner went up against the *contrabandistas* in West Texas."

"I'm not too crazy about hearing that. Who the hell told you that?" I asked, serious now. A banker and a woman as lovely as she was greedy had stolen my father's trust before I could even spend a penny of it, mixed it with drug money in a botched attempt to make a movie. Then my ex-partner and I, with Petey's help, had stolen it back. But not without considerable bloodshed and bruised law enforcement egos. "What did he say? And who the fuck was he?"

"I won't tell you his name," Molly McBride said, calm against my sudden seriousness, "but he told me enough about you to start me digging."

"And?"

"Mr. Milodragovitch," she said, turning to face me, "I mostly do criminal work. I know cops. I know crooks. And stories get around."

"What the hell do you want?" I asked, tired and angry now. What I really wanted even more than an answer to my question was another blast of that pure cocaine.

"I want you to sit down and listen to me for a moment," she said, her head bowed, then raised into the moonlight. "That's all. Please just listen to me."

"So let me get this straight. Let me get this perfectly straight, okay? I don't get laid, right? I get a bedtime story instead? Wonderful." But I sat down anyway.

"I don't blame you for being bitter," she said, sitting across from me and grabbing my hands. "Just listen, please."

"What have I got to lose? Except pride, dignity, and my bad reputation?"

"Four years ago," she said, clutching my hands harder, "my little sister was running down by the creek when she lost her dog—"

"I don't fucking do lost dogs these days," I said, perhaps a bit more angrily than I meant. She released my hands, then stood up to lean against the rail, her back to me.

"Ellie is a mutt," she said into the night, "a nothing dog, but Annette loved her. It had been a bad year. Our Daddy died early that year, and Annette's boyfriend had—well, white boys shouldn't smoke crack and hang around topless bars—and her favorite prof in the English Department killed himself. So when she lost Ellie, Annette went crazy.

"She stapled flyers to damn near every tree, took out a half-page ad in the paper, even tried to borrow money from me to rent a billboard . . ." Molly paused as if exhausted, her sigh full of some grief I didn't want to understand, then she turned to face me.

"Eventually," she continued, briskly now, "the man who had Ellie called, and offered to sell her back for a hundred dollars . . . They were to meet at the overlook above the spring, down there in the park. The cops know that much from Annette's answering machine tape . . ."

"The cops?"

"Two days later they found her body stuffed under a ledge above the spring," Molly said, nodding toward the sleeping dog, "and Ellie was sitting beside her. Maybe she'd never been lost at all.

"The son of a bitch had . . . he had raped and killed Annette . . .

he had tortured her, raped her, killed her, then, my God, the son of a bitch cut her head off . . . they never found her head . . . we had to bury her without a goddamned head . . ." Then Molly paused again, heaved a great breath, then let the rest gush out. "My mother couldn't take it. Six weeks later, she hanged herself."

"Jesus," I said. "What can I say?" Both my parents had been suicides, so I had some idea of the confusion and guilt it caused.

But Molly was already moving away, back to the bathroom, leaving the dog and me in the pitiless moonlight.

And when she came back, she came back into my arms. Naked. Just as she was supposed to. Whispering against my neck, "Don't say anything."

Nobody ever knows how much is only real for the moment. Or how much is real forever. Maybe the momentary is all we'll ever know, the woman open beneath you, her lips wild with laughter, or riding high over you, her tears like hot wax on your chest. Molly was muscular and willing and lovely, and there were moments when I felt as if I might die, and moments when I knew I'd live forever. And even worse, a moment when I convinced myself that I was doing the right thing, somehow giving support and comfort to this woman.

Afterward, we leaned again on the rail over the dark wrinkles of the hollow, ice ringing like tiny bells in our glasses, the moon still molten, but the wind had shifted to the southeast, suddenly warm in our faces, our sweat unslaked.

"I never lived any place where you could work up a sweat in November," I said. "Just standing still."

"I've never lived any place where piss froze before it hit the ground," she said.

"Maybe I made that part up," I admitted.

"I thought so," she said.

"But no matter how cold it is," I said, "you can always put more

clothes on." Then I paused. "But I've never figured out how to take
enough clothes off when it's hot down here." Then I paused again,
turned to face her, touched the dark stone on her chest. "What's this?"

"The only thing my mother left me," she said quietly. "It's called
the Shark of the Moon."

I looked more closely. The golden band no longer looked irreg-
ular now that I could see the snouts, dorsal fins, and tails of the
golden sharks circling the dark pool of the stone. And etched faintly
in the center I could feel another.

"So what the hell do you want from me?"

"Believe me. I've tried everything. I can't get anybody to help.
Not the cops. Not the most desperate and sleaziest PIs. Hell, I even
tried to put an ad in *Soldier of Fortune*, but they wouldn't take it. So
it's up to you, Milo. And as Mattie Ross said, 'I hear you have true
grit.'"

Jesus, I thought as I tried to remember if John Wayne got laid
in that movie, she's pulling out all the stops. "I'm guessing here, but
I'll bet you want to put an ad in the paper about a lost dog in Blue
Hole Park, right? And you hope the same bastard will answer it?"

"I'm meeting him at ten o'clock this morning," she said, "on the
same overlook where he took my sister . . ."

"What makes you think it's the same guy?"

"I knew it in my bones," she said, "when I heard his voice over
the telephone. I fucking knew it."

"You cut it pretty close."

She reached into the chest of drawers and pulled out a Glock 20.

"You know, I've yet to meet a woman in Texas who doesn't carry
a piece," I said. "It doesn't have a safety, it doesn't have a blow back
lock, and the FBI thinks it's perfect."

"They gave me a permit."

"Everybody's got a permit as far as I can tell," I said, wondering
why all the major decisions of my life had to be made while I was
slightly tipsy, mildly high, and stinking of bodily fluids. Or maybe
it wasn't just the bad decisions, maybe it included the good ones,
too. Whichever, I had no way to resist. "Okay. I've got a black cherry

El Dorado. Meet me in the parking lot at nine. I've got to look over the ground."

She put her arms around my neck, saying, "How can I ever thank you?"

"Consider me thanked, and I'll give you the family rate for a bodyguard day."

"Family rate?"

"Three hundred instead of five," I said, smiling, "in cash, in advance."

"The fuck doesn't count?" she asked.

"Nothing solidifies a deal like folding money. It doesn't change its mind and doesn't whine about respect the next morning."

"That's for sure," she said as she dug into her purse and handed me the money with a quick burst of nervous laughter. "That's what I always tell my clients," she added. "The ones who are guilty, that is." Then we laughed, shook hands, and I left her standing in the hard moonlight, listening to the faint murmur of the creek.

The upper reaches of Blue Creek wandered weakly through Betty's ranch, then crossed another ranch, before it wound onto her other uncle's place—Tom Ben Wallingford owned several sections— before it dropped in a small stream off the Balcones Escarpment to join the gush of the huge artesian spring at the base of the hollow, where Blue Creek became a wide, beautiful stream, pellucid water slipping over limestone ledges, pausing occasionally to form perfect swimming holes. Travis Lee, who had his job at the law school and later his private practice, donated most of his part of the old family ranch to the county for a park, taking a huge tax write-off and keeping a narrow strip of land on the north side of the creek. Leaving his older brother with his sections of mostly worthless scrub, particularly after the government dropped the mohair subsidy, land good only for deer leases, which the old man wouldn't allow. And, as Austin expanded northwesterly, development, which the old man hated. Tom Ben's sections nearly were surrounded by upscale devel-

opments, but the stubborn and childless old cowboy was dickering
with the Blue Creek Preservation Society, of which Betty Porterfield
was president and probably the major financial angel, to put the
land into a conservancy, but only if they could come up with a deal
to keep it a working ranch. But nobody could come up with the deal
he wanted, and it seemed that Tom Ben Wallingford was going to
dicker until he died, and he seemed to think he was going to live forever.

The Overlord Land and Cattle Company, a wholly owned sub-
sidiary of Overlord Minerals, Inc., owned most of the land around
the ranch—hell, most of Gatlin County—and the CEO, Hayden
Lomax, insisted the old man had signed an option to sell the ranch,
which Tom Ben Wallingford had denied completely. The whole
thing had been simmering toward court for a couple of years before
I came to stay in the Hill Country.

When Betty Porterfield asked me to move into her ranch house,
I told myself that I had buried my Montana past and intended to
finish out my life in the Hill Country. Betty and I had met over a
gunshot dog and fallen in love over stories of loss and gunfire. And
I loved Betty's ranch, a section of Hill Country heartland, and the
crippled animals Betty brought home from the emergency veteri-
narian clinic where she worked nights, loved the bright glow of the
plank floor and the homemade cedar furniture, the wood cookstove
and the hissing Coleman lanterns, the reassuring scratch and peep
of the chickens in the yard dust, the yawns of sleeping cats, throwing the tennis ball for the three-legged Lab, Sheba, until my arm
hurt, watching the sweep of weather across the wide Texas sky as I
sat on the front porch pointlessly whittling, turning cedar posts into
cookstove shavings.

Until it went bad, I'd never been closer to a woman than Betty.
She had healing hands; I'd seen her work, seen the undeniable hope
in an animal's eyes when she put those hands on them. A look, I suspected, I had when she first put her hands on me. So I tried really
hard. For the first time in my life I studied how to be home, studied every angle and plane of Betty's face, every freckle, every stray

wisp of red hair, the faint trace of the bullet scar across her right cheek, the dark leaden dimple on her left jawline where she'd fallen on a pencil in the third grade, which only showed when she occasionally laughed, wild and free.

And I studied Texas, too, because it seemed important to Betty, important in some way I didn't understand, but extremely important nonetheless. "Texans are proud people," her Travis Lee explained to me, "and Betty is a Texan." As if that explained everything. So during the mornings while she slept, I wandered the ranch with books. Hell, I knew more about flora and fauna on her ranch than I knew about my grandfather's land, which I had finally managed to give back to the Benewah tribe, one of the few places in Montana I had ever called home. Not the moldering mansion where I was raised, not the log cabin the garbage company goons had burned down. Those places weren't home. Except sometimes in the log cabin back home when I'd be sitting on the porch watching the first snow, and my big black tomcat, Eldridge Carver, would curl in my lap. That was home, sometimes. But that was easy. Making myself at home on Betty's ranch was work.

Month after month I wandered the ranch on foot in all kinds of weather. I sometimes thought I knew it better than Betty did. She'd torn out all the pasture and cross fences except for a small plot down the hill from the house where she kept a couple of saddle horses and occasionally ran a calf or two. On the back side of the ranch, I discovered a tiny outcropping of flint, no bigger than a freight car, and at the base of it, covered with limestone dust, a midden of arrowhead flakes, probably Comanche, since it seemed they had owned everything from there to southern Colorado for two hundred years. And I studied the Indians, too, nothing but ghosts now.

On other afternoons I'd gather up one of Betty's saddle horses, then drift easily for a couple of hours over to Tom Ben's place, where we'd sit on the veranda sipping iced tea and watching the sun soften the cedar breaks as it settled over the Hill Country while he shucked dried corn and doled it out cob by cob to the small herd of Spanish goats he kept for the occasional barbecue. During the Korean War

Tom Ben had been a twenty-eight-year-old captain in the Marine reserves who had been called to active duty when I was a sixteen-year-old Army private on falsified enlistment papers, and on those occasional afternoons we sometimes touched on those times, talking without talking too much. But he never talked about WW II, except to wonder about what might have happened if we had to invade Japan. And about Korea, Tom Ben mostly complained about the cold and bitched about his feet. Never married, he was as fond of his niece as if she were his child, and he extended that fondness to me. His place was a home place in a way Betty's never quite managed, but I didn't go over there often enough.

At Betty's place I read all the books I'd always meant to read, watched endless hours of movies on the battery-run portable television with a built-in VCR, which Betty allowed me to keep in the old smokehouse. She wouldn't watch them with me but sometimes she'd come in to lean on my back, briefly, her nose snuffling out the old smoke and salt smells. Then she'd leave me to the present and drift back to the nineteenth-century British novels she was addicted to.

Also, for the first time in my life, I had long stretches of solitude with which to consider my life, trying to connect everything from my father's lovesick suicide to my mother's aggressive lie that somehow forced me to endure three months of muddy Korean hell before a broken collarbone got me back to the States in time to hear about her drunken suicide drying out at a fat farm down in Arizona. I considered it all: the failed marriages, the drunk years, the boring dry years—and it only added up to anything when I was in the arms of this sad, redheaded woman.

But I couldn't make her happy. No matter how hard I studied. Hell, I knew better. A man can make a happy woman sad but he can't finally make a sad woman happy. Then I studied her sadness until the burden of that became too much for either of us to carry.

And the sorry truth was that I couldn't study Texas hard enough to make it home. It remained a foreign country, an undiscovered dimension, too large a place to be one place, a country held together by a semimystical history and a semihysterical pride. The more it became urbanized, the more it insisted on being country. The politics seemed like a cruel trick played by the rich on the poor. When I read copies of letters sent back home from the first settlers, the lies leapt off the page like billboards advertising hell: no hot weather, no mosquitoes, free land. Like every other place I had been, it was all about money. No more, no less. And even with money, I was still an outsider, more at home with whores, small-time drug dealers, musicians, and winos. And too old to change. It was as if I was spending a thousand dollars a month for a combination of graduate school, therapy, and serious frustration. But I tried and tried until I wore out my try, until it ached like a bad tooth.

Oddly enough, it was her other uncle who brought my unease to my attention first. Travis Lee drove up to the ranch house one silken fall morning as I sat in a rocking chair on the front porch, an unread novel in my lap, an unwhittled stick at my feet, the sun warm on my face, and Betty asleep in the house.

"What's happening, cowboy?" Travis Lee wanted to know as he rolled down the passenger's window of the huge pickup. "What the hell aren't you reading?"

"Something I always meant to read. *Anna Karenina*," I said.

"Ends badly, I hear," Travis Lee said as he kicked open the passenger door. "Let's go down to the creek and have a beer."

He drove silently down the pasture to the tiny creek and the spring box where I kept a case of Coors cans cooling among the crawdads and mint leaves, and silently drank a beer before Travis Lee spoke.

"Mind if I piss in your creek?" he said as he unbuttoned his jeans. Except in the courtroom, Travis Lee wore Levi's, cowboy boots, western shirts, and expensive leather vests, a wide-brimmed Stetson, plus a huge gold belt buckle decorated with what looked like a snake's head with ruby eyes.

"Ain't my creek," I said.

"Ain't mine either, anymore," Travis Lee said. I raised an eyebrow. "Blue Creek doesn't look like much here," the old man said, his large hands lifting his hat and rumpling his thick thatch of white hair, as if it could be any more rumpled, "and over there where it joins the branch that crosses my brother's ranch, it doesn't look like too much either, but by the time it drops off the escarpment into Blue Hole, it's the perfect Hill Country creek." I didn't think I was supposed to say anything, yet, so I didn't, just pulled two more beers out of the cold spring water. "But I guess you knew that. Betty says you've become something of a Texas expert."

"Self-defense," I admitted.

"Hey, I've been to Montana," Travis Lee said. "You people up there can go round and round about being land-proud, too."

"Right, but there ain't so many of us on the dance floor."

"I always suspected that too much solitude might make a man a bit cranky," Travis Lee said.

"I like to see the sunset without too many people in the way," I said. "This is nice out here, but Austin is just another city—same faces, different scenery—except for the food and the music, it could be anywhere. Besides, I was born cranky."

"I just bet you were, boy," the huge old man said, his laughter filling the small valley.

"An old friend of mine who grew up down here tells me Montana would be perfect if it had less February, more barbecue, and some decent Mexican food."

"Hell, boy," the old man said, "it's too nice a day to sit around just looking at your fuzzy navel. You're lookin' as stale as yesterday's beer fart. Let's go to town, celebrate, maybe choke down a whiskey or two."

"Celebrate?"

"One less day to live with that slick socialist son of a bitch in the White House," he said. "That always makes me happy."

"I thought you used to be a Democrat?"

"*Used to be* being the operative phrase. Where do you stand in this political morass?" he asked.

"I guess I'm against everything."

"A cynic, then."

"I prefer to think of myself as a realist," I said.

"Whatever, let's go have a drink."

For reasons I didn't quite understand—he was a lawyer who specialized in putting land deals together, which meant developer, which rhymed with dog turd, as far as I was concerned—I said yes, left Betty a note, then climbed into Travis Lee's silly four-wheel-drive Ford crew cab pickup, the ideal rig for every lawyer seeking muddy fields and hay bales to buck.

We started with a whiskey visit to Travis Lee's law office where we drank expensive Scotch sitting among the old man's collection of the War of Northern Aggression artifacts—sabers and muskets and company rosters among dozens of original photographs.

"Sorry for the museum clutter," Travis Lee said.

"Pretty impressive," I said.

Travis Lee propped his hand-tailored boots on the desk, leaned back in his chair, and said, "I pretty much missed my war, I guess—broke my ankle on the last jump before we were supposed to ship out for Korea—so I guess I adopted this one. But you made the Korean thing, right?"

Somehow Wallingford's question bothered me. As if Korea had been like a visit to a theme park. But he was Betty's uncle, so I answered politely and honestly, "I was sixteen and stupid and my mother wanted me out of the house after my Dad died."

"Sounds like she wanted you dead," Wallingford said with the oddly blunt honesty that Texans sometimes had, and which I sometimes enjoyed.

"Who knows?" I said. "According to my Dad, my great-grandfather was at the Battle of the Wilderness when he was younger than that. Fourteen. Survived into his nineties, but he was still sharp. Hell, he was the sheriff of Meriwether County into his seventies. Tended bar into his late eighties."

"What did he have to say about the Wilderness?"

"According to my Dad, he said it wasn't much worse than being down in the Pennsylvania mines as a child," I said. "But bad enough so that after he got wounded, he hid in a pile of brush and bones, playing dead until he could whittle a crutch and hobble back to his lines."

I didn't add that the wound was caused by a rebel younger than himself who had found my great-grandfather when he stumbled over the pile of bones he was hiding beneath. Almost by accident the kid stuck a bayonet through his calf as my great-grandfather ran his bayonet through the kid's throat. My great-grandfather cauterized the wound with a red-hot ramrod, then whittled a crutch, and hobbled west instead of back to his unit. What the hell, it wasn't his war—his father had sent him in place of an older, more favored brother—so he headed into the setting sun, away from the war. He didn't have much English or any skills except the ability to shatter a coal face with a pick and a certain native willingness to use a firearm without hesitation, and his only ambition was for more sunlight and fewer bosses shouting at him. So he hobbled across the Great Plains swabbing bar floors, slopping pigs, and shoveling horseshit and hay while he worked on his English. By the time he got to Montana, the Gold Rush was almost over, the war was long over, so the first Milodragovitch in Montana became a peace officer, and, as was the custom in those days, a saloon owner and a whoremaster.

"Whores aren't bad people," Travis Lee said when I finished the story. "Let's go have a drink with several, professional and political."

Then we proceeded to a round of visiting drinks with his old political cronies, cranky to a man, and ex-colleagues at the law school, plus cops, bartenders, and ex-hookers. Then a late lunch at a tiny barbecue shack above Blue Creek, the only commercial establishment on the strip of the old family ranch that Travis Lee still owned north of the creek, where we played dominoes, drank Shiner beer, and ate smoked brisket as tender as a fresh biscuit.

"Milo," he said in his best voice, his great shaggy head hanging over the table, "you're too young to be retired. You're chewin' on your ass like a mangy hound, sittin' out there at the ranch, doin' nothin'. You need somethin' to do." Then he leaned his huge face across the table and whispered, "I understand you know something about the bar business . . ."

"I certainly do," I said.

". . . and that you've got a bundle of cash sittin' fallow in the

Caymans," he said. "I can raise some money from friends, add yours to mine, funnel it in through an offshore loan, and boy we got a gold mine right here, clean and legal."

Which is how we became partners in the Blue Hollow Lodge. Once I was convinced of the "clean and legal" part. But I insisted on owning the bar outright, to which Travis Lee agreed without much fuss. Betty was against it at first, especially the part where I lent her uncle some of the start-up money, saying that I was just using it as an excuse to get out of the house. Then without explanation she changed her mind. I had more money than I could spend in two lifetimes, even if I lived as long as my great-grandfather, and it did sound like a good way to get out of the house occasionally. Or maybe I was just tired, as I once said during an argument with Betty, of being her fancy man.

Of course, later, quickly bored with the bar business, I got my Texas PI ticket and six weeks after that moved out of Betty's ranch house . . .

. . . and into a large, anonymous motel suite on the ground floor, a place that, except for the heavy bag and free-weight set, could have been anywhere, belonged to anyone. Perhaps it should have seemed a sad place, but coming from Molly McBride's bed and facing a day when something might actually happen to break the routine of my days, it didn't seem so bad.

I called Betty at the clinic to let her know that I wasn't driving out to the ranch for breakfast. When she asked why, I answered, almost truthfully, "I've got a client."

"Christ on a crutch, Milo," she said, "are you on drugs? Or just fucking drunk?"

"Neither, particularly. Why?"

"Oh, hell, I don't know," she sighed, and I could see her forearm brush the hair off her face, "between the bar and your fucking *clients*, we never seem to see each other anymore anyway—"

"Lady," I interrupted, "between your job and trying to save Blue Creek, we don't see each other at all."

So she hung up on me. Not for the first time, either. I'd seen

Montana, even with its terrible winters, destroyed by greed, miners and developers and logging companies—Christ, Hayden Lomax's corporation even owned a leaking cyanide leach gold mine in eastern Montana that the state had been trying to shut down for years. Also an undeveloped shallow gas field on the edge of the Crazies— so I didn't share Betty's hope to save Blue Creek.

Early on she asked me one morning on her front porch why I wouldn't investigate Hayden Lomax and his development corporation that wanted to steal her uncle's ranch and surround the South Fork of Blue Creek with country club developments and fill it with phosphates, drain-field sewage, and golf balls.

"Nobody pays enough money for me to go up against really big money," I admitted. "You might as well ask me to investigate the mob."

"I don't know if it's the bar, or your so-called job," she said, "but I hate it when you're a cynical son of a bitch," she said. "Get off my property."

"It's nice to know that at least you, among all people, actually have property rights."

"You haven't paid your rent this month," she pointed out.

I wrote her a check for the usual amount, a thousand dollars, packed my war bag quickly, and left that day. We didn't speak for a month, and I didn't move back in for six weeks.

And God knows how long the silence would last this time if I told her about Molly McBride, I thought as the telephone rang. I almost let it ring but finally answered.

"Milo," Betty said softly, "we've got to sit down and talk before we lose this thing. Can't you make breakfast in the morning? Can't you put whatever you're doing off for at least that long? Please."

"Goddammit," I growled, breaking into her plea, "if you had a gutshot dog on the table, and I needed my aching heart stitched back on my sleeve, I wouldn't ask you to drop your work. So don't fucking ask me."

Then I hung up, took a long hot shower, and slept like a baby through what remained of the mad night.

CHAPTER FOUR

WHEN MOLLY MCBRIDE pulled her Ford Probe rental into the parking lot above the overlook, I climbed out of the Caddy, dressed for my part as the innocent jogger. Except for the floppy camouflage jersey that covered the S&W Centennial Airweight .38 strapped to the small of my back. Molly still wore the Tulane jersey, which nearly covered the bulky Glock stuffed into a fanny pack at the base of her back, and baggy sweats, her hair tucked under a New Orleans Saints hat that almost hid her scrubbed face. Neither of us acted as if we expected to greet each other as lovers or friends, so we just walked down the trail to the overlook. To the left, the creek bounced down the limestone shelves to join the deep well of the artesian spring. From above, the Blue Hole looked like an eye into a better world, clear and cold, yet somehow warm with the shafts of mid-morning sunlight filling the water. The shifting wind had died, and the cloudless sky seemed endless.

"Don't you have any questions?" she asked, a bit nervously.

"What's to know? The guy makes a move on you, I stop him, then let the cops deal with him. He doesn't, I follow him back to his car and check him out. It should be simple."

"I wish you'd just kill the bastard," she said, then patted her fanny pack.

"You didn't hire me for that," I said. "And if you start letting off rounds from that cannon, you'll probably shoot me or some poor software engineer across the hollow. Why don't you put it back in the car?"

"Why don't you put yours back?"

I shook my head, patted her shoulder, she smiled nervously again, then I searched the broken rocks of the slope above the overlook until I found a shadowed nook between two scrub cedars ten feet above the overlook as Molly stretched her legs against the low stone wall below. And we waited.

The guy had picked a good time. Mid-morning the park was usually empty, the dawn joggers off to their offices, the lunchtime joggers still tied to their desks. Not much foot traffic at all: an older couple walking their ragged mop dog; a college couple more interested in grabbing each other than running; and three singleton joggers in expensive Lycra suits.

Then a fourth, a tall, gawky bald-headed man, shuffled up the switchback from the creek bottom. He ran like a duck, feet splayed, elbows flapping like his oversize shorts and belly pack. A classic nerd, even to the thick horn-rims he wore. But he paused as if to catch his breath as the trail opened into the overlook, so I rose on my haunches. Molly hadn't even turned. With a quickness I couldn't believe, the jogger was behind her, his bony forearm around her neck in a choke hold, hissing something I couldn't hear in her ear.

I didn't even consider the .38, just rushed down the rocky slope and slammed a right hook into the nerd's kidney. The duck-footed guy grunted like a man hit with an axe handle and dropped to one knee as Molly spun away. I caught a glimpse of her red, frightened face as she dumped her fanny pack and fled. But even as he dropped to his knee, the guy caught me in the right thigh with a hard back-thrust blow from his bony elbow. For a moment I thought I'd been shot but managed to roll away and scramble to my feet, my right leg no more use than a boneless tube of flesh. I reached for the Airweight now, but the skinny guy front-kicked me in the chest so hard I left my feet and landed on my butt against a clutter of limestone shards on the side of the trail. Once again I felt as if I'd been shot, in the heart this time, mortally wounded, nailed to the ground, my hands dangling uselessly in my lap. The skinny guy moved toward me in some sort of martial arts shuffle and he had death in his angry eyes. Mine. I had no doubt that the kick aimed at my chin meant to snap my neck like a match stick.

With trembling hands, I managed to lift a large, flat limestone rock from between my knees and raised it in front of my face. When the skinny guy kicked, he broke the large rock in half with his lower leg, and the sole of his running shoe clipped the skin at the edge of my chin. He stumbled backward. In the bright sun his shinbone gleamed as yellow as pus before the blood covered it. But he didn't go down. He lifted his face to the sky, growling with pain, then he looked down, stared at me, confused for a moment as if things hadn't gone as planned. Then his hand darted to the belly pack with the hidden holster. The holster's Velcro opening sounded like ripping flesh. I did the only thing I could, threw the piece of rock in my right hand. The bastard must have had the hammer cocked and his finger on the trigger as he started to draw the pistol out of the belly holster, because when the rock hit his wrist, he jerked the trigger, releasing a muffled explosion at his groin.

He went down this time, castrated or emasculated or both by the muzzle blast and the round, a froth of dark blood foaming from his crotch, mixing with the bright red gush pumping from the femoral artery in his left thigh. He sat there leaning against the low stone wall, tendrils of smoke from the melted nylon of the pack drifting around his face, his hands on his knees, the pistol forgotten between his legs, opening and closing his mouth as if his teeth hurt, as he bled out almost peacefully.

I just sat there, too. I couldn't have helped if I wanted to. The skinny guy's eyes frosted over before I managed to get a full breath into my lungs, and even that one was full of tiny knives. My chest hurt so badly, I could just manage to raise my arm high enough to touch the bloody scrape dripping from the point of my chin. And, hell, even if I could have gotten up, I probably would have put a round right between the bastard's eyes for good measure. I didn't know who this guy was, but he sure as hell took a lot of killing.

When I could finally get up, I hobbled carefully around the massive puddle of blood curdling in the dust, and I couldn't help but notice that his hand was wrapped around a S&W Ladysmith .357. Just like the one I'd given Betty for her birthday, so she could stop carrying the huge .40 Ruger semiautomatic in her purse. Then a cell phone rang from Molly's pack dumped on the edge of the bloody pool. But it seemed too much trouble and pain to pick it up, so I trudged up to the Caddy for my cell phone, trying not to think about it. Just as I refused to think what the sudden disappearance of Molly McBride and her car must mean.

The first deputy on the scene, a young man named Culbertson, took one look at the body sitting in a lake of crusted blood, ignored the ringing cell phone, then put me on my knees, my fingers laced behind my head while he patted me down and recited my rights, even while reminding me that I wasn't under arrest. Yet.

"Where's the piece?" he asked when he found the empty holster at the small of my back.

"In the front seat of my car, officer," I said, "unloaded and sitting on my carry permit and my PI license."

The deputy jerked me to my feet by the cuffs, and marched me up to his unit in the parking lot, leaving the crime scene unsecured. Frankly, in spite of the pain, I was already thinking like a lawyer. Not soon enough, though, as it turned out. When the kid held my head down to ease me into the back seat of the unit, I thanked him. Suddenly, the kid shoved me into the back seat.

"Thanks, kid," I said.

The deputy stepped back, his hand trembling on the handle of his service revolver. "If I were you, you old son of a bitch," he spat, "I'd keep my smart mouth shut. Ty Rooke had a lot of—" Then he shut up as another unit howled into the parking lot. He slammed the door so quickly, I just had time to get my feet inside.

Where I sat for a long sweaty time, watching the passage of a lot of cops. Gannon was first on the scene, walked stiffly past Culbertson's unit without looking at me, then sent the deputy to watch over me. Then came the crime scene crew burdened with useless gear; the medical examiner with his team, loaded with false smiles; and several plainclothes detectives, teetering on cowboy boots, hip-shot by heavy revolvers on tooled leather belts, their eyes sullen with the code of the west, squinting as if they were John Wayne and I already swinging from a live oak.

Finally, Gannon returned after twenty minutes down at the crime scene, his suit coat soaked at the neck and armpits, his shoes dusty. He dismissed the young deputy, opened the unit's door, rubbed his sweaty face, then bagged my hands after he helped me out of the unit.

"A little late to be bagging . . ."

"Don't say another word," he grunted, interrupting me. "Not one fucking word."

"What the hell is going on?"

"Milodragovitch," Gannon hissed from the corner of his mouth as he led me to his unit, "either shut up, or I'll have you gagged."

Which made me quite glad that after I called 911 on my cell phone, I left messages on the answering machines that picked up instead of Betty, Travis Lee, and Phil Thursby.

"Well, before you have me gagged, Captain, dig the cell phone out of the extra belly pack and hit star 69."

Gannon didn't even bother to look at me.

I kept my mouth shut all the way into Gatlinsburg and up to the jail on the top floor of the limestone courthouse, where they formally arrested me for capital murder, then held another reading of my rights, complete with three assistant DAs, Sheriff Benson in full dress uniform, and a television news crew. My buddy, Gannon, seemed to have disappeared. They booked me and let me piss into a jar and tested my hands for gunpowder residue before they roughly forced me into an orange jumpsuit and chained me to the table in an interrogation room for what seemed like a long time.

I knew they were watching me through the two-way mirror, so I tried to be calm without going to sleep, which I knew they'd take as a sure sign of guilt. Truth was I had killed men before, too many to suit me and several face-to-face, and I knew better than to dwell on it. Instead I concentrated on a lake high in the mountains of Glacier Park, Upper Quartz Lake, where the water was deep enough so that waterlogged firs hung upright in the clear water, where a single loon sang against the cliffs of the cirque just to hear himself. The other memories would have to take care of themselves.

And I'd had my share of dealings with police officers. I told myself I had nothing to worry about—no nitrates on my hands, I could feel the skinny guy's footprint blooming across my bruised chest, and in the mirror I could see the scrape leaking down my chin—but something caught my eye at the small wire-glass window set into the doorway. The face peering at me, except for the glasses, which were rimless, could have belonged to the dead man. And these eyes had a burning message in them, too. Whatever the eyes were saying, I knew it was not good news.

Before they took me down to the courtroom to arraign me—as Gannon had told me, things moved quickly in small Texas counties—Culbertson and another grim-faced deputy put me in ankle shackles and cuffed me to a waist chain, then threaded a chain through the handcuffs. They hustled me down the hallway as if they wanted me to do the guilty-man shuffle, but I refused. When they tried elbow lock come-alongs, I ate the pain, and refused to hurry. When they pushed, I collapsed into their arms and managed to knock off their cowboy hats.

"Watch it, you shitbag," the other one whispered harshly. "Either walk, or we'll throw you down the stairs instead of takin' the elevator."

"Fuck you kids," I said quietly as I grabbed the grim-faced one who reached for his night stick and stuck my thumb into the nerve center behind his thumb. "Push me again, asshole, and I'll take you straight to hell with me. A dead solid promise."

"Crazy old bastard," the white-faced one said as he jerked his hand back and then hit me in the small of the back with a stun gun.

After that, at least I had the pleasure of making them carry me into the almost empty courtroom for my arraignment. I did my best to slobber on their tooled cowboy boots.

A nervous young man stood at the defendant's table. My defender, I assumed, appointed by the judge since Texas didn't have a public defender program, but I neither listened to the kid's name nor shook his offered hand. The bald man who looked like the dead guy was standing at the prosecutor's table beside a chubby woman in a suit of an unfortunate shimmering electric blue. Then the judge stepped up to the bench and slapped it with a large, hard hand. Judge Steelhammer, his nameplate said, didn't need a gavel. Then he started talking, but I didn't listen too carefully. The effects of the stun gun were still ricocheting around my aching body.

The bald man stood up, wearing a perfectly fitted khaki twill suit. Judge Steelhammer spoke directly to him. "I want to express my deepest regrets to the district attorney for the loss of his brother and to thank him for standing aside in this matter at hand." The bald man nodded curtly, gave me a look, then left the courtroom.

Then the judge turned to me, his eyes as pale as ball bearings beneath his thick, dark brows. "Mr. Milodragovitch," the judge rumbled, "you stand before me accused of capital murder, and believe me this court takes the death of an officer of the law, on or off duty, very seriously. How do you plead to the charge?"

Before I could answer, the doors banged open as Betty and her uncle rushed into the courtroom, Travis Lee shouting, "Your Honor, if you please—a moment to confer with my client before the plea?"

Judge Steelhammer looked as if he were one of those conserva-

tives in Texas who hadn't found Wallingford's antics in the legislature amusing or his change in political parties convincing, but as an
elected official Judge Steelhammer was nobody's political fool. He
smiled grimly and said, "Mr. Wallingford, please. I didn't realize
you'd taken up criminal law, but, please, take all the time you need."

Betty, dressed in a Longhorn sweat suit and running shoes, as if
just back from a run, sat down in the front row. Wallingford pushed
through the gate, elbowed the public defender out of the way,
slapped his briefcase on the table, and pulled me into his shoulder.
I could swear that his blue pin-striped suit smelled of mothballs.
"Phil's in Houston, son," he whispered, "so you're going to have to
make do with me. What did you do to make a sheriff's detective assault you?"

I gave him the short version of the events and showed him the
leaking scrape on my chin and the bruise spreading across my chest,
the tread of the bald guy's running shoes stamped very clearly over
my sternum. Wallingford quickly convinced the judge to send an officer down to the lab for the dead man's shoes. Even from the bench
the judge could see that the arrow shapes on the running shoes' soles
matched my contusions. Then Steelhammer conferred with Travis
Lee and the chubby woman. I kept my eyes on her wide, shining
hips, afraid, or ashamed, to turn to look at Betty.

Everyone back in place, the judge conferred with the chubby
woman and reduced the charge, then set bail at two hundred fifty
thousand dollars, cash or property bond.

"Shit," I muttered to Wallingford, "I can't make that without
dipping into the offshore accounts."

"You fuck this up," Wallingford whispered, "I'll hunt you down
like an egg-suckin' hound." Then he took a folded document from
his coat pocket, turned to the judge, and said, "I have the deed to
the Blue Creek Ranch, which has been appraised at well over that
amount, and the owner, Miss Betty Porterfield, has agreed to post
the bond."

"I can't let her do that," I whispered as I turned to look at Betty.

She looked away quickly. But the judge slammed his hand on the bench again, and it was done.

"We'll see you outside," Wallingford said curtly as the deputies took me away.

To a cell this time—a bit more roughly and not wearing their name tags—where we waited together as the paperwork was processed, and where I learned the dead man's name for sure. "This is for Ty Rooke," the deputy with the sore hand whispered as he ground the stun gun into the base of my spine the first time. "And this one is for me, motherfucker," he hissed as he hit me with the stun gun the last time.

Or it was the last time as far as I knew.

The sunshine was flat by the time I climbed stiffly into the front seat of Wallingford's crew cab Ford pickup. Betty sat stolidly behind the steering wheel and stared blankly out the windshield as I quietly thanked her for putting up the ranch and promised to raise the cash to replace the bond as quickly as I could. Wallingford sprawled across the back seat like a man who had spent the day bucking bales. In his rumpled courtroom suit. The air-conditioning was on high, and I shivered in my running shorts and thin shirt.

"You okay?" Betty asked, as I grunted and wrestled with the seat belt. She still didn't look at me.

"For a guy who started the day by getting the shit kicked out of him," I groaned. "And ended it in a jail cell with two psychopaths, I'm fair to middling."

"There's a photographer and a forensic pathologist waiting at the emergency room," Wallingford said quietly from the back. "They work you over pretty good?"

"Nothing that will show," I said.

"What did they do?" Betty said, finally looking at me, her fingers soft on my cheek.

"Nothing I didn't deserve," I admitted. "One of theirs is dead. And I'm the chosen asshole."

"What else?" Wallingford said, sitting up now.

"They're holding the Beast, my license, and my piece," I said.

"How long?" Betty asked, as if it mattered.

"The Airweight's probably history, and I suspect the Caddy will come back in lots of little pieces. It's just stuff. Fuck it."

"They can't do that," Betty said, but neither of us looked at her. We knew they could do damn near anything they wanted.

"You want to give me the rest of it?" Wallingford said. "The long version."

"After the emergency room. In the bar," I said. "I need something solid to lean on."

When I didn't show up for my shift, Mike Herrera doubled over without complaint. He even made a joke when I hobbled to the bar on Betty's arm wearing a gray sweat suit we'd picked up at the nearest mall, Wallingford close behind me. But when I didn't smile, Mike closed his face into a well-learned expressionless Mexican mask and brought the drinks without comment as we huddled at the empty end of the bar. We ordered drinks, then I asked Mike for the telephone so I could call the front desk to ask the reception clerk to pull the security tape from Molly McBride's registration, and to make a copy and lock the original in the hotel safe.

I drank the Scotch in one long painful swallow, wiping out the taste of the pissant pain pills, which were all I could talk out of the ER doc. Well, it didn't have to go on too long. I had a stash of codeine in the gun safe on the north side of Austin. Wallingford sipped at a pint of draft beer as Betty stirred her coffee thoughtfully, her face carefully blank after she heard me mention Molly McBride's name. I didn't think much about it at the time, just ordered another Macallan, a water back this time.

"You sure you don't want to sit down?" Betty asked.

"Sitting down is the last thing on my mind."

"This isn't the best venue to tell your story," Wallingford suggested.

"Here or nowhere," I said. "This is the only time you're going to hear it." Then I turned to Betty. "Maybe you better have a drink, too, hon. This isn't going to be pretty."

Betty ordered a shot of Frangelico, dumped it into her coffee, then stared stiffly into the remains of the sunset. Wallingford reached for his notebook, but I stopped him with a look. Then I ran down the whole sordid story. Betty never flinched. Not even when I finished by saying, "Please don't ask me if I'm as stupid as I look, because I am. And Betty, before you say anything, I need a quick favor."

"What?"

"Go in the bathroom. Check the serial number of your revolver against your carry permit."

"Order me another drink," she said as she picked up her large purse and walked quickly out of the bar.

"What's that about?" Wallingford wanted to know. "What's going on?"

"Just hope I'm wrong," I said, then signaled for another drink.

She seemed to be gone a long time. Travis Lee put his hand on my shoulder, then said, "Milo, I know this might not seem the right time for this question, but given your troubles, maybe it is. Have you thought any more about that investment opportunity I was tellin' you about?" He had been nagging at me for weeks about some surefire investment he wanted me to help him with. I guess I must have looked at him as if he were insane. "Another time," he said quickly, patting me softly on the shoulder.

Betty came back, her tear-stained face white, her fingers trembling as she gunned the liqueur. "Serial numbers don't match," she said quietly. "Guess I should go to the range more often."

"Right," I said. "Shouldn't we all."

"And it's worse than that," she said, a sudden blush rising so hard up her face that her freckles nearly disappeared beneath the flushed skin. "I gave that woman the Annette McBride story," she said, then paused for a long moment. "And the dog, I gave her the goddamned dog. She came around saying she was doing a piece for

a San Francisco environmental paper about trying to save the Blue
Hole, and she pumped it all out of me." Then she added carefully,
"In a motel room bed. It started when you went to Montana."

"Wonderful," I said. "I'll be fucked." It was all I could think to
say. Her admission hit me like a jolt from the stun gun. Hell, I knew
that Betty had slept with several women in the years after she had
been raped. But I didn't know what to think about this. I shook my
head as if I'd just been hit, then laughed. Or something like a laugh,
only hollow and empty, like a sleeping dog's dreaming bark. "Well,
whoever the hell she is and whatever the fuck it is that she does for
a living," I said, "she's damned good at her job." Then I barked
again.

Betty's eyes brimmed with tears. I had to look away.

"But why?" Wallingford wanted to know.

"I don't know," I said. "I don't even know how to begin guessing."

Wallingford excused himself, leaving Betty and me alone in the
uncrowded bar.

A room service waiter came into the bar to hand me a videotape.
"Room clerk says it's in the right place."

"Thanks," I said, then when the kid left, turned to Betty, and
said as softly as I could, "And thank you, too."

"For what?" she asked quietly.

"You didn't have to tell me," I told her. "At least now I know
that we were both being set up. But I have to admit that I don't
know what to think or what to feel or anything. Except maybe I'd
like to hit somebody."

"Hit me."

"No, I'd rather hit a stranger," I said. "Or myself. Fuck it, I'll
think about it later."

Betty didn't say anything, just leaned over to hug me, her wet
cheek against mine. I leaned into her body and bit my lip when a series of back spasms hit under her hard embrace, but she felt it,
moved her hands lower to knead the jerking muscles.

"I'm off for a couple of days. I could . . . could stay with you tonight," she murmured with a soft sob. But she felt me shake my head. "What the hell, I've already been stood up once today."

My mind was cluttered with too many things to think about what she had said. One of the things we had fought most often and most bitterly about since I had moved out of the ranch house was Betty's constant refusal to stay with me at the Lodge. "I don't think so," I whispered into her shoulder.

Which is how Wallingford found us. "You folks are crazy," he said. "This is no time for spoonin'."

"Don't be stupid, Uncle Travis," Betty said over my shoulder. Sometimes she seemed constantly angry at her uncle.

I stood up as straight as I could, took a deep breath that felt as if somebody had hit me in the chest with an axe handle, then leaned heavily on the bar. "Look, folks," I said. "I really appreciate your help. Why don't you two take off? I'm going to have a couple of more drinks, then a double dose of these pissant pain pills, and I'm going to bed. I'll think about all this shit when I wake up. I'll call you two tomorrow."

Travis Lee slapped me on the shoulder and wished me a good night. Then Betty hugged me again, perhaps harder than she meant to. I sagged against the bar.

"Are you okay?" she asked.

"I'm fucking fine," I snapped.

They finally left, and I wrapped myself around my Scotch.

Which is how Gannon found me later as he served the search warrant for my room and the court order to confiscate my passport.

"Hell, I don't have even have a passport," I said—I *didn't* have a passport in my own name, but several in other names; I'd been prepared to run all my adult life—and my room was clean. Everything important was in the gun locker. Except for Billy Long's cocaine, which was taped inside the emergency light in the elevator.

"And I'd like you to watch the search," Gannon said. "If you don't mind, Mr. Milodragovitch."

"As long as you'll give me a hand, and I can take my drink," I said.

"You want your lawyer?" Gannon asked. "I think I saw him standing around the lobby phone bank."

"No fucking lawyers," I said, then held out my elbow for Gannon to grasp.

As Gannon helped me down the hall, he said quietly, "You're walking like an old man."

"It don't take much of this shit to make you old."

"I'm sorry about that."

"I'm not complaining," I told him honestly. "They're just kids. And sometimes payback is part of the job description."

"Right, but the stupid bastards were bragging and laughing in the locker room," Gannon said.

"It ain't the worst thing that ever happened to me."

"I don't want to hear the worst," Gannon said, almost smiling as we stopped at the unnumbered door of my room.

Gannon tossed the room with a quick and practiced expertise without leaving the least mess. I complimented him. "Good work, man, the only thing you didn't find was the mouse fart."

"Right lizard boot, you goddamned drunk," Gannon said as he wrote a number on the back of one of his cards and left it by the telephone. "This is my personal cell phone. Call me before you leave town. We'll have a drink somewhere down the road. In another county. Maybe you'll tell me what really happened."

"I've got no plans to leave town," I said.

"You better leave," Gannon said. "Believe me. Word around the courthouse is that Steelhammer plans to dismiss your charges tomorrow, so you'll get your bond, your piece, your car, and your license back. Until the grand jury convenes in three weeks and comes in with a capital murder indictment. Tobin Rooke is a mean, smart son of a bitch, and he and his twin brother were as tight as two baby snakes in a single egg. They've never lived apart. So you can bet your ass he's gonna nail you for something, and it won't be pleasant. You can count on that."

I used the arms of the chair to push myself upright, then said,

"He better bring his lunch this time, Captain, 'cause they fucked with the wrong dog."

"Forgive me for pointing it out," Gannon said, "but clearly you ain't as tough as you think."

"I dug my own grave once," I said, "but I ain't buried in it yet."

Gannon's face remained impassive. "You need a hand back to the bar?"

"You really want to know what really happened. Off the record?"

"Rooke was a complete asshole, man," he said, "but you know I can't go off the record with a suspect. Not on a mess like this."

"Well, fuck you then," I said. Then I told him the whole story. Except for the fact that it seemed that Molly McBride had stolen Betty's revolver.

"That doesn't make any sense," Gannon said.

"You're telling me," I said, "unless he was moonlighting as a hit man."

"I've always thought he was dirty—too tight with rich folks—but hiring out for a hit? I just don't know," Gannon mused.

"The son of a bitch was going to kill me," I said. "There's not a smidgin of a doubt in my mind."

"You sure you just didn't piss him off?"

"Right," I said. "Have you got the technology to get a photo off this tape?"

Gannon shook his head. "Not without involving other people in the department. And I don't think you want that. Try this guy downtown." Gannon picked up his card off the telephone table and scribbled another number on the back of it. "Let me know if I can help."

"You can help me back to the bar," I said. And he did. Later, I made it back to the room leaning on Mike Herrera's shoulder. But I couldn't sleep. I grabbed my smokes and a beer out of the small fridge and shuffled outside to the balcony that overlooked the hollow.

No matter how I looked at it, I couldn't come up with a reason why an off-duty sheriff's detective would want to kill me. Unless it had something to do with my vague campaign to save Enos Walker from an undeserved hit from the state's needle. The slice of the moon was smaller than the night before and it seemed somehow sharper, the soft rush of the Blue Hole somehow farther away.

It was two the next afternoon before I could struggle to the Jacuzzi. Mike brought me a Bloody Mary and a plate of Pete's hottest tacos. The weather had held, and I found myself basking in the sunlight like a lazy dog.

"So what are we going to do now?" Betty asked as she squatted behind me.

"First, stop sneaking up on me," I said.

"You didn't call," she said. "And I was afraid you never would."

I leaned back far enough to see her face. She looked as if she hadn't slept any better than I had. "You're right," I admitted. "I probably wouldn't have. I need to work some things out."

"Let me help," she said. "I've got to help. I'm involved, too, re-member."

"I don't know," I said. "I suspect that things are going to get worse before they get better."

"Some people are better in a crisis," she said, "than they are in day-to-day life."

"Don't I know it?"

She leaned down to help me out of the Jacuzzi. It was a little more difficult than either of us expected. "How do you feel?"

"As if I've been hit by a train, love."

"Well, keep it in mind, old man, you aren't as young as you used to be."

"Hell, I never was," I said.

CHAPTER FIVE

IT TOOK ANOTHER FULL DAY of moving carefully between my
bed and the Jacuzzi and gobbling pissy little pain pills before I
could climb into Betty's pickup so she could drive me by the locker,
where I gathered up enough drugs to allow me a little movement,
then she dropped me at Carver D's house. Carver D had been burning cyberspace oil. He hadn't dug up anything more on Sissy Duval,
except that she wouldn't come to the telephone or return messages
and that after her husband's death, she had sold the bar and license
to a chain of self-service laundries down in the Rio Grande Valley, a
chain that was suspected of washing more than dirty shorts. They
had kept Billy Long as a manager until his untimely death, then
quickly gave his job to the pudgy bartender, Leonard Wilbur. Carver
D had pulled the court files on the Dwayne Duval shooting. He had
been killed by a college kid from Mexia, Texas, a Richard Wylie
Oates, who, except for traffic tickets, had never run afoul of the law
before and whose folks were even cleaner. Oates had been convicted
of second-degree murder, with Steelhammer on the bench. The jury
had sentenced him to a huge jolt of hard time, which he was still
serving outside Huntsville. He'd done fifteen and had been twice de-

nied parole. Enos Walker had an older brother living in Austin, a preacher. But he didn't answer his telephone or return messages, either.

"Looks like you've got your work cut out for you," Carver D suggested as he handed me the Molly McBride registration tape back, along with a sheaf of head shots of the lady in question. "You want to borrow Hangas?"

"Thanks," I said, "but as soon as I get my ride back, Betty's going to chauffeur me around."

"Y'all back together?"

"Together might not exactly be the right word."

"What's that mean?" he asked, wiggling in his antique chair so hard that I thought the wheels were going to pop off.

"You don't want to know," I told him. "You have any luck with the serial number on the piece in Betty's purse?"

"Got it as far as a gun dealer in Little Rock," he said. "Usually a dead end there."

"Well, thanks."

"It's great to be nosy for a purpose," Carver D said. "Watch your back, man."

"Just as soon as I can stand to look at it," I said. "Now call me a cab."

"You're a cab."

A couple of days later when Phil Thursby got back from Houston, where he had managed to plead a capital murder down to manslaughter-one even though the crackhead rich kid from Clear Lake had been caught on video and confessed to killing a Vietnamese convenience store clerk, he came into the bar while I was behind the stick giving Mike a much needed break. Thursby hopped on a stool, and shook his head slowly, almost painfully. Thursby had a high forehead above thick black-rimmed glasses and looked like a teenager playing a criminal lawyer in a high school play. But he had pale blue eyes, as restless and mad as a rabid dog's, a thin mouth like a knife wound, a curiously deep and soothing voice, and he was one of the best criminal lawyers in the state. Except for an occasional glass of Veuve Cliquot champagne and a nose for trouble, Thursby seemed to have no vices. He bought his suits off the rack in the boys' section at Penney's, still lived in the small frame house off Red River where he'd been raised, and drove a battered Toyota Corolla with neither a radio nor air-conditioning. Wallingford said the little bastard didn't need a radio because he listened to the voices in his head, or air-conditioning because he had liquid nitrogen in his veins.

"Remember, Milo, if Carver D wasn't your buddy, I wouldn't even talk to you," Thursby rumbled as I pulled a cork and filled a flute for him. He took a tiny sip, nodded as if he approved, then added, "as far as I know Steelhammer plans to dismiss your charges, but when the grand jury convenes, and with your history, unless you happened to be hanging on the cross next to Jesus Christ that day and he'll climb down to swear to it, Gatlin County will indict you. Tobin Rooke is almost as good as I am, but he lacks my convictions." Thursby allowed himself a flicker of a smile, larger than an eyelash, but not much. "He knows he really hasn't got a duck's fart chance of stinkin' in a blue norther to finally get you in prison," Thursby continued, "but it'll cost you a couple hundred K just to get it to a jury verdict, and believe me, they'll convict, so then it's another hundred for the appeal, with no guarantee that we can beat this before we can get it into federal court." Thursby paused, sipped at a single champagne bubble, then added, "You want the best free advice I've ever given?"

"My father always told me free advice usually wasn't worth what it cost," I said. "What do you want for a retainer?"

"To hell with that. Sell everything you own," Thursby said, ignoring me, "and learn to speak Portuguese."

"Brazil?"

"You'll like it there," Thursby said, "the women are pretty and the drugs are cheap." Then Thursby took another tiny sip of the champagne, hopped off the stool, and turned to leave. "Let's start with fifty thousand."

"I'm too old to move again," I said as I waved him back. "Give me a couple of days," I said quietly as I leaned over the bar, "and I'll come up with the money."

"Clean?"

"As clean as I can make it. But if it isn't, will you take that case, too?" I asked.

"Not my style," Thursby said flatly. "Put it in my overseas account. You've got the number."

"If you had a sense of humor," I said, pushing a standard PI contract across the bar, "you'd be dangerous."

"Dead wrong," Thursby said as he signed it so I would at least have a little confidentiality coverage and left, saying, "Don't abuse this. I don't want to have to defend this thing in court."

Later that afternoon, as predicted, Judge Steelhammer dismissed the charges and released the bond, and the Sheriff's Department released the Cadillac and the Airweight. Of course, when I picked them up, the Beast came back with a location beeper under the gas tank and the Airweight with a broken firing pin. Gannon stopped by after work, so I complained to him about the alterations in my machinery. He just leaned on the bar as if trying to decide what to drink.

"You're lucky you're not dead," Gannon chuckled, "and the Caddy stashed in a chop-shop in Nuevo Laredo."

"I'd forgotten how lucky I was," I said. "Thanks for reminding me, Capt. Gannon."

"Call me Jimmy."

"Not yet," I said. "You're still on duty."

"Not now," he said.

"Well, we still haven't had that drink."

"Last time I saw you, Milo, you had them all," Gannon said. "I'll have whatever your lawyer drinks."

"I do that sometimes," I said as I filled two flutes with some of Thursby's champagne, "but I seem to remember an offer of help."

"I think I offered to help you pack."

"How about something else?" I asked.

Gannon lifted his glass and his eyes narrowed as he frowned. "What's in it for me?"

"Enos Walker," I said. "Lalo Herrera is coming out of retirement to cover my shifts and manage his sons and the bar, so I can give this my full attention."

"What the hell's Walker got to do with Rooke's death?"

"Damned if I know," I admitted, "but it sure seems like my troubles started there."

"What do you want?"

"The case files on the Dwayne Duval shooting. That's all."

"That was before my time," he said. "I think the state boys handled the investigations back then. I'd have to sign the files out."

"Whatever happened to interdepartmental cooperation?" I said.

"Not my department," Gannon sighed, then we clicked glasses. "But I'll see what I can do."

"Please," I said quietly.

Gannon savored the champagne. "Here's to the good life."

"And a copy of those files."

I didn't really have any real hope that Gannon could or would get them to me, but it seemed like a good idea to get him in the habit of at least trying to do favors for me. We finished the flutes, then he walked slowly out, as if the single glass of champagne had made him wistful.

Gannon was barely out of the bar when Travis Lee stepped through the door and pulled up a stool at the end of the bar next to the glass wall over the hollow. At least he set his cowboy hat on the bar, so I didn't have to point out the sign prohibiting umbrellas. He smiled, ran his fingers through his thick gray hair as if to remind himself that he still had it.

I held up the champagne bottle.

"A headache in every swallow," he snorted. "Turkey on the rocks," he said. "A double. And a beer back."

After I got his drink, I poured myself another glass of champagne. No sense in losing the expensive fizz. As I lit a cigarette, Travis Lee bummed one off me. "I didn't know you smoked."

"Haven't had one in twenty-five years," he said, then hit the cigarette so hard that he burned a half-inch of it into ash. "Damn, that's good."

"What's up?" I asked.

"Oh, I was just in the Lodge, so I thought I'd stop in and see how your back's coming along and remind you that we have a chance to make a lot of money very easily and very quickly," he said.

"I got some other stuff on my plate right now," I said.

"What? Tending bar?" he said.

"I'm just giving Mike a few days off so he'll cover my shifts while I try to dig out from under this load of crap that has fallen on me," I said. "Phil says I've got about three weeks."

"Where are you planning to start?" he asked, but he didn't sound either interested or confident.

"First I'm going to talk to the kid that shotgunned Dwayne Duval."

"What the hell does that have to do with anything?" Oddly enough, he seemed interested now.

"I don't know exactly," I admitted. "It's just a place to start." I didn't tell him that Sissy Duval had lied to me. If you can't follow the money, I thought, perhaps you should try to unravel the lies. "You didn't know this Duval character, did you?"

"I bought a drink or two off him in the old days," he said. "I've known his widow since she was a kid."

"Sissy?"

"Yeah," he sighed, then tossed off the Turkey. "She used to be a pistol. Haven't seen her in a while." Then he looked at me as if he knew I had. But I didn't say anything. "You think Duval's death is connected somehow to the, ah, young woman who, ah . . ." He paused to sip on his beer. "That killing was a long time ago."

"I don't know," I said. "Every case has to start somewhere," I added, "and what's the point of being a private eye if you can't follow a hunch. If I believed in a rational world, maybe I'd still be a cop."

Travis Lee looked at me as if I were insane, finished his beer, and my cigarette, then said, "Well, son, call me when you come back to the rational world." Then he picked up his cowboy hat, set it on his head carefully, and strolled away like a man without a care in the world.

Since I was Phil Thursby's investigator, I didn't have any trouble getting an appointment with Dickie Oates. The prison officials hated Thursby almost as much as they were frightened of him, so they even let me talk to Dickie in a small conference room. Somewhere beneath the hard-ass con who sat down across the table from me, I could see the lanky, snaggle-toothed lop-eared kid with a round, open face that Oates must have been at the time of the Duval killing. But now Oates was all busted knuckles and scars. A crooked nose parted his face, and dark shadows lurked deep in his bright blue eyes. All in all, though, he didn't look too bad for all his years as a guest of the Texas Department of Corrections. But we both knew the real story was worse than his face and body showed.

"So why the hell is Phil Thursby interested in reviving my appeal?" Oates asked, smiling cynically. He didn't have to ask who Phil Thursby was. "My fuckin' lawyer ain't."

"Look, Mr. Oates," I lied as I opened a leather legal-sized notebook, "we don't know if he's interested or not. Right now. But he has a team of interns who do nothing but read transcripts and old case files. One of them pointed out that there seemed to be something missing in your story."

"Like what?"

"Why don't you tell me the story," I suggested, "and I'll see if it's there."

For the first time, Oates smiled slightly, scratching at his left eyebrow, where a new scab nestled, then he locked his hands on the table, eager now, hopeful, it seemed, for the first time in a long time.

"Okay," Oates began, "so I'm playing pool in this joint with a bunch of my frat bro's, and somebody started bitching about table roll and scratching on the eight ball or some shit. Nothing too loud,

just guys mouthing, when this coked-up asshole who said he owned
the place threw us out.

"So what the hell, we had words, but we went. I was the last one
out the door and stepped around the corner to take a leak between
the wall and my pickup, and while I got my pecker in my hand, this
fucker slams my face into the rock wall with his forearm. When I
turned around, he blasted me good . . ." Oates touched his crooked
nose. "When I hit the ground, he put the boots to me. Pretty hard.
Till some women pulled him off, three or four of them, then one of
them helped me to my pickup."

"What do you remember about that woman?"

"Not much," Oates said. "Tall, lots of hair, blond maybe, nearly
as fucked up as the guy."

"What did she say to you?"

"Nothing much," Oates said. "Apologized, sort of, called him an
asshole. That sort of shit."

"She suggest payback?"

"Yeah, well, maybe," Oates said, frowning again. "Ain't you leading the witness, Counselor?"

"Ain't my problem. Your shotgun, was it in the gun rack?"

"Not a chance, sir," he answered. "It was my Daddy's quail gun,
and I wouldn't hang it up in a rack like some asshole redneck. I had
it in a case behind the seat." Oates shook his head sadly. "When that
little detail came out in court that was the end of any talk about a
manslaughter plea. My lawyer said I was lucky the prosecutor didn't
go for first degree. The jury was filled with Gatlin County corporate
crackers. They would have given the needle for sure."

I knew from the courthouse rumors that Steelhammer had a
record of coming down hard on college students who came into his
county to break the law. Then because I didn't have any other questions, I asked, "You ever do any cocaine back then?"

"Shit, man, it was Austin," he grumbled. "Back in those days
ever' third sorority girl had 'I Love Champagne, Cadillacs, and Cocaine Cowboys with Cash' tattooed under her pubic hair."

"Ever buy any out of Duval's Place?"

"Not me," he said. "There was a rumor that the guy who bought for the frat house got his product there. But, hell, I didn't know shit from wild honey in those days."

Then I wondered, "This lady you were talking about, she say anything else?"

"Sometimes when I dream about it, man, she does," Oates said. "She asked me if I had a gun in my truck."

"When you dream about it? Spare me the psychological bullshit," I said. "I know you've got more time on the couch than a retired hound dog."

"That couch shit doesn't happen much in the Texas Department of Corrections, man. Not much," Oates said seriously, refusing to be denied. "But I dream about that night all the time, almost every night when I can get to sleep, so how the hell am I supposed to remember what really happened? In the dream, most of the time, she calls him over, so I think he's coming after me again, and, man, I was already fucked up. Four cracked ribs, two broken fingers on my right hand, a crushed nut, and my nose, well, it felt like it was touching my ear. So I up and shot the motherfucker when he came after me. Once in the guts, then once in the face."

"In the face with the second barrel?"

"That's what they said."

"They said?"

"At the trial."

"You don't remember?" I asked.

"Not really," Oates whispered, shaking his head. "The first shot hurt my hand and my head so much, I don't remember the second one. Hell, for a while it looked like the bastard was gonna pull through, but he already had some kinda sinus infection, and it got into his brain. So that fucked the dog for me."

"You don't remember anything else about the women?" I asked as I closed the notebook. "I don't remember a single woman on the witness list."

"You know how it is. My lawyer couldn't find anybody who admitted they were even there. Not even my friends." Oates sucked a tooth and shook his head. "You think you can do anything?"

"All I can do is try," I said, then handed Oates a card. "You remember anything about the woman, even dream anything, you call me collect."

"You mean that?"

"Sure," I said. "Sometimes we don't remember things until we're talking about it."

"Thanks," Oates said. "I'll try not to take advantage of the offer."

"Take care," I said, resigning myself to collect conversations with Oates.

"Next time, bring in a lungful of smoke," Oates said quietly. "Secondhand smoke is the only kind we get in here."

"Right," I said, then started to leave. "How do your parole hearings go?"

"Man," he said, "I don't know. I don't have a record out in the world and not much bad time in here, but they treat me like I'm a fuckin' serial killer or something. That snakefucker of a prosecutor has showed up every time." Then he paused, a sly look flitting across his face. "You're the dude that killed his brother, ain't you?"

"It was an accident," I said. "And they dropped the charges."

"Those Gatlin County assholes," he said. "Those corrupt bastards will find some way to nail you."

"Maybe not," I said. But I didn't have any more hope than Dickie Oates did when I left.

When I climbed stiffly into the passenger seat of the El Dorado, Betty turned from behind the wheel and considered me. "We gotta do something about that back, Milo," she said. "Pills and hot tubs don't seem to be doing a bit of good."

"That's for damn sure," I said. "Thanks for taking the time off to drive me over. I don't think I could have made it without you."

"No problem," she said quietly, a stiff smile on her face. Then she started the car, saying, "I didn't take off. I quit. For a while."

"What?"

"Well, I didn't exactly quit," she said. "I just took an unpaid leave."

"What did they think about that?"

"I sort of own the practice," she said quietly, "so I don't much give a shit what they think."

"I didn't know that," I said, wondering why she worked nights in her own clinic. Maybe she was trying to stay out of trouble, working nights. That's what I had told myself back when I tended bar at night. I didn't know. But she had said she was better in a crisis than in everyday life. Maybe that explained it. Since it seems a crisis always pulls into your driveway after midnight.

"There's a lot of things about me you don't know," Betty said, a grim smile on her face as she eased out of the prison's parking lot.

I wondered what those other things might be, but right then they didn't seem very important.

"But about your back?"

"What?"

"You remember my friend Cathy Scoggins?"

"The ditsy broad who's always stoned?"

"She's a damn fine acupuncturist," she said, "not a broad. Why don't you let her work on your back?"

"Has she ever worked on you?"

Betty paused a moment, then said, "Not exactly, but she's had good luck with some of my patients."

"Dogs and horses and scabby calves?" I said. "Why not? Will she let me get stoned, too?"

"She'll probably insist on it," Betty said.

After a long pause, I said, "I don't know what to say about you taking off from work."

"Just say 'thank you,' you fucking idiot."

"Thank you, you fucking idiot," I said, but my heart didn't seem to be in it, so I popped a couple of codeine tablets and leaned the seat back, and drifted off as quickly as I could.

We were hunkering over barbecue plates at Black's in Lockhart before Betty asked me what I had learned from the Oates kid.

"Not much that makes sense," I admitted. "I know that he's doing too much time for the crime, and Steelhammer was the judge. But I've got this funny feeling about the shooting. I'd bet the farm that somebody else—probably this woman he dreams about—fired the second barrel into Dwayne Duval's face that night." And just that easily I picked up another chore: keep Enos Walker out of the execution chamber, get Dickie Oates out of prison, keep Betty Porterfield out of trouble, and keep my old ass out of jail. "Or something crazy like that," I said, then drifted off into worrying.

"Well, that's certainly an insane idea," Betty said sharply, bringing me back. "What the hell's that got to do with your troubles?"

"I don't know," I said. "The only thing I know is that when I talked to Dickie Oates, it's the first time I've felt like somebody's telling the truth since I had a drink with Enos Walker."

"Jesus, Milo, the kid's a convicted killer," she insisted. "He'd say anything, right? And Walker's a stone criminal."

I had to agree but I didn't want to let that go by, and continued, "Sissy Duval told me that this Mandy Rae character and Enos Walker showed up in town with twenty keys of Peruvian flake and went into business. It sounded like they cornered the market for a while, and I can't help but think that's somehow connected. But I don't know what it's connected to. All I know is that nobody was trying to shoot me until I went looking for Walker. Which is a question I intend to explore at some length with Sissy Duval tomorrow." Then I paused. "You said you knew those people a little bit?"

"A little bit," she said. "Austin was sort of a large small town in those days. Everybody knew everybody. And you know I was a little crazy in those days."

"Someday we'll have to talk about those days."

"Someday," Betty said. "But first, your back. We can't have a hard-nosed private dick being chauffeured around by his lady friend. Takes some of the glamour out of it." Then she smiled tiredly.

"That's for damn sure." Then my cell phone buzzed in Betty's purse. She tossed it across the table, and I answered.

"*Bueno*," I said.

"Milo, you son of a bitch," Thursby said, "a fake Mexican accent doesn't get you off that easy. I've got two messages from one of my less esteemed colleagues up in Gatlin County, one Jacky Ryman, who says he's Richard Wylie Oates's lawyer and who is threatening to haul me before the bar for client interference. First question, who the hell is Richard Wylie Oates? And two, what should I tell his lawyer?"

"I suspect Oates is doing a lot of hard time because Ryman is a jerk," I said, "and tell the asshole that you've got a client who's willing to finance a malpractice suit against him. Then tell him to messenger his case files over or you'll subpoena them."

After a long silence, Thursby said, "You've learned a lot from me, Milo, and I've not yet noticed a bulge in my bank account."

"I'm having trouble with my back," I said.

"Fix it," Thursby said, then hung up.

I handed the cell phone to Betty. "Why don't you see if your friend can work me in this afternoon? It's bad enough that I'm stupid, I don't need to be crippled, too."

Cathy Scoggins lived in a high-dollar development off Bull Creek Road in a large limestone-and-glass house that sat on the top of a ridge with a view in all directions. "She didn't get this place practicing alternative medicine," I suggested as we pulled into the driveway behind a brand-new Lexus. "Or that rig."

"She's a witch," Betty said. "She married well, several times, and divorced even better."

"But she forgot to get any furniture out of the deal," I said as we walked in without ringing or knocking. Except for large pillows and small Oriental rugs, the hardwood floors ran unimpeded to the stone-and-glass walls.

"Furniture just gets in the way," came a voice from behind one of the pillows, then a small woman with a smoky halo of wild dark hair shot with gray and dressed only in a black bodysuit popped up, an agile shadow against the late afternoon sky. "I like to keep my life simple," the woman said.

She embraced Betty, shook my hand, then led us upstairs, where she not only didn't have much furniture—a massage table, a wet bar, and a Chinese armoire—she had almost no interior walls. Although I knew Cathy Scoggins was middle-aged, she looked like a hyperactive teenager. She stood under five feet tall, and obviously had the metabolism of a ninety-six-pound hummingbird. She ate like a horse, drank like a sailor, and smoked dope like a stove, but as far as I could tell, nothing had any effect on her. She probably chattered like a monkey when she talked in her sleep. When I hesitated to take off my underwear in front of her, she slapped me on the butt with a tiny hand, and said, "Milo, if I had as many pricks sticking out of me as I had stuck in me, I'd look like a porcupine, so drop your drawers, sailor, and climb on the table."

I grumbled as a giggling Betty helped me out of my shorts and onto the padded table, where I sat on the side, surly as a hungry bear and terribly aware of the large scar on my abdomen running like a crooked arrow from my bruised chest almost to my limp dick dangling from the gray hair of my crotch.

Cathy touched the scar lightly, the question in her dark eyes.

"Gutshot," I explained.

Within moments, Cathy had fired up a crystal glass bong, let me have three large tokes of terrific marijuana, rolled me onto my stomach with minimal effort, and with her nimble little fingers found every muscle in my lower back that was as sore as a boil.

"What the hell did they do to you?" Cathy said.

"A stun gun," I said.

"More than once, I'd say," she murmured.

"Nazi bastards," Betty muttered from the corner.

"Let me work out some of the knots first," Cathy said, then began working at my neck and shoulders with her strong, tiny hands. Minutes after my first sigh and almost so quickly and easily that I didn't really notice it, she had smoothed the tight muscles of my back and had a dozen needles or more sticking in various parts of my body. Then she stepped back to admire her work. "That should do it," Cathy said quietly as she rattled in the armoire. "How's it feel?"

"I can't feel a thing," I admitted grudgingly as I suddenly slipped toward a doze, sniffing at some sort of sweet smoke that wasn't marijuana. If only my hippie ex-partner could see me.

"No shit, Sherlock," Cathy said, laughing. "Remember. The old jokes are the best."

"Talk about porcupines," Betty said from the corner of the room, which was the last thing I remembered until I woke as Cathy removed the needles. I could swear that some of them didn't seem to want to be pulled out.

"What the hell?" I said as she pulled out the last two, which seemed even more reluctant than the others. I felt some sort of electric pull as my skin tented as Cathy lifted the needles.

"Hold still," Cathy said once the needles were out, moving her hands in the air over my back. "I'm sweeping your aura clean."

I probably wouldn't admit it, even under torture, but I felt something, a rippling of skin, a shifting of muscles as Cathy's tiny hands swept over my back.

"What color's his aura?" Betty asked after a stifled laugh.

"You don't want to know," Cathy said, then slapped me on the butt lightly.

"I'll be damned," I said as I sat up and swung my legs off the side of the table without help, an errant erection poking its wary head out of my crotch.

"You folks want me to leave you alone?" Cathy asked.

"Milo's on a case," Betty complained.

As quick as a dragonfly, Cathy's hand flew at my dick and thumped it with her middle finger as she might a watermelon. It throbbed once, then disappeared. "I hope that's not permanent," I said as I hopped off the table. Amazingly, not only was the pain in my back gone, but my chest didn't hurt much at all either. Even the nagging burn of the spent .25 round's path through my guts seemed eased. "I'll be a son of a bitch," I said.

"You'll be a dead son of a bitch," Cathy said quietly, "if you do too much of that cocaine."

"What?" I said, reaching for my clothes. Cathy pressed one finger lightly into my back behind the liver. I flinched as if she had stuck a knife in me.

"You haven't done too much blow, but it's a bit too close to pure to be completely safe. Where the hell did you get it? I haven't felt anything like that in years." I didn't think it was any of her business, so I didn't answer. Betty looked worried and started to say something. But Cathy continued quickly, "Doesn't matter. Just don't do too much, man, quit when it's gone, and don't be buying none of that shit they sell on the street these days. I'll see you next week. You'll be okay for a while, but your back's a real mess. So we need a couple more sessions."

"What do I owe you?" I asked as I slipped back into my clothes and boots.

"Stop being such a dour son of a bitch," Cathy said, glancing at Betty. "Life's too short to be taken that seriously."

"I'm Slavic," I said. "I'm supposed to be dour and serious."

"You feel more like a black Irishman to me," Cathy said, laughing.

"That's the American mongrel peeking through," I said.

"Wear something warm on your back for the next few days. A sweater or a down vest or something like that." I must have looked confused. Cathy pointed out the glass wall with the northern exposure. A dark band hovered on the horizon. "Cold rain by dark. Freezing rain by midnight."

"Thanks for the news."

"And the next time you want to talk to Sissy Duval," Cathy said, "call me, and I'll go along. She owes me big-time." I assumed that Cathy and Betty had been talking while I had my little nap.

"Owes you?"

"I fixed her orgasms," Cathy said without a smile.

"I'll keep that in mind," I said.

"So will I," Betty giggled from the corner.

"It's happy hour," Cathy said. "One martini never hurt anybody."

By the time we left, my back felt so good I climbed into the driver's seat without thinking about it.

"Are you all right?" Betty asked.

"My back feels like the train wreck never happened."

"I was thinking about the three martinis," Betty said.

"Three martinis never hurt anyone my size," I assured her. "Besides, we've got a police escort." I nodded toward the unmarked car parked down the street from Cathy's driveway. We hadn't had any trouble losing the Gatlin County district attorney's investigator on the way to Huntsville, but as soon as we got back in range, the unmarked car latched on to our tail.

"What's wrong with your orgasms?" I asked as we drove away.

"Where'd you get the cocaine?" she replied.

"I took it off a dead man," I said, hoping she would take it as a joke, knowing she started having trouble with her orgasms after she killed the man who raped her.

The next morning Betty ran out to the ranch to check on her animals, so I slipped into the Lodge's airport van and rented a car when I got there. I didn't want Gatlin County following me when I called on Sissy Duval. No sense helping them make a case against me. I thought about picking up Cathy or the dead man's cocaine, but it wouldn't have mattered. Eldora answered my ring with a frown, as if she expected someone else.

"Mr. Electrolux. I don't know what you did to Mrs. Duval," she chattered nervously, blocking the doorway and making me stand in the cold rain, "but last time you paid her a visit, she spent the next three days in bed. Then decided she needed a vacation. She's gone away. On a long trip."

"Where?"

"None of your business," Eldora answered, an anxious smile flittering across her face. Then she tried to smirk, but that didn't fit either.

"Thanks," I grumbled, thinking I should have brought Hangas. Texas wasn't the South, but some people were still Southern.

"She say when she's coming back?"

"No, sir."

I realized that I'd have more luck squeezing gold from a whore's heart than getting Eldora to talk to me. So I went back to the rented Taurus. I waited in the plain brown sedan until Eldora, just as I expected with Sissy Duval gone, took off before lunch. I followed her new Ford station wagon to the HEB grocery store, then to a small, well-maintained frame house in West Travis Heights.

I called Carver D on my cell phone to leave a message for Hangas, asking him to take a gentle run at Eldora and a brief tour of the black community east of the Interstate for any word of Enos Walker.

"I'll run her through my machine," Carver D said, "and in half an hour, we'll know her whole life story."

"I don't need her life story. I just want to know where her boss is."

"Grist for the mill, Milo," Carver D sighed, then laughed.

"And if you can handle it," I said, "lend me fifty K for a couple of weeks. Put it into the Mad Dog's offshore account." Even though he lived like a hermit, Carver D was the last surviving member of a Texas family fortune based on those two popular commodities— pussy and politics—so unlike me he wouldn't have any trouble coming up with fifty K in clean money.

"I thought the fair Phillip had advised you to depart these fair climes," Carver D said.

"Yeah, but he didn't mean it."

"At his prices, man, he never says a word he doesn't mean."

"Tell Hangas I'll call him when I get back tonight."

"You going anyplace fun?"

"Someplace between Midland and Odessa, actually," I said. "Wherever that is."

"I know exactly where it is and I sure hope you enjoy it without hurting yourself," Carver D said, then hung up.

I sat in the car, watching the cold rain splatter against the windshield, then I tried Betty on her cell phone. But it was busy, and I didn't bother leaving a message. She was already deep enough in my troubles.

Since I couldn't find a lead on Sissy Duval, I thought I ought to pay a call on Paper Jack, who had insisted that he knew the Molly McBride woman and who, according to the Lodge desk clerk, lived between Midland and Odessa. I still felt good after Cathy's treatment, but not good enough to endure three hundred miles in the cold rain, so I went to the airport, dropped the rental car, hopped a shuttle to Dallas, changed planes, and landed at the Midland airport before dark. Just as the last light faded across the rain-dreary plain, I was parked in another rented car down the road from Jack Holbrook's house when he came home from his oil well supply company. Jack lived alone in a three-thousand-square-foot house setting on five of the barest acres I had ever seen a few miles northwest of the Interstate between Midland and Odessa. I waited long enough for Jack to get a drink in his stomach and a second one in his hand.

"Milo, what the hell are you doing here?" Jack asked when he opened the door to my knock. The old man had changed out of his suit and into a baggy jumpsuit, a tattered sweater, and heel-shot slippers.

"I hear there's nothing between here and the North Pole but a three-strand barbed wire fence. I want to get out of the cold and ask you a few questions about the other night."

"Talk to my lawyer, asshole," Jack growled, "because we're filing charges."

"Don't be an idiot," I said as I stepped around Jack's bulk. "And lead me to a drink."

Without too much grumbling, Jack led me to a large den at the back of the house. Jack flopped into a broken-backed La-Z-Boy. The room was crammed with fast-food debris and empty Wild Turkey bottles. A fuck movie played silently on a large-screen television standing in front of a gun case rack full of imported shotguns. I found a fairly clean glass and a dusty bottle of cheap Scotch on a battered sideboard.

"Trouble keeping a housekeeper, Jack?" I said as he raised the glass.

"Nobody wants to do a day's work for a day's pay anymore," Jack said without taking his eyes off the screen. "Fuckin' Meskins steal everything that isn't nailed down, widow-women want to marry my money, and the women from my wife's church keep trying to save my soul."

"How long's your wife been dead?"

"Since the day she died, asshole," Jack said.

"You said you knew that young woman at the bar the other night."

"I was drunk," Jack said. "Otherwise, I would have broken your back."

"You're not drunk now," I said standing over him. Perhaps the combination of drugs, pain, and legal peril had made my hair-trigger temper even more hairy. "And I've just gotten out of a train wreck, too, you old bastard."

Jack half-rose from the chair, then waved his hand as if it was too much trouble to get on his feet. "You're sure as hell on the prod," he said. "But you're damn near my age, Milo. You'll find out what it's like. Maybe it's time to walk easy."

"I don't have time to walk easy, Jack. Talk to me about the woman at the bar."

"I told you she was a whore," Jack said. "A fuckin' thousand-dollar piece of ass." Then Jack smiled slightly. "Damn near worth it, too, as I remember."

"Where'd you find her?"

"Not a clue," Jack said. "But it had to be someplace where they had gambling. Vegas, Lake Charles, Reno, Mobile. Any place but Indian reservation casinos; they're all run by some fucking guy named Guido Running Deer. That's about all I do these days. Drop five or ten grand at the tables, get drunk, then find a thousand-dollar hooker."

"How long ago was it?" I asked, thinking that Lake Charles rang some distant chime.

"Old lady's been gone three years," Jack whispered. "Had to be since then. After my heart attack, damned Edna wouldn't let me go to the pisser alone. Always thought I'd go before her . . . Life's a bitch, ain't it? And sometimes you don't die." Then Jack sat up straight. "How's your drink, ol' buddy? That's pretty shitty Scotch, ain't it? Let me get my clothes on, and we'll drift over to the Petro-leum Club. Everything's top-shelf there."

I thought it over for at least a second. "Why the hell not? I can't get a flight out until tomorrow morning, anyway."

But it turned out to be a late afternoon hangover flight. I kept the lonely old man company through the evening hours in the ghostly climes of the Petroleum Club, then sat up listening to com-plaints about the oil business long past midnight, hoping he'd either pass out or remember where he'd met the McBride woman before he died. Or I did. But I didn't learn anything else.

Except to be reminded the next morning once again that hang-overs at my age were crippling beasts. And airplanes were no place to endure them.

Hangas, the solid mass of his body perfectly draped in a tailored black suit that wasn't quite a chauffeur's uniform, met me at the gate when my flight arrived about dark-thirty. "You don't look all that chipper, Milo," Hangas said. "Can I buy you a couple of these over-priced airport drinks?"

"Let's go someplace where I can have a cigarette, too." I had called him before I climbed on the plane to see if he had talked to

Eldora. He said he didn't have much to tell me, but he knew by the sound of my voice that I could use a lift.

Half an hour later, we were bellied up to the lobby bar at the Four Seasons Hotel, a place where we could talk in the anonymous crowd. Hangas, who had never completely recovered from a tour as a Marine guard at the embassy in Paris, had a glass of an estate bottled Haut-Medoc while I went back to the smoky hair of the Scotty dog that had bitten me.

"If Enos Walker's in town," Hangas said after he tasted the wine and nodded to the bartender, "nobody's seen him. And a lot of folks down here know him. From his basketball time. He was big stuff when he transferred down from Oklahoma City College. Until he went bad and got kicked off the team. According to his brother, the preacher."

"You get a chance to talk to Eldora?" I asked.

"That Mrs. Grace, she's one fine-looking woman," Hangas said, then paused to savor the wine.

"And about your age, too," I suggested.

"Perhaps a mite older and more serious than I prefer," Hangas said, smiling. "I'm too busy taking care of Mr. Carver and keeping an eye on my younger children to have time for any serious women."

"I thought your youngest two were already in college?"

"One at Rice, one at Baylor. But college is the most dangerous time," Hangas said seriously. "Waco one weekend, Houston the next, and I'm sort of involved . . ."

"Both places?" I said, but Hangas just smiled as serenely as a black Buddha. "So what did Eldora have to say?"

"Not much," Hangas allowed, "but I got the distinct feeling that she was a bit worried and didn't actually know where Mrs. Duval had gone."

"I don't like that."

"I don't think Eldora does either," Hangas said. "You want me to ask her again tomorrow?"

"Day after tomorrow," I said. "If she's really worried, you'll know for sure."

"Sounds good to me," Hangas said as he finished the wine. "Mr. Carver says you're in some deep shit. If there's anything I can do, please don't forget to call."

"Thanks for the ride," I said. "I'll get the drinks, then grab a cab."

Hangas nodded politely, then eased through the crowd as easily as a shade in spite of his size. I had another before I settled the check, slightly surprised that Hangas's glass of wine had cost almost twenty dollars.

"Good price for a glass of wine," I said to the bartender. "Grapes mashed by virgin feet?"

"Some folks have taste—" the bartender started to say.

"Right," I interrupted, "but usually they pay for their own drinks."

"—but Mr. Hangas has great taste," he added with a gentle laugh.

When I taxied back to the Lodge, I found Betty in my room, wearing a silk nightgown I'd never seen, and propped up on my king-size bed, drinking Negra Modelo out of the bottle and eating shredded beef taquitos as she watched a rented movie.

"Looks like you've adjusted nicely to the twentieth century," I said as I kicked my boots off.

"It's not that I don't like it," Betty said. "It just wears me out sometimes."

"You mean you'd rather chop kindling for the cookstove and pump a Coleman lantern for light," I said flopping beside her, "than call room service."

"Most of the time," she said. "You remember calling me last night?"

"I don't recommend knee-walking nostalgic drunks more than once or twice a year," I advised. "I was homesick."

"I could tell," she said. "You must have asked me a dozen times to go to Montana with you. But not until spring."

"And what did you say?"

"Maybe. If you're not in prison," she said. "Or working some idiot case."

"Thanks," I said, slipping my arm under her neck and my mouth next to her ear, a new easiness between us. "Anybody call but me?"

"Fucking phone rang all day long," she said. "Until I finally turned it off. My Uncle Trav and Phil Thursby want you to call them at their offices tomorrow. Something about money."

"What?"

"Uncle Trav said he wanted to talk to you about that investment thing and Phil wanted a retainer."

"Wonderful."

"And some guy named Renfro wanted you to call him back no matter what time you got in. He said it was very important."

"Renfro? I don't know anybody by that name. He say what he wanted?"

"He said he couldn't say over the telephone," Betty said, then reluctantly added, "he claims to be a friend of Sissy Duval's. A good friend."

"I expect Sissy's got loads of good friends," I said, snuggling closer to Betty's soft, warm body.

"This one sounded more like her hairdresser than her boyfriend."

"Maybe I'll call him. Tomorrow. Maybe he's got work for me," I said. "I don't seem to be making any money working for myself."

"And some woman who wouldn't leave her name wants you to find somebody for her. But she wouldn't say who," Betty said. "She said she'll keep calling."

"Just what I need. More clients."

"You just use your clients as an excuse to be nosy," Betty said. "And me as a place to relieve your hangovers."

"Not every time," I said as I slipped the gown off her small breasts. "Not every time."

"Okay," she said, chuckling as she slipped the rest of the way out of the gown. "Just this once." Then she paused, naked in my arms. "I know you hate this," she added softly, "but we have to talk about the Molly McBride thing . . ."

"She conned me," I said. "I fucked her, and it nearly cost me what's left of my life. What's left to talk about?"

"Well," Betty said as she rolled away, then spooned against me, as if it was easier to talk to the drapes than me. "I slept with her five or six times . . ."

I clenched my tongue between my teeth to keep silent. "How'd it start?"

"At a meeting of the Preservation Society," Betty said. "She asked me for some background over a drink . . . and as soon as you came back from Montana you dove back into this idiot detective thing, and we seemed to be in the midst of an endless and silent fight, so much for so long, I guess I'd given up on us, and one thing led to another. I guess you know how it was."

"Yeah, unfortunately."

"You knew that I'd done it before . . . during the bad times . . . But this was different. More intense. At first, I felt terrifically guilty," Betty said, "so I was a bitch. Then I convinced myself that you were leaving, so I didn't feel guilty at all, which made me even more bitchy."

"I guess I should have noticed."

"Listen, I love you," she said, "and I know you love me. I even love the way we love each other. But I hate the life you live."

"I'm sorry," I said, meaning it, "but it's the only life I've always enjoyed, the only one I can bear to live. And it's far too late to change. But you were half-right about one thing."

"What's that?" she asked, the sneer loud in her voice.

"This bar thing was a mistake," I said.

"Well, that's wonderful news," she said. "Since I told you not to go into business with my uncle."

"Only once," I said, but she didn't smile. "And it's not him," I continued. "I'm used to being at home in a bar, and the people who come in here aren't my people. I got tired of them and taking care of business. I guess I felt that I had to go back to my kind of work or roll over and die."

"And it nearly killed you," she said sharply.

"Ah, fuck it," I said, thinking our moment had passed, and began to disentangle myself from her.

But she turned, rolled into my arms, weeping, and said, "No. Fuck me."

Afterward, I slumped into a brief nap, then woke out of a dream I couldn't remember, the hangover still jangling through my nerve sheaths. So I eased out of bed and into my clothes, then picked up the cell phone and Renfro's number, and went down to the bar, had a drink, then returned the call.

Renfro showed up so quickly, I suspected he had been waiting in his car outside the Lodge. He was a tall, bulky, but slightly effete man who couldn't talk without fluttering hands and a nervous giggle.

"So Sissy is an old friend of mine, you know," he said as he pulled up a stool next to mine," and she asked this favor, you know, so I said yes. I'd go by myself, but she insisted I bring you along for protection."

"Protection? From what?"

"It didn't make much sense, really. She said somebody's been following her," Renfro said, "and now that she's shaken the tail, she just wants to go away." Renfro patted a large envelope in his inside overcoat pocket. "And not come back for a while, you know." Then he spread five hundred-dollar bills in front of my drink. "She said to give you this. Okay?"

"How'd she get hold of you?"

"Called me at work on my cell phone," Renfro said. "From a pay phone, I think," he added. "She was worried about bugs on her phones."

"Should be all right," I said. "Okay, I'll go with you. I've got a bone to pick with her."

"You want to talk to her?"

"She fucking lied to me."

Renfro laughed. "If every man Sissy had lied to got to talk to her, it'd wear the hide off her little pink ears, you know." Then he laughed again. "She did mention something about that, though."

"Good. I'll hold the money," I said, "and if she wants it, she has to talk to me."

"I suppose that's okay."

"So where are we supposed to meet her?" I asked, then finished my drink.

"I'm not supposed to tell you that," Renfro said, "until we're there."

"We'll take my ride. We have to make a stop at my gun locker on the way."

"What for?"

"Well, it seems that I've pissed off somebody around here," I said, "so I'm not going off in the darkness with somebody I don't know without a Kevlar vest and my favorite piece under my arm."

"Wonderful," Renfro said, laughing and clapping his large hands. "I haven't played with guns since sixty-eight." I raised an eyebrow. "I was a company clerk with the Marines in Hue during Tet. We were all on the line. Even the cooks. We beat their asses silly that time, you know, had the war won, then the politicians sold us out. Chicken fuckers."

"That was a long time ago," I said, "and I'll bet you haven't fired a round since then."

"You'd win the bet," Renfro said, then shoved the five bills at me again. "Sissy told me she owed you at least this much. The price of her lie." Then he pulled the envelope out of his coat and handed it to me. "This is her getaway money."

"I wonder where she's going?" I said.

"Not very far," Renfro said, laughing as he stood up. "It's only ten grand, and a woman with Sissy's tastes can't get very far on that."

CHAPTER SIX

SOMETIME AFTER MIDNIGHT, Renfro and I were standing on the sixth green of a very dark golf course somewhere on the south side of the string of lakes along the Colorado River north and west of Austin, so far from town that the city lights were only a faint smudge against the low ceiling of the clouds. The sixth hole was raised and bunkered, nestled on the verge of a live oak motte. The norther still pumped a cold misty wind across the Hill Country, spiced with occasional bursts of even colder raindrops the size of dimes, which clattered like hail off our vests. We listened quietly as the wind rattled the live oaks madly. Renfro had insisted that if he couldn't have a weapon, he should at least have a flak jacket. The flag marking the hole flapped like a lost bird. The Browning Hi-Power felt oddly heavy under my arm, less comforting than I hoped.

"It's so dark I couldn't see my ass, if my head was up it," I said. "And she's a half-hour late."

"She's always late," Renfro whispered nervously. "I wish I could afford to get away. Sissy's great fun to travel with. Completely insane and terribly organized."

"Well, I won't give her the money," I said, "unless she promises to take you along."

The tall man nodded again.

Renfro had been very interested when I jerked the DA's location beeper off the Beast and stuck it under one of the Lodge's vans, but he didn't ask any questions. And during the detour to pick up the Browning, a couple of extra magazines, and my Kevlar vest, Renfro hadn't even commented. Except to insist on a vest, which I didn't much like, and to give me directions through the dark back roads.

"You think she's coming?"

"Of course," Renfro said, giggling. "She'll be late for her own funeral, but she'll be there with bells on . . . What the hell?"

Renfro started slapping at his chest, then at his other hand, muttering curses.

The red dot on the back of his glove exploded in a fluff of fake rabbit fur as I shoved him down and dove in the same direction, shamelessly using Renfro's bulk as cover and scrabbling for the Browning. Two more silenced subsonic rounds thumped into Renfro's vest as we rolled toward the nearest bunker. I fired back along the line of the laser sight glistening in the rainy mist. One round hit what sounded like a car; another snapped through glass; the third, fourth, fifth rounds disappeared into the heart of the dark wind.

But the sniper wasn't deterred. His rounds scattered divots from the green. As I shoved Renfro's unconscious bulk into the safety of the deep bunker, then rolled in behind him, a round skipped off the Kevlar vest over my left shoulder blade. It felt as if I'd been hit with a twelve-pound sledge. I pressed against the sand beneath the lip of the bunker as another half-dozen rounds chopped at the edge of the green above it. The sniper just wanted me to know that he knew where I was. My whole left side felt paralyzed, as if all the bones on that side of my body had been shattered as I flopped into the bunker.

Across the golf course, I heard the grumbling slide and clunk as a van door shut. Then it drove rather sedately off into the stormy night. Without lights.

I crawled up to the edge of the green, both hands on the Browning, and counted to a hundred before I checked on Renfro, who gasped at the cold air with shallow breaths and had a faint feathery pulse in his cold neck. I propped his feet high against the bunker, then slithered into the tangled oaks, where I waited on my knees for another hundred count. Impatience had killed a lot of people, and I didn't plan to be one of them. I had used up all my luck when the sniper decided he didn't want the sound of rifle shots in the night. If the rounds hadn't been suppressed and subsonic, the vests would have been useless.

Even with his, Renfro still might die of internal injuries. And without *mine*, the round would have shattered my shoulder blade, scattering bone chips like shrapnel through my viscera. Just the thought of it made me shiver long enough for my back to break out in spasms again. Even five years after the spent .25 round had hit me after it went through the general's elbow, I could still follow its twisting, burning path through my guts.

When I finally stopped shaking, I stood up as slowly and quietly as my battered back would let me, then pussyfooted through the motte, and eased into my car, turned the key, and ran down the windows in the hope that I would hear the killer's approach under the gusting wind. I waited a full five minutes by the lighted digital clock before I started the car and switched the heater on high. While I waited to warm up, I considered my problems.

Since I had followed Renfro's directions through the dark without paying much attention to them, I didn't know exactly where we were, and I didn't much fancy just driving off into the night. Even if Renfro was dead, my spent shell casings would be hell to find in the dark, even with a flashlight. If worst came to worst I could change the firing pin in the Browning, or melt the piece down. But there would be telephone records connecting me with Renfro, plus witnesses in the bar who had seen us leave together.

No way I could walk away from this, and being surrounded by police didn't sound like such a bad idea. Hell, even a jail cell didn't sound too bad at this moment. As long as it wasn't in Gatlin County.

So I dug Gannon's card out of my billfold, then called him at home. He answered on the first ring. He didn't sound like a man who had just been dragged out of a deep sleep at two-thirty in the morning. "What now?" he asked. He sounded wide awake and very annoyed.

"Sorry if I woke you," I said. "It's Milodragovitch and I've got a bit of a problem."

"Milo?" Gannon said, not happily. "You didn't wake me up. Somebody reported gunfire at the Arrowhead Country Club."

"That would be my problem," I interrupted. "I'll meet you on the sixth green with another body."

"You ever think of becoming a mortician?"

"Too late to change careers at my age," I said, "and this one may not be quite dead." Then I hung up. I grabbed a down vest and a clean T-shirt out of my travel gear, then a survival blanket out of the winter gear junk box I kept out of a long Montana habit, then trudged back to the bunker, wrapped Renfro's shattered hand as tightly as I could, then bundled him in the vest and the blanket. Then I just crouched there, waiting in the cold, wet wind. But I didn't unload the Browning and set it on the green until the first unit, complete with lights and sirens, roared down the cart path toward the green where I stood next to the flapping flag, my hands raised.

"Not you again," the deputy groaned as he climbed out of the unit and trudged up the bank. His face was shadowed under the plastic-covered cowboy hat, but I recognized the voice from the jail cell. The kid followed procedure, put me on my knees and cuffed my hands behind me, then checked on Renfro. But as the kid helped me to his feet, he muttered something under his breath.

"What's that?" I said, preparing myself for the worst.

"I said, 'Thanks.'"

"What the hell for?"

"For not snitching me off the other day," the kid said. "Looks like maybe I was a little bit out of hand."

"I was an asshole," I admitted, "so I've got no complaint. What's your name?"

"Bob Culbertson," he said quietly. "No hard feelings?"

"Not a one, Bob," I said. "You're the one working nights."

"Forever and a night, the captain said."

"I'd shake your hand, kid, but I seem to be tied up."

"Sorry," the kid said. "Procedure."

"Not a problem."

"I'd ask you what happened," Culbertson said, "but I'm sure the captain would want me to wait."

"This time," I said, "I ain't answering no questions until my lawyer is standing close by my side."

"That's sure as hell the way I'd play it," Culbertson said, smiling. Like most cops, if he was in trouble, he wouldn't talk to his mother without a lawyer present. Then he stuffed me in his unit one more time, and called a chopper for a Medevac.

The norther had finally blown itself out by daylight. Dawn came to a wide clear blue sky and cool, dry air. It could have been spring in eastern Montana. From the green, I could see the flagstone clubhouse where groups of irritated early morning golfers milled around their fancy carts and were obviously bitching about losing their tee times. Like cocaine junkies who had too much money and nothing to do with themselves.

"You ever play golf?" Gannon asked me as he led me up to the top of the green as the crime scene cleared.

"Never had the pleasure," I said, "but I hear that hitting a golf ball well is damn near as hard as hitting a major league slider."

"I wouldn't know about that," Gannon said. "I had a ton of other problems—couldn't hit the fucking Double A batting practice curveball, couldn't block a low fast slider, and my peg to second wasn't all that hot."

"Couldn't have been all that bad if you made it to Double A ball."

"Got a tryout because my Dad knew a scout for the Red Sox," Gannon admitted. "What about you? You ever play any ball?"

"Football. Pulling guard on the last small-college single-wing team in America," I said. "I could knock you out of your socks. If you were standing still."

"I always hated football," Gannon said. "Still do. And here I'm living in the hell of football heaven." Then he paused. "You still not going to talk to me without your lawyer?"

"Not one fucking word," I said.

"You're not even going to tell me why you boys were wearing vests?"

"Just luck," I said. "So why don't you put me in back of the unit or a cell or anyplace I can get these cuffs off. My back's killing me."

Gannon motioned to Culbertson, who unlocked the cuffs. "I've sure been seeing too much of you guys together," he said in an oddly flat voice, as if he was no longer amused by his own joke. "Go home, you old bastard, you're a victim here, and discharging a firearm is a misdemeanor," he said. "Besides, I know where you live. Unfortunately. I'm sure you've got another piece someplace, but I'm keeping this one."

I hesitated only long enough to ask two questions: where they had taken Renfro; and what number had answered when he pushed star 69 on the cell phone from Molly McBride's fanny pack.

"Crime scene crew didn't find a fanny pack, Milo," he said. "Maybe your ears were just ringing."

"Yeah, and maybe his nuts were calling his dick," I said. "Long distance."

Culbertson started to say something, but Gannon cut him off. "You're in enough trouble, old man, without making bad jokes," he said. Then gave the deputy a grim look when he didn't successfully stifle his giggle.

Renfro didn't look all that good late that afternoon when they let me visit him briefly in his room at Breckenridge Hospital—gray-faced and sprouting tubes like a space monster, his shattered hand wrapped like a mummy's—but he managed a slight smile when he saw me.

"How the hell did you get in?" Renfro whispered.

"I told them I worked for Hair de Temps," I admitted.

Renfro laughed so hard that his tubes rattled dangerously. "You don't look much like a hairdresser," he finally managed to say.

"I think they were afraid to ask. You okay?"

"Thanks to the vest," Renfro whispered. "But I won't be cuttin' hair for a while. They're not going to work on my hand until they make up their mind about my spleen. See if it stops bleeding, or something. They seem to think I'm going to lose my spleen, maybe. What the hell's a spleen do, anyway?"

"I'm not sure," I said, "but I know you can live without it."

"That's what they said, but it's nice to hear it from you," Renfro said. "They said they put all my stuff in a bag underneath the night stand. How come you put Sissy's money back in my pocket?"

"Didn't want the cops to take it off me."

"Thanks. Maybe you should take charge of it? I don't want to have to explain it to my mother. She's not fond of Sissy."

"Let me count it," I suggested, "then I'll give you a receipt, and stash it in the safe at the Lodge. If Sissy calls, tell her to messenger me a note at the Lodge—no telephone calls—and I'll get the money to her. It's probably not necessary, but be sure to tell her not to use her credit cards, no matter what." Then I counted the cash.

"You know," Renfro whispered hoarsely, "I thought she was just in one of her self-dramatization modes but I guess I was wrong."

"You know, you said ten grand didn't seem like enough cash for a woman like Sissy to get very far away. Any idea where she might be headed?"

"Sissy's got some kind of under-the-table income nobody knows about, a sugar daddy or something, you know," Renfro said, "and she can take care of herself. She comes from tough Texas root stock. Back in the twenties, her great-granddaddy, ol' Homer Logan, raised the cash to sink his first dry hole by standing ass-deep in an East

Texas slough from daylight to dark, skimming runoff crude with five-gallon cans."

"His first dry hole?"

"And his second," Renfro said, oddly proud, "but he finally brought in a well on his third try. The family's made the transition from oil field royalty to oil field trash two or three times, you know, and Sissy was along for the ride the last couple."

"You know Sissy's housekeeper?"

"Her cousin Eldora? She's a paid companion, not a house-keeper," Renfro said. "She keeps her from falling completely into the vodka and the cocaine. She's been watching out for Sissy since they were children."

"Any chance she might tell you where Sissy might be?"

"Only if she wanted to," he said, chuckling tiredly. "Eldora is tougher than a cheap steak."

Renfro chuckled once more, then began to fade under the weight of the drugs. I put the receipt in his night table sack, then turned to leave.

"I gotta ask, you know," Renfro whispered from the bed. "How come that guy was shooting at us?"

"Got tired of waiting for Sissy, I guess," I answered. "I'll check on you tomorrow," I said. "You take care of yourself."

Renfro smiled sleepily as I left.

Walking down the hallway I dug out the five hundred that Renfro had given me, then stuffed that into the envelope. Hell, I guess I've never done any of this shit for money. I tried to count up all the money I'd spent since beginning the search for Carol Jean Warren. But given the way things were going, it seemed a bit early to start counting the costs. Even if I could.

I went out to the Lodge to stash Sissy's money in the safe, then spent a bit of time making sure that I didn't have a tail, drove back to the safe locker, where I picked up a less bulky vest, another Browning Hi-Power, a stash of codeine, a pile of running cash, my second best set of false identity papers, and a bag of traveling clothes. Then it was back to Austin to the Four Seasons, where I used the fake identification to register, let the bellhop take my bag, then shouldered through the five o'clock crowd to have a quick drink before I went to the hotel down the street to use a pay phone. I called Betty on her cell phone.

"Where the hell've you been?" she asked. "You didn't even leave a note, you bastard."

"You wouldn't believe me if I told you," I said. "And I didn't think I'd be gone that long. Where are you right now?"

"Standing in your room and tapping my foot like a mad house-wife."

"This fuckin' shit's way out of hand," I said. A woman at the pay phone bank beside me, who could have been a hooker or an heiress, in a leather coat with a wolf fur collar and snakeskin boots, looked at my rumpled, sandy clothes, then crinkled her nose as if she smelled a fart. So I gave her the opportunity. Then I made the mistake of laughing as she huffed away. "Maybe you should take a trip or something, hon," I said to Betty.

"I don't take a step without you, bud," she answered sharply. "I don't know what you've got yourself into, but I'm in it with you."

"Somebody took a couple of shots at me last night," I said, knowing as soon as the words left my mouth that they were the wrong ones. Betty became even more adamant. Finally, she wore me down. I needed another drink, some food, and a long nap. "Fuck it," I said, sighing tiredly. "Pack a bag. I'll send somebody you know to pick you up and bring you to me."

"Are you sure you're all right?" Betty asked.

"I'm just tired, hon," I admitted. "I need a night's sleep before I think about this shit . . . I'll see you in a bit." Then I hung up and leaned my head against the wall beside the pay phone, wishing I had some way to ask Betty to spirit Long's cocaine out of the elevator. Somebody tapped me roughly on the shoulder. I whirled, my hands raised defensively, to find a clean-cut young man in a blue blazer and gray slacks, who held up his hands, open and placating. "What?" I said, then looked down at the cop shoes beneath the slacks. "Hotel security?" I asked. The kid nodded. "What's up?"

"Can I see some ID, sir?" the kid asked in his flat cop voice, his cold blue eyes checking out my rumpled jeans and muddy boots.

I started to complain but assumed I'd already called enough attention to myself, so I showed the kid a valid North Dakota driver's license, making sure that he saw the sheaf of credit cards and the retired Grand Forks deputy's card, too. "Airlines lost my bags during the delay in Denver," I explained.

"You staying with us, Mr. Malvern?"

"Too cold here," I said. "I'm running from an early winter dose of cabin fever and I don't think I've run far enough south. Just stopped in to use the telephone to let my wife know where to find me—crazy woman won't fly—and pick up some new clothes." The kid handed the driver's license back. "One more quick call," I said, "then back into a cab."

"Good luck," the kid said but he didn't mean it.

"Sorry. Guess I forgot how sensitive the ladies are down here," I said. "I knew I shouldn't have farted in front of her."

"You're lucky she didn't call the police," the kid said, shaking his head. "She has before. For less reason."

"Thanks," I said, shaking my head, too, then turned back to the telephone to call Hangas.

"Sarge, I need a quiet favor," I said when Hangas answered.

"Name it," Hangas rumbled, then added, "I need to talk to you, too."

"Remember that damned expensive glass of wine I bought you?" I asked. Hangas just chuckled. "Run out and pick up my woman, then bring her there. And maybe you should watch your back a little bit."

"It's like that, huh?"

"Probably just horsehit and gunsmoke," I said, turning to find the security kid's eyes on me, "but who knows when you're going to run into the typical Texas experience." I hung up, smiled at the kid, and hustled out of the lobby as quickly as I could.

I nursed a couple of Scotches at the Four Seasons bar until Hangas and Betty showed up just before eight o'clock.

"Sorry it took so long," Hangas said as Betty wrapped me in her arms.

"You look terrible, love," she whispered, her lips against my ear.

"I've been better," I said, then to Hangas, "Thanks, man. But maybe we'd better get a table." We found one in a dark corner, settled in, ordered drinks, and went to business. I told them about the aborted meeting with Sissy Duval and the shooter.

"Unless they were using four cars, they weren't on my tail," I said, "so the only way the shooter could know how to cover the meet would be a scanner tap on Renfro's cell phone, and I don't know why they would do that. Hell, he's just a hairdresser. And as far as I can figure, the only reason to whack her would be because she knows something about Enos Walker or Amanda Rae Quarrels. And right now I'm just too tired to think about it."

"You've got a room here?" Betty asked as the cocktail waitress brought the drinks. I nodded. "So can we go up when we finish our drinks?"

"But I don't think that Renfro and I were the real target," I said, "or they would have handled it differently." Hangas knew what I meant: Somebody would have walked over to put a couple of rounds into the backs of our heads. But Betty didn't realize that. Then I took a healthy slug of the double Macallan, relaxing for the first time since the silenced gunfire started. "Then I nearly got arrested because I farted in front of a woman dressed in the skins of endangered species."

"A good piece of luck that you picked up the vests," Hangas said.

"It wasn't luck, man. I guess I've been on a hair trigger ever since that Rooke asshole tried to kill me, and I've been watching my back ever since," I admitted, then turned to Betty. "The best piece of luck is that they haven't checked the serial number on your piece yet."

"See, I am involved," Betty said brightly, as if she'd just won a prize.

"I'm sorry, love," I said, then hit the whisky again, hard, and circled my finger at the cocktail waitress. "Shit. Molly McBride and Mandy Rae Quarrels don't exist, Enos Walker and Sissy Duval are in the wind, and I've got something less than three weeks before I'm indicted for capital murder. What the hell, let's have one more." For once, nobody argued with me.

"I caught up with Enos Walker's older brother," Hangas said quietly. "He's got a big church operation over on the East Side. He seems dead straight and mightily embarrassed by his little brother, but I'd bet anything that he knows where he is. Trouble is, we've got no leverage on him. Same trouble with Eldora Grace. She's nervous as a cat in a Vietnamese neighborhood."

"Bigot," I said, but Hangas just smiled like a man who had done three tours in the Mekong Delta as the cocktail waitress set another eighteen-dollar glass of wine in front of him.

"She knows something but she's one hard-nosed woman."

"Let's leave her alone," I said, "and leave this shit alone, too, tonight. I'll think about it tomorrow." I settled the tab with cash and asked the waitress for a telephone. I ordered a couple of cheeseburgers and a six-pack of Bohemia beer from room service to be delivered to my room, then a bellhop to pick up Betty's bags, which Hangas had stashed under the table. "And get me another key for my wife," I said. Hangas and Betty both looked at me. "Tomorrow," I added, "tomorrow, I'll explain everything. Maybe."

Hangas made his goodbyes, and we finished our drinks silently.

Up in the room Betty waited until we'd finished the cheeseburgers and I was on my second beer and she'd fired up one of Cathy Scoggins's bomber joints before she asked, "So what's my married name?"

"Malvern. An ugly name but give it a couple of days," I answered, tossing her the walletful of fake ID, "Mrs. Hardy P. Malvern."

"What's the P stand for?" she asked, handing it back.

"Peter," I admitted. "It took ten days in the Grand Forks cemeteries to come up with that one. It's only my second best fake ID, but it's a good one. Social Security number's valid, driver's license is current, and credit cards are live, all the other stuff is state-of-the-art."

"You should have been a criminal," she said, handing me the joint.

"I am," I said, hitting it, and handing it back. "And now you are, too."

"Well, Hardy Peter," she said, smiling, "what's next?"

"After this doobie," I said, grinning, "maybe you could help me out of these clothes and into a Hardy Peter nap . . ." Then a wave of giggles swept over us. When it was over, I said, "Fuck, I'm nearly sixty years old, I've been beat up, tortured, and shot at. I shouldn't be giggling like a kid."

"You'll live longer that way," Betty said.

After Betty pushed the rolling room service table out in the hallway, she stepped over to me, kissed me softly, then began helping me out of my clothes. I could feel the bullet bruise spreading across my back, so I tried to avoid questions by keeping my T-shirt on, but she eased it over my head before I could stop her.

"Jesus H. Christ," Betty whispered when she saw my back. "Honey, can't you find some other hobby? Something besides . . . besides whatever it is you're doing."

"Many are called," I allowed, "but few are chosen."

She wasn't amused. "How the hell do you know the shoulder blade's not broken?"

"Doesn't hurt enough?"

"How the hell would you know?" she asked angrily. "You've got half a quart of whisky in you."

"And four codeines, too," I admitted. Tears filled her eyes as Betty drew back her hand to slap me. I caught her wrist. "I'm old, babe, but not dead." The evening's fun seemed to be over. "I don't hit you," I said. "Don't hit me."

"No, you've got other ways of hurting me, you bastard," she

said, angrily jerking her wrist away, then storming off to the bath-room. "And you won't fucking quit," she snapped over her shoulder before she slammed the door.

When she came out of the bathroom, it seemed simpler just to pretend to be asleep. Then in a moment, I was.

When my cell phone woke me the next morning, Betty was gone, bags and emotional baggage, and only a terse unsigned note: *If you're still alive at four this afternoon, you bastard, meet me at Cathy's.* I answered the phone. Gannon.

"Wake up, Milo, it's a lovely day," the cop said. "And by the way, where the hell are you?"

"Who wants to know?"

"The district attorney's office," he said. "Among others."

"Why?"

"You're supposed to check in every day."

"Nobody told me," I said.

"Consider yourself told."

"Consider me checked in."

"And they want—" was all I heard before I turned the phone off and rolled over to finish my nap.

A couple of hours later, as I stood in a long, hot shower, I won-dered where this was going. No closer to an answer, further from Betty. All the money my father had left me and all the money I'd stolen from the *contrabandistas* hadn't changed my life that much. I stayed in hotels where the hot water didn't run out in the middle of a shower now, and drove a Cadillac instead of a beat-up Toyota rig. But now a Toyota Land Cruiser cost damn near as much as a Cadil-lac. And there was no place in the world for me to buy a new body. As far as I could tell under the solid beat of the water, this one had given up on me. I didn't check too closely but I couldn't find a place that didn't throb like a boil the size of my fist.

To hell with it. I had a quick room service breakfast, another couple of codeines, then decided I needed to keep my head down for the next few days. I stopped at the front desk to extend my stay, then called Hangas at home.

Hangas's family had worked for Carver D's family in various forms and functions since Reconstruction. Hangas's father had been a foreman for one of the family's construction firms in Houston, and the summer after Hangas had graduated from high school, he'd been banging concrete off forms on an August afternoon as hot and muggy as a barber's towel when Hangas had thrown down his shovel, told his father that the family had been in thrall to these white motherfuckers long enough, by God, and he was off to join the Marine Corps. The old man just shook his head, smiled sadly, and wished his youngest son the best of luck. But during his twenty years in the Corps and after four children, Hangas had mellowed. When he retired to Austin after his wife had died, Hangas had no qualms when Carver D, whose house had just been blown up by an angry state senator who lost his seat because Carver D's paper, *The Dark Coast*, had exposed the senator's affinity for beating up prostitutes, asked Hangas to hire on as a bodyguard. During their years together, Hangas had prospered, and he and Carver D had become more than friends. My ex-partner had been friends with Carver D when they were in the Army at Fort Lewis and the friendship had been extended to me. Carver D and Hangas had made me part of their world from the beginning. So Hangas was waiting on the front porch of his sprawling brick ranch house off Enfield Road when I drove up.

"You look a little bit rough, Milo. You okay?" Hangas asked as he climbed into the Caddy.

"I've been better," I said. "But I'm still moving."

"What are you planning to ask the Reverend Jonas Walker?"

"I'm not going to ask him anything," I said. "I'm just going to tell him what happened."

The Reverend Jonas Walker made his younger brother seem small. He was at least seven years older, two shades lighter but with the same light blue eyes on either side of an even larger hooked nose, plus he was bigger, a soft-spoken giant of a man in sweats with short gray hair and a matching beard. He met us on one of the composition basketball courts next to the Congregation of the Holy Ghost, a huge flagstone, tin-roofed church and basketball complex beyond the Interstate deep in East Austin. He did not seem pleased to see us, sweating heavily and dribbling a basketball as he confronted us.

"As I told this gentleman the other day," the huge man said to me so softly I had to lean into his shadow, "I've had no contact with my errant brother in many years. I left that life long behind me, many, many years ago."

Hangas and I glanced at each other. If Jonas Walker had walked on the wrong side of the street, he'd been luckier than his little brother. His name didn't show up on any of the criminal records that Carver D could access.

"I just have a favor to ask," I explained. "If you should hear from him, would you please tell him that I'll testify and I'll find the goddamned bartender and make him stand up in court and force him to tell the truth."

"The truth should not be forced," Reverend Walker said quietly. "And please don't take the Lord's name in vain in front of me."

"I'm sorry," I apologized. "With my help, at the very least your brother can cop a manslaughter plea."

"How much time will he have to do? I don't think he likes doing time."

"I don't know, but it's also certainly possible that he might walk on a self-defense plea," I said. "Billy Long obviously pulled the piece on him. I can testify that your brother didn't have it on him when he went into the office and a piece like that will probably have an ATF paperwork trail leading directly to Long."

"And what's your interest in this?"

"I'm not sure you'd understand, sir."

"Try me," Reverend Walker said, his voice no longer quite so soft. In fact, he sounded a bit like his brother.

So I sighed so deeply it hurt my back, then tried to explain to the giant about the bear cub's spit and Enos Walker's hard-timer breath.

"That's about the craziest thing I've ever heard," Reverend Walker said, glancing down at the end of one of the four basketball courts where half a dozen lanky kids were shooting baskets, "so I'm gonna assume you don't have any ulterior motives in this matter. But if I *were* to hear from my brother and I *happened* to see you in my congregation some Sunday morning, maybe we can work something out."

"Man," I said as I dug down for another deep and painful breath, "I've never been in church on purpose in my life and I'm not about to start now. What the hell, he's your brother, not mine."

"Sounds like you could have used some church time, *brother*."

"If you can't teach morality without superstition or hope without false promises of eternal life, *brother*, the human animal probably has outlived its usefulness," I said as I handed Reverend Walker a card. "You can leave a message on my voice mail," I added, then walked away.

As we climbed back into the Beast, Hangas said quietly, "That's pretty cold, man."

"Learned it in college," I said. "Besides, if I'd folded, he would have lost any respect he might have had for me after that damned story about the bear cub."

"Hell, I understood it perfectly," Hangas said, then chuckled. "Hey, man, can I ask you something kind of personal?"

"Sure."

"Did you ever find yourself praying in Korea, old man?" Hangas asked.

"Praying, shitting my pants, and crying for my mother," I had to admit. Hangas and I had survived the first of the stalemate wars. I'd spent three months in combat; Hangas had endured three years.

"But it didn't last?"

"Not too long after I ran the first clip through my M-1," I said. "Or maybe the second."

"Does that mean firepower is God?" Hangas asked, chuckling again.

"It'll have to do for this world, until something better comes along."

"Eldora Grace now?"

"She thinks I'm a vacuum cleaner salesman," I said. "Or something worse. I'll leave that one to you. Be sure to let her know that I've got Sissy's getaway money. And let me know how she responds to that."

"Voice mail?"

"Ain't modern life grand, Hangas?"

Since it seemed that Renfro's internal injuries were still causing him trouble, he still hovered between the conscious and unconscious worlds when I glanced into his room. A woman who looked remarkably like Renfro and a small, bald man with a ponytail hovered over his bed. So I left without bothering them. I had a couple of hours before I was due at Cathy's. I found a convenience store, bought a couple of beers and an *Austin American-Statesman* in which I checked the classified ads for firearms and used the pay phone. In less than two hours I had collected a twelve gauge Winchester Wingmaster pump with a full choke and a three-inch chamber, a .22 American derringer, and a Ruger Mini 14 carbine to stash in the trunk of the Caddy in case I needed some unregistered firepower, and still had enough time to slip by the Blue Hollow Lodge to retrieve one of the cocaine bindles from the emergency light before I drove over to Cathy's.

CHAPTER SEVEN

BETTY'S PICKUP and Cathy's rig were parked in the driveway, so I parked behind them, limped up the steps to ring the doorbell. When the tiny Judas gate opened in the door, I could see Betty's blue eyes smiling at me. She let me in quickly, double-locked the door, then held me tightly, whispering apologies against my lips. I could smell the *mota* and wine on her breath, could feel the smiling laughter on her face. It made my old heart sing.

"I'm sorry, honey," she said: "First, I badger you into letting me share your troubles, then first time I get scared, I turn on you. I'll forgive you, if you'll forgive me."

"Not necessary," I said, meaning it. "But no more running away, okay?"

"I promise," she said, stepping back so I could see her face. "But you have to promise not to treat me like a child."

"A child?"

"No more trying to protect me, okay?"

"That's going to be a little bit harder."

"Listen, you son of a bitch," she said, stomping her foot, "I'll never see forty again, I don't qualify as a vestal virgin, and you may be from Montana but you're not Gary Cooper."

"Love," I said, "that's a deeply stoned metaphor, but I'll do the best I can to do whatever you want."

"You'll do whatever I say?" she asked, laughing, her lovely face turned to the ceiling.

"Within reason."

"To hell with reason," she said. "Say yes. Or leave."

"Yes."

"And uncross your fingers."

I did.

"Cathy's ready to fix your back again," she said. "You shouldn't be taking off on long trips while your back is in such a mess."

"I can sure as hell go for that," I said and let her lead me upstairs into the lowering sun that burst through the glass wall with the western exposure, its bright shafts hanging in the smoky air like golden bars. But Cathy was not imprisoned. She flitted about the large, open room like a happy bat. Within moments she had me stoned senseless, naked, and stretched on the table. When she got a full view of my back, she didn't say anything, just sucked in her breath.

"What kind of drugs do you have in your system?" she asked calmly.

"Four codeines, three beers, and two short lines," I admitted dreamily.

"You got any more of that blow?" she asked.

"Inside pocket of my vest," I said. I heard the search, a couple of lines chopped and snorted—maybe even one by Betty, who never did coke—then Cathy touched the new bruise softly.

"What the hell did you do? Run into a bulldozer?" she said.

"Probably a light-loaded and suppressed five-point-six-millimeter round."

"Jesus," she sighed. "That's good blow. Makes me remember why I gave it up. Almost worth losing my license for."

"You don't have a license," Betty chuckled from the corner.

"I have a degree from the London school," Cathy said smartly, "and an idea."

"What?" Betty asked.

"Leeches," she said.

"Leeches?"

"I can have that bruise improved in a half-hour or so," she said. "If you can stand the sweet, squirmy little guys."

"Shove a couple more codeines down my throat, and let the squirmy little bastards loose."

The leeches felt like small strips of liver wriggling on my back, then no feeling at all. Even as Cathy removed them. Then she went back to the needles again. I didn't feel them at all.

Except for the smell of that even stronger incense, that was just about the last thing I remembered until Cathy slowly removed the needles. Once again they seemed to want to remain in my skin. My back felt wonderful, and I had another errant erection that almost hurt as Cathy flipped me over. Before I had a chance to even consider it or think about it, Cathy's mouth slid, wet and warm, over me, once, then twice, then so swiftly I didn't have time to protest, she slipped out of her leotard and mounted me, the slippery, tight hold of her cunt sliding quickly over me, gripping me like a living beast. I opened my mouth to say something, but what I'll never know, because the pink shadow of Betty's thigh swung over my face and her soft red pubic hair covered my mouth. My tongue, with its own volition, darted into the wet darkness, and I was lost in their dream for as long as they wanted.

Golden moments: the women lying side by side beneath me—Betty pale as a pink rose and as comfortably erotic as a sultan's odalisque, and Cathy as brown as a sunburnt bone and slippery as gristle—as I lapped and humped and snorted like a puppy; once paused inside Betty's softness while Cathy sat backward on her face, tiny, sharp teeth darting at my nipples; and that wonderful moment when all three of us convulsed in the throes of a single giant orgasm.

Other moments of startling clarity: still sitting on Betty's face, Cathy shoved a long nipple into my mouth, shouting "Bite!" Then came again like a freight train, and I realized that these women had made love before; when Betty came under Cathy's mouth it was as if a long cool sigh had rippled a crystalline pond; and when I came inside Cathy's tight cunt, Betty covered my mouth with hers in a long gentle kiss that almost eclipsed my orgasm.

After they were done with me, and I had recovered enough to pee, I slogged to the john, then rejoined the naked women on a pile of pillows against the western wall where we sipped vodka on ice and smoked dope until full dark. "By way of apology," was the only explanation Betty bothered giving me; "you can't leave me behind now," her only reason.

"A little fun never hurt anybody," Cathy suggested.

"What if I'd died?" I asked, holding up a glass of Absolut. Suddenly, recalling what the Molly McBride woman had told me about clear whiskey and her father in Lake Charles.

"We would have chopped you open with an axe, filled you with rocks, and dumped you in Town Lake," Cathy said. "Parked your pimp car on Ben White with the keys in it, stolen your clothes, snorted your cocaine, and fucked your friends. Assuming you have any left."

"Right," Betty said, laughing, open and happy.

"A good thing I kept my wits about me."

We chattered, as aimlessly as baby birds, until the sliver of moon scratched the top of the dark sky.

Late the next morning, bleary-eyed in spite of a long, tangled sleep, over a breakfast of chicory coffee, fresh fruit, and stale croissants, Cathy asked me, "Have any fun, cowboy?"

"Make that 'cowpoke,'" Betty said.

"Never done that before," I admitted.

"Never?" the women asked in unison.

"Had a chance once," I said, "but had to turn it down."

"Why?" they asked, but when I didn't answer, they rambled along without me.

But I couldn't help but think about the time I'd turned down a chance to sleep with two women. At the end of a long, tiresome domestic case back in the late sixties—one of my first—when I caught the young married woman with her lesbian lover in a Billings motel, both of them Meriwether high school teachers, she offered me their bodies whenever I wanted, if I'd just give her the pictures, and if I'd lie. If it got to court back in those days, she was sure she'd lose any claim to her children to her creep of a husband who headed the education department at Mountain States College. If I slept with the women, both solid Montana women, I'd feel obligated to lie. That didn't feel right. So I tossed her the film, gave the professor his retainer back, and walked away from the whole thing. Over the years, I had watched the young woman's children grow up rather nicely, then once they were off to college, she divorced her idiot husband, moved with her lover to Portland, and as far as I knew, lived happily ever after.

Unlike me, who always had wondered what it would have been like. And now that I knew, oddly enough, I felt slightly used, the memory blooming into a seed of doubt that clouded the lovely memories of the night. But these women—one who loved me, one who thought I was Irish—had no bones to pick with me. So I shook it off, poured more coffee, and took out a cigarette.

"Outside, cowboy," Cathy said gently.

I nodded and took my cup of coffee into the small enclosed patio off the kitchen that overlooked the dam-bound Colorado River. Betty said she needed a shower, and left as Cathy cleared the table. Outside it was as if clouds hadn't been invented yet. The high blue sky glistened like a baby's first tooth. Only the shadows held any trace of the norther as the morning blossomed with sun-warmed air. I was on my second cigarette when Cathy came out with the coffee pot to join me. She took the cigarette from me, had a long drag, then blew a series of perfect smoke rings that hung for a long time in the still air.

"You service other people's addictions well," she said as she handed me the cigarette.

"Thanks. I guess."

"You know, Betty and I have been friends all our lives," she said without preamble, "and I hope you have some idea how much she loves and depends on you, old man, and how hard this is for her. Maybe you should think hard about giving it up."

"It's too late to quit," I said, wondering again why everybody wanted me to stop the investigation.

"I don't know exactly what's going on with your troubles," she said, "but please take care of her. Please."

"She's already made me promise not to protect her," I said, then laughed.

"What did you say?"

"Yes," I said. "But I was lying," I admitted, laughing again, washing the shadows from the edges of my mind. "I'll keep her as far away from the trouble as I can. You can count on that."

"And you can count on me, too," Cathy said. "Anything I can do to help."

"How did you fix Sissy Duval's orgasms?"

"Went out to her great-granddaddy's place for two weeks," she said, "and fucked all the resistance out of her. Taught her that sexuality is best when it's bound to love, but it ain't all that bad when it's just random fun. Trouble was, she loved that asshole, Dwayne. For reasons nobody ever understood."

"When was this?"

"Oh, I don't know. Sometime after Dwayne took up with Mandy Rae," she said, "and before he got blown away. Skinny son of a bitch had destroyed her confidence."

"Where?"

"In bed, you idiot."

"No, where was her great-granddaddy's place?"

"A shack surrounded by abandoned pump jacks, old time oil patch machinery, and a bunch of slush pits somewhere near a hole in the road south of Lockhart," she said. "Town had some kind of funny name. I can't remember exactly. But it was on his first big-time producing lease."

"Can you show me where it is?"

"I'm not sure. The old man's name was Logan, though, and she called the place Logan's dump—that's about all I remember. Why?"

"I think somebody's trying to kill her."

"Why in hell would anybody want to kill Sissy," she said. "I've always liked her, but she's such a frivolous bitch."

"Maybe you better tell me about it," I said.

But before Cathy could start her story, Betty came out of the house, her smile as bright as a dew-sparkled rose, shaking her fluffy light red hair golden in the sunshine. "Okay, kids," she said, "no fooling around without me."

"Dammit all to hell," Cathy snorted. "I always knew you were a selfish bitch. Ever since you stole my four-colored pen in the third grade."

"It was mine in the first place," Betty said, grinning. "And besides, it was a three-colored pen in the fourth grade."

"Just proves my point," Cathy said, faking a sulk as she leaned her head on the flagstone wall. "And Miss Batson always liked you better."

"That's because I didn't shoot her in the butt with spit wads and rubber bands," Betty said.

"She had the kind of ass that invited pain," Cathy whispered into the shadows.

"What's on the agenda today?" Betty asked, her hand warm on my cheek.

"Road trip," I answered. "I've got to go to Houston, then Louisiana to look into some shit."

"How long?"

"Don't exactly know how long I'll be gone," I admitted.

"How long we'll be gone," she corrected me, "and if we're going, I've got to run out to the ranch, then see if Tom Ben's hands can look after the stock while we're gone."

"It would be safer if I went alone," I said.

"Not a chance, cowboy."

"Then I'll pick you up at Tom Ben's," I said. "We can leave your truck there."

"I'll give you a call on your cell phone before I head out to Tom Ben's place."

Betty gave Cathy a hug and me a long sweet kiss, then left.

"Alone at last," Cathy said, her wrist to her forehead. Then she ruffled her short dark hair. "You got time for this story?" she asked seriously. "It's going to take a couple of Bloody Marys."

"I counted on at least one."

Once we had drinks in hand and perched on stools at the breakfast bar, Cathy sighed, then said, "Austin in the seventies. What a fucking circus. It was like Hollywood with cowboy boots. Or maybe, what we thought Hollywood was like. Or maybe, we thought we were starring in our own movies. It was seventy-three and I'd just come back from acupuncture school in London, a fairly upright young woman—never as stuffy as Betty—but close. By eighty-five I'd been married and divorced three times, had the clap twice, and overdosed three times, twice on purpose, and spent most of my time hanging out with the kind of guys who were interesting when they were rebellious students at UT. But now they drove beer trucks and dealt the drugs they didn't smoke or stuff up their noses—Christ, I married two of them, much to their regret, and their daddy's trust funds—but at the lowest moment Betty and I hooked up with Sissy and Mandy Rae and their crowd." Then she paused for a long breath. "Nobody has the constitution for that kind of action. I don't know how I survived."

"How'd you get out?"

"Woke up one morning with Enos trying to strangle me with his dick," she said, "while fucking Dwayne was trying to squirm his skinny dick up my ass. It was too much. I stepped back, watched them go after each other without me as an excuse. Then I just stayed away, so unlike most of the rest of them, I survived those years without suffering rehab, jail, or death. Believe me, cowboy, I paid for this life. And I intend to enjoy it."

"I noticed that," I said. "I'm sort of interested in where Mandy Rae's cocaine came from."

"Nobody seemed to know," Cathy said. "Mandy Rae had dumped her first husband—some old guy who pushed tools on an offshore drilling rig out of Morgan City, or somewhere down in coonass country—then hooked up with Enos, maybe in New Orleans, I don't remember exactly. But they came to town with kilos, not ounces, and it kept coming—more coke than any of us had ever seen, and shit even purer than yours. By the way, why don't we do a short line?"

"It's always the people's cocaine," I said. "That keeps it simple."

"Good plan," she said.

Afterward, Cathy's story drifted through those lost days, which seemed so happy at the time, and for many of the people it had turned out so sadly. Some people should never have a drink. I knew at least a hundred people who were alcoholics midway through their first teenage beer. They either survived or didn't. And the drugs.

Just after my forced resignation from the Meriwether County Sheriff's Department, I had been on a toot, during which I offered an anthropology graduate student a hit off my doobie before we made love. The next weekend the young woman, behind three hits of Purple Haze acid, had tried to fly out her apartment window. Luckily, she lived on the second floor and landed in a snowbank. She broke three ribs and lost the tip of her little finger to what she called an interesting case of frostbite. Three months later, arguing with her new boyfriend over where they were going skiing, she shot him in the butt with a .22 short to get his attention. When that seemed to have no effect, she shot herself in the thigh. They drove all the way to Bozeman before they decided prescription painkillers sounded better than bleeding all over the chutes above Bridger Bowl, so they checked into the ER. The boyfriend later died in a Mexican prison, but the young woman grew up to be the head of a chain of drug rehab clinics in California.

Nobody knows when or where addiction begins. I also knew I couldn't count the number of people who had done cocaine without either becoming hooked, going crazy, or losing their jobs. But the dozen or so who had gone down the hard way, went that way from the beginning, and ended very badly.

"Maybe it wasn't us or the drugs or even the sex," a sad-faced Cathy said, "but the shitty moral force of all the whitebread assholes who tried to impress their will on us, make us behave, and live their frightened little lives."

I nodded, but slowly because I didn't know.

"Maybe it's always been a religious war," Cathy whispered, "like the abortion thing." Then she stood up, shouting, "Well, fuck 'em. When they die and find there ain't nothing afterward, think how silly they'll feel."

"I thought they were dead?"

"I've always hoped that there's just enough afterlife for the ass-holes, just a nanosecond where they understand that this is all there is," she said.

"Here's to the final answer," I said, raising my glass. We finished our drinks.

"I've got a client in about fifteen minutes," Cathy said, then gave me a fierce hug and a kiss like a punch in the face. "Kick ass and take names, cowboy. *Mi casa, su casa, mi amigo.* Stairtown. That's where Homer's place was."

"Thanks," I said, then left.

Down in the Caddy I checked my voice mail. Except for six hang-ups, it was empty. So I went down to the Four Seasons, grabbed my gear, stuffed the Browning into a shoulder holster under my vest, and checked out. I drove out to the gun safe to pick up some more traveling cash, then headed the Beast toward the Lodge, for a shower, packing, and a change of clothes. The Caddy felt good under my hands and butt, as close to home as I got to feel these days. I almost felt guilty when I checked the mirrors for a tail.

But it was a waste of time. When I unlocked the door of my suite, the drapes along the south wall were open, flooding the room with smoky sunlight. Two large men in dark suits and darker glasses were outlined against the glare. Another slimmer one in a light suit stood a bit apart from them, leaning lightly on the heavy bag hung from the ceiling, the strong sunlight gleaming off his glasses and bald head. A dark-haired woman wearing a round, black hat with a wide brim and a half-veil that hid her face sat in one of my easy chairs, a slim cigarillo smoking between her red-tipped fingers. A low-cut black dress exposed a soft round cleavage that seemed to glow in the shadow of the hat. She smelled like money all the way across the room. Beside her, the bulk of an old, fat woman moldered in an electric wheelchair. She was also dressed in black and wearing a veiled hat covering a square, heavy face. Even through the veil, though, I could tell that her skin was riddled with pitted scars and hairy moles. Her hooded eyes glared angrily at me. The visible wings of her hair were so deeply black they had to be a cheap wig or an oil spill.

I had the Browning from beneath the vest with a motion so quick and smooth it surprised even me, my two-handed combat stance solid, the sights locked on the younger woman, hammer cocked, safety off. But I hadn't bothered putting a round in the chamber.

"Very nice, Mr. Milodragovitch," the young woman said, her voice husky, tired, worn from smoke and drink, and deeply unimpressed. She spoke carefully, with a slight accent, as if English wasn't her first language. Maybe Spanish, I told myself. The old woman's eyes rose, glittered madly for a second, then dropped.

"Three days a week at the range," I said, only lying a little bit. I'd been avoiding the range more often than I'd been there for months. Even with earmuffs my ears rang for hours after fifty rounds. Just as I'd avoided the heavy bag because my hands ached so badly after a workout. "And clean living," I added.

"You won't be needing that." The woman tilted her head toward the corner of the room where a third man in a dark suit covered me with a shoulder-strapped mini-Uzi with a large suppressor on its barrel.

"You'll be the first, lady," I said.

The woman nodded to the third man, who calmly draped the assault weapon back under his coat. As my eyes adjusted to the light, I could see that the men in the dark suits seemed to be Latinos, Secret Service radio earplugs in their ears. They even had the easy but alert stances of real professionals, their faces in a bland, almost happy repose. They were on the job.

"Just calm down, Mr. Milodragovitch," the man in the tan suit, Tobin Rooke, said, his thin lips barely moving.

I moved the Browning slightly, aimed it at the heavy bag, then pulled the trigger. Although the hammer falling on the empty chamber sounded as loud as a grenade in the closed room, nobody even flinched, or even moved until the echoes of the hammer died, when Rooke lightly touched the heavy bag as if it were swinging.

"Fuck all of you," I said. "Whoever the fuck you are."

"I believe 'whomever' is the correct usage," Rooke said so quietly that I nearly didn't hear him.

"I've been to college," I said, charging the Browning and shoving it back into the shoulder holster. The next time I pulled it out, I wanted to have a round in the chamber. "It's obvious I ain't gonna impress anybody unless I put a round up their nose. So what's the deal, lady? Since I assume you're in charge." She nodded. "A nice hat, too. I haven't seen a hat with a veil since the forties." My mother had worn one just like it to my father's funeral, black gauze wreathed with expensive sherry fumes.

"Thank you," she said without irony. "I understand you are looking for the woman known as Molly McBride," she added.

"Molly McBride?" I said, more than somewhat surprised. "What's it to you?"

"I want to talk to her," the woman said. "She has something of mine, and since you don't have an actual client, I thought perhaps I might provide you one. If you would be so kind."

I had no idea what to say at this sudden turn.

So the woman continued: "I know you don't need the money,

Mr. Milodragovitch, so I'm going to offer you something much more important."

"What's that?"

"Your freedom," she said quietly.

"Who the hell are you, lady? And what do you have to do with my freedom?"

She took a long drag on the little cigar, then blew a long, slow billow of smoke into the stolid air. "I'm Mrs. Hayden Lomax," she said, "and this man, as you well know, is Tobin Rooke, the district attorney of Gatlin County, and he has an envelope containing a contract, a small check, a bench warrant for a material witness, the woman who calls herself Molly McBride, and a DA's special investigator badge and identification. Of course, he had to use your booking photo, so the picture's not too flattering, but it's clearly you." She didn't bother introducing me to the old lady in the wheelchair.

"A bail jumper warrant would be better," I said, "but isn't there some sort of conflict of interest here?"

Mrs. Lomax presented me with an icy sneer that should have frosted my balls, and she kept staring at me, silently, until the old woman pinched her arm. "As an officer of the law, you answer to me, not some crooked bail bondsman," she said quickly without a trace of irony and as if she had been waiting all day to say the line. Then she nodded to Rooke to answer the rest of the question.

"There are not now, and upon successful completion of your contract, will be no charges pending," Rooke said primly. "This McBride woman, whoever she might be, is a material witness in a homicide. So this is all, however personally abhorrent, perfectly legal. Your business partner, Mr. Wallingford, has examined the documents and approved them. You are certainly free to consult him at this time." Rooke slipped a cell phone out of his perfectly draped suit, punched redial, then crossed the room to hand me the phone.

"Where the hell are you?" I said when Travis Lee answered. "It sounds like you're next door."

"Sippin' Tennessee whiskey and lookin' at this pile of *caca de toro*

on my desk, and wonderin' where my next fortune's comin' from,"
he said.

"What the hell is going on with this Lomax woman?" I asked.

"Sounds to me like a chance to pull your ass out of the pigshit,"
he said. "I'd be on it like a duck on a June bug, if I were you."

"What's the woman want?"

"Who cares what she wants?" he said. "She's Hayden Lomax's
last trophy wife, so whatever Sylvie Lomax wants, she gets. So
maybe you better ask her yourself."

"Thanks. I will." I handed the cell phone back to Rooke, who
gave me a manila envelope. "What do you get out of this?" I asked
Mrs. Lomax. "Aside from the sheer pleasure of using your money
like a club?"

"Don't think of it as a club, Mr. Milodragovitch," she said, a
wisp of a smile like a thread of smoke flickering around her face,
"but more like a willow switch."

"Thanks for correcting me," I said. "I assume you mean that a
willow switch tickles before it stings? Believe me, lady, I'm tickled
shitless, but that doesn't answer my question."

"I was warned that you'd be like this."

"Who warned you?"

"Someone who knows your type," Mrs. Lomax crooned. "Like
a pup with a bone: You don't know if you should chew on it, bury
it, or hump it."

"Aside from the fact that I don't have any idea what you're talking about," I said, "what do you want from me?"

"When you locate this Molly McBride person and inform the
Gatlin County authorities," she said, "you've completed your chore.
They'll handle it from there. That's all you need to know."

"Why use me to find the woman," I said, "instead of the police
or one of the big firms?"

"It's in your interest to give this chore your full attention," she
said calmly. "I prefer the people who work for me to also be personally motivated." Then she stood up, leaving the little cigar smok-

ing in the ashtray. I was clearly dismissed, and Mrs. Lomax was already out of the room in her rich mind.

"Don't you have to swear me in?" I asked Rooke.

"I don't think that's necessary in this case," Rooke said, his steel gray eyes glittering with what had to be rage, madness, or both.

"Well, I sure as hell do," I said, "but not with these goons for witnesses. Let's go down to the bar. I feel safe in bars."

"I'm sure you do, Mr. Milodragovitch," Mrs. Lomax said with a coy smile. Then she snapped, "Handle it, Rooke." She swept past us with a rustle of silk, a waft of sandalwood, and the solid weight of a gold chain swinging at her waist, a golden snake curled up her arm. Up close the young woman obviously wasn't nearly as old as her makeup made her look from a distance—not even thirty, I guessed, wondering why a young woman would want to look old— she wasn't even as old as she sounded, but her green eyes, as hard and unyielding as malachite, looked older than the dark side of the moon. Her fine features, framed by coal black hair, seemed chiseled from an ancient marble as pink and bloody as the froth from a sucking chest wound. As she walked out the door, her hips swayed like willows in the wind and her bare white shoulders gleamed like a hot flame in the smoky shadows. The last bodyguard, a large man with a pair of puckered scars in the middle of both cheeks, paused long enough to put out the smoking cigarillo, then stepped behind the old woman's wheelchair.

"Of course, if you talk about this deal, man," the bodyguard whispered, in an accent that sounded as if it were from further away than Mexico, "I will personally cut you into small pieces and feed you to the pigs."

"Thanks," I said as the bodyguard walked past, pushing the old lady. "Sorry I called you a goon." But the tiny curl of the bodyguard's lip suggested that my apology wasn't even slightly accepted.

"Let's get this over with, Milodragovitch," Rooke said as he started to follow the procession out the suite doorway.

"Don't we need a Bible or something?"

Rooke spun in the doorway, his body obviously as quick and

well trained as his twin brother's had been, his jaw violently clenched, his words reduced to a thin, hard stream. "When this is over, you dumb son of a bitch," Rooke hissed, "I'm going to devote my life to destroying yours."

Given the attempts on my life, Rooke's threat didn't seem all that big a deal so I fumbled through drawers until I found a Gideon Bible, remembering that Gannon had said that the Rooke brothers had been closer than twin snakes in a single egg. The vision of baby snakes wearing glasses popped into my head. The laughter just bubbled out.

"What the fuck are you laughing about?"

"Just wondering if you slept with your forked tongue up the rich lady's ass," I said, "or took off your glasses and stuck your whole fucking head in?"

He would have come for me, but the bodyguard with the scarred cheeks laid a hand on his shoulder.

So, oddly nervous and slightly excited and more solemn than I would have imagined, in the middle of a bright fall afternoon in the Texas Hill Country, with Lalo Herrera in all his ancient Latin elegance as one of my witnesses and a bored software salesman the other, I became a peace officer for the second time in my rowdy, misbegotten life.

After Rooke slithered hastily out of the bar followed by the salesman, Lalo poured two shots of Herradura, then raised his shot glass. "*Buena suerte,*" Lalo said, then Lalo and I sipped the smooth fire of the tequila. Lalo ran his hand through his thick hair, still crow-wing black in his seventies, and leaned over the bar.

"Milo," he said quietly, "I was born in this country of skulls . . ."

"Skulls?"

"Before you Anglos came, my people called this place La Tierra de Calaveras," he said. "The land of skulls."

"Any particular reason?"

"Perhaps some *bandidos* who used to raid down in that country south of the Nueces River had a hideout or a cave around here. Or some other people say maybe the Tonkawas left the skulls of men they had eaten piled around old campsites. No one knows. I'm just certain that many bodies are buried in this county," he said as he poured us another shot, "and many of them entombed by people very much like those who just departed. *Buena suerte, amigo.*"

"But when I'm down to bones and ashes, *mi viejo*," I said, "I plan to sleep in my grandfather's ground."

I detoured through the lobby on my way back to my room. The Lomax gang was loading up. The old woman's wheelchair whirred quietly up a ramp and into the side of an extended frame black Mercedes limo with darkly smoked glass windows as Sylvie Lomax supervised. The bodyguards climbed into a Mercedes sedan of their own. A better work ride than I'd ever had.

Back in my suite, as I showered and packed my war bag, I did a casual and unsuccessful sweep of the rooms for bugs, wondering how the hell Mrs. Lomax had known I was coming by my place. When I finished, I stood in the middle of the room. Her scent still hung in the air, sweet and light beneath the burning rope stink of her cigarillo. I reconsidered the job I had taken. Maybe I should have called Thursby instead of Travis Lee. I used the room phone to call Phil Thursby, but he was in court and wouldn't be out for hours. I promised to call back. I called Travis Lee again at his office but only got his machine.

It took almost an hour to wind my way through traffic almost back to Austin, then around the lake west to the southern entrance of Tom Ben's twelve brush-choked, gully-broken, hardscrabble sections along the southern fork of Blue Creek. The entrance to his place was marked only by a battered mailbox in front of an electronic security gate. Cattle rustling was back in style these days. After somebody buzzed me in, I knew I had to cross half a dozen cattle guards and go through as many electronic gates at the electrified cross fences before I got to the main house. Tom Ben didn't much care for trespassers or modern-day cattle rustlers. His place covered a patch of land that was flatter than Betty's but broken by a series of shallow branches and dry washes so that it seemed rougher country than Betty's place. His place had suffered more from the thorny invasion of South Texas brush. But he worked it harder. At several places I saw teams of D-9 cats pulling anchor chains or root plows to clear the brush for grass pasture and hay fields to feed the small herd of Brangus cattle he ran, along with small bunches of Spanish goats he kept for barbecues.

Tom Ben still lived in the simple tin-roofed single-story field-stone structure surrounded by a wide, shaded veranda that his great-grandfather had built. Except for electricity and indoor plumbing, it hadn't changed since it had been built just before the Mexican-American war. But the outbuildings—a hay barn, an abandoned dairy barn, and half a dozen sheds—were structural steel and as shiny as a new dime.

Betty and her uncle sat in cedar rockers on a small deck under a trio of live oaks, a pitcher of iced tea between them. Tom Ben looked nothing like his younger brother. The old man was short and sturdy, solid arms and legs and a round, drum-tight belly that jutted angrily from his thick-chested body. He almost always dressed in bib over-alls, rundown cowboy boots, and a battered banker's Stetson that looked as if it had been used a dozen times to swab a newly born calf or reinsert a cow's prolapsed cervix.

"You're gonna tear the bottom out of that fancy car, boy!" Tom Ben shouted as he always did, except when I arrived on horseback. "When the hell are you going to get some real Texas transportation?"

"When I want a sore ass more than a bad reputation," I answered.

"You're walking like a man who's been throwed and stomped, anyway, Milo," the old man growled.

"You should see the other guy."

"Yeah, I should have burned out that fuckin' Rooke family thirty years ago when I caught that trashy bunch roastin' one of my prize billy goats."

"You ready?" I asked Betty. She nodded. I tossed her my keys.

"Why don't you move your stuff, love. I need to confer with your uncle for a minute."

Betty hesitated for a second, then took off.

"What's up, Milo?"

"I seem to have gotten even more mixed up with the Lomaxes this morning," I said. "And I wanted to ask you about a story I heard a few years ago."

" 'Bout that option to sell I supposedly signed? According to what Betty told me, you and me maybe crossed paths with the same slippery cooze."

"Maybe."

"Well, I'm glad Betty ain't here to hear this," Tom Ben said, " 'cause it don't make me sound like much of a gentleman. Ah, hell, this young woman came out one Sunday when I was watching the Cowboys. Said she wanted to write a piece about my Brangus bulls for *American Cattleman.* Had a camera and a tape recorder and copies of some of her articles and everything. Even said she'd pay me for my time. And, hell, she knew her cattle and she was driving a cherry Jimmy pickup. She was as polite as she could be—apologized for coming during the Cowboys game, offered to come back when I wasn't busy. Of course she was as pretty as a new colt—looked more like a movie star than a journalist. But I was having my evening Jack Daniel's early that day, like I always do when the Cowboys are playing, and I offered her a splash, and hell . . . one thing led to another. Goddamned woman could drink, boy. Before I knew it, I'd done an interview, and some other stuff, signed a release, taken a check without looking at it, and made a damned fool of myself . . . Well, I bet you know the rest." The old man paused, removed the limp Stetson from his thinning gray thatch, then blushed.

"What did you do?"

"When I got my clothes back on, looked at the size of the check, and realized that I hadn't even looked at that release, I locked all the gates, and sent some hands on horseback to drag the bitch back. When she found a locked gate, she tried to head cross-country. Banged up her pickup a little bit and tore up 'bout ten thousand dollars' worth of fence-line, and hid that signed option before my hands caught up with her." He paused, dug in the pocket of his overalls for a blackened stub of a pipe. "Wouldn't have done her no good anyway," he added, but I wasn't listening.

"What happened then?"

"She fought my boys like a wet cat till they got her hog-tied and locked in the corn crib in the dairy barn with a pile of unshucked ears I keep for the goats, then I told her about the rats and mice in the corn, and reminded her that wherever you find rats and mice, you're bound to find rattlesnakes. Hell, she spent ten days in there drinking stale water and doing her business in a bucket, but she wouldn't say a word. Though I was damn sure it was that fuckin' Lomax who sent her. So we stashed her classic Jimmy pickup in an old line shack over there on the northwest pasture beside the catch pond."

I remembered seeing the shack and the pond one of the times I had ridden one of Betty's saddle horses over to the old man's ranch.

"Hell, I had half a mind to bury it in the bottom of the pond 'cause we'd just dug it, but that model is such a great truck, I couldn't bring myself to do that. Then my hands dropped the bitch off in downtown Austin, and I tried to forget about the whole mess.

"Believe me, boy, these days when I have my evening whiskey, I lock all the doors and windows first," Tom Ben said, then laughed bitterly. "And I keep waiting for that piece of paper to show up. That fuckin' Lomax will get this place over my dead body." He paused to light his pipe, then a snort of laughter blew out the match. "And not even then actually," he added.

"Is this the woman?" I unfolded one of the head shots Carver D had scanned off the Lodge registration videotape.

The old man nodded, suddenly sad. "If that goddamned Travis Lee hadn't come limping back from jump school all shiny in his uniform while I was still in Korea, everything would have been different."

"Sir?" I said, confused by this sudden turn in the conversation.

"You didn't know? Son of a bitch ran off with the woman I was supposed to marry when I got back from Korea," he said, stood, then jammed his shapeless Stetson back on his head, and rolled on his old bow legs and frozen feet back to the veranda steps where he stopped and turned. "Betty said you gave away a piece of family land one time."

"I kept enough to be buried in," I said.

"What'd it feel like?"

"Since my great-grandfather had sort of stolen the land from the Benewah Indian tribe," I confessed, "it didn't exactly feel like a family place."

Tom Ben thought about that for a moment, rubbed his chin, puffed on the stubby pipe, then said, "Goddamned little brother of mine brought home the mumps from high school, too, so there was never going to be any children for me, either." Then he shook his head, grinned ruefully, then stepped into the shadows of his house.

I looked at the photograph one more time, folded it, and stuffed it back into my pocket, then stepped off the porch, and walked to the Caddy where Betty waited. I grabbed the manila envelope out of the front seat, and we stepped away from the car.

"I should have known she was a professional," I said.

"He told you about the woman?" she said. "He must really like you," she added. "He's never even told me the whole story. Just hinted about it."

"Right," I said, "and he mentioned something about Travis Lee running off with his fiancée."

She nodded sharply.

"What happened?"

"After a fling," Betty said, "Travis Lee dumped her to marry a rich girl, and she committed suicide. Tom Ben never spoke to him again."

"You mean your uncles never speak?"

"Sometimes through lawyers. Sometimes through me."

"And you never said a word to me?" I said, amazed.

"Down here people aren't raised to talk with your mouth full or about family stuff," she said. I assumed that by "down here" she meant Texas, which seemed to have a different set of rules of family behavior than the rest of the world. "Why? Is it important?"

"At this point I don't have any idea what's important," I said, "but it's sure as hell interesting. Wait until I tell you why I'm late." I handed her the manila envelope.

"You're kidding," Betty said after she discovered Gatlin County's new approach. "How's it feel? One minute behind bars. The next behind a badge."

"Actually, I'm not going to wear it. I'm going to carry it in my pocket."

"What now?"

"We're going to cash this little check," I said, "Then we'll find out how Mrs. Lomax knew I was going by my place."

CHAPTER EIGHT

WHEN THE ELECTRONICS guy's meter hit the peg, he had me drive the Caddy into a soundproofed and electronically baffled garage where he worked until late afternoon carefully and silently removing the bug from behind the dome-light casing, where it drew its power from the car's battery. "State-of-the-art for this kind of equipment," he said, "good up to a quarter mile." Then he stuck it to the headliner inside a plastic thimble. "Should approximate the sound," he said.

As I paid the bill for sweeping the Caddy, I whistled. "Shit, I'm in the wrong part of the business."

"Somebody's got to protect us against the government, man," he said. "They can read the newspaper headlines on your front porch and hear an ant fart if there's a telephone in the house."

"I'd like to get my hands on the creeps who put that piece in my car," I said as I counted off the last hundred-dollar bill. "Nothing personal, buddy. But I always thought you electronics guys jacked off too much."

"Gotta do something since we don't have to pound the shoe leather," the guy said, then laughed.

"Ex-cop?" I said.

"Shit, man, nobody can afford to be a cop these days."

I should have listened to him. Before I climbed into the Caddy, I pulled out my cell phone and started to check my voice mail one last time.

"Excuse me, boss," the guy said. "I wouldn't use one of those gadgets if I was worried about electronic surveillance. They're a pretty easy tap."

"Could I borrow your telephone?"

"Make yourself at home," he said. "But if you're interested, I can do better than that."

"How?"

"It'll cost you a bundle up front and a fairly stiff monthly fee—in cash—but I can come up with five scrambled cell phones. Of course they can only talk to each other."

"Perfect," I said.

The only message on my voice mail was from Gannon. He wanted me to call him on a land line.

"Don't you trust your own people?" I asked without preamble when he answered.

"There's a prize in every Cracker Jack box," Gannon said, "and a devious heart in every fucking cracker down here. Where the hell are you?"

I gave him the name of the chain motel bar just off I-35 North.

"I'll turn the siren on and be there in thirty minutes."

"Why?"

"Now that we're colleagues, Milo, we should talk."

Gannon showed up looking very uncomfortable in a full-dress uniform. The leather straps of his Sam Browne belt stretched tightly over his jacket, as if he were restrained, and each time one of his new cowboy boots hit the floor, he grimaced as if he had just stepped on a thorn. He looked as if his cowboy hat hurt like a migraine.

"Joining the enemy?" I asked.

"You're now looking at the chief of patrol," he grumbled as he pulled up a stool to our stand-up table and ordered a cup of coffee. "Sheriff said either get into uniform or get *gone*. He didn't have to add that he'd prefer gone."

"What brought this on?" I asked.

"I think they're pissed because I didn't shoot you at the golf course," he said. "They let Culbertson go, too."

"Why?"

"Nobody tells me anything these days," he said.

"So what did you want to tell me?"

"If I were you, Milo . . ." Gannon started to say.

A lanky cocktail waitress with a smile like a classic Buick grille stopped at our table and waited until I removed the gray plastic case of cell phones so she could set our oversized happy hour drinks down. She wanted to run a tab, peddle plates of appetizers, work on her tip, and maybe even tell us the story of her life. Sometimes the friendliness of the natives drove me nuts. I threw a wadded fifty on the tray and told her to keep it. When she smiled, the Buick seemed to be speeding into my face.

"If I were you, Milo, I'd mail my badge back to the bastards. Preferably from a foreign country. They're setting you up for something."

"That's old news. Finding out what for will be half the fun. You have any ideas? They want me out of town and not looking for Enos Walker? Or they want me to finger the McBride broad? Or maybe they're planning to frame me for my own attempted murder? What the hell do they have in mind?"

"I don't have a clue," Gannon said. "And there's not a single rumor around the courthouse. That's the frightening part."

"Lomax owns most of the county," I said. "Maybe he's got something in mind?"

"I did some checking around," Gannon said, "moving easy and slow. Lomax draws more water than just owning the county. He's asshole buddies with every political bigwig from the new governor all the way up and down. But Lomax has been down in Central

America for the past three weeks. Some kind of mine disaster. And with his clout, if he wanted you dead, buddy, you'd be meat fragments floating in cowfeed or recycled aluminum or holding up a bridge on some highway down in Mexico." Then he paused to rub his chin thoughtfully. He looked like a man polishing a middle-buster plow. "Do you have any chance at all to find the McBride woman?"

"I've got some notions," I said, "and in the past I've had some luck finding people. And having a badge might not make it any harder."

"Notions? What kind? What have you got in mind? Where are you going to look first?"

"You don't want to know."

"You're probably right," he said, but he didn't seem convinced.

"But I might need your help, Gannon," I said.

"You can count on me, sure, but I've got to walk easy. My job is hanging by a thread of gnat's snot," Gannon said quietly. "So call me, if you can figure out a safe way."

"I've got a clean cell phone," I said, digging one of the new telephones out of the case. "But you can't call me. I can only call you."

"Whatever," he said. "Detective work must be nice when you have unlimited funds."

"Believe me, man, I've paid for every dollar I've got. The hard way," I said, "and it's still the same job—sticking your face in a pile of crap and hoping you find a rose instead of a shitty thorn."

Gannon shook his head without smiling, gunned his drink, and shook my hand. "Good luck," he said. Then thumped out of the bar.

"You trust him?" Betty asked quietly.

"I don't know," I said, "I'm not sure I trust anybody anymore. Not even myself." But I was used to that sort of thing. "Your uncle said this deal sounded okay."

"Try to remember he's a lawyer," Betty said looking away. Which was exactly the same thing she had said when she first tried to talk me out of going into business with Travis Lee. And a version of what she had said when she changed her mind about the project: At least he's a lawyer.

After we stopped by Carver D's to leave him one of the scrambled phones, we drove southeast to spend the night in an old-fashioned roadside court outside Bastrop. Snug behind the rock walls, stretched on a lumpy double-bed, and covered by a blanket as thin as a sheet and sheets we could see through, Betty and I shared a doobie and a couple of beers. Because of the bug, our conversation in the Caddy had been limited to scenery, the deep insanity of far-right-wing talk radio, and other mundane topics. But once stoned, Betty had a lot of things to say as she snuggled against my shoulder.

Finally, she ran down, paused, then asked me, "Are you okay about yesterday? You know, the thing with Cathy?"

"Oh, yeah, that. I remember that." She slugged me in the ribs hard enough to roll me out of bed. "It was wonderful while it was happening," I admitted as I climbed back between the covers, "but thinking about it now—well, I'd rather not think about it right now." Then I paused, thinking about it. Then said, "Cathy is a friend, whatever, and you and I are together."

"You realize that I'd slept with her a few times before," Betty said, giggling, "but never with a guy around."

"How about a goat?"

"Italian dwarves," she whispered.

"Well, that's okay then."

Once we controlled our stoned giggles, we curled into each other slowly and softly, like walking wounded careful not to disturb our bloody bandages. Afterward, Betty still sitting on my hips, I felt her tears hot against my chest.

"What?" I said.

"Nothing," she said. "Nothing."

"Tell me," I whispered, amazed all over again how quickly she could go from love or laughter to tears.

"Nothing, really," she said, then wiped her eyes, laughing again. "I'm just crazy like always."

"This kind of shit would make anybody crazy," I said, then shrugged, slipped into sweats and running shoes, grabbed my cigarettes and a beer, then stepped outside for a couple of smokes while she watched the news on the ratty television.

The night loomed clear and cold, the stars sparkling away from Austin's ambient light and in the heart of the dark of the moon. I was running on something slimmer than a hunch, and, right or wrong, I didn't want anybody dogging my ass.

"Can I ask a couple of questions?" she said as I came back into the motel room. "Just a couple?"

"Sure," I said, expecting another serious conversation about our future. But I was wrong.

"What are you going to do about the car?"

"I don't know," I said, hesitating. "We'll have to see if we can find out who's bugging us before we go to Stairtown."

"Stairtown?" she said, looking very confused. "Where's that?"

"The place where Cathy fixed Sissy's orgasms," I said.

"Oh," she said quietly. "And how are we going to do that?"

"We're going to lead the son of a bitch up a dead-end road," I said, "then beat the shit out of him."

But I was wrong again. It turned out to be a stout young woman operative in a white van loaded with what I guessed was at least ten thousand dollars' worth of electronic gear that I led up the dead end. Hoping that the guy who had swept the Caddy had been right when he told me that the receiver had to be within a quarter-mile to pick up the bug's transmissions, when we checked out of the motel that morning, we stopped by a hardware store for a battery, wire cutters, and a pry bar, then drove back country roads discussing a meeting with an important witness to the assault in Blue Hole Park, drove until we found the narrow dirt lane that dead-ended against a small county park nestled down by the river not too far from Smithville.

After I parked, I clipped the feed off the bug and hooked it to the small twelve-volt battery, set it in the thimble, stuffed the Browning under my arm and a set of cuffs in my vest pocket. I let the pry bar dangle under my shirt sleeve. Betty and I chatted aimlessly as we walked back up the roadside until we found the van pulled into the shallow ditch. The short-haired woman behind the wheel still had earphones on her head.

"Hello, darling," I shouted into my hand.

Betty walked to the back of the van to cut the valve stems off the rear tires with the wire cutters. The woman swept the earphones off her head. I knocked on the window, but she wouldn't roll it down.

"I believe this belongs to you," I said, holding up the bug. When she still didn't roll the window down, I set the bug on the thin, rough pavement and raised my boot heel. "No?" She wasn't impressed, so I slipped the pry bar into my hand, popped the door, then reached in to stick the pistol under her nose.

"All right, you son of a bitch," she said as she climbed out of the van, her hands not raised very high or very convincingly.

When I frisked her, I didn't find a weapon of any kind, so I holstered the Browning, backed up a step, and dangled the bug in front of her face, asking, "Does this belong to you?" She didn't want to answer, but when she reached for it, I snapped one cuff around her wrist, then the other to the door handle.

"Shit," she said, then tried to kick me in the shins.

"Lady," I said, "you can either behave or you can take a little nap. At this point I don't give a damn which."

"He means it," Betty said as she handed the wire cutters to me.

The woman decided she wanted to behave so she remained silent as I disabled the van—popped the hood to cut the cable to the oversized battery and the fuel line—and disrupted her communications. I tore the mobile telephone out of its cradle, dumped the batteries out of the cell phone, then snipped every wire I could find in the back of the van. "That's criminal vandalism, buddy," she said when I finished.

"You want to call the sheriff, lady?" I said, more angry than I in-

tended to be. "He knows you're conducting illegal electronic surveillance in his county, right? I'm going to call him as soon as we
find a telephone. I'll just bet he'll be happy as a pig in shit when he
sees all this stuff. Probably hasn't got a bit of it in his office."

The woman just looked at the ground, scuffling the gravel with
her jogging shoe. "Please," she whispered.

"You an ex-cop?" I asked.

"Ex-Army," she admitted.

"Who hired you?"

"I work for a firm," she said. "They don't tell us who the client
is."

"Must be cheap bastards to make you work this gig alone," I
said. "You are alone, aren't you." She didn't glance over her shoulder.
"You got a card?"

"I just send the tapes in, man," she said, then the woman dug
her wallet out of her jeans pocket and handed me a card.

"Doris Fairchild, Poulis Investigations, Dallas," I read aloud.
"How long have you been on me?"

"Since the night after you were arrested."

"Shit," I said. "Tell your fucking boss that I'm a cranky old bastard and I'm really pissed. I'll be standing in front of his desk one of
these days. Soon. You got off easy, lady," I said. "Given my attitude,
I'm likely to gutshoot the next one of you assholes I run into."

"Lucky?" she said, glancing at the van.

"Lady, if you'd been a man, I would've broken both your arms
and burned your van," I said. "I'll call a tow truck when we get back
to civilization."

"Thanks a lot," she said, sarcasm thick in her voice. "You can
shove your fucking chivalry up your ass."

"Listen," I said, "I hate you lazy electronic sneaks. So don't push
your luck."

I threw Ms. Fairchild's cell phone into a patch of prickly pear
the size of a small house, tossed her the key to the cuffs, then Betty
and I walked silently back to the Caddy.

"You're really angry, aren't you?" Betty asked as we climbed into the car. When I didn't answer, she said, "I guess so."

"Last straw, I guess," I said and punched the Caddy hard back up the potholed road. I passed the van so fast that it rocked with the draft. Doris Fairchild shot us the finger.

"I don't think that's happened to me since junior high," Betty said quietly.

I sighed, chuckled, then slowed down. "And how long's it been since you've done it?"

Betty paused, then answered, "I don't think I've ever done it."

"Cathy said you were kind of stuffy."

"Well, fuck her," Betty said, then punched me on the shoulder.

"You gotta stop pounding on me, love. Remember my back."

"Your back was all right last night."

"I was faking it."

We laughed all the way to a small country store at a crossroads. I stopped, used the pay telephone while Betty grabbed us some coffee and doughnuts.

"You call a tow truck?" Betty asked as we drove away.

"Actually, I called the Bastrop County sheriff's office," I said. "I don't know who's fucking with me, but I'm tired of it."

"What'd he have to say?" Betty asked.

"Well, he didn't say thanks," I said. "At least now I know how the shooter followed Renfro and me to the golf course the other night. And that's probably also how the Lomax party knew to meet me back at the Lodge yesterday. But I still don't have the vaguest notion why the Lomax family or the county would want Sissy dead. Or me. Or Renfro."

"Maybe it's his wife," she suggested.

"If she wanted me dead, why did she send me after the McBride woman? I don't know. Hell, I saw her up close. She's way too young to be involved in the Duval shooting," I said, "and too rich to bother with dealing cocaine. Besides rich people don't bother killing people in public places. They just disappear them. It's not worth the trouble or the risk. Shit, love, I don't know. Where's the nearest big town in the other direction?"

"Probably San Marcos. Why?"

"I need to look a little different."

After our purchases in San Marcos, we checked into a motel to prepare me for my visit to the Caldwell County courthouse in Lockhart. It took longer than it should have at the plat office because the old woman helping me was full of chatter. She had grown up when there was still a bit of town left in Stairtown. I was glad I had taken the time to buy a cheap suit and a theatrical quality fake beard and wig. She was bound to remember me.

So the sun was still high in the western sky, pale behind a thin haze, when we reached the turnoff to Stairtown between Lockhart and Luling. The sharp stink of sulfur and crude oil filled the air. I checked the county map again, then eased up a small, crooked country road. At first, it was just a pleasant rural drive—small farms, a church, a creek—but as the road rose up a shallow rise, we saw the first pump jacks of the small oil field with its maze of lease roads. It took a while, but finally I found a wide spot to park high enough to give me a view through the spotting scope of Homer Logan's lease.

The shack sat among abandoned oil field equipment—rusted tank batteries, draw-works engines that hadn't run in years, wooden pipe racks filled with tubing and rods, and a slush pit. Sissy Duval's BMW was parked beside the shack. Nothing moved behind the thin curtains, or on the surrounding land. I drove down to the turnoff, left the Caddy idling on the road while I checked the tire prints on the dirt track to the shack. The foreign treads of the Beemer had been in and out a few times. A larger tire, from a pickup or a van, had been in and out once.

"We're not going in?" Betty asked as I drove away.

"I'm going in alone," I said. "Later tonight. I gotta get some stuff first."

"You're not going in there without me," she said.

"You can either stay in the motel room," I said, "Or I'll lock you in the trunk."

"You would, wouldn't you, you son of a bitch?"

"You ain't seen nothing yet."

"I've seen enough," she said, flaring. "I'll just call a cab and follow you."

"Listen to me. Please," I said. She nodded slightly. "The only thing that scene lacks is a flock of buzzards circling overhead," I said. "It's going to be hard enough for me to make sure that I don't leave any trace evidence. I don't have time to worry about you, too."

This time she nodded as if she understood.

So I dropped her at the motel, rented another car for cash from a lot just down the block from the motel on the outskirts of San Marcos, bought dark blue coveralls, a large and a small flashlight, surgical gloves, an extra roll of duct tape, a roll of electric tape, and two pairs of huge socks.

At three A.M., dressed in coveralls, my running shoes covered by the socks, I crept out of the rented junker and slowly up the side of the dirt road by the thin flashlight beam. The shack was dark and silent, the door unlocked. I sat in the doorway, slipped the other pair of socks over the dusty ones, then began a careful search. Except for Sissy's traveling mess, the small cabin was empty. Sissy had found some cocaine. About half a quarter-ounce bindle remained among the clutter of cut straws, smudged glass surfaces, and glasses of unfinished vodka. Also, a hypo and some used works.

Then I searched outside among the machinery and empty tool sheds until I found the outline of a body mostly buried in an old slush pit, at the edge of the crumbling dirt bank. A light brown crust covered the darker mud below, and it was unmarked except for long scratches beyond the arms and two pieces of discarded water pipe, which I assumed they had used to hold the body down in the mud. I risked the big flashlight long enough to spot a stand of streaked hair waving above the sun-blackened neck. The lighter mud had been in the sun long enough to dry and crack. There didn't seem much point in checking the body. Whoever had killed her had killed her in broad daylight, gotten her toasted on the coke, and held her face in the mud until she stopped struggling.

I went back to the shack and spent another hour cleaning up the cocaine traces with a bottle of bleach I found under the sink. Then I shoved the rest of the cocaine into my pocket, and the works into a trash bag that I carried away. Whatever happened, this wouldn't go down as an accidental overdose or a psychotic episode, so they would have to mount a full-scale investigation. Just in case I never found out what was going on, or if I got killed before I did.

The search of the Beemer didn't take long and only yielded a telephone number without an area code on a piece of paper crumpled around a hunk of chewing gum in the ashtray, which I shoved into the same pocket with the cocaine. I drove the Beemer into one of the empty sheds, then left.

Sissy Duval had lied to me and she probably was, as Cathy said, a frivolous woman, but she deserved a better death than this. Another chore on my tool belt.

Back in the motel room, I hesitated to tell Betty what had happened, but she quickly asked, "She's dead, isn't she?"

"I think two guys came in a truck," I said quietly, "and knocked her out—probably in some way only a forensic pathologist can discover, if they're lucky—then filled her with coke, tossed her into the slush pit and held her face in the mud until she smothered. They'll probably write it off as just another cocaine accident."

"Why? How? What for?" she stammered. "Nobody knew we were looking for her. Except Cathy."

"Don't start doubting your friends," I said. "But Sissy damn sure knew something somebody didn't want me to know," I added calmly. "Maybe about Mandy Rae. Maybe Enos Walker. Maybe something entirely different."

"What now? We can't call the Sheriff's Department, can we?"

"They're going to have to figure it out without my help. Another day in the sun, maybe the buzzards will find her," I said.

She wailed again, her teeth chattering as she hovered near shock. I wrapped her in all the blankets in the room, got a little Scotch down her throat, and held her until she stopped trembling, then started the long drift into an exhausted sleep.

"What now?" she muttered sleepily.

"Houston," I said. "Then on to Lake Charles."

"What?" she asked, waking briefly.

"Molly McBride went to a great deal of trouble to convince you that she was from San Francisco," I pointed out, "and to convince me she was from New Orleans. But I remember the Houston address on her phony lawyer card, and she let something slip about Lake Charles. I'd bet a dollar to a doughnut that I can pick up her trail one place or the other."

"I don't want a fucking doughnut," Betty said, wiping at her eyes. "I want ham and eggs and red-eye gravy on my grits."

"I'll buy you a boxcarful if you'll just smile again."

She did. For a second before she plunged into sleep like a woman leaping off a bridge.

Driving toward Houston on I-10 after a breakfast stop to eat and dump my garbage bag, as Betty napped curled in the back seat, I called Hangas to ask him to keep an eye on Eldora Grace in the hope that he might be around when she got the bad news. He told me that she hadn't been home the last two times he stopped at her house. I suggested she might be staying at Sissy's place. Hangas said he would try there.

As I drove, I found myself in another world of shallow rolling hills broken by thick, dark broadleaf forests, which after a few hours gave way to industrial chaos, nothing like the open spaces of the Hill Country. I'd never been in East Texas but I suspected that it was going to be different from anything I knew anything about, more like the South than the West.

Houston seemed to be the world's largest construction site combined with the world's worst traffic jam, all of it plopped down with neither rhyme nor reason among as many shacks as tall shining buildings, all buried in an uncommon grave under a humid, shallow sea. Even the Caddy's air conditioner couldn't keep the hot, heavy, stinking moisture out of the car.

When I pulled off the freeway, I parked in a residential area, then opened the Houston street map. Betty climbed over the seat, rubbing her eyes.

"What's up?"

"I told you. The McBride woman swiped her phony calling card out of my shirt pocket when she snagged a cigarette."

"Or when you had it off," Betty said. I tried to keep my face grim. "You did take your shirt off, didn't you?" she asked, grinning as she poked me in the ribs.

"But I remember the address," I continued. "Navigation Boulevard. Sometimes people make mistakes when they make fake business cards." Then I paused. "I took my shirt off but not my socks," I said, grinning, too.

"That's disgusting," Betty said. "Like one of those old black-and-white porno films." I glanced at her. "I'm not as stuffy as some people seem to think."

I shook my head, chuckling, then wound south toward the ship channel and Navigation Boulevard. The address turned out to be a rundown joint with black-painted windows called the Longhorn Tavern, the sort of place where, when I parked the Caddy in front, I imagined I could hear the hacking coughs of day-drinkers, the snicker of switchblades swinging open, the metallic click as the hammers of cheap revolvers were drawn back.

"It'd be easier if you stayed in the car," I said, "and without argument." Betty glanced at the place, then nodded solemnly. I took a picture of Molly McBride from the glove box, then climbed slowly out of the car, and trudged up the sagging steps of the tavern. I wondered if my pace looked as ancient as it felt.

Inside, every bar stool was filled, every bleary eye aimed at the morning game shows murmuring on the two televisions at either end of the bar. The clientele seemed to be an interracial cross-gender mob of the unemployed mixed with the unemployable: construction workers, semiretired whores, shore-bound sailors, longshoremen, and street-level drug dealers. Even in scuffed boots and faded jeans, I felt overdressed because I wore a clean shirt. I found a small space at the front of the bar next to a fairly clean fellow about my own age with one arm of his khaki shirt pinned to his shoulder. It seemed the safest place.

When the bartender, an enormous black woman with scarred, ham-sized fists and the wary eyes of a street fighter, lumbered down to my end of the bar, I ordered a bottle of Lone Star, trying to fit in.

"No bottles," she rumbled. "Nothin' but cans," she added as she cracked one for me.

Looking around, I agreed with the bartender. I wouldn't put anything resembling a weapon into the hands of this crowd, either. Not that the bartender would need one. "Thanks," I said, shoving a ten at her. "Keep the change," I said, then pulled the picture out of my jacket pocket. "You haven't seen this woman around here, have you?"

"Annie," the one-armed guy on the stool murmured as he spun to face me.

"You ain't a fuckin' cop, are you?" the bartender asked, tugging on her ear with the thick fingers of her right hand.

"I'm a private in—" was all I got out of my mouth before the large woman threw the straight right at me. I tried to shove my stool backward to slip the punch, but the one-armed guy stuck his boot against my stool, and the large fist slammed against my forehead, hard enough to knock me off the stool. I hit the floor, rolled, then stumbled backward all the way across the room. The bartender shouted, "We don't allow out-of-town pigs in here, do we boys?" Then half her customers swarmed me. My last clear thought was that I was going to die, with perfect irony, at the hands and feet of a crowd of winos.

Then it was all bar-fight confusion and chaos. Tables and chairs, teeth and hair, blood and primal grunts. It seemed I remembered the one-armed guy kicking viciously at my crotch. And that I'd never been quite so happy to hear the sounds of sirens and hoping they were coming for me.

I came back to the world sitting on a rickety chair at one of the dirty tables. Two young cops—one black, one Chicano—wearing surgical gloves swabbed delicately at my bleeding face, Betty and the bartender hovering in the background. The rest of the bar had cleared as if by magic.

"How are you doing, buddy?" the black cop asked.

"I've been worse," I said after I had checked my teeth and nose, then the rest of my face. A fairly deep gash in my left eyebrow. Another long shallow one under my chin. A dozen fingernail gouges. "Nothing a couple of butterfly bandages can't handle," I told the cops. "Sore ribs. Both pupils the same size, I hope." Betty nodded. "And it feels like they missed my nose and nuts." My right fist echoed with the memory of at least a single solid blow.

"You got any ID, buddy?" the Chicano kid asked, seemingly uninterested in my injuries.

I dug out my real driver's and PI license. Luckily, I'd left the badge case and the fake ID in the trunk of the Caddy. This was no time to have a badge. The photo of Molly McBride had disappeared.

"So what happened in here?" the black kid asked.

"Ah, hell," I said quietly, "we're on our way to New Orleans, and I'd heard that an old skip I've been chasing for a couple of years had been seen in here. Guy named Bill Ripley. Thought I'd stop in and ask. Guess I asked the wrong guy. My fault entirely."

"You see any of your attackers?"

"It all happened too quick," I said. "The bartender tried to stop them, but there were too many, too fast."

"Recognize anybody, Annie?" the black officer asked the bartender.

"Place was plum-full of strangers this morning, Officer."

"Guess the fleet's in," the Chicano officer snorted. Then he handed me a stack of sterile pads and a roll of gauze tape. "It would be a good idea to get out of this part of town, sir. Why don't you let your wife drive? They have a lot of good doctors on your way. Over in Beaumont, maybe."

"Sounds good to me," I said, then I stood up, forcing myself not to wobble. "Thanks," I said to the bartender, who gave me a hairy eyeball and a sneer. "Let's go, honey," I said to Betty, as blandly as a tourist, then put my hand on her shoulder and let her lead me to the safety of the Beast.

"What the hell happened in there?" Betty asked as she eased out from the curb.

"I got knocked down by a fat woman," I answered, "and damn near kicked to death by an alcoholic mob."

"But why?"

"They don't like strangers, I guess," I said. "You call the cops?"

"They were roaring by when this guy tumbled out the front door."

"Great. At least I got in one shot," I said, checking my face in the visor mirror. "Let's get the fuck out of this town," I said. I gobbled a couple of codeines, then used Betty's Swiss Army knife scissors to trim some butterfly bandages to try to seal the cuts on my face.

"It's about ninety miles to Beaumont," Betty said. "You going to bleed to death?"

"Why do you ask?"

"Because you're going to have some stitches when I get there."

"No fucking way am I going to sit around some goddamned emergency room."

"You may not have to," Betty said, then reached for the cell phone in her purse as I reached for the codeine bottle again.

Stunned by the codeine, I didn't exactly pay much attention to where Betty led me in the medical office complex next to the Beaumont Hospital, but when she hugged the tall, black doctor with a short gray beard before she introduced us, I knew exactly where I was.

"Warren Reeves," the doctor said as he shook my hand.

"Good to meet you," I said. And I meant it. Reeves and Betty had been engaged when she had killed the black kid who had raped her. Reeves had stuck by Betty all through the troubles afterward, but her guilt had driven a wedge between them that no amount of love could extract.

Reeves led me into the examining room filled with children's toys, cleaned me up quickly, and deadened the cuts. Then hit me with tetanus and antibiotic shots. "I hope I remember how to do this," he said, " but from the look of your face it doesn't need to be plastic surgery. This isn't your first rodeo."

"I only agreed to the needle work because she made me," I said. "She's a hard woman."

"Don't I know," Reeves responded, grinning.

"You boys want me to leave the room while you talk about me?" Betty asked.

"I love it when she's shy," I said.

"Me, too," Reeves said, then began stitching.

Afterward, Reeves refused payment, but I stuck five hundred dollars in his pocket. "Donate it to your favorite charity."

"You sure y'all won't stick around for dinner?" Reeves said to Betty. "I know Anna and the kids would love to see you. It's been too long."

"Milo's hot on the trail of something or other," Betty said. "Maybe on the way back. I'll call."

"Do that," Reeves said. Then to me, "Any doctor can take those stitches out for you."

"I can do it myself."

"Of course you can," Reeves said. "Just sterilize the fingernail clippers before you do it."

We laughed, shook hands again, then I left Betty and Reeves to make their goodbyes alone. But Reeves shouted at me before I got out the office door. "You sure you won't spend the night? The guest house is always ready, and there's forty pounds of blue cat in the freezer."

I was suddenly very old and tired, the pain of the beating seeping through the drugs, and the invitation so warm and generous. "Why the hell not? Lake Charles ain't going anywhere."

Later that night, Reeves and I, stuffed with catfish and hush puppies, loafed on the patio listening to the frogs and insects sing along the brackish slough that stretched just behind the dark screen of thick brush at the edge of the yard. Domestic sounds came from the kitchen—the rattle of pots going into the dishwasher, the soft murmurs of the children, and Anna's lilting voice, her accent a charming mixture of French, Vietnamese, and Southern—Reeves and I sipped Cognac and smoked good Havanas.

"Keeps the mosquitoes off," Reeves said quietly as if apologizing for the cigar.

"Maybe for you," I said as I slapped one on my wrist, leaving a large freckle of blood on my skin and an odd pain in my hand. "I think they're using me as a drug smorgasbord. At least they're easy to kill. Too fat and stoned to fly." I slapped another one on my forehead.

"You been rustling cattle?" he asked.

"No. Why?"

"Looks like you've been butchering a calf with a chain saw."

"Don't believe I've ever had that pleasure."

We chuckled softly, then sat quietly for several minutes, listening again to the buzz saw of the night. Then Reeves said, "Betty's as happy as she's been in a while. You should be proud."

"If I thought I had anything to do with it, man, I might be proud," I admitted, "but sometimes I think she's just a slave to her moods."

"I blame her folks for that," Reeves said. "Distant father. And a mother who should have been on lithium."

"She never talks about them."

"Her old man wasn't my favorite person, but he was interesting," Reeves said. "Really the last of the great country doctors. House calls and the whole number. Also, a great mechanic. He could stitch up your ranch hand, tune your pickup truck, pull a calf, then take a flat of free-range brown eggs in payment. But the money changed all that."

"Money?"

"He patented an improvement to a surgical staple gun or something that made him a considerable fortune. Then the gravel company that owned the dump truck that hit her folks head-on settled a heavy piece of change on Betty," he said. "Lord knows her mother's ranch never made a dime after they gave up deer leases."

"Her father wasn't your favorite person, though?"

"He was a hard son of a bitch," Reeves said. "Betty told me that after her first menses, he never touched her again. Never a hug, never a held hand, never even a hand ruffling her hair, or an encouraging word. She was a mess when I met her. Nobody could live up to Dr. Porterfield. Same kind of charmingly arrogant Southern jerk as her lawyer uncle."

"Travis Lee?"

"You know the old boy?"

"We're sort of partners," I said.

"Well, I'd surely watch him," Reeves said. "He started off as the sort of lawyer who'd start a fistfight just to drum up clients, then graduated down to politics, and further down to shady land deals."

"I thought he was too rich for that kind of sleazy," I said.

"Last time I was over in Austin, an old friend of mine suggested that Wallingford had taken a bath in the last oil glut, mis-read the computer boom, and was badly overextended. Very badly."

"When was that?"

"I don't know. Five or six years ago."

"Hell, I'm supposed to be suspicious by nature. And profession," I said, "so I had my lawyer go through the contracts. Travis

Lee's always come up with his share of the payments. And he is Betty's uncle."

"I've been wrong before."

"And I've misjudged a few women."

"And Betty a few men . . ."

"The rape?"

"Not just that," Reeves sighed. "After her mother and father were killed in the wreck, she took off two years before she started medical school, and I suspect she ran a little wild, cocaine cowboys and that ilk. In fact she just eased back to a seminormal life when . . ." Reeves paused, puffed on the cigar, then blew a perfect smoke ring into the humid air. "Ah, hell, the rape and the killing and all the troubles afterward."

"Troubles?"

"She put five rounds in the guy's back. If he'd been white, and if she couldn't have afforded Phil Thursby," Reeves said, "she would have done hard time. And she knew that. She was guilty, and nothing I could do or say seemed to ease that guilt. She quit medical school, ran wild again until she went to vet school somewhere in California, then left the twentieth century and moved out to the ranch.

"I didn't see her again until Anna and I got married. And as far as I know, you're the first man she's been involved with for any length of time for a long time," Reeves added, then paused again. "I suspect it hasn't been easy."

"Since people started trying to kill me, she's been a lot easier to be around," I said.

Reeves gave me an odd look.

"I haven't exactly lived a citizen's life. Now my chickens are coming home to roost. Turns out they're turkey buzzards."

Betty and Anna stepped out of the kitchen, arm in arm, smiling.

"If you ol' boys done gossipin' 'bout us girls," Anna said to her husband, "the children are in bed and waitin' for their Daddy to read to them."

Betty said, "And I should get my patient into bed."

Reeves and I stood, shook hands, and I said seriously, "Thanks for everything, Doc."

"Anytime, man, anytime."

We made our good nights, then Betty slipped her arm around my waist and I draped my arm over her shoulder as we walked slowly through the thick grass, slick with dew and littered with shards of streetlight, to the small guest house at the back of the yard.

"You're walking heavy tonight, honey," Betty said.

"Long day."

But Betty went to sleep first. So I slipped into my jeans, popped a couple of pain pills, found a couple of beers in the refrigerator, grabbed the cell phone, and stepped into the muggy night and fog knee-deep on the damp grass. Time to call Carver D to see if I could find out if Sissy Duval's body had been found without actually asking him.

"Did I wake you up?" I asked when he answered.

"It's hard to tell these days if I'm sleeping or awake, old man."

"Anything happening back in that world?"

"Nothing much. Where the hell are you?"

"Beaumont."

"Lord, you're making tours of the classiest cities in Texas, aren't you," he said, laughing. "Midland. Odessa. Beaumont. Don't forget Waco and Van Horn." Then I heard the sound of the bourbon bottle splashing. "By the way, I heard an ugly rumor to the effect that you have joined the enemies of official repression," he said. "Surely a lie, Milo."

"Nope."

"Now why would you go and do something like that?"

"Trying to keep my tired old ass out of jail."

"Hope it's worth it," he said. "And hope it actually works."

"Well, it hasn't caused me any trouble yet."

"Speaking of trouble. What have you been up to?"

"Drinking, fistfighting, and running up my expense account," I said.

"Sylvie Lomax might have been able to shove you down Tobin Rooke's throat," Carver D said, "but I know that skinny son of a bitch never approved an expense account."

"Well, I can try," I said. "But I need another favor. Check out a Doris Fairchild who works for Poulis Investigations in Dallas. That's who had my Caddy bugged. And while you're at it, partner, why don't you start building me a file on the Lomaxes."

"I'll see what I can do," Carver D said. "You stay in touch."

"Right," I said. "Did Hangas have any luck talking to Eldora Grace?"

"Hell, he can't even find her."

I clicked off the phone, hoping I wasn't going to have to find some way to report Sissy Duval's death myself. Then I opened my second beer, lit a last cigarette, and watched the smoke drift in the murky air while the mosquitoes feasted on me until, bloated with blood and stoned on codeine and Cognac, they fluttered fat and happy into the thick grass. For a long moment, I envied their simplicity. Eat, drink, try to fly, fall to soft earth, and sleep.

CHAPTER NINE

PERHAPS I HAD EXPECTED Lake Charles to be full of Southern mansions and live oaks dripping with Spanish moss. But I
didn't expect two casinos as garish as jukeboxes on either side of a
brackish lake, one perched on the edge of downtown like a fat wa-
terbird on the edge of a swamp, and the other lodged among industrial facilities. Sand and gravel mountains were heaped everywhere,
and mazes of petrochemical pipes seemed designed to pump pay-
checks right into the riverboat moored to the flat shoreline.

"Doesn't look like a place where a working girl might hang out,"
Betty said as we crossed the Interstate bridge. "Of course, I wouldn't
know about that."

"Any place they turn cards, honey, somebody turns tricks," I
said.

After giving the Players Casino a once-over, we recrossed the
bridge and lodged at the Isle of Capri, checked into the nearby
hotel, dressed in casual but expensive western clothes, then went to
work.

After four days and nights of checking out every bar in the area without even a smidgen of success, we gave up on the last evening, and went back to the room. Betty slumped in front of the television, more tired than drunk. I stood at the mirror with a bottle of hydrogen peroxide and a pair of nail clippers, removing the stitches and trying not to look at the fading bruises.

"Jesus Christ, Milo," Betty complained, "I've been in more bars the last four days than I've been in the rest of my life put together. Let's give this up, please, and go home."

"Patience is a virtue in this business," I said as I clipped the last stitch out of my eyebrow, then started on the ones under my chin.

"Well, what now, cowboy?" The plaint in her voice hovered on the edge of tired anger now.

"Let's go over to the casino and lose some money," I suggested, hoping to jolly her out of the mood.

"So much for patience," she said.

"You can hang out here, hon," I said. "I just need some mindless abstraction to shut my brain down."

"Believe me, honey," she said finally, "I'm about as mindless and abstract as they come."

I tried to talk her out of it, but, as she had every step of the way on this trip, she insisted on following.

Out of habit we walked directly to the bar down the narrow aisle between the clattering slot machines and crowded tables beneath a low ceiling. Also out of habit, we went into our routine. Betty ordered an Absolut on the rocks with a twist from the young, round-faced bartender, then she suggested that I join her.

I said, as required by our script, "The only people who drink white liquor are sissies or drunks, and the only people who drink bourbon are white trash, con men, chicken fuckers, or phony Confederate gentlemen . . . I'll have a beer."

"Nice talk," the bartender said as he delivered the drinks. "That where you got that mouse?" I started to laugh, but the bartender shouted to another young man shoveling quarters into a nearby slot. "Andre! Who was that one-armed son of a bitch that used to say that all the time?"

"Molineaux," Andre answered without looking up from the slot. "Fastest one-armed bartender in the world. And unluckiest."

Betty and I smiled at each other. "Better to be lucky than good," I said. "And sometimes the bad guys are too smart for their own good." Then to the bartender: "Double Absolut on the rocks. And keep them coming, partner."

Two mornings later back in Houston, dressed by the Salvation Army—dirty coveralls, work boots, a battered hardhat pulled down over my eyes, and my nose stuffed with blow—I was the first customer through the door when I heard Annie unlock it. Betty had insisted on following me. She was dressed in ripped jeans, her gloved right hand in the pocket of an old Navy pea coat, wrapped around the derringer. Except for Annie and an elderly black swamper, the place was empty. I pulled up a stool. Annie leaned against the bar, her huge hands resting on the edge.

"What can I do for you, mister?" she said.

"I'll have the address of that one-armed fucker," I said, then slammed the back of her left hand with the flat sap. Probably harder than I meant to. Betty snapped the doors locked, then turned to cover the swamper with the little pistol.

"Motherfuck!" Annie screamed, then, undeterred, reached across the bar for my shirt, so I slapped her on the fat right elbow with the sap.

"You ain't going to be popping nobody with that hand," I said, "and if you don't tell me where to find that Molineaux son of a bitch, I'm gonna put knots on your head a goat can't climb."

"I don't know nobody by that name," she said. A fat tear slipped out of her eye as she cradled her arm.

"That one-armed bastard, lady."

"He goes by the name of Morrison, mister," the swamper said

quietly behind me. "I'll show you where he lives. Just don't hurt her no more. Please."

"You best be right, old man," I said, "or I'll be back and burn this fucking place to the ground and barbecue this sucker-punching bitch with it."

"Don't worry, sir," the swamper said, shuffling toward the front doors. "Rollie pays good but not that good."

Before they left, Betty said to the fat woman, "You better put that hand in the ice, ma'am. It might be broken."

"What about my elbow?" she wailed.

"Just a stinger, I'll bet," Betty said. "He's good with his hands."

Annie didn't seem mollified, but she stuffed her huge hand deep into the ice.

"You're out of fucking control," Betty whispered as she touched my nose lightly as we went out the door. I had no way to disagree. Just kept sniffling through the day.

The swamper directed us to an older but fairly well-maintained brick house a few blocks from the bar. "Roland Morrison" was printed on the mailbox.

"You want me to knock?" the swamper asked.

"Fuck that," I said. "Honey, if this old fart runs, shoot him in the foot."

The swamper smiled. "Hell, man, I ain't run in thirty years."

"This ain't no time to take it up again," I said, then, guessing that this wasn't the sort of neighborhood where any of the residents would bother to investigate any sound short of automatic gunfire, I kicked in the hollowcore door.

The front room was cold enough to hang meat, the air conditioner blasting on high. Molineaux slept, even through the crashing of the door, passed out on the couch, wrapped in a dirty blanket, one knobby knee sticking out, his single arm dangling to the floor. A bottle of Lagavulin Scotch—probably a gift from his daughter—

and several empty beer cans sat on the coffee table. The large, new television murmured in the corner. Stale beer farts filled the room.

I eased my boot down on Molineaux's fingers, pinning them to the carpet, then placed my right hand over his face, pinching off his nose and covering his mouth, and holding his stump with my left.

The one-armed man struggled to breathe, but I held on until he turned blue. I let him have a quick breath, then cut his air off again until his face turned a deep, painful purple.

After Molineaux sucked in a couple of ragged breaths, he growled, "You son of a bitch, if I had both arms, I'd beat your fucking head in."

"Forget it, man," I said. "You've probably always been the kind of yellow-bellied bastard who had some excuse." I turned him loose and stood up, saying, "But if you want, asshole, I'll tie one arm behind my back."

Molineaux struggled to sit up. "Shit, man, I've got such a hangover I can't even see straight. Mind if I have a taste?" He jerked his head toward the half-empty bottle of Scotch, and I nodded. He grabbed the bottle, had a hit that made it bubble, then tried to backhand me with it.

While his arm was drawn back, I broke Molineaux's nose with a quick left jab, then I suddenly flashed on the one-armed man aiming vicious kicks at my crotch, so I let him have a full-bore right cross. I felt teeth and jawbone break under my fist. Molineaux flew over the couch, crashed into the wall, then sprawled, unconscious, on the couch, blood and teeth dribbling out of his mouth.

"Dammit," I said, turning him on his side so he wouldn't strangle on his own blood.

"Jesus," Betty said quietly.

"Reckon you killed him?" the swamper asked.

"He's not dead," I said, "but he's going to be difficult to interrogate with his jaw flapping loose." I turned to the swamper. "What's your name, sir?"

"Joe Willie," the black man said softly.

"Well, Mr. Willie—"

"Joe Willie Custer," the black man corrected me.

"Well, Mr. Custer," I continued, "would you mind answering a few questions?"

"Not the way you ask them, man."

"Dont worry, sir," I said, pulling my money clip out. "Name your price."

"How about a hundred?"

"How about two fifties?"

"Better than a poke in the eye with your right hand, man," Joe Willie said, stuffing the bills into his shirt pocket.

"Listen, I've already beaten up a fat lady and a one-armed man," I said, "so be cool. I'm not about to start roughing up senior citizens now."

"I'm cool, man."

I asked, "What was this asshole doing here?"

"Hiding from the law, everybody thought, but I don't know exactly. Mr. Morrison showed up six or seven years ago with too much money for this neighborhood," Joe Willie said. "Then a couple of weeks ago, he started spreading money around, saying if anybody came around looking for his daughter, we were to discourage him. But I guess you weren't discouraged."

"No, but I'm sure as hell confused," I said. "You take off, Mr. Custer. And please, keep your mouth shut. You know I'm the kind of son of a bitch who will come back." Then I pulled off two more fifties. "Give this to Annie. But don't tell her I'm sorry, because I'm fucking not."

Joe Willie added to his stash, thanked me, then shuffled out of the room.

"What now?" Betty wondered.

"Toss the apartment and hope for the best," I said. Without much hope.

But once again, good luck prevailed over hard work. I found the crumpled envelope in a plastic trash bag in the Dumpster in the alley with a return address for a Molly Molineaux just off the Strip in Las Vegas. I went back to the apartment, filled a homemade bindle with baking powder, left it open on the coffee table, then decided against binding Molineaux's good arm to his ankles, and fixed the door as best I could. A few minutes later I found a pay phone at a convenience store on our way to Hobby Airport and called 911.

"That should keep Molineaux busy for a few days," I said to Betty as I climbed back into the Caddy with a couple of cold beers. "At least until the lab finds time to test the baking powder." I cracked one of the beers and sucked about half of it down in a single swallow. "Jesus, what a morning."

"Honey, I've got to say something," Betty ventured.

"What?" I said, braced for some conversation I didn't want to have. "Want to go home just because I lost it?"

"I've never been afraid of you before," Betty said softly, "but I saw your face when you whopped that fat lady and when you hit the guy so hard that teeth flew out, and quite frankly it scared the hell out of me. Perhaps it's time to take a break."

I worked my way through the maze of construction and crazed traffic toward the airport without answering her.

"You know, sometimes you have to be as crazy as the people you deal with," I said. "Good old Annie didn't pull that punch or hesitate to sic her customers on me. And you saw the bruises on the inside of my thighs where Molineaux tried to kick me in the nuts. Violence was their choice, not mine. So to hell with them."

"But you enjoyed it," she said softly. Betty had assumed the stone face of a die-hard liberal, I thought, so I didn't say anything else, didn't remind her that she shot her rapist five times in the back as he left the bedroom.

"I fucking hate it," I said. But knew she didn't believe me. Hell, I wasn't exactly sure I believed myself.

"Where are we going?" she finally asked.

"Houston Hobby," I said. "I'm flying to Vegas. I have to get there before they wire Molineaux's jaw together."

"What about me?"

"I was hoping you'd drive the Caddy out to Vegas for me," I said. "Maybe I can wrap this thing up by the time you get there, then we can drive out to Big Sur, spend a few quiet days, cool out."

"I think you're just trying to get rid of me," she said stiffly. "Why don't we just drive straight through?"

"I'm too beat up," I admitted.

"All right," she agreed, very reluctantly. "But you leave all the firearms in the trunk. And all the coke. And that nasty little sap, too."

"No problem," I said.

"Listen," she said. "I'm only going to ask you this one more time. Drop this crazy stuff. Let's go home. You can dump the badge, and this silly chore. We can afford to fight them in court. Let the Lomaxes find somebody else to follow their crap around."

"I'm sorry," I said, "but it's way too late for that. Try to remember what's at stake. Whatever Enos Walker did, he doesn't deserve to die for it. Dickie Oates has been in prison for a long time. If he doesn't get out soon, he'll never have a chance on the outside. And perhaps I should remind you that I'm a little old to start serving time." I didn't have the heart to remind Betty that Ty Rooke had blown his nuts off with her pistol. "I could run but I couldn't hide from myself."

"I don't know. Maybe you're right," she huffed tiredly, the days of drinking and the morning of adrenaline sapping her energy. "I think you're absolutely insane, but I'll do this one last thing. But you have to promise me that you won't do anything until I get there. Just find the woman and wait. All right? Promise?"

"It doesn't always work that way," I said.

"Promise, Goddammit."

"Okay," I promised. "I'll try it your way."

She didn't answer. Just looked at me. We pulled to the curb so Betty could drive the rest of the way to the airport, and I could un-strap the Browning from under my arm and repack my war bag. I made a point of showing her the bindle I had taken from Billy Long's desk, but didn't say anything about the one I had taken out of Sissy's cabin. As we pulled up to the departure area of the curb, I gave her one of the scrambled cell phones, then leaned over to kiss her cheek. It was as stiff as rawhide. She didn't turn her head.

"I'll call you when I get there."

"Whatever," she said. "I may stop at home to spend the night."

"Whatever," I echoed, then kissed her cheek one last time, and climbed out. She drove away without looking back.

As I waited for the next Southwest shuttle to Dallas Love Field, I worked the phones. I called Carver D. He told me that Doris Fairchild seemed to be carrying somebody else's driver's license. Nobody caught it until after the lady in question had made bail through a Dallas firm, disappeared without a trace, forfeiting her bond. The real Doris Fairchild was a waitress in Big Spring. Lewis Poulis of Poulis Investigations, on the other hand, was the real deal, although a bit too good and clean to be true. Carver D asked me what I wanted him to do with the Lomax file. I told him to fax it to me at the Hyatt Regency in Dallas. "Hayden Lomax is pretty much an open book," he said, "but Sylvie is a blank page." Then he added that Hangas had mentioned that he still couldn't find Eldora Grace, and nobody seemed to know where she had gone. I wanted to call Gannon to see if he could check with the Caldwell County Sheriff's Department to see if Sissy Duval's body had been found but thought I'd best wait until he was home.

So I called the bar to check on my other business. Lalo Herrera informed me that the bar seemed to be attracting several on-duty and off-duty Gatlin County deputies, but I told him not to worry. I'd take care of it when I got back. Then I called Phil Thursby. He suggested that since I had the money, I might be better off fighting the case in court, instead of getting involved with Sylvie Lomax and whatever shifty shenanigans she had devised. I agreed with him. But the sorry truth was that I was having more fun than I had in years. When I talked to him, the sheriff of Bastrop County sounded happy, too. He didn't seem to mind that the woman had jumped bail or that somebody had abandoned a van-load of high-tech electronic gear in his county. He just hoped the FBI didn't bigfoot all over his treasure before he could get his paperwork through the court.

"Who'd the van belong to?" I asked.

"Texas plates were stolen off a wrecked van," he said. "And the VIN is on a hot list out of Howard County. Paperwork is top-drawer. It would have passed anything but a felony stop. Wonder what that little dyke was doing down in my county?"

"Up to no good," I said.

"By the way, what was your name?"

"Hayden Lomax," I said, then replaced the telephone in the hook.

When I got to Love Field, I cabbed to the Hyatt, picked up my fax from Carver D, checked in, showered, and changed clothes, had a room service lunch, then called Lewis Poulis, who agreed to see me as soon as possible. Perhaps because I used my own name. Then I called one of the national security outfits to arrange for a couple of bodyguards to escort me from the hotel to Poulis Investigations, then to DFW. I did a couple of lines of Sissy Duval's coke, which tasted surprisingly like Billy Long's personal stash, then grabbed my bag, dropped the key on the television, and went down to meet my protection. It was expensive and the paperwork a bore but at least I knew I'd get out of Poulis Investigations alive. As we drove away, in a Lincoln Town Car, the shoulders of the two hugely muscled salt-and-pepper bodyguards filling the front seat, their necks as thick as elephant legs, and their eyes as bright as foxes, I wondered why I'd never thought of doing things this way before. Asking for help turned out not to be as tough as it sounded. I asked them about the layout at Poulis Investigations, then asked them to stop at a hardware store on the way.

Poulis Investigations was located in an industrial slum not too far from Love Field in a cinder block building surrounded by a chain

link fence topped with razor wire and security cameras. The bodyguards didn't say a word when we pulled up in front.

"You picking up something, sir?" the driver asked.

"Delivering something," I said. "If I'm not back in an hour,
boys, call the cops."

The driver looked at me with a smirk. "That won't be necessary,
boss. We'll bring you out," he said. "These fucking guys are all ex-
Army. Think they're tough because they're Gulf War vets."

"They never played in Green Bay in December," the other one
growled, chuckling. "By the way, sir," he added politely, "you might
want to wipe your nose."

Clean-faced and through the gate, I was ushered directly into
the boss's office. The nameplate on Poulis's desk identified him as
Col. Lewis Poulis, USA, Ret., and the large retouched photograph
of an ex-president behind him suggested he was either a deeply committed Republican or an ex-CIA asset. Poulis was a small, compact
man with a potbelly that looked as dyspeptic as his shaved head and
smirking face. He looked as if he fancied himself as a pretty tough
nut, but I could tell from the 8x10 photo of him in his dress uniform that he didn't wear any combat badges. I sat down in the
padded chair across from Poulis, a chair subtly tilted forward to keep
the person sitting in it slightly off balance. As if I needed anything
to tilt me off dead center.

"You know who I am, Colonel," I said, "and you probably know
more about me than I do, so you know what I'm here about."

"Actually, sir, I don't," Poulis said, exchanging his smirk for a
smug smile.

"One of your operatives—Doris Fairchild, she said her name
was," I said, "left a van full of electronic equipment that is in the
custody of the Bastrop County sheriff."

"As I told the sheriff when he called, and, as I'm sure you know,
anybody can have a business card printed up. No one by that name
has ever been employed by this firm," Poulis said calmly, "and I offered to open my personnel files to him. I'll make you the same
offer, Mr. Milodragovitch. Professional courtesy, you understand."

"Give me a break," I said. "How about the lawyers who arranged her bail? Ever work for them?"

"We do a lot of work for a lot of law firms," Poulis said. "And the lawyers for major corporations."

"And, of course, your client contracts are confidential," I said.

"Of course." The smug smile again. Which drove me nuts. I recognized that smile, the smirk of chickenshit Army officers who had never heard a shot fired in anger, the bland simper of corporate criminals in front of Congress, the toothy, cynical, self-righteous beam of money and corruption, the smile that never dies. "Of course, you understand, they have to be." And that shit-eating grin again.

"Well, let me suggest that if anybody," I said tightly as I suddenly felt the coke boiling through my blood. "Let me fucking suggest," I growled as I stood up and pushed the heavy desk hard into Poulis's tight little belly, so hard I knocked the short man's breath out and tore all the wires underneath loose, and pinned him like a bug against the wall under the large photograph, "if anybody, lawyer, doctor, or corporation chief, mentions my name, and you take the case, I'll spend the rest of my life wiping that fucking little smile off your face."

"The rest of your life may not be all that long," Poulis wheezed angrily.

"You fucking assholes have been trying to kill me since I was sixteen," I said as I grabbed his stubby nose and twisted it until it bled, "and it ain't worked yet." Then I slammed Poulis's head against the ex-presidential portrait until it fell off the wall and Poulis's eyes flickered back into his head.

"How did it go?" the driver asked, leaning against the car, the back door open, his partner standing by the gate. But then he saw the three guys in uniforms dashing out the front door. "You probably want to go now, sir?" he said.

"I think it'd be best," I admitted. "And it might be best if those assholes didn't follow us."

"I figured something like that," he said. "Earl's got it covered."

I glanced back. Earl had picked up my hardware purchases, looped the short length of chain around the gate posts and slammed the large padlock on it, then stepped over to the car. "Delivery complete, boss?" he said.

"Little bastard's nose is badly out of joint and bleeding a bit, but the spooky little fucker had probably been doing coke all afternoon."

"Of course," they answered in unison, Earl with a grin as sharp and large as a linoleum knife. I never did get the driver's name.

On the flight from DFW to Vegas, I went through the Lomax files that Carver D had collected. Carver D hadn't just gathered the facts. He had spiced the information with choice bits of gossip, rumor, and innuendo.

Hayden Lomax might be on the Fortune 500 list now but he had been born in a small town in East Texas. His mother, the women's basketball coach at a small religious college, had died during the emergency cesarean section, and his father, a semialcoholic itinerant roughneck, had abandoned the child into the arms of his wife's horse-faced sister, Alma, a Baptist spinster high school English teacher, a strict, dour woman known for her jump shot, the passionate length of her prayers, and the fiery depths of her anger. She, like her sister, had been a hard-nosed point guard on the college's basketball team. Although Alma was occasionally known to beat the young Hayden senseless, then pray with him until he forgave her, mostly she doted on the boy, alternately spoiling him, then working him like a Trojan, forcing long hours at the backyard hoop, and at least one weekend a month driving the boy to Houston, Austin, or Dallas so he could see major college basketball. Alma made the boy keep his grades up, too, stay out of trouble, mostly, and kept him away from the dinner table every night until he sank twenty straight free throws. She had plans for the boy, but genetics defeated her. Try as he might, practice as much as he could, Hayden Lomax never grew a smidgen past five nine. When his father died in a beer joint fracas, rumors, which spread like a laughing flu through the small town, suggested that Alma had hired a hit man to revenge herself on Stubby Lomax for his short genes, but no proof was ever forthcoming.

So the only scholarship offers Hayden received were from small colleges. Alma did what she could: cashed in her teacher's retirement, moved to Austin, took the only job she wanted, a night janitor at the university field house, and spent her days grooming Hayden for his walk-on debut at the university. He was a good ball-handler, a sharp, accurate passer, a dead-solid foul shooter, a bit too quick with his fists for a short guy, but full of hustle, and he would not quit. In spite of his lack of an outside shot, he was the perfect whitebread complement to the playground moves of the urban kids on the team. If he'd been taller and had a better outside shot, Hayden might have made the perfect sixth man, the guy who could spark a slumping team, could make the right steal, draw the right foul, sucker-punch the right point guard. But no matter how hard he tried, how hard Alma prayed, how much she leaned on him, he never quite made the transition from walk-on to star. He had his moments, but spent most of his college career riding the bench. And he never started a game. Not once in his years of college ball.

After graduating with a business degree, Hayden married a horse-faced girl from Brazoria, who looked a lot like Alma, and whose father had just inherited three junkhouse offshore drilling rigs from his father-in-law. Hayden's father-in-law was a high school principal and knew nothing about the oil business. Neither did Hayden, but he learned. He went at business as he had at basketball, with more ruthless hustle than talent. In the oil patch success didn't depend on his height. During the early years, he had survived the Arab oil embargo, the boom, the next bust, acquired his first ten million dollars—and a double-handful of lawsuits filed by disgruntled partners. After his first wife had fallen to her death from the floor of one of his offshore rigs, he acquired a small construction company in Gatlin County, Overlord Sand and Gravel. Overlord Minerals grew like a refrigerator fungus in the cold darkness of states and countries that fostered a lack of regulation with the love of a bribe. His oil interests spanned the world from Maracaibo to Burundi to Ghana to the North Slope; his construction companies paved bits and pieces all over the planet; his petrochemical plants and gold mines polluted a dozen countries; his political ties spread like a cancer; Hayden Lomax moved like a hyena in the rotten wake of the multinational prides, living well on their scraps because he never went completely public, he owned most of it, he owed no one an explanation.

Except the pack of his silent, swarthy foreign partners. And his aunt, who still lived with him on Almadura, his ranch estate that took up more of Gatlin County than Tom Ben owned. Lomax had all the money in his part of the world but for some reason he never explained, he wanted more, he wanted Tom Ben's ranch, wanted to develop the last large piece of open land in the county. Maybe it was simply greed, maybe just madness. He seemed to have no other vices, except for beautiful women and having his way like a spoiled child. He didn't drink and there had never been even a rumor of drugs in his life. After the death of his first wife, Hayden had dallied and married and divorced several actresses and models and heiresses over the years. About three years was the usual length of their stay, but he had been married to Sylvie for almost seven.

Sylvie Catherine Bessiere had arrived at the University of Texas with an American passport and a transcript and diploma from a boarding school in Marseilles, which had since closed its doors. She was allowed to register provisionally as a first-year graduate student in French, but at such a late date it suggested to Carver D that some sort of regents or alumni pressure had been applied. She met Hayden Lomax at the dedication ceremony for an athletic dormitory annex bearing his name. Sylvie hadn't bothered withdrawing from the university. They were married the next weekend. A few months later Sylvie's crippled French aunt joined Alma at the ranch, one big happy family. Or so it seemed.

Access to information about the big happy family was tightly controlled, Carver D wrote—when they left the estate they traveled like royalty: closed limos, private airplanes, and a phalanx of bodyguards—but neither Hayden nor Sylvie were particularly circumspect about their sexual liaisons. Although a persistent rumor insisted that they had agreed not to see just one other person at a time, thus preventing the complications of infatuation or romance. For people like that, I supposed, it made a perverse sense.

CHAPTER TEN

I HAD BEEN GOING to Vegas for various things for thirty years. Foolishness, mostly—gambling, whoring, that sort of thing—and I also had married my fourth wife there on a cocaine toot almost twenty years before, one of my several marriages in which the divorce seemed to take longer than the marriage. Except for my second wife, who had died in a car wreck with four sailors on a mountain curve outside Susanville, California, it seemed all my divorces were like that. Maybe that's one of the reasons I stopped getting married. Eventually. And I seemed to have stopped gambling about the same time, too.

I had heard that the new corporate Vegas—which was as unfamiliar to me as if I had never been there—was just as sharp, shifty, and greedy as the old one but not quite as friendly. I rented a Mustang convertible at the airport, then checked into one of the less expensive Strip hotels, a faux-stucco castle not too far from Molly Molineaux's address, using the Malvern ID, hoping to lose myself in the crowd of nickel slots players.

During a room service meal and a couple of beers, I skimmed the classified ads, found a 10mm Glock 20 for sale—a pistol I didn't particularly like—called the number, slipped into a pair of thin leather gloves, then drove into a bedroom neighborhood beyond the UNLV campus, where I paid an out-of-work pit boss as much cash as he wanted without dickering for the pistol, a nylon holster, and three loaded clips. Judging from the man's shaking hands and sweating face, the cash would be up his nose before I got back to the hotel. I found a twenty-four-hour auto parts store, bought a can of Armor All, then went back to the room, broke the piece down, unloaded the clips, and sprayed every surface that might hold a fingerprint. Often, buying a pistol in America is easier than buying drugs. I wondered if perhaps it shouldn't be the other way around. Then I packed the pistol, the fake ID, the cocaine, and my badge into a briefcase, dropped the briefcase at the desk to be locked in the hotel's safe, then drove through the sparkling electrical night into the soft dark of the desert to call Betty on the scrambled cell phone.

"I'm at Cathy's," she explained when she answered. "The ranch house, it seemed so . . . I don't know," she said. "Lonesome, maybe."

"I hope I haven't ruined your lifestyle by taking you out into the world," I said, then chuckled.

But she didn't. "It's a goddamned wild-goose chase," she said seriously. "That's what's ruining *our* lives. Where are you staying?"

"I'll probably be moving around," I said. "Take your time on the way out here, love. Take I-10 to Phoenix, then go north to I-40, cross at Bullhead City, then check into the Golden Nugget in Laughlin, and call me on the scrambled cell phone. I'll meet you there."

"And just how fucking long am I supposed to wait?" I could almost hear her foot tapping on the other end of the connection.

"Trust me. I'll be there."

"Trust you?" she said. "Ha. Isn't that a little far out of town?"

"We've had a lot of luck so far," I said. "There's no need to push it. I don't want you in Vegas until I'm sure what's going on."

"Remember, cowboy, you don't do a single goddamned thing until I'm there," she said. "Just look around, all right?"

"Trust me," I repeated.

"I sure as hell hope I can," she said, sounding very far away, "I feel very goddamned left out." In the background I could hear Willie Nelson singing the opening bars of "Redheaded Stranger."

"And tell Cathy to kiss my ass," I said, but Betty didn't laugh, so I hung up.

The next morning, though, my luck ran out big-time. Molly Molineaux's address was one of those chain mailbox drop and packing outfits instead of an apartment complex, and on a busy street, not exactly a place I could stake out without drawing the attention of the local police. So I took myself down to the police station like a good little boy. It took two hours to work my way past a bored desk sergeant, a surly lieutenant, and into the office of a deputy chief, a tall, thin man named G. Donald Willow, with drooping jowls and wispy hair. Somebody once told me that when you meet a man who uses an initial in front of his name, you should at the very least lock up the hen house. And not because you're worried about him stealing the eggs. Even a sardonic smile didn't lift his wattles as he tossed my license back to me. I hadn't used my badge because I didn't want anybody in Gatlin County to know where I was in case Willow checked.

"Okay, partner," he drawled. "What the hell do you want?"

"Well, sir, I wanted to let the local law enforcement know that I was in town," I said. "I'm looking for a skip," I added even though I suspected it was already a lost cause.

"If you've got a name and address and a warrant," Willow said, "I'll have him picked up."

"All I have is a picture and places he sometimes hangs out," I said.

"Degenerate gambler?"

"That's what his boss says."

"No criminal charges involved?"

"No, sir. The boss is his brother-in-law. He just wants him back."

Willow looked out the window into a desert sunshine as thin as his hair. "I just love you out-of-town assholes. Do you have any idea how many of you creeps show up every day," Willow said. "If you had a bail-jumping warrant, maybe, instead of a license that means as much to me as a sheet of used toilet paper, I might give you permission to hang around my town. But being as how you're some low-rent peeper without a warrant, my advice for you is to gather up some local licensed professional help."

"I'm sorry?" I said, confused.

"Hire yourself a licensed private investigator here in town," Willow said, handing me a card, "because if I catch you on the street—loitering, shadowing, or spitting—you'll spend your Vegas vacation in a holding cell. But you probably called it the drunk tank back in the old days."

I started to tear up the card and toss it on the desk, and tell the asshole something about the old days, but I swallowed my anger, glanced at the card, and stuffed it in my pocket. J. Michael Fresno, Investigations. Another one.

"Well, thanks for your advice," I said, then left, figuring to take my chances on my own.

I stopped at the hotel, checked out, picked up the briefcase, and found a gun locker where I could stash the briefcase and the phones. Then I drifted down the Strip until I found a suite with a Jacuzzi at one of the more expensive hotels, where I checked in, threw my war bag on the bed, and went to work. I didn't have any interest in subcontracting my case to some other PI but I hoped that if I hired a cab and some help it would pay my dues into the local economy. So I gave the doorman a fifty-dollar tip and asked him to find me an independent cab or car service that would be on call twenty-four hours a day. With a driver who only answered to himself. Or almost only to himself, as it turned out.

The first car was driven by the doorman's cousin, and the second two by guys with heavy beards and the superficial politeness of ex-cons, so I declined. Then a perfectly maintained shiny black classic Buick Invicta station wagon with heavily tinted windows pulled under the hotel's portico. "Red's Car Service/The Last of the True Independents" was lettered on the side. The doorman waved it toward me. As the Buick stopped in front of me, I opened the front passenger door. But somebody was already in the front seat.

"Excuse me," I said as I climbed into the back.

"No, excuse me, please," the shadowy figure said with a soft elegant voice, then turned to offer a gloved hand. "I'm Mrs. Eileen McCravey, and this is my son, Craig, who prefers the unfortunate sobriquet, 'Red.'" Mrs. McCravey was as tall and darkly majestic as an Ashanti queen—so much so that I nearly kissed her hand—but her son's face was as white as the Nevada sun except for a faint trace of freckles across his cheeks and a pair of sunglasses that were large and dark. A vague notion of pink nestled at the roots of his white kinky hair that poked out from under his soft cap. Even sitting on a pillow, Red was almost short enough to see under the steering wheel, and he had padded extensions on the pedals. I introduced myself to the McCraveys as politely as if they were long-lost family.

"How's it hangin', man," the driver said, holding out a palm to be tapped lightly, then he handed me a card. "Doorman says you looking for a long-term investment in car time. You making a movie or what?"

"Or what, more likely," I said as I placed ten hundred-dollar bills in Red's hand. If this notion was going to work, I wanted it to work quickly. I had to trust somebody. "I'm looking for a woman."

"That ain't my style, man," Red said stiffly, glancing at his mother.

I dug out my PI license and showed it to them. "A long-time stakeout, then maybe a long time tailing. Let me know when this runs out."

Red handed the money back to his mother. "She your wife? Or she steal your money?"

"More like my pride," I said. "She set me up to be killed." I had no reason to be candid with this strange couple, but perhaps it was easy to be honest with them because they seemed so odd, as far outside the norm as I was.

"Killed, man? That's cold. You gonna pop her?" Red asked.

Mrs. McCravey gave her son a hard look and a sardonic moue, then folded the bills and stuffed them into her purse. "Thank you, sir. And please forgive my son for his curious candor. He's both cynical and excitable."

"Whooee, that's me, man. The excitable cynic," Red said. "You mind if I drop my Mom off before we go to work?"

"Not a bit. It's a pleasure to ride in a classic station wagon big enough to be a hearse."

"Hell, man, it's big enough to live in," Red said.

As we drove down the Strip toward downtown, Mrs. McCravey continued, "We're at your service, sir. The cards have been remarkably unkind for several weeks now."

"She's a professional poker player," Red said proudly, "with a Ph.D. in economics from Wharton. So she knows her numbers, man. Me, I'm more a people person. I ain't into numbers. Not like she is."

"Actually, it was just a master's," she explained. "And a long time ago. When I tried to go to work on the Street, my race and my gender seemed an insurmountable problem. Or if surmountable, certainly not worth the effort on my part. So I went back to Detroit and another sort of life altogether. Then moved down here on the arm of a second-rate Sammy Davis wannabe." She paused, smiling like a woman who had enjoyed this other sort of life as well as she could. "Mr. Milodragovitch—is that right?—have you been in the investigation business for a long time?" she asked.

"Except for forays into the bar business, I've been a PI since I got out of law enforcement thirty years ago," I told her.

"But you have no Texas in your accent."

"Texas is a fairly new vice," I admitted. "I grew up in Montana. Meriwether."

"You must have known Big John Reynolds?" she said.

"Sure. John owned the game at the Slumgullion, where I made

my first foray behind the stick. He and my father were cronies. I can't remember when I didn't know John."

"I played against him a few times down here," she said. "He was charming, but lord was he tough. There aren't too many players like him anymore."

"He was a great friend," I said.

"So what can we do for you?"

"There's this mailbox place over on Trocadero," I said, handing her a picture of Molly Molineaux. "Maybe we can park somewhere around there until she shows up. Then follow her home."

"Then what?" Mrs. McCravey wanted to know.

"Then I try to talk her into going back to Texas with me," I said.

"I've seen this woman somewhere," Mrs. McCravey said as she handed the picture back. "And it is not my impression that she was exactly a hooker. If she is, she's one of the few true freelances in town. Which means she's either very connected or very tough."

"If she's expensive, maybe she'll respond to money," I said as we parked in front of Benion's. "That would make it easier," I said, "if she'll talk to me for money."

"Be cautious, sir, and remember that everything in this town turns on money," she said, "but not always the way you want it to turn out." Then she climbed out, and walked into the front door as I climbed into the front seat.

Driving to the Strip, Red prattled at me. "Hey, man, I thought about bein' a PI. Hell, driving a cab, that's a perfect cover. 'Course my ride is more like a bus than a cab—the longest production station wagon in Detroit history—but I got two other classic cherry rides. A Checker and one of them English hacks. 'Course in Vegas, between the cops and casino security, a PI license ain't all that easy to get.

"'Course I got a little record back in Detroit to deal with, too," he continued. "Did a little collecting for a shy named King Kong Elmo. You ever hear of him? No. Well, he is big, man, so big now he's almost legit. But that should count for me, you dig, collecting. Some of them people are tougher to find than a whole peanut in a pile of elephant shit. But you just gotta know how to ask the right question, you dig?"

I had to agree. "Didn't we just drive past the place?"

"Oh, shit," Red muttered, then popped a U-turn that parked us right down the street from the mailbox drop. When I saw the light bar on the police unit behind us fire up, I thought Red was about to get a ticket. Until the unmarked unit pulled in behind the marked one.

"Maybe if you just drive away," I said as I stuffed another ten C-notes into his hand and opened the door, "they'll be satisfied with me." Then I added, "See what you can dig up, man. I'll call when I get out of jail. Now go."

Willow didn't even bother getting out of his unit until the two young officers had patted me down thoroughly and cuffed my wrists tightly behind me.

"No weapons, huh? I would have thought an asshole as dumb as you are would surely be carrying a piece," Willow said.

"Didn't seem necessary," I said. "This looks like the kind of place where I could shake a piece off the first skateboarder I saw, or buy one off the nearest cop. Who turned me?"

"What makes you think that little albino asshole McCravey didn't burn you?"

"He doesn't hardly seem the type."

"If you weren't going to use the doorman's cousin, man, you should have given him a C-note, you cheap asshole, because it's going to turn out to be an expensive economy," Willow said.

"I guess I haven't kept up with the price of graft in this shithole," I said.

"This is a family town," he said. But he didn't say which family.

Even in the middle of the afternoon among the scrubbed walls of the jail, even empty, the holding tank didn't look like any place I wanted to be. And I knew it wasn't going to get any better as the sun fell. At least the other prisoners wouldn't be fighting over my clothes: everybody's jailhouse sweats and slippers would be the same. I didn't know how long the Vegas police thought they could hold me before letting me make a call, but I assumed it would be a considerably uncomfortable length of time, so I found a corner where I could pretty much cover my back, slid to my haunches, and pretended to sleep, while I tried to figure out what the hell was going on.

The confusion must have started fifteen or twenty years before, either with the death of Dwayne Duval or the failure of Enos Walker's last cocaine scam. Already three people were dead, one was still in the hospital, another was on the run, and I didn't have the faintest idea what I'd done to stir up this ancient hornet's nest of death and disaster. And I couldn't even begin to guess why the hell somebody had sent the Molineaux woman to charm me and a cop to kill me. And how the hell did Betty end up in bed with the McBride woman before I did? Just to steal her piece to shoot me with? And what the hell did Sylvie Lomax want with the Molineaux woman? Shit, I thought as I went back to pretending to be asleep. At least I could do that.

It was a long pretend, broken only when they allowed me my telephone call.

The first customer to try me was a drunken college kid about midnight who poked me on the thigh with his foot and asked, "Whattcha you in for, old man?" I ignored the first kick, then the second, but when the third came, I dropped the kid with a leg-lock, rolled up his body, kneed him hard in the crotch and jammed a thumb against the kid's eye.

"First jailhouse lesson, punk," I said softly, "people don't like being in here, so you'll want to leave them alone. First lesson's free. Second one costs you an eye."

"You best pay attention, gringo," growled a huge, tattooed Chicano from the far corner.

I moved back to my corner, leaving the crying kid curled in the middle of the cell. Things actually stayed so quiet that I drifted off about three A.M., and only woke when I heard my name being called just before six. A sleepy young man in a rumpled sport coat stood beside one of the jailhouse bulls.

I rose slowly, too long on the cold floor, creaked to the cell door, only able to say "Yes" very quietly.

"Let's get your stuff and get out of here," the sleepy man said.

"Who the hell are you?"

"Me? Me, I'm the unfortunate son of a bitch who went to law school with that fucking Thursby," the young man said as he handed me a card. "Byron Fels," he added, "but don't shake my hand. Please. I don't want to catch whatever you caught from Chief Willow."

"He's not a pleasant fellow, I take it."

"He's a mean son of a bitch," Fels said. "And such a degenerate gambler that if he wasn't a cop, not a single casino in the state of Nevada would let him in the door."

"So I guess I don't get to file a complaint or anything, huh?" I said without any real hope of getting even. Legally or otherwise.

"Charges are dropped. Paperwork has disappeared. Just get out of town as soon as you can. And don't come back until Willow is retired or, preferably, dead."

"Thanks," I said. "Can I get a ride back to the hotel?"

"What do I look like? Taxi service?" he grumbled, but gave me a ride anyway.

"Send me a bill," I said as Fels dropped me at the hotel.

"Forget it," he said. "I owe that fucking Thursby."

Thanks to the wonderful twenty-four-hour ambience of Las Vegas, I found a quiet lounge where I had three slow drinks until Fresno's office was open, when I called to make an appointment with the boss as soon as possible that morning. Then I climbed into the Jacuzzi. Half an hour later, after some stretches Cathy had shown me, and a light breakfast, I was almost human again. I called Red. He came over, filled me in, and we agreed to meet that afternoon.

On the way to Fresno's office I took a quick detour by the safe locker to pick up the Glock and call Carver D. He did a bit of Internet sleuthing for me, then I stopped at a bank before I went to the courthouse, where I discovered that George Donald Willow was married to one Patricia Kay Fresno. Interesting but not unexpected. Fresno's offices were in a glass cube set among a landscaped greensward. Inside they looked more like law offices than the lair of a tough, intrepid investigator. Obviously, there was more PI work in Vegas and it paid better, much better than Meriwether, Montana, or any other place I had ever worked. J. Michael dressed like a successful lawyer, but the diplomas framed on his wall suggested a more violent education: Navy SEAL, State Department Security Service, Clark County Sheriff's Department. J. Michael was somewhat larger than his brother-in-law and looked considerably more fit and he seemed to have a smaller greedy gleam in his eye and no smug little smile.

"What can I do for you, Mr. Milodragovitch?"

I tossed a certified check face down on the desk. "You know who I am. Let's cut the shit," I said.

"I understand that you're looking for somebody. And that you've done some investigative work yourself," J. Michael said smoothly, carefully ignoring the check. "So I'm certain that you understand the high risk of failure and the cost of such an investigation—"

"How much would you want for a retainer?" I interrupted.

"Five thousand," J. Michael answered immediately. "Surely your client can afford that."

"I'm the client in this matter," I said.

"That's unusual," he said. "In that case, I suspect my retainer should be more substantial."

"At least I don't have to worry about my client lying to me," I said. "I'll give you two grand."

"It's my understanding that you've already spent one night in jail over this," J. Michael said. "I wouldn't think you would want to bargain over something as unpleasant as that?"

"You know," I said, "I've been a PI off and on for years. And I did some shit I didn't particularly like. For the money. Protected people and things I didn't particularly approve of or care for. Committed the occasional misdemeanor, but lately I've had cause to suspect that as bad as I've been, some of my fellow PIs are truly pieces of shit."

"I'm sorry to hear that—" he started to say, and for a moment he sounded sincere.

"For five thousand dollars, asshole," I interrupted, "I can make you and your loser of a brother-in-law disappear into the desert." I signed the back of the check. "This is a cashier's check for two grand made out to cash. Pick it up, call Willow, and let's say 'so long.'"

"I don't—" he started to say.

"Whatever you're going to say, don't," I said. "You're not the only asshole in the world with a computer. Don't let your bulldog mouth overload your bullfrog ass. Like you did in Reno last year. How old was that guy who kicked your ass with his cane? Seventy-two?"

"Goddammit, he was a kendo master."

"Whatever," I said.

J. Michael put the check into his desk drawer, called Willow to tell him that we had a deal, then turned to me, saying, "I hope you realize that this isn't my idea. But I've got to keep my sister out of the poorhouse. Maybe I can actually help you find this person?"

I almost believed him, but I was already mad. "Buddy, I wouldn't trust you to find the fucking men's room."

After lunch I followed Red's directions out into the desert a few miles off the Interstate up Highway 93, where I turned on a dirt road that led behind a stony, brush-smudged ridge, then to the edge of a deep wash. When I got out of the Mustang, Red climbed out of the station wagon dressed in a rumpled camouflage suit covered with faded paint ball spots, a floppy bush hat covering his hair, large dark goggles protecting his eyes, and his facial skin slathered with sunblock. His mother sat in the front seat, cool and elegant in floral gauze over silk and a floppy straw hat, a painted fan in her hand.

"Where in the world did you get this tank?" I asked as I admired the classic station wagon.

"Out of a junkyard, man, brought it back from total death," he said proudly.

"Beautiful," I agreed.

"And clean, too. Dude it's registered to don't know he owns it. And in the right clothes, man, I just look like another fancy redneck."

"Perfect," I said. "You get the ammo?"

"Right here," Red said, holding up a small duffel bag. "Targets already pinned up down the wash. Brought my piece, too, man. Hope you don't mind?"

"No problem," I said.

"Craig, you take the gear on down," Mrs. McCravey said quietly, then stepped over to me and placed her hand gently on my arm. "Mr. Milodragovitch, can I speak to you for a moment?"

"Certainly, ma'am," I said.

"I am in your debt," she said, "that is for sure. Your infusion of cash has turned the cards around for me. You must know how it is. Sometimes one hits a slump and, for no valid reason, loses one's confidence. That no longer seems to be a problem. But no matter how deeply I feel my obligation to you, I must ask a favor."

"Anything, Mrs. McCravey."

"I suggest two things are going to happen—one, that Craig has already found this woman for you and won't tell me; two, that she will not return willingly to Texas with you." I nodded. "Because of his height and his . . . condition, Craig has always felt he had to prove himself, to be tougher than normal men, so if at all possible and whatever the circumstances, please encourage restraint."

"I'll treat him like he's my own flesh and blood," I said.

"And I'll pray that will be sufficient to keep him safe."

"I don't pray, ma'am," I admitted, "but I'll do my best."

Mrs. McCravey leaned over to brush my cheek, her lips soft on my skin, her scent fragrant on the desert air. I realized that she was much older than she looked. Older than me even. And I felt even older than a dinosaur turd. Because I already knew what Red and I faced.

Thirty yards down in the arroyo, Red had propped two silhouette targets against the dry wall where the wash bent sharply about twenty-five yards away. A Dirty Harry .44 Magnum revolver dangled from his hand.

"Can you hit anything with that cannon?" I asked as I dug a pair of earmuffs out of the duffel. "And don't you have any ear protection?"

"Never needed it, man."

"How often you fire that thing?"

"Three or four times a year, maybe," Red said.

"Listen, kid," I said as I broke the filters off two cigarettes, "if you don't wear ear protection, you'll be deaf quicker than a rock and roll drummer." I stuffed the filters into his ears. "Now, let's see what you can do."

"Shit, man, I already look funny enough," he said as he touched his ears, and we smiled. Then he turned and fired six rounds from the Magnum and put two outside the thorax area and four on the edge of the target, filling the narrow arroyo with the enormous blasts that started small sand avalanches along the steep edges.

I racked the slide on the Glock, then quietly said, "Maybe the noise will scare them to death."

"What's that you said, man?"

"Not bad," I said a bit louder.

"Shit, man," he said. "Hit some motherfucker in the toe with this piece, they hit the dirt."

"Chances are, my friend," I pointed out, "if they're that far away, moving and shooting back, a handgun is probably a waste of time." I took fifteen steps closer toward the targets, ran a clip three rounds at a time until I got the feel of the Glock, then finished the three loaded clips from various stances, most rounds either dead center or just off. "It's not great, but it'll do," I said as I coated the rounds Red had brought with Armor All and reloaded the clips.

"Shit, I'm just an amateur," Red said. "Man, you're a pro."

"Man, if you don't go to the range once a week and fire at least fifty rounds, you're not just an amateur with a handgun, you're a danger to your friends and associates."

Red pulled himself up to his full five foot six, his eyes flaring behind his dark goggles, and started to take offense, then he let out a sigh. "I suspect you know what you're talking about, don't you?" he said, sounding more like his mother than he usually did. "And I suspect you're not giving me advice because I took your money or because I'm a poor, pitiful albino nigger. I guess it's like my Mom says. For no good reason, you trust me. Well, man, you can trust me to hold up my end."

"Truth is, Craig, I've never had any control over who I trusted," I said. "You offered, I accepted. Maybe we'll get lucky, and all this hardware will just be an extra load."

"Call me Red, man," he said. "I got a cooler of cold, cold beer in the rig, so let's have one."

Which we did. Afterward I gave Red one of the cell phones, then we all went back to our jobs. Red to pick up a few things I thought I might need before he picked me up, Mrs. McCravey to a table stakes hold 'em game downtown, and I went back to my chores. On the way into town I remembered something I had heard early on in the search. So I dug out the card Byron Fels had reluctantly given me. He wasn't all that glad to see me but he didn't gouge me too badly for a casino contact. Just as I suspected, no degenerate gambler ever left Vegas with any money. I began to wonder if all Texans' notorious reputation for lying wasn't well deserved after all.

While I was in jail, Red McCravey had taken over my search. And Red quickly proved his ability to find people before they got lost. He came up with her address—a high-security high-rise, where she hadn't been seen in weeks—but he assumed that a woman who looked like Molly Molineaux probably had logged considerable time in limos. Sure enough one of his friends not only knew the woman, he knew where she was hidden. He had spotted her on the front porch at the desert house of a second-rate but wildly successful Vegas comic named Jimmy Fish, who had supplemented his comic career by playing gangsters and heavies in movies.

Jimmy Fish had a round, unpleasant face dominated by widely spaced, wild eyes. Even his curly hair looked as if it were psychotic. He had a loud, grating voice, an accent that sounded half-Brooklyn and half-Southern, and he had the manners of an ugly spoiled child. Something about his screen persona suggested that his movie roles didn't call for much acting skill. He was a natural asshole. If only I'd known how right I was, I could have saved us all a great deal of trouble and pain.

Jimmy Fish had a mansion in town where his wife lived but since they had separated he spent most of his time at his desert place outside Blue Diamond. It only took a couple of hours to find out that he was in town and that he didn't have a show on Thanksgiving night. I hoped he'd be at the desert place and not having a party. I planned to ring his doorbell when least expected and use my badge to bluff my way to Molly Molineaux. Once I had my hands on her, I wasn't planning to turn her loose until I found out who had hired her. I resigned myself to the fact that she wouldn't talk easily. I would try money first, then fear, and if it came down to it, pain.

Red dropped me off near Jimmy Fish's place a couple hours before sundown, then went back to Nellis Air Force Base to pick up the last of our purchases. I lugged a new pack stuffed with gear and water up a hogback that overlooked his house from the west. The house, a fake adobe, snuggled like a rock spill at the end of a blind canyon. A pool as dark and blue as the devil's eye sat in a stone patio behind the house. Gleaming razor wire topping a chain link fence outlined the five rocky acres around it. The only opening seemed to be a sliding gate in front of a cattle guard where the driveway ran into the highway. Except for the cactus and creosote bushes, not a spot of green showed. It could have been a rock garden. Perhaps Jimmy hated the sight of green unless it came from money. A battered old pickup was parked in front of a three-car garage.

I set up the spotting scope, checked my weapons, and settled in to watch. For a long time nothing moved but the long shadows creeping black across the desert. Then a small, dark man came out to clean the pool. Overhead long strings of high, dry clouds drifted across the sky. As the sun slipped behind the mountains the clouds fired red, then faded into a soft powdered pink that dissolved in the light breeze. When the pool man put his things away I put my eye to the scope just in time to catch sight of the woman as she stepped out of the sliding glass doors and into the deep shadow around the pool, her white one-piece suit shining against her dark tan, then she threw a bundle of towels on a deck chair, dove in, and began swimming laps with long, smooth strokes, swimming as if she never planned to stop.

Then I spotted a white blob behind sliding doors. I kicked the power on the scope up to full and focused on the round, hungry face of Jimmy Fish hanging like a bad moon behind the pool. Beyond him I could see Mexican furniture grouped around a fireplace. Off to the side a short woman set a large table with silver and linen. I worried about a party until she stopped after only two place settings. When she finished the table, she laid a fire in the fireplace, turned the lights on, then disappeared into the kitchen. Molly finished her laps, wrapped her hair in a towel, draped another over her shoulders, then tied a third one over her wet suit. When she went through the doors, Jimmy—head and shoulders shorter than her and rotund in a running suit that had never run—raised his face like a man looking into the sun. She patted him on the cheek and then walked quickly away toward the back of the house.

At full dark I pulled a windbreaker out of the pack, drank some water, then waited. For an hour nothing much happened. Jimmy sprawled on the couch and watched a football game on a television set into a carved armoire beside the fireplace. The short woman brought in two bottles of champagne in iced buckets and put them and two flutes on the end table beside him. Jimmy cracked one, took the first slug out of the bottle, then filled his glass. The pool man came back outside wearing a blanket-lined denim jacket and a straw cowboy hat that had seen better days. A cup of coffee steamed in his hands. He sat in one of the deck chairs, rolling cigarettes and smoking. When Molly came into the living room dressed in a worn sweat suit, Jimmy waved her over and poured a glass of champagne, patted the couch beside him, but she took her flute and sat on the hearth in front of the fire. She had a sip, then opened a small purse and began to work on her nails. I called Red, told him that this looked like the right night, asked him to head out right now, and hurry.

Then I gutted up and called Betty. I knew she wasn't going to be happy.

She answered in a motel bar outside Phoenix.

"You didn't call last night," she said without preamble. "I don't like that. I had to spend the night in El Paso. I don't like El Paso. It's not Texas. Fuck, I'm not even sure it's America."

"Maybe that's why I liked it," I said, then immediately regretted it. "I'm sorry, but I was locked up."

"Right. Locked up with a thousand-dollar hooker, you asshole."

"Not yet," I said, trying for a joke, but she didn't laugh. "I haven't found her yet," I lied, "but I've got a line on her. Seems like you would want me to find her. After what she did to you. And me."

"I'm sure," she scoffed. "Maybe I should just drop your car and fly back to Austin."

"That sounds like a great idea," I said, tired of trying to convince her that I was doing what I had to do. "Just let me know where the fuck it is."

"Or you could come get me, Milo," she whispered, changing tunes. "We could go home."

"We're in a ton of trouble, and a long ton of other people's futures depend on me working this out," I reminded her.

"You don't even know any of those people," she hissed, angry again.

"It doesn't make a damn bit of difference," I said, then paused a long moment to catch the anger in my throat.

"Well, it fucking should!" she shouted. Then whispered hoarsely, "Just give it up, Milo. Give it up."

"How many drinks have you had?" I asked after a long pause.

"Three. And I'm going to have three more and a turkey sandwich," she said flatly, "and call it Thanksgiving."

"Sounds good to me," I said. "I think I'll do the same. I'll meet you at the casino tomorrow night." Then I switched off the phone, and dug a granola bar out of the pack. When I finished it, I had a nip of brandy and a small toot. I didn't have either the time or energy to deal with a jealous woman as she dithered between anger and whining, or even time for a turkey sandwich. I had another granola bar, then waited again.

Betty called me back shortly, the ringing of the phone loud in the desert night, but I told her I was on a stakeout, that I couldn't talk, to please not call me. I promised to call her. She called me an idiot, then hung up. She called me back twenty minutes later to tell me that a good-looking cowboy was giving her the eye. We had words, the kind of words that are hard to take back, even if you want to catch them as soon as they're out of your mouth. This time I hung up on her. A sliver of the waxing moon tried to peek through the ambient glare of seductive neon hanging over Las Vegas.

When the short woman brought a turkey to the dining room table, I called Red again and caught him just as he was going through Blue Diamond. Jimmy cracked the second bottle and refilled the flutes as the short woman brought the rest of the trimmings to the table. She said something to Jimmy, but he just waved her away.

A few minutes later she came out the kitchen door wrapped in a short jacket, said something to the man, then they walked slowly around the house to the battered pickup. I moved the spotting scope and the bipod to focus it on the end of the driveway. I could see the interior of the pickup cab clearly in the outdoor light at the gate. The man took a remote out of the glove box and pointed it at the gate. When the gate began to trundle sideways, he tossed the remote back into the glove box. Red was waiting for them when the pickup rattled over the cattle guard. I hoped they didn't live twenty miles away or something. But it didn't matter. They stopped at the first bar down the road. Red said he'd call back when he had the remote.

It took a lot longer than it should have. I hoped he hadn't been caught. Jimmy and Molly picked at their Thanksgiving meal for a while, then moved back to the living room. He went over to the armoire to fetch a silver tray heaped with cocaine with a silver straw sticking out of the pile like a dagger. He cut a couple of lines as big as snakes, but Molly only did part of hers. I said to hell with it and joined them for a brief snort of my own. She switched the television to a black-and-white movie I didn't recognize, while he put half a dozen CDs into the rack, then proceeded to boogie. He waved at Molly to join him, but she didn't seem to want to. She sat down on the hearth again and poked the fire. He took her by the hand, tugging at her, until she waved the poker at him. He laughed and gave up, decided to dance alone, pausing only to gun champagne and snort a line. He strutted his stuff like a bantam rooster in front of her, but Molly seemed more interested in the movie. Like some short, pudgy men, Jimmy had quick feet and an odd grace. He was probably stronger than he looked, I thought, but didn't keep the thought in the front of my head.

I was cold, my nose was running, the brandy in the half-pint had almost disappeared, and I was worried about Red. I couldn't call him. I'd probably catch him with a slim jim down the pickup window as the phone rang in his pocket. In the blind canyon the faux adobe walls gleamed like teeth. Jimmy had gone back to trying to get Molly to dance, but she kept refusing. It looked as if it was going to get rough. But there wasn't anything I could do until Red called. Finally, the phone rang.

"Where the hell have you been?" I said.

"None of your damn business," Betty said.

"Goddammit," I said, "will you please stop calling me? You're going to get me killed."

"You seem to be doing a fine job by your own damn self," she mumbled, then hung up on me. Which was probably the reason she had called.

The night went on, completely out of control.

When Red finally called, I asked him where he'd been. The man had gone in the bar while the woman sat in the pickup listening to Mexican music. Red had sat in the parking lot, turning away drunk fares, until the woman stormed into the bar to drag her husband out. The only good news was that she hadn't locked the pickup, and Red was on his way. I dug a flashlight out of the bag, stuffed my gear back in, then headed down the hogback toward the road. When I reached it, the dark bulk of the Checker cab loomed beside it. Even in the dark I could see how cherry it was, the hand-rubbed black paint job gleaming even in the night. I fancied I could see stars shining in the finish.

"You sure he won't recognize my car, man?" Red said as he handed me the rest of my kidnapping gear.

"Right now, kid, I don't think he would recognize his own mother," I said. "Assuming he has one."

"I guess I could repaint it," he said. "Go back to the original yellow."

"Nervous?" I asked as I pulled on the surgical gloves and checked the loads of the Glock.

"Just about my car, man."

"Let's do it," I said. "There'll never be a better time."

"Then I guess it's now, man."

I climbed into the Checker. When Red stopped at the gate, I climbed out, then crawled under the cattle guard where I wrapped a bundle of det cord around the supports. Red had a homeboy who was a supply sergeant out at Nellis. For a price he was happy to provide the det cord, a straitjacket, and a cache of "twilight sleep" ampules from an Air Force nurse with a habit. I didn't know what I was getting into with this woman but I intended to get her out of the house and keep her one way or another.

"Should I leave the lights on?" Red asked as I climbed back into the Checker.

"Let's act like we're supposed to be here," I said as I punched the remote. "We don't want anybody to think we're sneaking in."

Red drove through the open gate, then up the driveway. He parked beside the porch facing down the driveway for a quick exit. I slipped out of the cab, checked my weapons, got out my badge, and went up the low steps to ring the doorbell, then stand aside.

Even through the thick door and the roar of music crashing into the still night, I could hear Jimmy Fish curse loudly and wonder who the hell was at the door. The porch light came on and the door swung open. He stormed out on the porch, saw the cab, and muttered "How the hell—"

I stepped in front of him. "Mr. Fish, I have an arrest warrant—" I started to say, my badge in one hand, a makeshift sap in the other. In case he wasn't impressed by the badge. He wasn't. He had a shiny automatic hanging in his hand. He started to lift it, so I laid the sockful of ashtray sand just under his ear. He went to his knees, confused but not out. I kicked the pistol out of his hand and off the side of the porch and stuffed the badge back in my pocket.

"Stay down, asshole!" I shouted at him. "And I won't tell your wife."

Behind him I could see Molly stretched out on the couch. She looked unconscious, her sweatshirt bunched around her neck, her hair down and disheveled. I slammed the sockful of sand against the side of Jimmy's head again. A little harder this time, and he rolled over on his side, moaning.

This wasn't working exactly the way I had planned it. *When in doubt, try kidnapping,* I must have thought, because I ran over to the couch, pulled Molly's sweatshirt down over her breasts, grabbed her purse, and tossed her over my shoulder. Even unconscious, her body felt strong and lithe against me. I carried her out the front door, down the steps, and dumped her into the back seat of the Checker.

"Duct tape!" I shouted at Red, and he tossed me a roll. I lashed her hands together, then to the hand grip above the door. It didn't seem to take too long, but the little bastard had obviously gotten to his feet, dashed back into the house, and dug up another pistol. When I turned my head, Jimmy Fish was staggering down the steps, another shiny semiautomatic pistol in his hand, screaming, "I don't even have a fucking wife!"

Maybe the divorce had gone through already. Maybe I should have hit him harder. His first shot glanced off the roof of the Checker. Before I could stop him, Red was out of the cab running toward Jimmy Fish, the big pistol wobbling in his hand, shouting, "Shoot my ride, motherfucker!"

The two of them engaged in a serious firefight about ten or fifteen yards apart. How they missed each other I'll never know. Red blew a large chunk of plaster off the house with his first round. His second went through the open door and out the sliding glass door at the back of the house. The third hit something inside the house that exploded like a vacuum tube. At the same time Jimmy Fish gouged several rips in the fenders and doors of the Checker and punched a hole through the front window and out the back. They might have hurt each other, eventually, but I slammed the back door shut, leaned over the trunk as I unholstered the Glock, and put a round in the fat meat of Jimmy's thigh. He went down like a broken puppet and screamed like a wounded rabbit.

"Go!" I shouted at Red.

He looked at me wildly, then turned to the little fat man in a heap at the bottom of the steps, and raised his pistol. "Don't fucking kill him! Let's just go!"

He slid behind the steering wheel as I dove into the back seat.

"Where?" he said as he rammed the Checker into gear.

But I didn't have an answer. I was too busy trying to stanch the blood pouring thickly down the side of the woman's face, cursing myself. "Goddamn!" I felt as if I had been searching for this woman all my life, and now some fucking idiot had shot her in the head. "Goddamn motherfucking son of a bitch!"

"What the hell's your problem, man? The asshole didn't put holes in your ride," Red said as he bounced across the cattle guard and stopped so I could ignite the det cord. But when he turned to look at me, he saw the sheet of blood covering the side of the woman's face. "Shit, man, what are we going to do?"

I jumped out, dove under the cattle guard, wrapped the Glock in the extra lengths of det cord, pulled the ignition string, then jumped back in, shouting, "Drive like the wind, my friend."

We fled into the dark, heading into the desert away from the bright lights, the big city, and the disaster of the night. Perhaps in the desert, like an ancient hermit, I could find the answers.

CHAPTER ELEVEN

ONCE AGAIN in the presence of Molly I was exhausted and re-alized that perhaps I hadn't planned too carefully. I had her but didn't know what to do with her. She was the sort of woman who had been designed to drive men mad. She would have been a trial for a saint. I felt trapped and confused, unable to think. Even after I dug my flashlight out of the pack to check her wound. When I got a good look at it, I sighed so loudly that it sounded like a shot. Ei-ther a glass or metal fragment had sliced as cleanly as a razor blade across her high cheekbone, then punched a tiny hole in her ear next to the skull. Lots of blood but no real damage. The bleeding stopped under pressure, and the slice could be closed with butterfly bandages when we got to Red's garage in North Las Vegas, which he had of-fered as a temporary lockup. When the bleeding stopped I jabbed an ampule of the twilight sleep into her hip, then climbed into the front seat, as if just a little distance from her would clear my mind.

Maybe it did. We drifted all the way west and north to Pahrump, where we stopped behind a convenience store. We couldn't drive back to Vegas in a car with bullet holes in it. While Red took a ballpeen hammer and made the holes in the front and rear window look as if they had been made with rocks, I went inside to get two large coffees, a six-pack of beer, a pile of cardboard sandwiches, a spray bottle of cleanser, and rolls of clear strapping tape and paper towels. I cleaned up the blood while he called his Mom, then we hid the bullet holes as best we could, and headed up to Highway 95. I stayed awake long enough to drink two beers, a sip of coffee, and half an egg salad sandwich before I drifted off. I fell into a dark hole of dreamless sleep so deep I might as well have given myself the shot instead of Molly.

We were both dead until Red pulled into his garage tucked under the Interstate in North Las Vegas. Mrs. McCravey was waiting with first-aid supplies, a clean pair of sweats, and a sheet spread across one of the workbenches. I placed Molly on the sheet. Mrs. McCravey scissored Molly out of her bloody sweats, and we began to clean the dried blood out of her hair and off her body. Mrs. McCravey, her palms as golden as old ivory, her fingers as supple as a professional card dealer's, did most of the work. She even took the scissors from me and cut perfect little winged bandages.

Afterward, even swaddled in a new pair of loose sweats and with butterfly bandages marching across her high cheekbones like tiny insects, Molly McBride or Molineaux or whatever the hell her name was still a strikingly attractive woman.

"What are you going to do with her?" Mrs. McCravey said.

"Take her back to Texas," I said, without really thinking about it, "and lock her in a corn crib until she comes up with the answers to some questions." Maybe nobody would think to look for her in the same place twice.

"Sounds like a frightful chore."

"What makes a girl as beautiful as this sell herself?" I asked stupidly.

"Who knows?" Mrs. McCravey said. "Drugs, sexual abuse, revenge, money—all I know is that most whores are stone lazy sluts at heart. They'd rather fuck than work."

"Revenge?"

"They're like junkies—if they aren't junkies—all their failures are the fault of the world around them," she said quietly, then she added, "and maybe this one is trying to shed the guilt of passing."

"Passing?" I said.

"This lady doesn't have just a good tan, Mr. Milodragovitch," she said as she stroked Molly's forehead with a damp cloth. "She's as black as I am."

Without a flicker of an eyelid to warn us that she was conscious, Molly suddenly grabbed Mrs. McCravey's wrist, hissing, "You watch your mouth, you fuckin' old nigger bitch."

Without a moment's hesitation, Mrs. McCravey slapped Molly's face. Then the fight was on. It was like two drunks trying to put a monkey into a sack: It simply has more appendages than they do.

The struggle was silent, serious, and still in doubt when Red stepped in. He lay on her legs, and I leaned on her chest, but she bucked her hips so wildly that Mrs. McCravey didn't have a chance to plunge the needle into her hip. Exasperated, Mrs. McCravey stood back, picked up a wrench, and said, "Honey, if you don't hold still, I'm gonna knock out your front teeth with this Crescent wrench."

As Molly paused to consider this, Mrs. McCravey managed to pop her in her shapely buttock with the dose. Molly calmed down, a bit, but I could still feel her fighting the drugs. So we stayed on her until her buttocks relaxed. Weak as she was, the straitjacket was still a struggle. Once she was trussed, I got the badge out of my back pocket.

"Okay, Miss whatever-the-fuck-your-name-is," I said, still breathing hard, "I've got a warrant for your arrest as a material witness in a homicide case in Gatlin County, Texas, and you're going back with me. Either in a straitjacket and a diaper, or like a civilized person."

"Why don't you just shoot me now? Get it over with," she said, her words softly slurred, her dusky eyelids fluttering closed. "Just put one right between my fuckin' eyes," she muttered as she drifted under again.

Red and his mother sat down on rolling mechanics' stools, sighing. Red popped the last beer, but his mother took it away from him before he got it to his lips. "A frightful chore," she said after a long pull, then handed it back to him.

"Shit, man," Red said, "I can find you a dozen hookers prettier than this one. And they might fight back, if you pay 'em enough. But they'll fight fair." He giggled weakly, handed the beer to me, then sat back down as worn as the seat of a cheap suit.

I shackled Molly's ankle to the vise at the end of the bench, then asked the McCraveys to watch her while I checked out of the hotel, retrieved my goods from the gun locker, and picked up some burgers and beers. On the way, I called Betty and caught her just before she crossed the Nevada line. Her hangover was too bad for her to argue about the change of plans. For a change.

Some hours later Betty honked at the garage door, then rolled the Caddy through after Red opened it. Then she climbed out looking a bit frazzled, deeply tired, more than slightly hungover, and madder than a flock of constipated hens. She saw Molly stretched out on the workbench, surrounded by fast food wrappers and empty beer cans, and then she really flew off the broom handle.

"You were supposed to wait!" she shouted, ignoring my introductions to the McCraveys.

"It just didn't work out that way, honey," I said.

"Don't 'honey' me, you son of a bitch!" she shouted. "You were supposed to wait!"

Then I told her that I'd hoped that she'd help me carry Molly back to a quiet place where we might straighten out some of my questions, and she went off like a rocket. I finally had to drag her to the other side of the garage, so the McCraveys wouldn't have to listen to her tirade.

"If you think I'm riding anywhere with that bitch," she hissed, "you've got another goddamned think coming, buddy."

"So what do you want me to do?"

"Do what you said you would goddamned do," she said. "Call

the Gatlin County Sheriff's Department, and let them take care of it. We're out of it."

"She'll end up as dead as her phony sister," I said.

"You've got me confused with somebody who gives a shit."

I didn't know exactly what to do with this escalation of her attitude. But I sure as hell didn't like it.

"I guess I'd have to say that you're right, *honey*," I said. And the words wafted between us like the stench of a decaying body. "Maybe if you took your sorry red-haired ass out to the airport, lady, it might clear up your mind."

Betty slapped me so hard my ears rang, then, with tears in her eyes, stormed around me, grabbed her shoulder bag out of the Caddy, then hurried off down the alley.

"You want me to give her a ride, boss?" Red asked quietly behind me as I stepped out the door of the garage.

"Please," I said. "I'll pick up the fare."

"Not a problem," he said, then hurried after her in the Buick.

I flopped on one of the stools, finally bone-tired. I wondered how she knew that Sylvie Lomax had told me my job was over when I found Molly and called the Gatlin County authorities. But I was just too tired to think about it.

Mrs. McCravey handed me a beer. It was cold comfort but it was all I had. "How long have you two been together?"

"Not long enough, obviously," I said. "Or too long."

"You sleep with the hooker?"

"Not as many times as she did," I said. I sounded too bitter even to myself.

"Oh," Mrs. McCravey said gently. As if that explained everything.

We slumped silently in dim corners of the garage like mourners for what seemed like a long time until Red came back.

"She say anything?" I asked.

"Not even thanks," Red answered. "What now?"

"I've got some ideas," I said. "But not any good ones."

After two days and nights under the sedative, when she woke up that first morning she was almost as fuzzy as I was after the long, cocaine-fueled drive from Vegas to Tom Ben's place. The crib set in the front corner of the large unused dairy barn. The windowless walls were steel, as were the bars around the corn crib. The only exits were the locked sliding doors at either end. The faint odor of milk and cowshit drifted out of the large drain that ran down the center of the barn between the unused headstalls.

Without speaking, she took the aspirin and water from my hand, then looked around the small metal corner room, her eyes moving slowly over the comforts of home: a port-a-potty, a milkhouse heater, an upright cooler with hot and cold running water, a small chest of drawers with a mirror on top, a small refrigerator with a television on top, and the metal cot she lay on. She leaned down to stretch, touching her feet, finding the thick socks, the sweat pants, and the shackle on her left ankle. Then she touched the bandage on the right side of her face.

"What the hell?" she said, then focused on my face. "You son of a bitch," she said softly. "I should have known." Then glancing around the room again, she spotted the pile of unshucked corn in the far corner. "Oh, shit," she moaned. "Not again."

"A little more comfortable than your last visit," I said. "What do you want me to call you?"

"What?"

"Your name," I said. "You seem to have several."

"Call me 'shit out of luck,' " she grouched.

"Okay, shit."

"Just call me Molly," she said. "Where's your stuffy girlfriend? You guys looking for a ménage à trois? You didn't have to kidnap me. I'm a working girl. To tell the truth, though, I don't think she really gets off on girls." I let her ramble on until she either ran out of energy or lost track of the thought. She recovered quickly, though, a crooked smile blossomed on her face, and her eyes brightened as the drug flushed out of her system. "Where are my contacts?" she said. "And what the fuck do you want?"

"Just a couple of answers," I said as I pitched her purse to her. "Everything's in there. Except your little gun." I had put her der- ringer in my war bag. "We can get this over quickly. Just a couple of questions."

"You're more likely to get me to fuck that old man again, or one of his goats, than get me to answer a question," she said.

"I can be an unpleasant guy," I said. "Ask your Daddy. When he can talk again."

"Maybe you are an unpleasant guy," she said. "But listen, you jerk, I slept with you. I know you. I'd bet my life that you don't have it in you to really hurt me. As long as I don't try to hurt you."

"That's an interesting approach to reality," I said.

"What the hell happened to Jimmy Fish?" she said, touching the bandage again. "And my face?"

"Jimmy decided to defend your honor, I guess."

"What?"

"He came out of the house shooting. A fragment of one of his rounds poked a tiny hole in your ear and a little scratch across the top of your cheek."

"Stupid asshole," she said, touching her face again. "Is my face going to be all right?"

"The slice on your cheek is clean. The scar will give you charac- ter. Like the one at the corner of your mouth," I said. "But I fear the hole he put in your ear is sort of permanent."

"I hope you put a round in his fat head."

"Actually, in his fat thigh."

"You should have killed him. He turned out to be a hitter in middle age," she said. "He used to just want to spank me, but lately he's taken up hitting."

"Maybe I should have brought him along."

"Wouldn't have done you any good, man. You might beat the shit out of me for a month of Sundays," she said, "but the people who hired me would run me through a limb chipper. Alive. After

half the Third World gangsters in South-Central had a piece of my
ass."

"Don't give me any ideas."

"What the hell are you so mad about, anyway?" she asked. "You
got a prime piece of ass, and you must have broken up with what's-
her-name."

"They didn't mention anything about blowing my head off?"

She paused a moment, reconsidered her position, then shook
her head. "That was a surprise. I didn't know about it until that doo-
fus cop said something about it that morning."

"What did he say?"

"First, you. Then me. Eventually."

"Lovely."

"They knew I wouldn't go for something like that," she said. "I
was just supposed to break you two up. Seduce her, then come back
and seduce you. That's what he said."

"He?"

"Just a voice on the phone."

"What the hell was the business with Betty's revolver?" I asked.
"Why did you swap her pistol?"

"I don't know anything about that, either," she said, glancing
away. "But the rest was just a straight deal. Fuck you, fuck her, watch
the cop beat the shit out of you, then pick up my cash."

"From who?"

"I told you, man, I don't know. Just a voice on the phone. So
forget it."

"Why did you dump your fanny pack that morning?"

"Get rid of the piece and the cell phone," she said.

"Somebody called you just after you split," I said. "You know
who?"

"No idea."

"We'll see how you feel after a couple of weeks," I said. "See if
you can't remember some names."

"Shit, this is like a vacation for me," she said, then smiled,
pointed at the television. "I'm not much for TV, except old movies,

but I could be awfully sweet if I had a stack of crime novels. The good hard-nosed ones, you know. None of that namby-pamby shit."

"Namby-pamby?"

"You know. Nice guy meets bad people. Justice prevails. That kind of shit," she said.

"I don't know anything about that," I admitted, so I rolled up my sleeping bag and pad. Wondering if I could torture Molly with a stack of Agatha Christie novels. Or get a blowjob for the collected Hammett.

"I'll see what I can do," I said.

"How about some coffee? And maybe some orange juice? And a buttered roll?"

"I ain't the room service waiter, lady," I said. But it seemed I was for now.

Luckily, I didn't have to get the crib ready. I'd called Carver D from the road, told him what I needed, and asked about Eldora Grace and Sissy Duval, but there had been no word about either. I'd thought about calling Betty, but she had left the scrambled cell phone in the Caddy. I left the other one with Red. I wanted to know what sort of shit-storm we'd stirred up and which way it was blowing.

When we had gotten to Tom Ben's about dusk the second day I had carried the woman into the crib, removed the straitjacket, changed her diaper, then dressed her in new socks and sweats, and locked her ankle back into the hardened steel shackles. I gave her the last of the sedatives, then grabbed a handful of Coors, the scrambled cell phone, then stepped outside.

The sun had just dropped below the horizon. Except the stars blinking through the darkness and the stain of ambient light from Austin to the east, the sky deepened until it was nearly as blue as the woman's eyes. A random, cold breeze licked at my face to remind me that it was nearly December. I opened a beer, then dialed Red.

"Hey, man, it's cool," he said quickly when he answered. "Fucking Jimmy Fish is making a joke out of it, pushing the free press as hard as he can. Says he's already been offered half a dozen script deals about the incident."

"What about the word on the street?"

"It's all a big joke, man," Red said. "Most people seem to think that there wasn't even a woman with him. He just got coked up and shot himself. Either by accident or for the publicity."

"And the cattle guard?"

"Hell, nobody's even mentioned that," he said. "They had it fixed the next morning."

"You went out there," I said. "Be careful, dammit."

"Hey, man, I rode out in a limo. I'll be sending you the charge."

"Fuck the money," I said. "You just stay clean and easy, man."

"I'm cool," he said. "You want me to mail you this cell phone?"

I told Red to keep it for a week or two just in case. Then I drank another beer, had a couple of cigarettes, and checked my voice mail. A cool message from Sylvie Lomax inquiring as to my progress in the search for Molly McBride. Travis Lee had called twice, his voice deep and troubled as he said we needed to talk about business. Important business. Very important business. I assumed that he was still talking about his unnamed investment opportunity. Phil Thursby had left a crisp message asking me to call. But nothing from Betty. So I called Gannon on the scrambled cell phone. When he answered, it sounded as if he were in a bar.

"Where the hell are you?" I said.

"It's my night off. So I'm leaning on your fancy bar, buddy," he said, sounding a bit worse for drink. "Where the hell are you?"

"I'm running down a lead outside Houston," I lied. "How's business at my place?"

"Booming, man," he said. "Looks like you could use another bartender, though. I've had some experience."

"How are things around the cop shop?"

"The usual bullshit. Nobody seems to miss you but me," he said, then quickly added, "Oh, there's word that my walking papers are in the works. That's why I was down here looking for a job. When are you coming back?"

"Just as soon as I find that goddamned woman," I said. "Tell Mike to let you have one on me," I added, then cut off the connection. I called Betty on the other phone, but got her voice mail, and had no idea what to say, so I cut that one off, too. Called Phil Thursby, but no human response there, either. So I cracked the other beer. As I drank it leaning against the Caddy, I realized my knees were ticking like bombs. Cocaine and road miles. So I grabbed a pad and a sleeping bag, went back into the barn, locked it, then lay down like a dog on the floor next to the woman who had nearly gotten me killed. Sometime later in the night, maybe in a dream, maybe with the chill seeping out of the concrete floor into my back, I found myself standing beside the cot as if I were about to crawl into bed with the woman. It seemed that changing her diapers and cleaning up her shit hadn't diminished her charm in my unconscious mind. But she moaned softly, turned in her chemical sleep, so I pulled the covers over her shoulders, tucked them tightly, then returned to the floor.

After I finished my room service duties that first morning, I took a shower in the corner of the barn, changed clothes, then opened the barn door, and stopped there. "There's some fruit and sandwich stuff in the reefer," I said, "and I'll bring something when I come back."

As I rolled the door shut, Molly shouted at me. "Are you just going to leave me here alone?"

"If you hear the shucks rustling, lady, don't put your feet on the floor!" I shouted back, then locked up and drove away, at least as far as the main house.

The old man sat in one of the porch rockers, puffing nervously on the stub of an old pipe. "Milo," he said, tapping his knuckles on the foot locker I had shipped from Vegas. "UPS delivered this a while ago. What the hell is it?"

"Just some stuff," I said, not wanting to tell the old man it was full of guns and drugs and cash money. "Just leave it there," I said. "I'll move it later."

"You sure all this shit is going to be all right?"

"She doesn't seem inclined to file a complaint," I said. "Hell, she's acting like she's on vacation. Like I did her a favor, or something." Then I realized that Molly hadn't been at Jimmy's by accident. She was hiding out. That changed everything.

"She's a piece of work, that's for damn sure," he said, then chuckled. "It took my hands a whole day to clean the rats and mice and snakes out of that corn pile. But I told them to leave the cowshit." Then Tom Ben laughed. "She might have been my last piece of ass," he said, "and she sure as hell did cost me more than just ten thousand dollars' worth of fence line. But it was damn near worth it."

"Cowshit's not bad. But that old milk stink might drive her over the edge," I said. "How come you gave up on milk cows?"

"Hell, them goddamned Angora goats were bad enough. Selling mohair was like living on government welfare," he said. "But milk cows, that seemed too close to farming to suit me. And my hands kept saying that they were cowboys, not milk boys. At least that was better than Betty's first idea. Chicken houses. Jesus, I'd rather raise Barbary apes."

"The dairy herd was Betty's idea?" I said.

"Yeah, hell, she put up the money for it when I incorporated."

Well, it wasn't the first time I'd been involved with a woman who lived her life as if it were a closely guarded secret. But that didn't make me feel any less foolish.

"Any idea how long you might keep that woman locked in my corn crib?" he asked.

"Probably not long," I said. "I'm not going to give her to the Lomax woman and I don't seem to be very good at this warden shit. She's already got me fetching and carrying like a house slave. Next thing you know she'll be sending me downtown to buy her underwear."

Tom Ben smiled as if he didn't think it was such a bad idea.

"You stay out of that barn, you old bastard," I said, but the old man's smile grew even larger. "Can I borrow your pickup? I got some chores in town, and my ride is too visible. But I'll be back."

"Keys are in it," he said, still grinning.

I carried the foot locker over to the barn, set it inside the door. Molly was asleep, though, so I took off to do my chores.

Albert Homer still hadn't cut the dead grass in front of his stu-dio–cum–house. I parked on the street because a pink Cadillac was in the dirt driveway. The burglar bars on the front door had been left unlocked and even outside I could smell the burnt rope stink of marijuana, so I didn't bother with the buzzer, just put my shoulder to the door until the inside frame splintered.

A chubby woman in heavy makeup with tiny feet and hands, dressed in a complicated leather bra-less and crotch-less teddy and garter belt arrangement, lay across the velvet bedspread beneath the warm glow of the raised light stands, all a-titter as she scrambled for a wrap. Homer turned quickly, his eyes wild and wide open like a man who had seen more than one husband advancing from the front door, then whirled back as if to flee.

Before he could take a step, I grabbed him by the throat and lifted him off the floor. "You lying son of a bitch," I said. Then I dropped him. Or perhaps threw him down. "Excuse me, ma'am, this won't take a moment." But she ignored me. I noticed that she had stopped looking for something to cover her naked body parts, and was digging through her purse. I nudged Homer in the ribs with my boot, and he curled up like a sow-bug, then I stepped over to the chubby little woman just as she pulled a small semiautomatic pistol out of her purse. "Give me that, you fucking idiot," I said as I jerked it out of her hand. I wanted to slap the makeup off her tiny face. Instead I fired the pistol into Homer's round bed, emptied the magazine, broke the slide off, then threw the two pieces out oppo-site windows. The woman jumped more at the sound of breaking glass than she had at the shots. "Does everybody in this fucking state have a gun?"

"My husband gave it to me," she whined.

"He give you that outfit, too?" I asked. She blushed, covered her breasts, shook her oddly small, well-formed head, then sat, weeping among the bits of charred cotton stuffing I'd blown out of the mattress. I handed her the purse. "Why don't you put some clothes on and head into the bathroom and fix your face?" She nodded slowly, then fled toward the back of the house.

I walked back to Homer, picked him up by his ear. "You shouldn't have told me the Vegas lie," I said. "And perhaps you should have suggested to the law that they might look a little closer into your father's death."

"I'm sorry," Homer blubbered, tears pouring down his face.

"Stop crying," I said, "and tell me what happened. He ask them for more money?" Homer nodded. "And they killed him?" I wondered how many kinds of drugs it took for Homer to gather up the courage to follow in his father's footsteps. "Let me guess. You've got one picture of Amanda Rae Quarrels in a safe-deposit box? One in the house? And another with a lawyer?"

"Becky's husband," he stammered.

"And I assume that's Becky in the john?" He nodded as he scrubbed at his slobbery face. "How much money do you get?"

"Five hundred a month. That's all."

"Cheaper than killing you, I guess," I said.

"That's what they said. They gave my Daddy a hundred grand," he said. "Then when he asked for more, he went fishing for the last time. They said they killed him for lying to them."

"Who said?"

"The voice on the telephone." Then he rattled off a local number.

"How do they pay?"

"Cash in the mailbox."

"Outside?"

"Yeah."

"When?"

"First Saturday night of the month."

"Always."

"As regular as clockwork."

"How long's this been going on?"

"I don't know," he said. "Seven years or so."

"Get me the picture you've got here," I said. He hesitated. "I'll tear your fucking ear out by the roots, kid," I said, giving it a tug. Homer scrambled around, unscrewing a light stand, then pulling a rolled 8x10 photograph out of it. He handed it to me. "If I were you, son, I'd find another way to supplement my income." He nodded. "Are you going to be all right?" He nodded again, snuffling. "Be nice to Becky. She looks like a good woman, if a bit over-dressed," I said on my way to the broken door.

"I'll do that, sir," Homer said.

"And fix your goddamned door, man," I said before I left. "I think I've already paid for it."

"Yes, sir," he said sadly.

I didn't know what I was looking for as I sat in the car and un-rolled the photo of Amanda Rae Quarrels. She had long, straight sil-ver-blond hair, mischievous green eyes, and a cocked, smart-ass smile on her wide mouth, high cheekbones, a slightly aquiline nose, and long beaded earrings. *Trouble* was the first word that came to mind. *Outrageous fun*, the second and third. But she didn't remind me of anybody I knew. Maybe that's what I was hoping to find.

I wrote the telephone number Homer had recited on the back of the photo, then checked it against the number wrapped around the chewing gum from Sissy's BMW. They were the same. When I dialed it, a disembodied voice answered by repeating the number and suggesting that if I had any business, I could leave my name and number. I did neither.

Leonard Wilbur wasn't any more happy to see me than Albert Homer had been. At least he didn't run. Over the Line was almost empty just after lunch. Wilbur was still behind the bar, but today he carried a clipboard as he filled out a liquor order and he wore a nice gray suit, a white shirt, and an expensive silk tie, plus a new toupee as thick and stiff as combed porcupine quills. His smile was as phony as his hair. The lame Chicano kid with the flattened nose seemed to be the bartender now. Several other Latinos, who probably had more words of English between them than Green Cards, seemed to be remodeling Long's office. Wilbur flinched as if I was going to tear his snotty lip off when I held my hand across the bar to shake his hand. I introduced myself as politely as I could, showed him my license, and gave him my card.

"Yeah, I remember you," he grumped. "Let me buy you a drink, then you can be on your way. Crown Royal, wasn't it?"

"Actually a can of Coors would be fine," I said. "You mind taking a look at this picture?"

Wilbur glanced at it, shook his head, then handed me the beer. "I can probably guess who she is," he said, "Mandy Rae Quarrels, but I ain't seen the woman in years and I didn't know her name when I saw her."

"You sure?"

"Partner, a man doesn't forget a woman like that."

"So how do you know her name?"

"Hell, man, she's a legend," Wilbur said. "Word was, she came to town, fucked everybody worth knowing from Willie to the Governor, his wife, and his pet bullfrog . . ."

"Bulldog?"

"Bullfrog," he said. "Then disappeared like a government check in East Austin. Not even a broken Thunderbird bottle left behind. Plus, that murdering son of a bitch who came in with you last month, he said her name, and I knew that Duval used to hang out with her."

"Let me ask you something else," I said. "Why do you think Mr. Long went for his pistol?"

"Well, Billy Long was always pretty touchy and . . ."

"And?"

"He hated niggers," he said, "and I suspect that one in particular. Maybe they'd had some trouble over business or something. Maybe a woman."

"And you, Mr. Wilbur?"

"What about me?"

"You ever have any trouble with Duval or Walker?"

"Hell, man, I just work here, and to folks like that, we're all niggers of one sort or another."

As soon as afternoon visiting hours at Breckenridge Hospital started, I went up to check out Renfro. He lay propped up in bed, the tangle of tubes gone, and his right hand in a small cast. The small ponytailed man sat beside his bed, fussing over him. Renfro introduced us.

"I guess I should thank you for saving his worthless hide," Richie said. "But what he was doing out there in the middle of the night, I hesitate to guess. He just won't take care of himself, no matter what, I—"

"I'm going to be fine," Renfro interrupted, holding up his hand. "Spleen's fine, and the bullet just clipped the big bone in the middle of my hand. I'll be out of the cast in six weeks."

"Just missed the ligament by a hair," Richie continued breathlessly. "Would have ruined his hand. Forever."

"Richie, darling, would you get me a Coke?" Renfro said. "Mr. Milodragovitch, you want something?" I shook my head as Richie headed for the door. "And that's a real Coke, Richie, not a diet one." Richie paused long enough to give Renfro a disgusted look, then hustled away. "If I'd wanted a Jewish mother," he said, "I'd have had one. Jeez. Any word from Sissy?"

"Nothing," I lied. "You said she had some sort of secret income, some kind of sugar daddy."

"Yeah, she's been pretty flush the last five or six years," he said, "ever since she quit selling lots for Hayden Lomax, but she never said a word about where it came from."

"I didn't know she worked for Lomax," I said, then suggested, "she must have been highly motivated to keep her mouth shut."

"You know, that makes sense," he said, then chuckled. "You'd probably have to shove dirt into her mouth to keep her quiet."

He didn't know how right he was. "Her money's safe. I'll get it back to you in a few days," I said. He might need it for hospital bills. He'd certainly earned it. "You take care."

"Hey, man, I'm going home tomorrow, you know," he said, then looked terribly embarrassed. "Thank you again."

"What for?"

"Saving my life, man."

"Part of the job description," I said, then waved goodbye, and left quickly before Richie could return to give me another lecture about Renfro's bad habits. I had enough of my own.

I called Cathy from a pay phone in the hospital lobby. She didn't sound all that glad to hear from me, but it had been that kind of day.

"Have you seen her?" I asked.

"I picked her up at the airport," she said coldly.

"How is she?"

"Mad enough to chew up ten-penny nails and shit upholstery tacks."

"I guess I just didn't do what she wanted me to do."

"You've always been pretty good at that, haven't you?"

"You could say that," I said.

"Well, she's my oldest friend, man, and you're just some guy I did drugs with and fucked," she said.

"So I'm not on the old friend list, huh?" I asked, followed by an empty chuckle. Her silence was answer enough. "When she stops spitting tacks," I said, "tell her to give me a call. I should be back by then."

Cathy just sighed, said she'd try, then added, "How's your back?"

"It's there."

"I could give you another number."

"It wouldn't be the same, honey," I said, and this time I hung up without saying goodbye.

Molly's face brightened when I showed up with two paper bags hanging from my hands. A bag full of sandwiches and salads from Central Market and a bag full of detective novels from Bookstop, but I wouldn't let her look in the bags until I cleaned up her wound and replaced the butterfly bandages.

Tough as she was, I suspected she'd be a whiner about this part. I loosened the butterflies with alcohol. When I tried to get to the hole in her ear, she squealed like a baby.

"If you're going to be a sissy about this," I said, "I'll bet I can find some tin snips and just cut the goddamned thing off."

"Well, it hurts," she said. "I don't mind big pains, but these little stinging things drive me as crazy as swamp skeeters." She stayed quiet, though, until I finished the rest of the job. "What's the verdict?"

"You'll live," I said. "You've got good bones and great skin. You'll be lovely into your old age."

"Thank you," she said, smiling. "Can I ask you something?"

"Ask, and I'll tell you."

"What did you mean about my Daddy knowing how unpleasant you could be?"

"The first time I found him in Houston, he tried to kick me in the nuts while a crowd of drunks held me down," I said. "The second time, he tried to hit me with a Scotch bottle. I broke his jaw and knocked out half a dozen teeth."

"Poor old Rollie," she said, "he never had any luck, the cathead tongs took his arm, the drinking took his bar, then the government took his boat." She broke into a thoughtful smile. "You son of a bitch, you remembered the address on the card, didn't you?" I nodded. "When you took that old man down that way, I guess I should have realized that you had more than muscle between your ears." I nodded again. "I wondered how the hell you found me."

"You dropped so many hints, lady, that it almost seemed you wanted me to find you."

"What an odd idea," she said. "What the hell makes you think that?"

"Just guessing," I said. "And also just guessing that Rollie Molineaux isn't really your father."

"He took my mother and me in," she said quietly, "he gave me his name, raised me from a pup after she died, and he was always as good to me as he could be. He never judged me and he always tried to help. Whatever kind of trouble I managed to stir up. You can't ask for more than that."

"He's pretty tough for a one-armed guy."

"He's pretty tough, period," she said. "He and another guy beat a man to death in the parking lot outside the bar when I was a kid."

"The other guy wouldn't be Jimmy Fish?" I said, guessing.

"How the hell did you come up with that?"

"Just a guess," I said. "I've got to go out of town this afternoon and I can't get back until about this time tomorrow."

"I get to go home then?"

"You get to go home when I find out what the hell is going on."

"Oh, you'll get tired of having me around," she said. "Everybody does, eventually."

"You going to be all right?" I said as I handed her the bags.

"I'll be fine," she said. "I noticed that you slept on the floor last night. Somebody cleaned the critters out of the corn?"

"I wouldn't know," I said. "Don't make too much noise," I added. "Right now not too many people know you're here. And I suspect your health sort of depends on some other people not knowing you're here."

"What the hell's that mean?"

"Some very heavy people went to a great deal of trouble to get me to come looking for you, honey," I said.

"Jeez, I thought you were just mad about your girlfriend."

"And her pistol."

"I told you, man," she said, "I don't know anything about that. I've done a lot of things in my life but I've never fingered anybody."

"What kind of things?"

"You don't want to know," she said quietly, then hung her head for a moment, then lifted it brightly. "So who's looking for me?" she asked casually.

"A woman named Lomax," I said.

"I don't know anybody named Lomax," she protested, then leaned back.

"Mrs. Lomax said you had something of hers."

"Since I don't know who she is, I can't think what it might be," she said, thinking it over, and didn't look up when I slipped out the door.

I traded rides with Tom Ben again, then headed out.

Thursby was sitting on a bench outside the Hays County courthouse in San Marcos, just where his secretary said he would be.

"What the hell are you doing out here?" I asked.

"Thinking about moving to California," he said.

"What?"

"We're being homered in the courtroom so bad that I'm letting one of my junior partners handle the cross examination of the local idiot deputy who put three rounds in my client, who fit the drug runner profile in his little, pointy head, at a phony traffic stop," Thursby said. "One of them missed him completely and killed his girlfriend."

"I don't understand."

"Unfortunately, he had just enough marijuana in the trunk of his old Camaro to make it a felony possession. The deputy said my client resisted, which is stupid because the kid has a tremor from brain damage in a car wreck. The death of his girlfriend makes it a capital murder. Interesting case," he said. "We'll beat them like a monkey's dick on appeal, but I'm getting tired of dealing with these idiots." Then he sighed, shook his head, and suddenly looked like an old man. "Speaking of idiots," he continued. "I glanced through the Oates case file. Something's wrong, Milo. I know Steelhammer can't be bought, but he was new on the bench then, and he might have been handled. The whole thing stinks like your lazy brother-in-law's shorts."

"I was just on my way to Huntsville," I said.

"I'll call ahead," he said, "to see if I can't ease the way. Tell the kid we're going for a new trial."

"Thanks," I said. "I'll cover the cost."

"Save your money," he said, pointing his thumb over his shoulder toward the courthouse. "I'll do it like this one. For fun. And headlines."

"I hope you have some."

"So where do you stand with Sylvie Lomax?"

"I haven't talked to her yet," I said. "I've got the McBride woman stashed in a safe place, but she's not talking. I'll cut her loose before I give her up to Rooke or Lomax."

"Not a wise decision," he said, "but one I approve of highly."

I left Thursby sitting there, his short legs swinging in the air. His feet didn't quite touch the ground, but his balls surely did.

After a troubled, almost sleepless night in a local motel not too far from Huntsville, I went out to the prison unit where Dickie Oates was lodged. Thursby's call hadn't eased my way at all. I had to use my Gatlin County DA's badge and a threat of a lawsuit to get an interview. More than my welcome had changed. This time we talked through thick Plexiglas with worn telephones in an oddly empty visiting room. Dickie Oates, who looked ten years older, sat down quickly, picked up the phone, then placed his other hand against the barrier. I read the ballpoint message on his palm.

"Can you do that, man?" he said. "My folks will pay you back. That's the only way I could get out of the ad-seg." When I looked confused at the term, he added, "The hole, man."

"You got it," I said, nodding to the officer who stood against the wall behind Dickie Oates. But the CO's face was as blank as the wall. "Cooley," his nametag said. "Two things," I said. "Phil Thursby's office will be in touch with you shortly. He's going to try for a new trial."

"Great," he said. "What's the other thing?" I unrolled the picture of Amanda Rae Quarrels against the Plexiglas. "That's one of them."

"One of them?"

"Before they put me in the hole," he said, "I had this guy on the yard—a shrink in on a drug rap—hypnotize me. There were a bunch of women there, kicking the shit out of that Duval asshole when he went down. I was on the ground by then and I was still there when the shotgun went off the second time." Then he paused. "Does that help?"

"Sure," I said, "sure." Though I didn't have the vaguest idea if it helped or not. I didn't even know what it meant. "What did you do to get put in the hole?"

"Looked at somebody the wrong way," he said. "That's all it takes these days."

"Hang tough, kid," I said, then left.

The Attitude Adjustment was a bunkerlike cinder block bar set in the middle of an asphalt parking lot just off the Interstate across the Madison County line. Although it wasn't quite ten o'clock in the morning, I had trouble finding a parking place among the pickups and four-wheel-drive units sporting Department of Correction parking stickers. The off-shift COs who filled the bar all stared at me when I opened the front door. Pool players hung over their shots, their heads turned, many drinks paused in midair. I tried not to look guilty but the looks on their faces suggested that I failed. I found an empty table in the darkest corner I could find. The cocktail waitress, a tall, skinny woman with stringy black hair, showed up quickly, her bony jaw working at a piece of chewing gum.

"What can I do for y'all, partner?" she asked.

"A can of Coors," I said. "Is Ramona Cooley working today?"

"I'm Ramona," she said. "You got something for me?" I nodded, but she took off for the bar, her tray winging before her. She was back in a moment with my beer. When she leaned over to set it down, she popped out her gum, and stuck it under the table as she whispered, "Stick it there." Then louder she said, "You passin' through or visitin'?"

"Heading for Houston," I said.

I stuck the envelopeful of cash to Ramona Cooley's gum, then drank my beer rather quickly and uncomfortably. She brought me another without being asked. The envelope went away with her. People had stopped looking at me with narrowed eyes, so I stopped chugging my beer. She brought me a third, again without being asked. I gave her a ten and told her to keep the change. But she made change anyway, leaning over me as she counted it out.

"Cooley's worked inside a long time, buddy, and he thinks Dickie Oates is bein' screwed," she whispered, "and we hate to take the money. But you know how it is. Thanks a bunch, hon."

I finished my beer, left the change, and walked through the silent stares.

CHAPTER TWELVE

THE COPY OF THE FILE on Dickie Oates was still at Carver D's, so I stopped there when I got back to Austin. The fat man was oddly somber and sober, sitting in his antique wheelchair, warming in the sun broken by the live oak branches.

"What's up?" I asked. "You look like something the dog threw up and the cat drug home."

"Petey just got accepted at Harvard Business," he said.

"And that's bad? Isn't an MBA a license to steal?"

"He won't let me go with him unless I stop drinkin', man," he said. "So I've stopped. You stopped once, didn't you?"

"I took a ten-year break," I said.

"How'd you do it?"

"Smoked a lot of dope, drank a lot of tonic water," I said, "read a lot of books, saw a lot of movies, and found the extra time hard to fill."

"You were tending bar, weren't you? Didn't that make it harder?"

"Hell, I worked all the time because the people on the other side of the bar showed me where I was headed if I didn't slow down."

"Well, I can't imagine life without Petey," he said, "so I'm gonna give it a try."

"Good luck," I said. And meant it. "Hangas going with you?"

"No. Hangas has too much family down here," Carver D said, then chortled. "He's gonna handle my affairs down here. Gonna be my bidness manager. Take care of things till we get back." As if cheered by the notion of coming back home, Carver D smiled. "So what the hell do you want, Mr. Nosy?"

"Dwayne Duval's autopsy report," I said.

And there it was. From ankle to scalp, Duval's body was covered with more than fifty fading contusions.

"Looks like somebody tried to kick the asshole to death before they shot him," Carver D said. "Makes you wonder."

"Makes me wonder where Enos Walker was that night," I said as I thumbed through the rest of the file. No matter how hard I looked, no female names appeared on the witness list, just Billy Long and one of Dickie's frat buddies. Of course, Long was inside and Dickie's buddy was around the corner in the parking lot on the side and just heard the shots. They claimed they never saw any particular women. "Makes me wonder what he was doing."

"According to the stuff that wasn't in the trial record, I'm guessing he might have been pretty close to Tulsa," Carver D said. "Maybe waitin' for a cocaine delivery around that time."

"What about his brother?"

"That'll be a little harder to dig up," the fat man said. "Call me in a couple of days."

"Maybe you should do this computer thing professionally," I suggested.

"And take all the fun out of it," he said, then laughed as he wheeled himself toward his office.

As I left, I realized that Carver D wasn't the only one who needed Petey. Shit, I was going to have to find another silent partner to help me launder the drug money. Which made me think about Travis Lee, so I returned his call.

Travis Lee's wife, who had died in a car wreck some years before, had left him a rambling house that sprawled along the crest of a small ridge overlooking one of the string of lakes along the Colorado River, a large but ordinary house except for the view. Travis Lee hadn't changed the house in the years since his wife's death, except to fill it with enough junk to start a Civil War museum. I had been to a couple of parties at his place—without Betty—but his friends were either too young, too old, or too Texas to be interested in anything I had to say.

Travis Lee waited out on the patio, a new pair of custom-made alligator boots propped on a small table. The boots and their matching belt gleamed in the late afternoon sunlight. At this angle, his golden buckle looked more like a golden frog than a snake. He lifted his can of Tecate in my direction as I came out the back door. "Thanks for coming out," he said, a grin large on his face as he waved at his Chicano butler standing by the back door to bring us a beer. "You ain't been exactly religious about returning my phone calls lately."

"I've been busier than a whore at a meat cutter's convention," I said. "What's up?"

"You know, son, I'm just an old country boy," he said as he started his routine.

"Spare me the preface," I said, grinning as I held up my hands in surrender. "I told you, Travis Lee, I just don't have the time to worry about investments now."

"Spare me," he said. "At some point, you're gonna have to piss on the fire and call the dogs."

"Trav, I've been long on busy, and you've been short of details," I said. "You think we could talk about this later? Then maybe my voice mail won't be quite so full of bullshit."

"Yeah," he said, his face large with concern. "Sorry to hear about you and Betty. Women come and women go, but business lasts. How much money you got in that offshore bank?"

"Enough. Why?"

"If you've got a million to lend me for thirty days," he said, ruffling his wild white hair as he stood up, "I can move it just across the street and turn it into three million clean and clear in a New York bank. We can split the profit down the middle." When I didn't answer, he added, "I'd even be more than willing to put up my share of the Lodge as collateral."

"Hell, man, if it goes bad, I don't want to end up with a fucking motel," I said, laughing. "I don't even want the bar, if you get right down to it."

"Hell, boy," he said, laughing and slapping my shoulder, "I thought you loved that place."

"I do," I admitted. "But it's always full of the wrong people." *And in the wrong part of the world,* I thought but didn't say. "Besides, the kind of profit you're talking about can only come from insider trading or drug deals, and I don't need that kind of heat."

"Don't be silly," Travis Lee said, still grinning. "I wouldn't do anything like that. Straight property deal, and we're covered all the way down the line anyway." He could tell I didn't like the sound of that. "And speaking of heat, there's another damn good reason to consider this deal," he said. "You might be needing a dose of clean cash. Like I started to say, I'm just a country boy, but I'm aware that you and that kid have been washing cash through the bar."

"I'm just a country boy myself," I said, "and even if I was running a laundry, it'd just be chump change, and I'd be covered like your Granny's ass."

"Leave my poor old dead Granny out of this," he said, his smile unbroken. "An old buddy of mine in D.C. whistled a little bird song in my ear last week. You're about to have tax people all over you like stink on a dead hog's ass."

"That's not a problem," I said, hoping I wasn't lying. At least not to myself.

"Not a problem? Tax people are always a problem," he said. "They can bury you, and nobody can do a thing about it. And there's some suggestion that the little whoredogs are sittin' in your bar as we speak."

I didn't say anything. I guess I didn't have anything to say. I just stared north like some dumb beast, not really looking at the dark bank of clouds moving down the long, empty plains toward me. Another goddamned norther.

"And speaking of whores? Any luck finding that woman for Sylvie Lomax?" he said. "If I were in your boots, son, I'd look for a double dose of clean money, and all the influential friends I could find. Hayden Lomax draws a lot of water around here. And I can guarantee that she draws a lot of water with him."

"I've been back and forth across five states and came up empty." I wasn't sure why I lied to him, but I had promised myself that once Molly told me what the hell this was all about, I'd see her home safely.

"Well, if you find her, don't tell my big brother. I understand that he's still got the bejesus hots for her," he said, and jerked his dimpled chin at Tom Ben's pickup sitting in front of his house, then he laughed long and loud, the laughter guttering on the rising north wind like a dying candle.

"I'll keep that in mind," I said, thinking that, given his history, it was a strange thing to say. And I wondered how Travis Lee knew about the incident. Unless Betty had told him.

"Well, you call me now," Travis Lee said, "sooner rather than later." He stood up abruptly, slapped me on the shoulder again, then headed for the back door of his house. "You want a real drink?" he said.

"No thanks," I said. "Not right now. And thanks for the warning."

"My pleasure, son. You're a stranger down here," he said, "and Texas hospitality is the rule, not the exception."

When I climbed out of the pickup in front of Tom Ben's dairy barn, I could hear the laughter cracking against the metal walls. The light, fading behind the rolling storm, had drawn the shine from the steel, leeching it to an ashen gray. Inside, in the corn crib, Tom Ben sat on a milking stool and Molly on her cot, her long hair combed out and her face made up. They huddled over a bottle of Jack Daniel's, laughing and slapping their knees. Tom Ben's glass was as dark as raw molasses, but Molly's was very light.

"Wow," she said as I came in. "My master returns."

The old man stood up quickly, stumbling a bit, a guilty boy's grin lopsided on his unshaven face. "Hell, Milo," he said, "I just thought I'd check on the girl."

"Thanks," I said. "I appreciate it."

"Well, I best be headin' out to the house," the old man said as he picked up the half-empty bottle of bourbon.

"I'll give you a hand," I said, but the old man turned on me.

"I got every place I ever started to go, boy," he said quickly. "One of them was back from the Yalu River. Ever hear of that fucking place, boy?"

"Yes, sir," I said. "I spent part of a spring staring in that direction once." Then watched the old man wobble out the door and into the dim evening. I guess I could see my legs wobbling in my future. He was only twelve years older than me. Then I looked at Molly.

"Don't look at me," she said. "I didn't invite him in."

"I'm sure you didn't," I said. "But one more of those drinks, honey, you would have had to help me carry him out."

Molly held up her foot with the shackle on it, smiling like a child. "We could work something out."

"Don't tempt me."

"So what did you find out, Mr. PI? When can I go home?"

"Where the hell do you call home?" I said.

She looked briefly puzzled. "Vegas, I guess," she said. "I've got some business there."

"I'm sure you do," I said. "You want some Mexican food?"

"What?"

"You want some Mexican food for dinner?" I said. "I've got one more chore to do before dark, then I'll bring you some dinner."

"And some cold beer?" she said. "Can't eat Mexican food without cold beer."

"Sure," I said, then checked the locks on her shackle.

"You've changed my diaper and you still don't trust me?" She sounded almost hurt.

"Not much," I said, then locked the door to the corn crib, and then the barn door.

As I leaned on Betty's gate in the rising north wind, it seemed like a hundred years instead of five since the first time I stood there. But it's always that way when things go bad between two people. The first time I had leaned on her gate, she held a pistol on me. But she let me inside that time. This time she just looked at me with dead eyes, holding back the three-legged lab, Sheba, who had the slobbery tennis ball in her mouth.

"What the hell do you want?" she said flatly.

"Thought I'd see how you're doing."

"As you can see, I'm fine," she said. "You brought that fucking woman back down here, didn't you," she said. "I told you not to do that, I told you to let the law handle it. You didn't do that, did you? No? So what do you want?"

"I guess I came to see if I could heal the breach."

"It's long past that time," she snorted. "You chose your life, Milo, now you can sleep in it," she added, then turned away, pulling the whining dog behind her as she walked back to the house.

It would be pretty to say that the cold rain and the biting wind started as I climbed back into the Beast, but the norther held back its sharp teeth and hard rain until I got back to the barn.

The wind and rain rattled the barn and the small milk-house heater roared as Molly and I shared the food from Taco Cabaña and a six-pack of cold Negra Modelo.

"You know what that old man told me?" she said.

"Hard to imagine."

"He said that he had hated the cold ever since he had carried one of his dead buddies until his body froze solid as a cedar post," she said. "Why would he tell me something like that? And what was he talking about?"

"Tom Ben was a Marine company commander in the Korean War. He was proud of it. And maybe he was trying to impress you."

"Oh," she said as if she wasn't quite sure where Korea was. Hell, I wasn't quite sure either and I'd been there for almost three months before the broken collarbone got me out of combat and into a hospital, and some doctor suggested that I wasn't really eighteen. "Why would he want to impress me?"

"Who knows," I said. "Tom Ben's a tough old bird, but maybe he was trying to get in your pants."

Molly giggled for a second, then suddenly became serious. "Can I tell you something?"

"Sure."

"It's a lot different meeting him like this, instead of on the job."

"Maybe it's you that's different," I said.

Molly paused for a moment, tore off a piece of brisket, and held it in front of the heater. "You're always trying to look inside my head," she said. "I'm not sure I like it."

"That's my job," I said, remembering what Betty had said at the gate.

"Do you like it?"

"Not always," I admitted. "How about you? You like your job?" Then I paused. "I'm sorry. I've no right to say something like that."

But she didn't answer. We finished our meal in silence, then a couple of beers and cigarettes. When she finally spoke, it was to ask if the shower in the corner of the barn had any hot water. I told her it did.

"Do you trust me enough to let me take a shower?"

"That's the wrong question to ask, lady," I said as I unlocked the shackle from her ankle. "There's soap and stuff on the shelf," I added as she picked up a clean pair of sweats and a T-shirt, then walked over to the dark corner where the shower stood. I tried not to watch as she slipped out of the sweats and under the rushing water, her long silken body shining darkly in the shadows. In spite of everything, she was still the most beautiful woman I had ever seen, and I could not stop looking at her, not while she showered, not while she came back to the crib to brush out the long, black ribbons of her hair, the soft weight of her breasts bobbing beneath the T-shirt. Finally, I busied myself unrolling two down sleeping bags, one on her cot, the other on my pad.

"It's going to be chilly tonight," I said. "This wet Texas cold seeps into your bones."

"You know," she said softly, paused with her face turned to me, the brush still in her thick hair. "You know, of all the men I've conned in my life, you were the hardest." Then she touched me on the forehead softly with the brush handle. "Of all the men I conned, you believed me the most."

"I guess I've always been a fool," I said. "How hard did you sting Paper Jack?"

"Thirty or forty grand," she said, yawning. "I don't remember the actual figure."

"How?" Reminded that yet another Texan had lied to me.

"Probably promised to make a single copy video just for him," she said. "Sometimes I block the details of a job."

"Why?"

"Why what?" she said. "I did it for the money. You think I want to be a whore all my life?"

"No," I said. "Why Paper Jack?"

"He slugged some old guy at a poker table in Vegas," she said calmly. "They were going to kill him, but somebody talked them into just spanking his billfold."

"I guess they thought he got what he deserved."

"Given the guy he hit," she said, "he's damn lucky to be alive." Then she paused. "You're sleeping here again tonight?"

"You're my only lead."

"Then you're shit out of luck, man," she said, but she was smiling.

When she finished with her toilet, I locked the shackle around her ankle, snapped off the lights, and we shared a few drinks of Scotch in the light of the milk-house heater almost without conversation, then slipped into our beds.

Later that night I had a version of the dream, the one where I stood beside her cot. This time, though, she reached her hands down from the cot, took my hands, and pulled me into the cot with her, saying, "Get in here, you old fart. It's cold down there." But this time it was no dream. I just had to act as if it was one to live with myself. Then I blamed the Scotch for making me open the cocaine and the shackle, then the cocaine for Molly, then I blamed myself for everything. But for a few hours the dead kept their eyes closed and the living shut their flapping mouths. And the dream lived. For the moment.

Although the storm still loomed cold and ashen outside, it was nearly bright noon when the nightmare began. When the scrambled cell phone began to ring, I untangled myself from Molly, then stumbled around the corn crib until I found the phone in my war bag.

"What the hell," I muttered.

"Milodragovitch," an oddly familiar voice shouted, "I've got your fuckin' nigger, I want my whore back."

"Shit," I said. Molly looked up at me from the cot. "What? Who is this? What are you talking about?"

"Listen to this, you asshole," the voice said, then I heard a grunt of pain, as if somebody had been hit with a truck. "We're standing here in North Las Vegas, asshole," the voice came again, "and your nigger's head is in a vise. If she ain't back here in forty-eight hours, I'm going to take a hammer to his face until he looks like crawdad shit. Not even his Momma will recognize his body. Of course it won't matter because she'll be fishbait floating in Lake Mead. Forty-eight hours, dickwad." Then the connection was broken.

"What's up?" Molly asked.

"Your buddy, Jimmy Fish, has got a friend of mine and his mother," I said, "and he's going to butcher them if I don't bring you back. He claims you're his whore."

"Oh God," she said, "that little fuck will kill them," then buried her face in her hands. "What are you going to do?"

"Put your clothes on," I said, then found my pants, dug out Fresno's card, and dialed the number. It took a few minutes to argue my way past secretaries and into the august presence of himself.

"Mr. Milodragovitch," he crooned, "what can I do for you now?"

"You can earn your money for a change," I said, then explained before he could interrupt.

The next four hours clicked by like the passage of death beetles. Molly and I drank coffee, chewed on oranges, and smoked like wood stoves. But neither of us said an extraneous word, just waited quietly. When the cell phone rang, it sounded as if we were trapped in a bell tower, as the ringing crashed off the metal walls.

"Milodragovitch," Fresno said.

"I'm here."

"Well, I don't know exactly what happened, but it went okay."

"What the hell's that mean?"

"The McCraveys are okay. Not fine, but okay. Red has a bunch of scrapes and bruises. And his mother had some kind of heart spell, but the paramedics said it's nothing serious. But Mr. Jimmy Fish, he'd been watching too many of his own movies."

"Yeah."

"I don't know why, but he decided to shoot it out with me and my boys. Tossed his crutch aside and grabbed for his piece," Fresno said. "I took a chance and put one in his shoulder. Little fucker dropped the piece, but before he hit the floor, one of the goons with him—some slick Frenchman, Red says—put one in Jimmy's head, then threw his piece down and slipped out the back door. I don't fucking know how he got away, but he did."

"Are we covered?" I asked.

"As far as I can tell, the two other guys don't speak English. So we're covered. I stuck one of our alarm shields on the outside of the building," he said. "Jimmy Fish had a gunshot crease in his thigh, but everybody around here knows that he did that himself. So as long as your friends keep their mouths shut, you're covered."

"Can you get the cell phone to Red?"

"I'll run it by the hospital. He rode along with his Mom."

"Thanks," I said, then asked him how much I owed him. He said he'd send a bill. I said I'd send a check.

"I guess I should thank you for more than the money," he said.

"Why?"

"I don't know. After the way we met, I guess I should thank you for even thinking that I might help."

"You didn't seem all that happy about your situation," I said. "I had to hope I read you right." Once again, asking for help seemed to have worked out.

"Maybe someday you'll tell me what's going on," he said, "but thanks anyway." And we left it like that.

"Jimmy Fish is dead," I said as I turned to Molly.

"I guess I can go home then," she said.

"What?"

"I don't know anything, man. Jimmy Fish set up the job on you," she said. "Hell, he's been getting me jobs since he turned me out running cons. One of his so-called buddies—Vegas, Hollywood, or Richboy Land—would want to fuck a guy up, and I'd be the instrument of revenge."

"Isn't that just fucking lovely."

Then Molly explained just how lovely it had been.

Jimmy Fish and Rollie Molineaux had been childhood buddies, had grown up together, and gone to work roughnecking offshore out of Morgan City to support their garage band habit. They had been working on the rig floor together the day the backup cable on the cathead tongs broke and snapped Rollie's arm off clean as a police whistle. They had gone into the bar business with the insurance settlement. Rollie became the world's best one-armed bartender. Jimmy discovered that nobody wanted to listen to him sing, but he had a real talent for handling hecklers, running whores, and setting up cons. Even during his run as a semifamous comic and character actor, Jimmy Fish couldn't stop the gangster life.

"He never recovered from the fact that he wasn't going to be the Cajun Frank Sinatra," Molly said. "He always thought the audiences hated his act and him, that they were just laughing at him, so the gangster life gave him a way to be in charge. Running drugs and whores and cons."

"Sounds like a sweetheart."

"Except for the fact that he sort of raped me when I was thirteen, he had his moments," she said softly. "Sort of."

"Sort of?"

"Oh, hell," she sighed. "I was a goofy, gawky teenager, and he was Rollie's best friend, almost a member of the family, and sort of a celebrity, and we'd been drinking wine, so maybe I flirted with him a little bit. He'd bought Rollie a fishing boat, and I think maybe they were running a little coke or something for somebody, so one night when Rollie hadn't made it back yet . . . I don't know. You know what they say, shit's what happens while you're waitin' for life to start."

"That's what they say, I guess."

"But I don't think they really know," she said, then released a bark of laughter, short and sharp as if she was biting off a sob. "But what the hell, man, he paid for college all the way through my first year of law school, and he didn't bother me too much, then . . ."

"Then?"

"Oh, hell, the usual story. Some rich guy I was datin', he OD'd one night and suddenly I was in the middle of a cocaine bust I couldn't skate," she said slowly, "without help from Jimmy and his connections, then suddenly there didn't seem any sense in finishing law school, right, and I wasn't skinny anymore, so I started taking my clothes off for a living, and believe me I made a good living . . . until Jimmy showed me how to make a better one."

"When did you start running cons?" I asked.

"It seems like a long time ago," she said. "A hundred years. Jimmy turned me out on the cons, but I had already turned myself out as a whore. It started out as a way to get even with a john, a rich bastard who had fucked me over badly, then the next thing I knew, I discovered a talent for it . . ."

"I guess I can vouch for that," I said.

"And Jimmy had his moments. But they had become few and far between. Shit, I thought if I made the son of a bitch pay for it, he'd feel guilty enough to leave me alone. But he wouldn't stop. No matter how high I raised my price, he paid it. Until the other day when he decided to pound on me when I wouldn't give it up."

"What changed your mind?"

"I don't know," she whispered. "We've got too much history. I didn't know where else to hide after all this stuff down here went bad. I was scared, man. There was a dead cop, Jimmy wouldn't tell me what was going on, and I guess I got tired of him treating me like a whore.

"He wasn't always like that. After Rollie drank his way out of the bar business, Jimmy took care of him when I couldn't. Then the feds took his boat and started hanging on his ass like fat ticks like he was some kind of big-shit smuggler." Then she stopped, shook her head. "In the beginning, man, it was fun. More fun than the other part. Not that I hated the other part—the money and the clothes, the guys kissing my ass, the limos, the low-rent movie stars. But now . . . I don't know."

"Now?"

"I don't know," she repeated. "Sometimes it starts to feel like I'm just another fuckin' whore."

"But you don't have any idea who set me up?" I asked again.

"Not the vaguest," she said. "Jimmy set it up." Then she paused. "Did your friend shoot him?"

"Hell, no," I said, unlocking the shackle. "Jimmy's own hired help put one in his ear. So I guess that's the end of it. I'll take you to the airport when you're ready."

Molly glanced up quickly, a wild look in her eyes as they cut around the corn crib. "You know, man, suddenly I'm thinking maybe I should stay here for a while."

"What?"

"I don't know," she said, a small frightened grin on her face. "I don't know who hired you or for what and I don't know what the hell you've got in mind but maybe I can help."

"What?"

She stood up quickly. "Hey, man, listen. I think you're right. Maybe I should stay out of sight. Just until you clear this shit up."

"That'll be the day," I said, then suddenly tired and confused, I sighed and slumped over to sit on the cot. "How's your mother fit into all this?"

"I don't know," she said. "She was just some whitebread hard-shell Baptist kid from a little town outside Shreveport. Vivian, I think. She came down to Baton Rouge to do some cheerleading and sow a few wild oats, then got knocked up, so her redneck parents run her off and she wandered down to Lake Charles and went to work hopping tables for Rollie. That's what she was doing when I was born."

"So who knocked her up?" I asked, a question as aimless and pointless as when I asked Albert Homer why his wife left or how his father died.

"Some black basketball player at LSU," she said.

"Maybe you can help," I said, standing up. "Maybe you can help after all." I was on the scrambled cell phone to Carver D in a long heartbeat.

When I walked through the driving rainstorm to borrow Tom Ben's pickup again, he was sitting in the living room in his recliner, wrapped in his bathrobe, and sipping something that smelled like bourbon and honey. "Shit, son," he said, his voice hoarse and gravelly, "I should have let you walk me home last night."

"What happened?"

"Like an idiot I fell asleep in the rocking chair on the front porch, and woke up with this throat," he said, then tilted up his mug to finish the dregs. "Maria," he shouted over his shoulder, "*otra copa*." As I picked up the keys off the table, Maria, the tiny, stooped cook-housekeeper, came bustling into the living room bearing a steaming mug in her small hands. "So where you headed, son?"

"It's Saturday, man, and I'm going downtown to shop for ladies underwear," I said, and the old man smiled a moment before he started coughing.

Molly walked into the fancy woman's store like a queen wearing a sweat suit and plastic slippers, trailing me like a royal guardian. We'd stopped at a western store on the way to buy me a black cowboy hat and a black leather jacket, and I didn't make any secret of the Browning strapped under my arm. I hoped we looked like rich, eccentric Texans. If the response of the sales clerks was any indication, it worked. They nearly trampled us in their haste to serve. Molly was a quick study and obviously had shopped with other people's money before. We were in and out in thirty minutes. Molly looked like something worth guarding, elegant in a lilac cashmere suit, high-heeled knee-high boots, and a long sueded lambskin coat, and a matching floppy hat.

"How do I look?" she asked as she settled into the cluttered cab of Tom Ben's pickup.

"You have to ask?"

"A woman likes to hear it."

"Pretty classy," I said.

"Thanks," she said. "I feel pretty classy. So what am I supposed to do?"

"Just stand outside the pickup," I said, "and don't run away."

"That's easy enough," she said, then patted my leg, smiling.

Jonas Walker stood just inside the doorway of his church, as he said he would over the telephone, glaring at me through the slanting rain as I walked up the steps. I stopped beside him, then turned to watch Molly climb out of the pickup, then lean against the pickup, professionally elegant.

"What do you want?" Jonas Walker asked without hesitation. "What the hell is so important that you'd take me away from my family on Saturday night?" he demanded, drawing himself up to his full height as if he could intimidate me.

"Well, let's see," I said. "First off, I want a little respect."

"What?" The large man doubled up his giant fists.

"Respect," I said. "That's important. Then I want to introduce you to the daughter you abandoned all those years ago. She's a high-class hooker and a professional con artist, but compared to you, man, she's a saint. I'm sure your congregation will appreciate meeting her."

"My flock knows about my troubled life and the sinful days in my youth," he said without much conviction.

"You've told them, of course, about the cocaine bust that got you thrown off the LSU basketball team and would have gotten you a jolt in Angola if the coach hadn't called in some political favors." Jonas Walker had nothing to say. The deep, angry lines around his mouth said it all. "And if that's not enough to gain your respect, you phony asshole, I've got enough financial information about you, your church, and Mr. Hayden Lomax to keep the IRS and a dozen forensic accountants busy for years."

"I'll ask you one last time," he growled. "What do you want?"

"Where's your brother?"

"Montana," he answered slowly, as if he didn't want to give him up but had no choice. "Up in Montana."

Of all the answers I might have expected, that was the last. "What the hell? Where?" was all I could say.

"Lomax has a place north of Livingston," he said. "Some kind of experimental mine site. Trying to cook minerals out of bad ore, I think. It's about halfway between Wilsall and Ringling, off to the east. You'll see some dirt roads leading to some gas leases. At the end of one of those roads, you'll find an abandoned mine called Punky Creek and a small steel building. Enos is guarding the machinery or some such bullshit while it's being sold off." Then he paused.

"That's a hell of a place to hide a black man that size," I said.

"That's the point," he said. "He gets bored, he drives to Billings, gets on a plane, flies to Denver or Seattle, flies back when he gets tired." Once again he hesitated.

"Is he up there alone?"

"He was when I dropped him there," he admitted grimly.

"You drove him up?" I asked.

"In the church van," Walker muttered, finally ashamed.

"What's the rest of it?"

"Ah, hell, man, I think he's cooking crank, too. He's a crazy man. Always has been." Then he began to explain like a lowlife talking to the law, "You don't appreciate my problem, man. I owe him."

"I know exactly how it is," I said. "He took the Tulsa bust and left you out of it, right? You better goddamn understand, I'd appreciate it if he didn't know I was coming to visit," I said. "And believe me, man, I'll tear this fucking church scam down around your ears."

"Believe me, brother," he said, "I've regretted abandoning my daughter all these many years. I've spent many, many hours on my knees in prayer, asking for God's forgiveness."

"Hey, man," I said, "people who actually give a shit do something about it. Praying is for people who ain't doing anything. As far as I'm concerned, you're an unforgivable asshole. And by the way, I am not your fucking brother."

Jonas Walker nodded once, sadness heavy on his giant face,

glanced once at Molly, then stepped into the church, slamming the heavy door, locking himself inside with his God and his memories. I didn't envy either one of them.

"What was that all about?" Molly wanted to know as we drove away in the fading light.

"That was a man's past coming home to roost on his shoulder like a dead crow," I said, sliding out of my shoulder holster, then she shoved the rig into my war bag for me.

"That was my father, wasn't it?" she said.

"No. Your father is the man who raised you," I pointed out. "And much as I dislike Rollie, he wouldn't have given you up even if I had put his last hand into the fire." Molly seemed to engender loyalty in even the worst of men. I suspected that even Jimmy Fish had been killed because he wouldn't give her up. At least not until he got her back. "Rollie's your father."

"You're right," she said calmly as if suddenly cheered. "Thanks. What now?"

"Let's find a place to eat that deserves your new wardrobe," I said. "Then I've got an all-night stakeout."

"Sounds like a date," she said. "Can I come along?"

"Damn right it's a date," I said, grinning suddenly as she kissed me, our faces hot in the cold rain, a fire that not even this cold Texas rain could quench. Whatever had happened between Betty and me, this wasn't part of it. "Then tomorrow morning I've got to stash you somewhere so I can go to Montana. I don't seem to be doing any good down here."

"Great," she said, then punched me on the shoulder. "I've never been to Montana. Went to Pocatello, Idaho, once to ruin a state senator's life for a timber company."

"Montana isn't the same sort of place," I said, "or this the same kind of job." Molly turned her face to the rain-streaked window. "Shit, I'm sorry," I said quickly. "Really sorry. You didn't deserve that. These people down here are making me into an asshole." She didn't deserve my judgment. Molly was just another version of the capitalist success story: buy low, sell high, fuck the consumer. "I could probably use some help with the driving," I said by way of apology. "Please."

"You're going to drive? Why not fly?" she asked. She seemed to have forgiven my mean-spirited witlessness.

"Airplanes leave tracks," I said. Then admitted, "It's never a good time of the year to fly to Montana, and only February is worse than December. If the weather holds, we can make it in two hard days. Or three easy ones."

"I could go for some easy times," she said. "Somehow I feel like I've earned them."

"Me, too. Let's start with a decent meal," I said, then dialed Jeffrey's to see if they'd had a reservation cancellation.

"Good idea," she said, patting my leg again, leaving her warm hand on my thigh as we crossed town on our way to dinner.

Red called during dinner, so I stepped outside the restaurant to talk to him. He was fine, his mother was fine, and things had gone down pretty much as Fresno had recounted them, Red said, except he didn't point out how calm the Frenchman had been when he put the round in Jimmy Fish's head.

"Man," he squealed, "I seen some cold shit in Detroit, and I wouldn't have minded puttin' a pill in the little motherfucker's head myself, but that Frenchman was one cold piece of work."

"I'll send you a check, Red, and you send me the phone."

There was a long pause on the other end of the phone. "You done overpaid me, man," he said, sounding hurt. "We're cool."

"I'm the old guy here, Red. I'll decide when we're cool."

Austin was so full of pickups, I didn't think another one would look out of place in Albert Homer's neighborhood, and Tom Ben had told me in a hoarse growl that he didn't think he'd be needing his this night, so Molly and I parked it down the street from Homer's studio just after midnight. Just a couple of rednecks spooning. We changed locations a couple of times, and Molly proved to be a good companion on a stakeout. She didn't have any trouble holding her bladder and she held up her end of the hushed conversations. I wished for a touch of Billy Long's coke, which was still stashed in the foot locker. I had to make do with convenience store coffee that was almost thick enough to snort. Then maybe we got a little deep into our ruse toward false dawn. Molly saw the black van with its headlights off stopped in front of Homer's mailbox before I did.

Except for Molly's soft company, the night was a waste. The van sped away from Homer's so quickly that it was already on the Interstate heading south before it turned its headlights on, but by that time I was too far behind it to read the license plate or even tell what kind of van it was.

"Well, that was a waste of time," I said.

"Not completely," Molly said, her voice muffled against my leg as she slipped into an easy sleep, her breath warm on my thigh.

CHAPTER THIRTEEN

By THE TIME we got back to Tom Ben's, the sun had risen to obscurity behind the avalanche of roiling, slate-gray clouds that filled the sky. When I parked the truck in front of the main house, the housekeeper, Maria, rushed out on the porch, waving her arms and shouting at me. I couldn't make out the Spanish but I could tell it wasn't good.

I jumped out of the cab, Molly right behind me. The housekeeper looked at us oddly, rumpled and sleepy in our fancy clothes. Inside, the old man was slumped in the recliner. He had his bib overalls on but only one boot, and his mouth gaped open and shut like a fish as he struggled for breath. The front of his shirt was soaked but his pale forehead was as dry and hot as a stove pipe. A thick string of spittle drifted down his chin. The gnarled fingers of his trembling right hand clutched the black stub of his pipe.

"He don't wake up," the housekeeper kept moaning. "He don't wake up."

"Where the hell is everybody?"

"The bulls," she muttered, "the bulls are in the road. The men round them up . . ."

"Probably a case of raging pneumonia," I said to Molly, "but maybe he's had a stroke, too. I'm going to call a chopper. Get some blankets."

The old man was still alive and, according to the paramedics, stabilized as the chopper took off from the front yard half an hour later. Even his color was better as soon as they got an oxygen mask on him. The distraught housekeeper fell back on the household routine. Before Molly and I could leave, we had to sit down to huge plates of *huevos rancheros* and eat just to keep the old woman from bursting into tears.

So by the time we got back to the barn to pack for the trip to Montana, we were yawning so hard our jaws cracked. We were stretched out on the cot in our clothes and almost asleep when the rounds started punching through the Caddy. First, I heard the pops and tinkle of glass as a headlight was shot out, then the following echoes of the rifle's fire. Then the flat slaps as the shooter ran half a dozen rounds into the body of the Caddy. The sniper hadn't bothered with a suppressor this time and had brought a larger bore assault rifle. It sounded larger, maybe an M-14 or an AK. I found a crack to peer through. A dark van was parked to block the road on a rise just out of pistol range, semiautomatic gunfire pouring out of the dark interior through the open side door. They had probably cut the fences so Tom Ben and hands would have their hands full horsing his bulls out of the highway.

"Some son of a bitch is shooting holes in my Cadillac," I said. "And if we go outside, he's gonna shoot holes in us," I said, unlocking the foot locker. I grabbed the Mini 14, stuck it through the crack in the main door, and ran a clip through it. Mostly the rounds just raised dust, but a couple smacked into the side of the van. It backed off a hundred yards or so, then the firing began again. I turned to Molly. "Grab whatever you can carry," I said. "It's time to run." I gathered the cash, the fake ID, the cocaine, and a bagful of clips and stuffed them into my war bag when the rounds started punching through the metal walls about waist-high, moving back and forth, steady searching fire.

No time for explanations now. I grabbed Molly's arm, pulled her down to the floor, then dragged her out of the corn crib over to the large drain in the center of the barn, jerked off the iron grate, and stuffed her inside. The drain would give us a little cover. I went in right behind her. It was just large enough for us to slither through the old milk and cowshit, while round after round punched through the tin walls, ricocheted off the concrete floor, whirring like shrapnel until they slammed into a stall or one of the opposite walls. We bellied our way out to the abandoned drain pit behind the barn, where we rested for a few moments, then dashed for the safety of a dry wash. I leaned over the side of the wash with the Mini 14, but the black van remained hidden, pumping rounds into the barn.

"What the hell's going on?" she asked breathlessly.

"I guess whoever's been trying to kill me has decided that they don't have to be subtle anymore," I said, and she managed a wry, smudged smile, and didn't complain as we trudged up a muddy path out of the wash, then ran toward the safety of a low rise just beyond.

Without the sun and no real sense of the lay of the ranch land, I just assumed that the wind and rain came from the northwest, so we marched straight into it as best we could across the broken terrain. We only paused for short rests and to take down electric fences in our way. In the second or third pasture, we came across an idle D-9 Cat with a root plow attached to it. I bent the barrel of the Mini 14 prying the padlock off the toolbox, then discarded it. I picked out a large screwdriver, a pair of pliers, and a roll of duct tape, then used the pliers to steal the battery.

"Okay," she said, "I gotta ask. Where the hell are we going?"

"You'll never guess," I said, tucked the battery under my arm, then led the way into the storm. Neither of us looked behind us at the soft explosion and the plume of smoke that had to be my Cadillac burning to the ground.

"Goddammit, I loved that car," I said. "I'm gonna have the hide and hair off somebody's ass for that little deal."

"It's just a car," Molly said.

"You got to be kidding," I said. "That was my last permanent address."

She chuckled a moment, then we moved on silently into the brisk wind.

Several hours later, convinced that the van hadn't followed us, we crossed the final ridge. The rain eased into a light mist, but the wind and scudding clouds didn't relent. Down in a shallow hollow, the catch pond gleamed like a dull silver dollar, the line shack leaning beside it.

The tires could have used some air, the Cat's battery had to be duct taped into place, but it was a classic short box GMC V-6 four-wheel-drive, the keys were in the ignition, and the engine nearly fired on the first try. It didn't take too long, though, until the tough little V-6 ran fairly smoothly. While I cleaned up as best I could in the shallow pond, Molly turned the heater on high and disposed of the spiderwebs and dirt dauber nests in the cab of the pickup. While I dried out in the blowing heater vents, Molly went to the pond to clean up.

I had just washed the mud and cowshit off my clothes with wet rags, but as I watched through the broken door of the line shack, Molly took off her clothes and waded into the pond. Standing thigh-deep in the chill wind and water as she washed her clothes, her skin darkened into a coppery, ebony shine I would have never seen without that ashen light, and when I stood naked on the edge of the pond, she raised her nose into the wind as if she could smell me coming. Her nipples were as hard as ice cubes, but inside she was as warm and soft as the ashes of a cooking fire. As I stood anchored in the soft mud of the bottom of the pond, my toes curled like talons, her long legs locked around my hips, one arm around my neck, the other pounding on my shoulders, her head back, neck arched into a quivering cord of muscle, her teeth gleaming in the feral Texas light.

Once we were back in the pickup, dressed and drying out, I removed the butterfly bandages and cleaned the faint wound, and

Molly smiled and asked me, "Two questions, old man? What the hell was that about?"

"Just about as much fun as old men get to have, lady."

"And how the hell did you know how to find this place?"

"Tom Ben told me where it was when he told me about you," I said. "He thought the truck was too fine a piece of machinery to bury in the pond. And we had a little luck."

"A little luck?"

"It's Sunday."

"I'm sorry, but what the hell's that got to do with it?"

"I don't believe that bulldozer driver would have let me have his battery," I said. "But it was his day off."

"So what do we do now?"

"Somebody got it in here," I said, "so we can get it out. A little air in the tires, a little gas in the tank, and a couple of stolen license plates, then we're goin' to Montan' to throw the hoolihan."

"What the hell's that?"

"Either some kind of cowboy party or a double-looped rope. Nobody seems to be exactly sure."

"I vote for the cowboy party part," she said. "But you're going to have to do something about that hat."

"Now I've got a couple of questions for you."

"What's that?"

"Where'd you get this truck?"

"It was waiting in the airport parking lot," she said. "Keys over the visor, directions to the old man's place in the glove box. I'd done all my research before I left Vegas—law school was at least good for something."

"What did you do with the option you got Tom Ben to sign?" I asked.

She laughed, kissed me on the cheek, then whispered in my ear.

I had to laugh, then asked, "You still have it?"

"Nope," she said. "When I finally got back to Vegas, I gave it to Jimmy Fish, but I think it stunk too much to do anybody any good."

"Just the rumor of it made a lot of people uncomfortable," I said.

"They weren't the only ones," she said, then laughed again.

We picked up a set of stolen plates off a closed used car lot in Junction, then swapped again in Del Rio, driving straight through all the way to El Paso, where we checked into the El Camino downtown as Mr. & Mrs. Hardy P. Malvern the next afternoon. I left Molly lolling in a bubble bath while I drove across the border and parked around the corner from the Kentucky Club, leaving the keys in the truck, then had two margaritas at the Kentucky Club, and assumed the classic pickup had disappeared before I crossed the murky, shallow waters of the Rio Bravo del Norte. I called Carver D on the scrambled cell phone, asked him to check out the expired plates and the VIN on the pickup, then woke Molly long enough for room service Mexican food, and to send our clothes out to be cleaned, then we made love and slept the sleep of the newly alive until they returned our clothes the next morning. Then we took a cab to the airport where Hardy P. Malvern rented a Jeep Cherokee, and we headed north to Montana.

It had been so long since I had been in Livingston that the last thing I expected was to see somebody I knew when we checked into the Murray Hotel two nights later. When I handed the night clerk, a woman who looked remarkably like Carol Channing's little sister, enough cash for three nights, she looked at the Hardy P. Malvern name on the registration card, then glanced back up at me, saying "Don't I know you, partner?"

"Never been here before, ma'am," I lied, but she looked as if she didn't believe me. I couldn't remember when I last stood in front of her, but she almost remembered.

"I'll need your license plate number," she said, tapping the registration card with a long fingernail, "and some ID."

"I thought Montana was supposed to be a neighborly place," I said, then turned my back to the counter to dig into my billfold for Hardy's driver's license. In the reflection of the plate glass window, I looked like the survivor of a terrible car wreck that only my hat survived. Then I couldn't remember the license plate number on the Jeep. We had driven straight through from El Paso, and my head was still ringing with road miles, my eyes blurred with the images of drifting snow, and my nose burning with the bitter cut of the coke. "Honey," I said, "I've forgotten the plate number again. You want to check it for me?"

"Your driver's license expires next month, sir," the night clerk said suspiciously as she handed it back to me.

But Molly saved us. She touched my arm, smiled, then turned, walked through the front door on her high-heeled boots as steady as a schooner in a freshening breeze. I might look like death microwaved, but Molly was a lady.

"You better take care of it, Mr. Malvern," the night clerk said, then smiled happily as she handed the license back to me.

"You don't have a typewriter I can borrow?" I said.

"Be careful," she said as she pulled a battered portable from under the desk. "It's an antique. And supposedly haunted. If it starts cussing at you, throw a shot of Wild Turkey down its throat."

When the rented Jeep was finally stuck in the lot, and the Macallan poured over ice, I sighed. The room was long and narrow, filled with comfortable old furniture. Outside, the Livingston wind, as cold as a developer's heart and as hard as a crap shooter's luck, roared down out of the Absarokas, throwing pellets of corn snow against the windows like a rattle of distant automatic gunfire. But we were safe and warm and home.

"We made it," Molly said. "I can't believe it."

"At least we're this far," I said. "Maybe tomorrow we'll make it the rest of the way." On the endless trip I had told Molly everything I knew about what had happened to me. I had left out the part about her hypocrite of a natural father because I assumed that she didn't need to know that. I had learned a long time before that my father had killed himself because he was in love with another woman and afraid to tell my mother. It wasn't a decision I would have made, but it was a long time ago. It had to be better for Molly to think of her father as a tough little one-armed son of a bitch who would take me on with a bottle rather than tell me where she was. "But that won't be the end," I said. "I still have to go back to Texas."

"Do what you have to," she said, picking up my hand and holding it to her lips, "and we'll work it out."

I was back in Montana, right, but that wasn't the only reason my heart sang like the wind. Molly's blue eyes no longer looked like a false dawn but were shining with what I hoped was hope. Then I turned to the typewriter.

It took all the next morning to get some cold weather clothes— winter underwear, insulated coveralls, gloves, and pacs—and a set of chains for the Jeep. We were heading for dirt roads and the weather on this side of the Divide could change quicker than the price of wheat futures. I packed the remaining cocaine and weapons in my war bag, checked with Molly one more time, who sat in front of the dresser mirror trying to make her hair fit attractively under a Scotch plaid hat.

"I'm along for the ride, honey," she said.

"I'll be back in a minute," I said.

Downstairs I stopped by the desk and returned the typewriter to a tall man with a dark beard, then hiked across the street to the dark, dingy bar where I had spent some time in the past.

The same ex-biker still stood behind the stick, waiting for something. He bounced down the bar toward me, and I held my finger up to my lips.

"Hell, it wouldn't have mattered, man," the bartender said. "I almost didn't recognize you in that get-up. Where did you get that hat?"

"Ran over a cowboy outside Laramie."

"That explains it," he said. "What can I do for you?"

"Let me have a shot of schnapps and a cup of coffee," I said, pulling an envelope out of the insulated Carhart's. "Then I want you to hold this for a while. If I don't show up in a few days, mail it."

The bartender looked at the address. "He's in fucking law school? Jesus, I thought he'd be in the slam by now."

"Me, too, man. Me, too."

When we were ready, we drove north toward winter.

The only constant things about the drive up Highway 89 were the wind falling in icy flows off the Crazies and the stretches of black ice covering the old highway. We made it to the lease roads with plenty of light left. They were hard-frozen, so I didn't bother putting the chains on the Jeep. Mostly we found dead ends, but just at dark I spotted a small, bullet-pocked sign pointing to the Punky Creek Mine. Except for random skiffs of scudding clouds, the sky had cleared, and the rising moon gave me enough light to follow the quickly freezing ruts up a dry creek that looked as if it had been washed, then dredged, and now the company was working the tailings for lost seeds and misplaced figments of gold-limned quartz.

At the head of the draw, the switchbacks led to a flat place just in front of a small metal building beside a large rock crusher and in front of a dark adit. Off to the side, a small Christmas tree set over the natural gas well that powered the machinery and heated the building. A Chevy Suburban was parked in front. All the lights in the building were on and light smoke poured sideways from the natural gas heater's stove pipes on the roof. Through the sweep of the wind, I could hear the rumble of a generator and the boom of a bass line. A satellite dish loomed like a gray moon from the southeast corner. All the comforts of home. I turned around at the bottom of the first switchback, left the Jeep idling, then stepped out, telling Molly, "I'm going to check it out. Any trouble, baby, you run."

"What kind of partnership is that?"

"The kind that survives," I said, then took off up the trail.

The building's windows hadn't been washed in a long time, but

I could still see Enos sitting at a table, listlessly playing solitaire while the large television boomed with rap music, half a bottle of Crown Royal on the table in front of him beside a large pile of white powder. At the end of the table a stack of cardboard boxes sat like a wall. He was alone and didn't look like he was going anywhere anytime soon. I assumed that daylight would be a better time to renew our acquaintance. So I slipped back down to the Jeep and drove us back to Livingston just as the weather changed again. The wind suddenly boomed in from the Canadian border like an invasion of geese, thick feathers of downy snow rippling down the dark sky.

While I had a couple of warm-up drinks at the Owl, Molly had done a good job cleaning up the remains of our traveling clothes. Even my cowboy hat looked as if it had new life, and Molly looked like a million dollars in the soft sweep of the cashmere suit, the dark drapes of her black hair swinging back from her high, smooth forehead. I kissed the faint scar, then said, "Tired of eating in the room?"

"Won't somebody recognize us?" she asked, laughing.

"We'll keep our sunglasses on," I said. "Maybe they'll think we're from Hollywood."

"I gotta ask," she said. "What happens when this shit's over?"

"Drift through Vegas, pick up your stuff, and disappear," I said.

"I've always wanted to go to Paris," she said softly.

"Look out, Paris," I said. "Here we come."

And we laughed as if life could begin all over again.

We found a quiet dinner at Chatham's Bar & Grill, a couple of good Scotches, a bottle of wine, and a couple of steaks worth dying for. Then we walked back to the hotel in the blizzard.

"What do people do here in the wintertime?" she asked, the wind nearly whipping away her words.

"Well, when winter really starts," I said, "they drink and fight and fuck and bet on when the chicken shits. Get divorced, kill each other, fall in love," I added. "Just like normal life. Or what passes for normal life in a Montana winter."

"Sounds like fun," she said as she struggled with the hotel door. "How come you left?"

"I guess I made the mistake of thinking love was more important than fun," I said.

"Or disconnected from it," Molly said, then we stepped into the
warm safety of the hotel. "I guess I grew up so fast I never knew
much about it."

As it turned out, neither did I. Not until now. We spent the rest
of the night doing our best to discover what we had both missed. We
nearly made it.

The next afternoon we checked out of the hotel, then drove out
to Punky Creek. As we parked in front of the small steel building,
the music boomed and the snowstorm rattled, but the noise must
not have covered the sound of our arrival, because when Enos
opened the front door, he had the huge automatic stuffed into his
belt. "You folks lost?" he said, waving us in out of the blizzard.

"Not exactly, Mr. Walker," I said, "but we could use some directions."

"You ought not to be out in this kind of shit," he said. "Ain't fit
for visiting."

"It's important that I talk to you, Mr. Walker," I said as I removed my gloves, hood, and sunglasses.

"What the fuck? You're that old son of a bitch from Duval's
place," Walker said, then stepped back to consider us and our arrival
at his hideout. At the end of the table one of the large cardboard
boxes was half-unloaded. It didn't take a genius to realize that Enos
was unpacking a meth lab.

"What the fuck are you doin' here?"

"Pat me down," I said, leaning into a steel support. "I'm clean."
I had assumed that this wasn't the time to be armed.

"Pat you down, my ass," he said, pulling the large pistol out of
his belt and flopping into a chair. "Man, you strip. And you, bitch,
you lock your hands behind your head, and don't fucking move. I'll
deal with you later."

"This is a hell of a place to be cooking meth," I said as I was undressing.

"I can't get off on that fuckin' coke anymore," Enos said. "And the bastards who stole my money, this is the only stake they'll give me to get back in the coke business. So I'm working my way back into the good times."

"Lomax?" I said.

But Walker just laughed. Once I was down to my T-shirt and shorts, Walker made me lock my hands behind my neck, while Molly stripped to her thermal underwear.

"Well, at least you people are clean," he said, "so come over here and sit down." He motioned to a worktable with several swivel chairs around it. I sat beside him. Molly sat on the other side of the table. Walker shoved a partially eaten microwave dinner to one side. An almost full bottle of Crown Royal stood beside ten or twelve long, sloppy lines of cocaine, lines like drifts or sand dunes, that had been chopped along the side of the table. As we sat down, Walker grabbed a straw and huffed two of the huge lines. "You understand, this ain't exactly an ideal time for me, man. I'm up here all alone, with this fuckin' meth to cook, and you two are the first human beings I've seen in two weeks. So I gotta ask what the hell you're doin'? If you ain't delivering money, drugs, or pussy, what business you got botherin' me?"

"I started off looking for you so I could keep the state of Texas from jabbing a needle in your arm," I said calmly, "then somebody started popping caps in my direction, and now I guess I'm looking for Mandy Rae and some answers."

The burst of his laughter banged the sides of the building like a twelve-pound sledge. "Mandy Rae. Shit, man, she's been dead for years. After Duval got shot that night, there was too much heat to work, so she split for France to move into the heroin trade. Perfect business for a bitch like that. When I was in the slam, I heard that the Corsicans blew up her car. She was a real pain in the ass, man, she always had to be running things, to be in charge of everything. Hell, if she wasn't dead, I'd kill her myself. I know damn well she dropped the dime on me when me and my brother went into business on our own."

"I think it's a quarter now," I said. "Where'd she get the cocaine?"

Walker laughed and reached for the bottle, saying maybe we should have a drink. "You think she'd give up her source to a Mandingo nigger like me? Hell, no. Not a chance." He hit the bottle hard, then looked at me and said, "But you still be wanting something else, don't you? You one of them unsatisfied white motherfuckers. You think if you know some shit, it'll make everything better? You don't know shit."

"You might be right. But I think if you'll come back to Texas with me, Walker," I said. "And roll over on Mandy Rae, Sissy Duval, and Hayden Lomax, I can help you beat the Billy Long murder charges."

"Billy Long's murder charges," he said, then laughed for a long time before he did another line, then hit the bottle again. "Fuck the small stuff. Mandy Rae, man, she's long dead. Hayden Lomax, hell, he owns the world down there, and you couldn't touch him in a hundred years. And Sissy Duval, she's just a silly piece of ass. She liked it up the old dirt track even better than her husband did. Fuck her. And all them other cunts." Then he paused to hit the bottle again. "Billy Long, that racist fucker, he don't count for nothin'. Nobody gives a shit that he's dead. I'm clean on that one. I'm clean here. Come spring, I'll sell all this shit to some Mexicans over in Yakima, then I've got some South American plans." He hit the bottle again. "Look at it from my point of view," he said, then stood up.

"That's what got me in trouble, Walker," I said. "Looking at it from your point of view. Now I'm thinking I should have just walked away."

"Maybe you should have walked away, man. What's to keep me from poppin' your ass, then runnin' it through the rock crusher?"

"Just me," I said.

"Milo," Molly whispered.

"By the way, who is that fine lady?" Enos asked. I didn't tell him.

"Maybe we ought to forget all this and go," she whispered, staring at the pistol swinging casually in his hand.

"Go!" Enos shouted before I could agree with her. "Shit, the party's just gettin' off the ground, girl. Hey, girl, let's see what you got under that other shit."

"Don't fuck with me, man," I said. "I'll sic Lomax on your ass."

Walker was suddenly no longer interested in Molly. "What's that you say?"

"Lomax sent me to look for you," I said, lying as fast as I could.

"That's your bad luck, old man," Walker muttered. "I ain't ever doin' no more time." Then without another word, Walker backhanded me on the side of the head so hard that I lifted out of the chair and fairly flew across the room, smacked into the side of one of the roaring gas heaters with the side of my neck and shoulder, then bounced hard to the concrete floor. I didn't have a second to appreciate my scrapes and burns before Walker kicked me in the side with his work boots. I had a moment to feel the left arm and several ribs crack before he stuffed the pistol in his waistband and jerked me upright to smash me full in the face with his giant fist. I felt my nose flatten and several teeth splinter. I guess I should have been surprised that he hadn't knocked my eyes right out of their sockets. When he picked me up again, at least I got the remains of my nose out of the way of his fist, but he caught me high on the forehead. I rolled over the heater again, then landed on a pile of rock-crusher bits. Then Walker picked me up again. I was done, all my strings were broken, my limbs dangling like broken wings. Piss ran down my leg, shit dribbled whenever it wanted, blood filled my eyes.

Before he could hit me again, through the billowing fog of shock, I heard Molly scream "No!" Then a sharp pop. I grabbed weakly at Walker's pistol, but he swatted me away like a gnat, then I heard another crack, followed by an explosion, then he released me. I tumbled to the cold floor as softly as a black feather, glancing off the bulk of the gas heater again, the smell of burning skin rank in the bloody, crooked remains of my nose.

Sometimes you don't get a chance to say goodbye. Sounds maudlin, but it's true. I don't know how long it took Molly to die. The .50 Magnum round had taken her just two fingers to the left of her right hipbone, right in the center of that lovely dimple which I would never taste again, then essentially blown her right buttock off. Even if I'd been conscious, I probably couldn't have saved her. Enos Walker was beyond saving, too. One of the .22 rounds from the derringer she had stolen out of my war bag and secreted in her purse had glanced off his teeth and harmlessly out of his cheek. The other, though, had gone up his left nostril, and, I suspected, kicked around his brain pan like a marble in a urinal. He probably was dead when he pulled the trigger. No one will ever know.

Once I was vaguely mobile, I crawled to Molly but there was nothing beyond her eyes, just that other country where the dead go, and when I held my face to hers, I just stained her beauty with my bloody snot. Then I crawled to the door and into the blizzard, burying myself into a small snowbank beside the shed, just long enough to stop the burning on my neck and back, then staggered to the pickup, and gobbled a handful of codeine. When I stumbled back inside, I struggled into my insulated Carhart's and pacs, listening to the tiny rat's teeth of bone grinding every time I moved my left elbow. Next came the first of many hard parts. To make my nose resemble one. It took three tries, even packed with wads of Walker's cocaine. The result wasn't anything that my friends would recognize, but it stopped flopping around my face. It didn't work as well as it once did, either, but I had enough coke left to pack the nostrils, plus some left over to pack into the bloody slots where teeth used to hang out. Then the necessary shit. Somehow I had to get out of there.

By the time I had taken care of everything, the snowstorm had blown itself out, and the sun sat low in the southwestern sky, hanging just over the snow-packed peaks of the Bridgers, the bare golden ridges of short grass banked by blue clots of snow glittering like frozen rivers. The wind had turned. Icy torrents roared off the Crazies behind me, blasted the afternoon, blowing the tears off my cheeks before they could freeze. South, the Absarokas gleamed with frozen snow and even harder rock, shining distant and dangerous like polar mirages against the clotted sky.

Welcome home, I thought, *welcome fucking home.*

CHAPTER FOURTEEN

ALTHOUGH IT WAS not yet April, it could have passed for a summer dusk in the real world, except for a small, aimless wind and the lingering chill of the last in a series of wet northers that had plagued the Hill Country winter. The pungent, musky cedar fragrance mingled lightly with the damp but dry limestone wafting on the cool air. The cloudless horizon burned like a distant grass fire. CJ, as Carol Jean Warren said we should call her, stepped out of the front door of Tom Ben's house as former deputy sheriff Bob Culbertson drove up. She patted my shoulder and tucked my windbreaker closer around my shoulders as if I was some ancient grandfather, and the movement set the rocking chair in motion for a long second. I waited for the black discs and the waves of nausea, echoes of the concussion, that sometimes still came with the rocking, but they didn't come, so I continued whittling at the scrap of cedar in my hands. I wished her good luck. CJ told me good night, kissed the top of my head, then headed down the walk to Bob's pickup, her pool cue case cocky over her shoulder. Bob climbed out of his pickup to meet her at the bottom of the walk. They chatted a few minutes standing beside the pickup. With skinny butts tightly packed into jeans, cowboy shirts topped by down vests, they could have been siblings. Or lovers. Which I suspected they had become in the weeks they had been working for me. But they showed no sign as they parted. She climbed into his pickup and drove away. Bob ambled up to the veranda, scattering the small goats, then stopped in front of me, smiling.

"You ready to beat the shit out of somebody, old man?" Out of uniform, Bob had the face of a boy scout.

I stood up and stretched. The dead man's ligament in my right knee felt a little stiff in spite of, or because of, the long workout I had endured that morning; I would have sworn that the pins in my elbow ached in the unseasonable evening chill. The skin grafts on my neck and shoulder felt like sun-dried leather. But when I stiff-armed Bob's shoulder with my right palm, he stepped back, grinning.

"Who are you calling an old man, kid?" I said. "Besides, we're just looking for some polite conversation."

Well, I was old, true enough. A man can't turn sixty in a hospital bed without feeling old. I was old even before I made it to the hospital in Billings. It took hours and almost all the rest of Enos Walker's cocaine to organize the scene at the Punky Creek Mine building. At least Carver D said it was nine o'clock his time when I called him on the scrambled cell phone as soon as I reached the back door of the Owl, called to ask him to call my ex-partner to ask him to drive over from Meriwether to help me. Then I pulled up my jacket hood, and hobbled into the bar, almost invisible among the other late night drinkers. The bartender handed me the worthless manila envelope full of worthless truths. I tore it into small pieces and fed it into the toilet. Then I settled into a long wait of nips of cocaine and slow sips of Absolut.

I'd wanted to carry Molly's torn body away with me but I couldn't think what to do with it. Wear it around my neck like the fatal, final albatross of my life, a sign of all my mistakes and foolishness. I didn't think I was going to need a visible sign of all that. But I did take the Shark of the Moon and hang it around my neck.

I had used up most of my energy to pile up the meth lab and drag the bodies into the stacks. My attitude toward Enos Walker was oddly benign. Whatever mistakes he had made in his life, I had to admit that my half-assed quest was at least as much for my own benefit as his. I didn't even complain too much that the son of a bitch weighed nearly three hundred pounds. Getting him under the meth lab was like dragging a live bull calf to a denutting. And when I got him under the end table, I hooked his thumb around the trigger of the Desert Eagle pistol and blew most of his fucking head off. The pathologist, should one ever turn up, would have a hell of a time tracing the path of the .22 round that had bounded around inside his skull like a crazed mouse and scrambled his brains like an omelet.

I was afraid to drag Molly into the pile, afraid her destroyed leg would rip off her body. I didn't think I could stand that. So I picked her up, even with my broken arm, then carried her to the table and placed her among the meth chemicals. As the winter dusk settled like an ashen cloud, I closed her eyes and stroked her face until I knew I had to go.

First, I turned off the gas to the heaters until the flames died, then turned it back on again, and set the crude cigarette and matchbox fuse, and finally staggered out to drive shakily away. I was halfway to Wilsall when the gas-filled building went off. It lit up the sky like a bomb, like the end of the world, and with any luck the natural gas and the ether would burn hot enough and long enough to destroy any fingerprints I might have missed inside the building. Whatever tire prints I might have left on the frozen road would be wiped out by the first rural fire truck up the track.

During the endless, wandering drive to Livingston, I discovered a long sharp pain in my right knee that somehow I hadn't noticed yet, plus the disturbing fact that the little finger on my right hand was half its normal size. But it didn't hurt. I stopped in Wilsall, did another bump of cocaine, and pulled my little finger out of my hand. That got me to the Owl.

Where I huddled on a stool near the front door, sick with the waste of Enos Walker's life. I could have saved him—saved all of us—if he'd just given me a chance. Molly's death had left me as empty as a whiskey bottle in a Hangtown gutter. Whatever she might have been in her earlier life, in my part of it she had been a beauty, a tough, stand-up, fearless partner, and I knew that I would never be able to replace her. Those light blue eyes fading to gray, then into impenetrable, dark distance—that would never go away. No matter how many times I lifted the water glass of vodka, no matter how much shit I stuffed into my broken nose, the black stone was going to hang cold over my heart until the end.

By driving like a madman, my ex-partner managed to show up from Meriwether just before closing time. He didn't ask any questions he didn't want to know the answers to, and dealt with the shit. On the way to Billings, he dumped the weapons, the cocaine, the codeine, and the fake identification into the depths of a deserted construction site in Columbus, followed by a sack of traction sand, a hole where once spring arrived and the cement was poured and the asphalt laid, except for memories, that part of my life would disappear. Then he took most of my extra cash and promised to mail it to Petey, then dropped me down the street from the emergency room entrance of Deaconess in Billings before he drove up to the airport to leave the Cherokee in the rental car lot. He would take the bus to Livingston the next morning, and we would leave no tracks. I wandered over to sit on the curb, stoned and drunk, waiting to die.

"Tell me about it some time, old man," was the last thing he said before he drove away.

I couldn't tell if it was the cold wind, pain, or just my life that filled my swelling eyes with salty tears.

My insurance was current, plus my checks cleared, and I even had a stash of cash in a hidden compartment in my war bag, and it was Montana so the hospital treated me like a human being, once I was willing to pay for a private room, and the police finally got bored and bought my story that I'd picked up a couple of hitchhikers who'd beaten me senseless and stolen my Caddy at a rest area outside Columbus. Of course, I didn't have any idea how I'd gotten burned or have the slightest memories who had dropped me at the ER.

I was a bit more damaged than I had any idea at first. They had to break my nose to reset it, so I could keep breathing through it. That was a pleasant experience. Even deep under the anesthesia I could swear I felt it. Some of the burns were deep enough to require skin grafts, which was about as painful as anything I had ever endured. My left arm had been smashed badly enough above the elbow to require pins to hold the bones together. There was some uncomfortable dental surgery and some new partial plates. And the mystery pain in my right knee turned out to be a torn ACL. They said the easiest and quickest recovery would require the ligament from a dead person.

"Shit, I'm half dead," I told them, "and your drugs are shitty, so do it before I change my mind and sue you."

They weren't amused. They hadn't seen as many dead people as I had recently. Nor did they find it as amusing as I did that the surgery was scheduled for the day I turned sixty. But by the end of February, though, my ribs had knit, and I was deeply and successfully into physical therapy, the grafts had taken, and they had given me a light plastic cast for the arm. Finally, I'd had enough bad food and sterility, and checked myself out against doctor's advice before the bastards committed me, for drug abuse and a generally bad attitude, to the state hospital over in Warm Springs.

As I combed my hair that day—completely white now—as I considered my new white beard and my ravaged face—I'd lost twenty pounds during the six weeks in the hospital—I thought perhaps they were right—it occurred to me that I resembled my great-grandfather a great deal—but my grin was still my grin, and I still had some shit to deal with back down in Texas before I moved on.

There is nothing like weeks of drugged fog equally mixed with severe pain and damned expensive bureaucratic torture plus a complete dearth of recreational drugs to make an old boy cranky. And in spite of Johnson's quip about the prospect of being hanged in a fortnight wonderfully concentrating the mind, when a man doesn't care if he lives or dies, the concentration upon revenge acquires a fearful clarity. It shines like the point of a poisoned dagger, shadows as dark and deep as the barrel of a sawed-off ten gauge double-barrel, and echoes like a tornado's thunder. Just in case my anger wasn't enough to carry me sensibly through the rest of my time, as soon as I was semimobile I had Petey fly up and check me out on a new laptop that connected me to a world of information, that even in spite of all the facts Carver D had dug out for me, I'd never realized existed.

"You've become a fair to middling one-handed keyboard man," Petey said.

"Thanks," I said. "Are you still planning to go to Harvard Business?"

Petey looked uncomfortable for a second, fiddling with the single piece of ornamental metal left on his head, a small earring. He had taken up normal clothes, too. Today he sported a dark tweed jacket, khakis, and loafers.

"If I can get Carver to stop drinking," he said softly. "He's the only family I've ever had." One winter day, Carver D and Hangas had found the fifteen-year-old Petey passed out in an alley off Sixth Street with only a skateboard for warmth. "I'd hate to leave him, man, but he's the one who encouraged me to go to school. And thanks to you, I don't need his money for this."

"I've been meaning to talk to you about that," I said. "It's time to shut our little laundry down." Then told him about my plans for the bar. "If you and your buddies would make one more haul to the Caymans for me, I'd appreciate the chore. Double your cut." Petey and his buddies usually went to the bank for me, then came back with legal amounts of cash to wash. "Can you shut down the program from Carver D's house?" I asked.

"Hell, man, I can shut it down from here."

Since both Molly and Enos Walker were dead and no longer threats to the Lomaxes or anybody else, I had made no secret of my location during the weeks in the hospital. As a result, I received odd lots of information from down in Texas. I had returned my Gatlin County badge and credentials, with a polite letter of resignation, a gesture received without comment. Carver D called daily until he decided to take a month off himself to spend it in a spin dry in Tucson, and to let me know that the GMC pickup had been a dead end, stolen in Lubbock, the plates stolen in Tyler. But he called a second time that day to let me know that Tom Ben hadn't made it. The stroke and the pneumonia had been too much for the old boy. I bribed a nurse to bring me a pint of Jack Daniel's, a taste I'd never much liked, but I drank it anyway, my hangover as grim as my grief the next morning.

I got on the phone that afternoon. Lalo told me that there didn't seem to be any cops hanging around the bar, but for some reason we were making money hand over fist. Hangas kept looking for Eldora Grace, but she hadn't surfaced for so long that her daughter up in Fort Worth reported her as a missing person. He also added that Travis Lee seemed to have Sissy Duval's power of attorney and was taking care of her investments and condo. Joe Warren had left several messages to ask me to find his wife again, but I didn't return any of them. Sylvie Lomax hadn't called, which was news with its own value.

But the strangest message came just about the time I had decided that I was not only going to survive, I was going to enjoy getting even. It came in a registered letter from a lawyer whose name I didn't recognize.

It was a scribbled note from Tom Ben: *Well, kid, if you're reading this, I'm dead meat. Hell, I've been half dead since Mary killed herself before I could get back from Korea and beat the shit out of my worthless little brother. But it's too late for regrets. And I don't have the energy for them today. I did as well as I could, given my failures. I'm sure you won't understand what this is about or what's going to happen next, but trust me, I did it in all good faith. For reasons you don't need to know anything about, the girl can't protect my place against the fuck-ing greed-mongering whores. So I'm leaving you my shares in the ranch corporation. And a note with my lawyer. I pray you'll figure out what to do with the land, and maybe with a little luck you can keep them from completely fucking over that small part of the world it has been my pride and joy to inhabit. Good luck, my friend.*

The note was signed: *Thomas Benjamin Wallingford, Capt. USMC.*

I had no idea what it meant then, but when I got hold of his lawyer, I found out. Tom Ben had incorporated the ranch some years before, dividing the shares equally between himself and Betty. He left me his shares, which wouldn't have been a controlling inter-est, except that, for reasons I didn't understand, and perhaps never would, Betty had outsmarted herself. Every time she cashed one of my rent checks, she transferred ten shares of her stock into my name, so I owned the controlling interest of the corporation. Per-haps trying to protect Tom Ben's ranch from Lomax and Overlord Land and Cattle, thinking I might go up against big money if I had something personal at stake. Just another touch of her desire for a secret life, I assumed. And I was sure that Betty didn't know just how fucking personally I was taking it now. Whatever her reasons, I now owned a controlling interest in Tom Ben's ranch.

Travis Lee showed up unexpectedly a few days later, bearing gifts, a crooked grin, and a complaint. "Hellfire, son, you should have let me know," he said as he stepped into the door. "You look like a man who's been rode hard, put up wet, then run over by a shit-storm."

"I don't have much hospital experience," I admitted. "And I don't want much more." Recovering in an El Paso hospital from a gunshot wound had been enough for me.

"Can't blame you for that," he said. "It's sure as hell hard to get up here in the wintertime. I sure didn't plan on spending a major part of my remaining years in the Salt Lake airport." He nodded to-ward the snow squall outside my room's windows.

"The price you pay for splendid isolation," I said. "What the hell are you doing up here?"

"Thought you might need something to read," he said, then handed me a sackful of paperback books, canned treats, and two half-pints of vodka.

"Where's the heroin?" I asked, after I glanced through the sack. I had to admit that the small cans of pâté, smoked oysters, and clams looked good. Travis Lee had even included a small jar of Dijon mustard and a package of water crackers. "Thanks," I said, oddly touched by the old man's visit. "You came a long way to see me laid up."

"Down at the nurses' station, they said that you're comin' along fine," he expounded. "Said you should be outa here in a couple shakes of a puppy's tail."

"That's not what they tell me," I said. "I'm wearing pieces of my ass on my neck, a dead man's ligament in my knee, and an assortment of screws and pins in my elbow worthy of a hardware store." Then I wondered, "How did you know I was in the hospital?"

"Hell, I don't know," he said, "somebody must have mentioned it. Austin may be on the verge of making Gatlin County look like a city, son, but you know it's a small town as far as gossip goes. And speaking of gossip, I hear you've settled your cash flow problem."

"I don't have a cash flow problem," I said, "so I don't know what the hell you're talking about."

"I'm talking about your sudden acquisition of my brother's ranch."

"Shit, Trav," I said. "That's not gossip, that's criminal behavior. The goddamned will hasn't been probated yet. So how the hell did you know about the will?"

"Word gets around," he said innocently.

"Then maybe you can tell me what the hell Tom Ben had in mind?" I said. "Leaving his place to me?"

"Couldn't speak to that, son," he said, "but I have some idea what that land is worth. Particularly if it's parceled out to the right people at the right time."

"It all seems like a long way away," I said. "I'm going to be in this bed for a time."

"You're coming back to Texas, aren't you?" he said, his face furrowed with worry. "You got a passel of business interests down there, son."

"I don't know what I'm going to do," I said, suddenly very tired and reaching for the nurse's call button. I wasn't going to criticize Tom Ben—he was clearly a man of some honor—but I sure as hell wasn't all that happy about being dropped into the middle of the Wallingford family's troubles. "Right now I'm going to see if I can't beg a shot out of these stingy bastards," I said, "then see about a *siesta*."

We chatted aimlessly until the nurse came, and I begged like an egg-sucking dog until she gave me a jolt of Demerol just to shut me up. Travis Lee made his exit, explaining that he had spent so much time on the ground at the Salt Lake airport that he had to turn around and head right back to Texas. I wanted to ask him about Sissy Duval, but it slipped my mind. As I drifted off behind the painkiller, I thought that it was nice of Travis Lee to come all the way up here to see me, then I wondered, sleepily, why he had gone to the trouble—he hadn't bothered to mention his investment ideas—but then I let it go as I slipped into the warm, drugged slumber.

Once out of the hospital, I went over to Meriwether to spend a couple of weeks with my ex-partner and his family. Baby Lester wasn't a baby anymore. Which he reminded me every time I slipped and called him that. And they were too busy with law school and a growing Lester to spend much time with me and my problems, and I got tired of watching them try, so I climbed on a plane and hopped back to Texas. I didn't really care if anybody knew I was back, but for some reason I didn't want to return to my room in the Lodge to wait for Tom Ben's will to go into probate. So I rented a car and stopped by my place to check with Lalo and ran into one of my grass widows, Sherry. She invited me up for a drink that turned into a few pleasant days. And nights. Until her big-shot computer-chip-on-the-English-tweed-shoulder husband came back from Boston. Then I crashed with Renfro and Richie at their place off Bee Caves Road for a few more days, but they took such good care of me that I began to feel as if I was either an invalid or a leeching guest at a chichi bed-and-breakfast. A guy can stand out-of-season strawberries and clotted cream for breakfast only so many days in a row.

So I went over to Travis Lee's office to ask him if I could borrow his place down on the Gulf for a few weeks, but he said he was having some work done on the place. When I thought about that last weekend Betty and I had spent there, I decided perhaps I didn't mind too much not going. I asked him if he couldn't get Gatlin County to speed up the probate process.

"Oh, son, I don't know," he groaned, a Confederate cavalry saber balanced on his knee, "down here a favor always calls for a favor in return. You scratch my balls, I'll scratch yours. I strongly suspect those old boys around the courthouse are a little worried that you might be considerin' removing my brother's land from the tax rolls. 'Cause of your former relations with my niece." Travis Lee stood up, holding the old saber in front of him. From this angle I realized that his golden belt buckle wasn't a snake's head but a bull-frog's head, and now I knew what it meant. He pointed the saber at me. "Now if I could go over there and give them some reassurance in this rather important matter," he continued, "I'm sure they would be more than happy to move things along."

"You tell them," I said, fighting to keep the anger out of my voice. "You tell them old boys that I don't have any plans to take the ranch off the tax rolls." Truth was I didn't have any plans about the ranch at all. But I had some plans for Mr. Wallingford, plans he wasn't going to like.

"You sure you didn't check out of that hospital too soon?" he asked.

"Maybe," I admitted. "But I was bored."

Travis Lee nodded his head as if he understood exactly. But he didn't understand anything at all. I didn't understand why I didn't jerk the saber out of his hands and shove it up his ass. Maybe I was learning restraint in my golden years.

When the will went through probate the next day, I decided to move into Tom Ben's ranch house. Over the fervent objections of Betty and some lawyer I didn't know, objections that Tom Ben's lawyer quickly stifled. When it was over, he handed me a sealed envelope. Betty watched, her face with a haunted look, as if she hadn't slept in weeks. When she had first seen my new old man's face in the judge's chambers, a ripple of concern crossed her pale face, and she took one small step in my direction, then pulled herself up, stopped, and just stood there, her face angry with hurt and betrayal, staring at me. But I didn't understand any of it. Not how we had gotten together, or how we'd fallen apart.

That afternoon I bought a four-wheel-drive crew cab pickup just like any other all-hat-and-no-cattle Texan, picked up my new gear, and moved myself into Tom Ben's house. It seemed like a good center of operations for what I had planned. I made a few quick changes: two more telephone lines installed; a wall between two bedrooms removed to make space for the computers and the exercise equipment; and had one of the bulldozer guys build me a new road out the backside of the ranch so my comings and goings wouldn't be quite so visible.

Tom Ben's foreman had towed the burned hulk of my Caddy out into the pasture with a bulldozer, then buried it. I told him to keep the hands doing whatever the old man had been doing, then went about my business.

The afternoon Red's scrambled cell phone came by FedEx with a sweet note from Mrs. McCravey, I decided to pick up Gannon's. When I called, I caught him in the office. I still used one crutch and kept a fiberglass cast on my left elbow, mostly for cover, and with the white beard probably looked like my grandfather's ghost. At least Gannon looked at me as startled as if I were some kind of specter.

"Jesus, man," he said. Today he was dressed like the rest of the boys in cowboy boots and a western-cut suit. "I heard that you'd been in a car wreck, but I had no idea."

"You should see the other motherfucker," I said.

"You have any luck with your notions?"

"Not a bit," I said. "It was a long tiresome chase into a pile of slick, slippery gooseshit with not a rose petal in sight. And as you can see, I'm a little too beat up to go on with it."

"I can see that," he said. "Are you going to be all right?"

"The rumors of my near demise haven't been exaggerated," I said, "but unfortunately for my enemies, I'm not dead yet."

"Well, if there's anything I can do, let me know," he said, ignoring my line about enemies. He honestly seemed to have no idea of the real story.

"Absolutely," I said. "Hey, how's that kid doing? Culbertson, I think his name was."

"Released when we downsized last month," Gannon said, but I suspected I knew the real reason.

"How's your job looking these days?" I asked. "You're not in uniform. They put you back in the detective division?"

"For a few weeks," he said. "While they decide if they're going to fire me. I'm keeping my fingers crossed." Then he paused. "You spending any time at the bar these days?"

"I was just on my way over there right now," I said. "You want to have a drink?"

"Sounds good to me," he said quickly, glancing around as if the walls were listening. "I'll meet you there in a few minutes. I've got something you ought to hear."

On the way out of the courthouse I made a point to clunk slowly past the county prosecutor's offices. Rooke glanced up from where he leaned on his secretary's desk. I gave him a friendly wave. Then he stood up straight, his hard gray eyes slightly confused, not a sign of recognition on his narrow face. He even tried to grin as if I were a voter.

As I walked through the lobby of the Lodge, Travis Lee came striding out of the office, his boots slapping heavily on the Mexican tile floor, his large Stetson sailing like a large white bird on his head. He planted himself right in front of me, so I stopped. He took a step toward me, smiling, saying, "Jesus, son, I'm worried about you. You're hobbled like an old mare with a stone bruise."

"I'm getting around," I said. That suited me perfectly. I wanted Gatlin County to think of me as an old man, to dismiss me as a threat. "I've got business to tend to down here. I'm meeting Gannon for a drink," I added as I turned to the bar.

"What business have you got with him?" Travis Lee asked, then stepped in front of me. The bottom of my right crutch, which I had filled with six ounces of melted lead sinkers while I was in Meriwether, caught him on the shin. Travis Lee jumped back as if he'd been shot.

"Sorry," I said. "We're just having a drink."

"What the hell you got in there, son? An anchor?"

I ignored him. "By the way," I said, "there's an envelope with Sissy Duval's name on it in the Lodge safe with ten thousand five hundred dollars in it. But it isn't really hers. I've got to give it back when I get a chance." But from the look on his face, I knew something was wrong. "What's up?"

"Well, I don't know if you knew," he said. "Sissy dropped me a note and asked me to take care of her affairs. She gave me her power of attorney a long time ago. Since the cash had her name on it, I took it. I'm sorry, I didn't know."

"Oh, hell," I said. "I'll figure something out. Where'd it come from?"

"What?"

"The note. Where was it mailed from?"

"Somewhere in the Caribbean, I think," he said, then started to walk away. "Enjoy your drink," he added over his shoulder.

Gannon and I had a pleasant drink, both lightly pumping each other to no avail. He suspected I hadn't been in any car wreck, suspected somehow that I had found the McBride woman, and that I knew more about what was going on than he did. So I gave him a taste.

"Enos Walker is dead," I said. "I'm sorry. I did my best to get him to come back. With my testimony, we could have worked a deal."

"A deal? Anything less than the needle wouldn't have done me any good," he admitted. "That's how you got busted up?"

I didn't bother answering that one. If he had to ask, he didn't need to know the answer. "I don't know how to tell you this, Gannon, but while I was nosing around I kept coming up with bits and pieces of information that Walker was somehow connected to Hayden Lomax."

"That doesn't make any sense," Gannon said. "A man like Lomax wouldn't fuck with cocaine. Christ, he's got to be worth three or four hundred million."

"I don't know," I said.

"Speaking of odd information," he said. "The other day I heard that Tobin Rooke is trying to convince the grand jury to indict you for Billy Long's murder. Since he can't indict you for his brother's death."

"Thanks," I said. "I haven't heard anything about that. Can you nail it down?" But I didn't really care. Tobin Rooke was about to have problems of his own.

"I'll nose around, but you know—"

"—your job's hanging by a thread," I interrupted.

"Yeah," he said standing. "I guess I better get back to it. I've got some paperwork to take home."

CHAPTER FIFTEEN

Now that I had a place to live and get ready for the endgame, I had to find some professional help. I usually worked alone, but my experience with the salt-and-pepper bodyguard team in Dallas and Fresno's rescue of the McCraveys had changed my mind about a lot of things. This job seemed to call for help. So I crutched out to my giant pickup, hopped in, and drove to a turnout at the top of the Blue Hollow Rim, then unlimbered my cell phone.

Bob Culbertson had moved back in with his folks when he lost his job, and his mother told me that Bob was supposed to be out looking for work, but she suspected that this time of the afternoon he was probably drowning his sorrows in some low-rent beer joint. "I don't understand it," she said. "That kid really liked that job, and if he can't find something soon, I'm afraid he'll just go back in the Army. He was an MP, you know."

She said Bob would probably be checking in shortly, so I left my number and told her that I might have something for him involving law enforcement. But I didn't explain that the job was going to be along the lines of breaking the law, instead of enforcing it. My cell phone trilled before I could start the pickup.

I told him the beers were on me. He said thanks, then walked out of the bar, still unsteady on his new cowboy boots.

"Guys from New Jersey shouldn't wear cowboy boots," Lalo said as he brought me a fresh beer.

"Well, *mi amigo*," I said raising the glass, "I think my days of cowboy boots are over. A man in my condition could fall off them high heels and hurt myself." Lalo chuckled happily. Coming back to work seemed to have knocked ten years off his face. "You're looking good, *viejo*," I said.

"Perhaps I retired too soon," he said. "But running your bar, my friend, is a pleasure instead of a job."

I saw no reason to tell him that as soon as things settled out, my lawyer had arranged to sell the bar to the Herrera family at fairly reasonable terms. Nothing down, with a small piece of the action every month as payment. Travis Lee wouldn't be happy, but lying in that hospital bed, I had decided to get out of the bar business as easily and quickly as I could.

Lalo poured two shots of tequila out of the Herradura bottle. We toasted the clear, bright day outside the glass walls of the bar. No buildings or houses troubled the tangled expanse of the Blue Creek Park. It could have been a different world, an easier world. But for the shadows still drifting behind my eyes. I shook Lalo's soft, satin hand, then went about my business.

The terrible force of coincidence that had plagued me since the day I had followed Enos Walker into the bar took one more shot at me. Bob Culbertson and Carol Jean Warren were playing pool at Over the Line. Leonard Wilbur was even behind the bar, holding a clipboard and counting bottles again. Even though he looked me directly in the face as the bartender handed me a beer, Wilbur didn't recognize me. I took that as a good sign.

I took my beer and walked down to the pool table where they were playing for ten dollars a stick. Culbertson looked a bit down in the mouth.

"You kids looking for work?" I said. They looked up startled. Neither of them had any idea who I was. I promised myself that if I survived all this, I was going to shear the hair and shave the beard. I couldn't do anything about the mustache, but maybe it wouldn't make me look like a dead man.

After I straightened out the confusion and introduced them, I took them into town for a late lunch at Threadgill's to explain to them what I wanted.

Carol Jean, who had discovered, as one often does, that working in beer joints wasn't nearly as much fun as hanging out in them, said yes without even asking what the job might be or how much it might pay. Bob was a bit more reluctant. He still wanted to pursue a career in law enforcement. So instead of explaining, I asked him a question.

"How'd you lose your job?" I asked.

"County budget cuts, they said."

"When you went down to check on Ty Rooke's body, did you hear a cell phone ringing in the other fanny pack?"

"Sure. Why?"

"That's why you lost your job," I said. "They wanted to be sure that your testimony would be suspect. I'd bet money that you'll find a letter in your file, dismissing you for fucking up evidence somehow."

"Well, that's a goddamned lie."

"That's how they work it," I said. "They write the lies on official documents. That way they're almost impossible to deny. But I think I can fix it."

"I think I'd be interested," Bob said slowly.

"Just where the hell do I fit in?" Carol Jean asked, a hunk of chicken-fried steak speared on her fork.

"I don't know exactly," I admitted, "but you strike me as the best sort of Texas woman," I said. "You can drive a stick shift, shoot a weapon, you're computer-literate, you're dead solid honest, and you're probably dangerous."

"And not all that hard to look at, either, Carol Jean," Bob said, smiling as she blushed.

"My friends call me CJ," she said, then turned to me. "How did you know I could shoot?"

"Honey, between your mother and your soon-to-be ex-husband I knew your whole life story before I found you the first time," I said.

"My mother! Goddammit, she gave me up?" she squealed. "If it hadn't been for her, I would never have married that lame son of a bitch anyway. At least there were no kids and no foolin' around. Those are the hardest things to get over in a divorce. I remember that from my mother's two disasters."

"Hey, I need a couple of drivers, a couple of bodyguards who don't look like thugs, and a couple of smart snoops," I said. "So a cowgirl and a boy scout will suit me fine. Maybe the bad guys won't pay any attention. I can only promise the work will be interesting and the pay excessive."

"Jesus, what do you need protection for?" Bob said. "Ty Rooke was just about the toughest motherfucker I ever saw—"

"You don't have to say 'motherfucker' in front of me, Bob," CJ interrupted, "just to prove you're not a Boy Scout."

"— and you took him out," Bob finished, trying hard neither to blush nor glance at CJ.

"That was pure luck, kiddo," I said. "Unfortunately, the most important element in survival is luck. I'm just trying to reduce the factor that luck plays in this little effort to wind things up."

"Sounds good to me," CJ said, and Bob nodded eagerly. "So what do we do now?" CJ said. "What you said, it's all true," she added blushing. "All but the part about the stick shift."

"So what do we do now?" Bob said.

"Gather up your shit and let's move deeper into the Hill Country," I said. "And you can teach CJ how to drive a stick shift."

"I'm sorta without wheels," CJ said.

I told her to toss her stuff in Bob's pickup and ride out with him. Once she learned to drive a stick, she could use Tom Ben's ranch truck.

So we had six weeks of relative calm, working the phones and the computers, working the exercise machines, and eating Maria's great food. She missed Tom Ben, her loneliness eating at her like a cold wind, but she kept our systems running on *chili verde*, chicken enchiladas, and *carne asada*. We ate so well that a night out for us was a visit to McDonald's to soothe our fiery gastrointestinal tracts. The three of us had taken a couple of quick trips in rental cars—one to Little Rock and one to Albuquerque—to pick up two Remington 7mm Magnum rifles with Weaver scopes, a stun gun, a little Sundance .22 derringer, and a S&W stainless steel Ladysmith from private party newspaper ads or gun shows. We also picked up a used telephone van for cash.

Back at the ranch Bob and CJ sighted in the rifles and ran rounds through them until the weapons felt like parts of their bodies. CJ ran me through two-a-day workouts as if I was training for the senior Olympics. When she wasn't trying to kill me, CJ spent her daylight hours digging in the dust of courthouse records in the five counties around Gatlin. When I wasn't working out or recovering, Bob and I worked the phones, mostly international calls. In the early evening hours Petey hacked his way into most of the computers we needed. Even if he couldn't get in, we could find out who to bribe. They left that to me, resplendent in my new wardrobe of tweed suits. At night, Bob and I followed CJ around the pool tables, bars, and beer joints of Gatlin and Travis counties, picking up bits and pieces of information, tracking tidbits of gossip, following the rills of rumors. I continued my ruse with the crutch and the light cast on my left arm, and discovered that more people talked to me about more things in my guise as a crippled old codger than they ever had when I was a hard-nosed private dick.

But finally the picture was as clear as we could make it without getting personally involved. But before I visited Tobin Rooke, I had to face Rollie Molineaux with the death of his daughter. And confess my sorry part in that loss. I wanted that chore out of the way before we moved onto the really hard part of the job.

Although I didn't have a clear picture in my head of what had happened that night at Duval's so long ago and the endless repercussions that echoed through a dozen people's lives, I climbed into the pickup and slipped out the back gate in the middle of a star-shot night, hoping to at least clear my conscience.

When I got to Houston, I discovered that the Longhorn Tavern had fallen prey to a new freeway exit, which made me oddly sad. I wondered what had happened to Fat Annie and Joe Willie Custer, where they had gone when the beer joint had closed, wondered where we were going to go when the last good beer joint finally fell all the way down. Rollie's house was empty, too, a for sale sign in the yard. He wasn't hiding, so he wasn't hard to find. But Rollie Molineaux was the last person I expected to help fill in the picture.

I found him sitting in a worn lawn chair on a dock jutting into the dark, sluggish water behind a bait shop on one of the many unnamed arms of Bayou Teche. A cigarette jutting out of his crooked, gray-stubbled jaw, a beer between his legs, and a battered captain's hat tilted at a rakish angle on the back of his head.

"Mr. Molineaux," I said when I stepped onto the dock. "I'd like to talk to you."

Rollie turned, a half-grin exposing a brown stain on the partial plate in the side of his mouth. "Hey there," he said. "You be lookin' like you might be that bastard who broke my jaw, but you're a mite older."

"Not as old as I feel," I admitted.

"Sit a bit and have a brew," he said, nodding toward the lawn chair beside him, then digging into the cooler at his feet. "Unless you're lookin' to beat on me some more, man."

"Sorry," I said as I sat down.

"Ain't no big thing," he said, handing me a beer.

"I've got some bad news for you."

"Ain't nobody brought me much good news lately."

"Your daughter is dead," I said, laying it out as quickly as I could.

"Yeah. I figured when I didn't hear from her when Jimmy Fish went down that no news might be bad news. He do her?"

"No, it was an accident," I said. "She got shot up in Montana."

"Montana," he said as if it was a foreign country. "What she be doin' up in that cold country?"

"Helping me on a job."

"Well, ain't that the shits."

"Yes, sir," I said.

"They said Jimmy got shot, too," he said. "You do him?"

"Some French guy put one in his ear."

"Guess I'm not surprised," he said. "He was bound to get shot someday. I should have put one in his head years ago when I thought he was foolin' around with my baby girl. You know how it is, man. Sometimes you got a best friend like a bad woman. No matter what they do, you keep hangin' around." Then he paused to open another beer, his odd apology ended. "What happened? Up there in Montana."

"Oh, hell," I said. "This guy I was looking for, he was beating me to death, and she put a .22 round up his nose. But he pulled the trigger at the same time. He pulled the trigger, but the people who started this, they're the ones who killed her."

"Ain't that the shits," he said again.

"I couldn't stop it," I admitted. "It tore the heart right out of me." I pulled the Shark of the Moon out of my pocket. "She was a fine woman," I said. "She talked about you a lot. I think she'd want you to have this."

Rollie looked momentarily uncomfortable, then he held up the stone to watch it shine in the sunlight, and he smiled. "She must have thought well of you to tell you about this ol' thing. Belonged to her Momma. I picked it up down in Belize on a run once." He didn't have to say what kind of run. "The mortal shits."

"You know, the people who got her mixed up in all this, I think they should pay," I said. "I intend to make them pay. But I need your help."

"Anything, man." I showed him the photo of Amanda Rae Quarrels. "Sure," he said. "That would be Amelia Fontinot, you bet, after she bleached her hair. This is her Daddy's old place. Jimmy left it to me. She'd be his half-sister, you know, younger. She married that old Desmond Quarries fellow from Morgan City, but I think Jimmy was fuckin' her and he sold her off to Des. He'd do things like that, you know. But she don't much look like that no more. Last time I saw her, I didn't even recognize her."

"When's the last time you saw her?" I asked.

"Shit, I don't know. Seven, maybe eight years ago," he said. "Back when I still had a boat. Jimmy and I picked her up off a tanker in the Gulf and brought her home. With some young girl. Hell, she didn't even say kiss my ass, thanks, or goodbye. But I sure got fucked over later. Couple of weeks later the DEA came calling. They found a bag of smack on my boat and that was all she wrote. Goddamned woman must have left it there. I was lucky to stay out of the joint. But they finally believed me. I never ran any coke or heroin. Nothing but smoke. That was my rule."

"When you and Jimmy were working offshore, you ever work for Hayden Lomax?"

"That cheap son of a bitch," he said. "Nobody with any sense ever worked for that sorry junkhouse outfit. Only people ever worked for Lomax was three-fingered winos like ol' Des."

"Thanks," I said, finishing my beer and standing up. "I got to be going now."

"Let me know what happens," he said.

"You already know too much," I said. "Thanks again."

Then I left him sitting in the warm, soft sunshine, left him with his memories, and the dark shadows of the stone. And a clear conscience, I hoped.

As I walked back through the bait shop, I glanced once more into the dusty webbed shadows. A dozen glass-eyed deer and boar heads glittered in the shadows. I didn't have to ask who had killed them. An old woman, her face blurred behind fat and great hairy moles, sat in a funky heap behind the counter, knitting at an unidentifiable hunk of clothing, her hooded eyes gleaming, the wings of her coal-black hair shining like a pair of obsidian axe blades.

Driving back from Houston I took a quick detour by Stairtown and Homer's place. Of course, there was no body in the mudpit. Sissy's BMW had disappeared, too. The old shack was scrubbed as clean as a dog's plate. No crime scene, no evidence, no past or future. The pumpjacks rocked and buzzards drifted across an empty sky while I had a beer and a couple of cigarettes, mourning the dead woman in the pit.

On the outskirts of Austin I called Reverend Walker. He said he didn't want me at his church and he didn't want to be seen in public with me, but I didn't give him any choice.

He stood at the bar of the Four Seasons, a large, uncomfortable man sipping at a tonic water. He turned to glower at me as I edged in beside him but smiled aimlessly when he saw the white hair and the crutch and nodded politely without a glimmer of recognition. Once I had a drink, I leaned over to whisper, "I'm sorry, man, but your brother is dead."

Walker spun quickly, recognizing me now. "Watch yourself, old man," he growled. "Just watch it."

I had a slow swallow of Scotch, then faced him. "It's true," I said. "He's dead, and I am very sorry."

"What happened?"

"Nothing that's going to come back on you."

"And the girl?" I nodded. "Damn," he said grimly. "It didn't have to happen that way."

"It's done," I said. "You've been doing good work for a long time. Keep it up. But what you need to do now is get a lawyer and an accountant to destroy every trace of any connection with Hayden Lomax."

"Why?"

"Just do it."

"You can't go up against Lomax," he said. "He'll turn you into fish food."

"Maybe not," I said. "Not if I've got the mortal nuts on him."

"Good luck," he said. "You'll need it."

"Thanks."

As I left, I heard Walker order a double Wild Turkey rocks from the bartender. I hoped he stopped after one. A man carrying that sort of guilt shouldn't be drinking hard. It could kill him.

I sent the kids off to Vegas with a bundle of cash for Fresno and to get them out of town. I had a couple of days to waste until Friday night, so I spent it reloading some .22 hollow point shorts and sitting on the porch carving seasoned cedar sticks into thin, sharp strips that would fit under my cast.

Late one afternoon as stately storm cells drifted up from the Gulf, trailing rain like silver skirts, Carver D and Hangas showed up without calling. I didn't even bother to ask how they had gotten through the gates. Hangas climbed out of the driver's seat, then walked slowly around to open the back door of the old Lincoln, his grin bright in the spring sunshine.

"My man looks good, doesn't he?" Hangas said as Carver D slipped out of the limo.

Carver D had dropped thirty or forty pounds. His eyes were clear, his voice resonant, and although he wasn't exactly nimble on two canes, he was moving. And smiling as he eased into the rocker beside me.

"What the hell are you guys doing out here?" I said.

"If you'd answer your telephone or return your calls," he said, "we wouldn't have to break into your solitude."

"I've been busy," I said.

"Busy," he said, sweeping his cane through the pile of shavings between my feet. "Busy as a beaver, I see." When I just kept running the blade of the Old Timer down a length of cedar, Carver D continued. "You're planning something awful, aren't you? Some kind of terrible revenge?"

"I'm retired."

"You're a base liar," he said. "You need Hangas to help?"

I glanced at Hangas resplendent in his tailored suit, smiling as calmly as a cobra might smile. "He's the most dangerous man I know," I said, "and I appreciate the offer. But nothing's happening."

"Milo, you shouldn't lie to your friends."

I had no answer for that. So we left it there, chatted until one of the thundershowers rattled the tin roof, then they left.

Tom Ben was never able to talk about the Rooke family without including the phrase "carpet-bagging goat-fucking white trash." The family had moved down after the Civil War, had scammed a section of land in the hills behind the Bad Corner, but as far as I could find out, they never had been charged with sexual congress with farm animals. Over the years the family had sold off pieces of the land, drifted off to California, or various institutions, penal or otherwise, leaving the twins sole owners of a five-acre plot right in the center of the unzoned tangle of the old home place, a jungle of variously sized lots, crooked roads, and Hill Country scrub land, and a gravel pit. Shortly after Tobin finished law school and Ty had been promoted to plainclothes, with financing that should have raised IRS flags, the boys had built a rambling brick home. They dated enough to forestall rumors of homosexuality, but never married. And except for a reputation left over from their college years for being particularly vicious bar fighters, their characters were beyond reproach in Gatlin County. Or as a retired deputy had said to me one night in a beer joint out on Lake Travis, "The best reputations money can buy."

Every Friday after he finished at the courthouse, Ty Rooke stopped for a couple of glasses of white wine at the only upscale bar in Gatlinsburg, then drove down to Austin for a stop at the Whole Foods Market, then home for whatever he did on his lonely Friday nights. We had followed him for weeks, and his pattern never changed. But I followed him in the repainted van this Friday night just to be sure.

I let him put his car in the garage, watched the lights come on, then pulled the van in front, and went up to the door. He opened the door when I rang the bell. He had no reason not to open the door: a telephone company van in front of his house, an old man in a telephone company uniform and carrying a telephone company tool kit at his door. He couldn't see the stun gun in my hand, the latex gloves, or the hand with the sap glove on it. I let him say, "Yes?" before I hit him in the chest with the stun gun.

Maybe I missed with one of the electrodes. Maybe his suit coat got in the way. Or maybe these Rookes were impossible to get down. Whatever, he got enough charge to fling him backward off his feet, knock his glasses off, and scatter health food across the carpet. But he didn't pause, just rolled up to his feet ready to kill as I stepped through the door.

He was on me like a spider, sweeping the stun gun aside as if I wasn't there, then had me in a choke hold a moment later. We crashed around the living room for a few seconds as I tried to buck him off. Unsuccessfully. I was a dead man until I finally managed to dig the derringer out of my pocket and fire the two rounds over my shoulder. I missed him, but the powder burns and percussion cone got him off my back long enough for me to slap him with the sap glove, cracking the skin over his cheekbone. He still didn't go down, but at least he paused, his hands protecting his face. I hit him in the liver hard enough to lift him off his feet. He finally went down.

When Rooke came back, after the third or fourth glass of ice water in his face, he found himself stripped to his shorts, his hands and legs cuffed to the legs of a metal kitchen chair leaning against the refrigerator door. I didn't trust duct tape to hold him any more than I trusted myself not to shoot the crazy bastard in the eye. He came back to consciousness as if he had never been away.

"Do you know who I am, old man?" he said. "You're in a shit-load of trouble."

"Do you know who I am, asshole?" I said. "You're probably in more trouble than I am."

"What do you want?" he asked, not missing a beat. He knew who I was now. "We can work something out, Mr. Milodragovitch."

"I'd really like to know who hired your brother to kill me."

"That's going to be a problem—" he started to say.

I interrupted by placing the derringer against the fold of his armpit and pulling the trigger. It was a light load, but the powder burn seared the skin and the notched hollow point carved a deep groove through his flesh, a painful red, white, and black furrow. I had some idea of how much this must have hurt, but Rooke seemed totally surprised. Before he got his breath back, I sloshed a bit of or-ganic *habanero* salsa onto a dish towel. He looked as if he couldn't believe what was happening. Then I snuggled the cloth into the wound, and taped the towel over his shoulder.

Rooke didn't have much to say. He seemed to have fainted. He just sprawled in the chair and drooled while I cleaned him up and started my search of the house.

"Well," I said half an hour later—the bastard hadn't even bothered to lock the entrance to the basement—"since you know who I am, asshole, and if I don't care that you know who I am, then you probably realize that when I leave here, you don't have much of a chance of being alive. It's simply a matter of how much pain you can stand."

"Bring it on, you son of a bitch."

"Since you threatened to ruin my life, and as far as I can tell you're still trying—rumor has it that you're planning to convince the grand jury to indict me for Billy Long's death—there's some other stuff you should consider," I said. "Credit card records put either you, your brother, or both of you in six cities across the country in the past six years where young women have been raped, tortured, mutilated, and killed. You never came to the FBI's attention because you bastards are law enforcement. You covered your tracks perfectly, cleaned the crime scenes professionally. You used different setups and took different parts of the body each time. Was Annette McBride the first? Or just another one? What the fuck were you doing? And how stupid was it to keep your souvenirs in a freezer in the basement?

"Oh, you're surprised that I know about the basement, you sick son of a bitch?" I said. I'd been around some bad people in my life, but I'd never been in the presence of a monster. I could have wished that some genetic malfunction in the egg had created these bastards, but I didn't believe it. Evil just exists. I could only hope it wouldn't infect me when I destroyed this particular version. "The basement's not in the building plans, sure, but what the hell did you do with all that cement you bought? And you bastards sold a dozen dump truck loads of topsoil. How fucking stupid and greedy can you be? Why didn't you just dump it in the lake?"

Rooke shook his head so hard that drops of sweat flew off his bald head. I could see his lips moving but no words came out as I removed the salsa-soaked dish towel from under his armpit. I found a pile of dish towels neatly stacked in a broom closet, wet one and used it to mop the salsa off his wound, then filled another with ice cubes, and placed it under his arm. I could almost hear the sigh of relief and could see the smile forming on his thin lips.

"So you want to tell me who hired your brother, Rooke?" I asked as I replaced the empty rounds in the derringer. "Or you want me to put another round in you? I know some places that will hurt even more. A hell of a lot more."

He wanted to tell me but he just couldn't bring himself to do it. Over the next hour or so, I thought I was going to either run out of rounds, hot sauce, or soft tissue before he broke. He wept like an angry child as I carried his naked, bloody body over my shoulder down the hidden basement stairs behind a workbench in the garage.

"Tell me who hired your brother," I said as I sat him on a desk chair and rolled him into the walk-in freezer, "and I'll let you live." Rooke wanted to believe me, but he couldn't quite bring himself to do it. He shook his head wildly. "Fuck it," I said, and put a point-blank round into the maze of tiny bones in his left wrist, then another, then dumped the rest of the *habanero* sauce into the wounds.

He couldn't get the name out fast enough. I was mildly surprised. But only mildly.

This sort of thing was more my ex-partner's style than mine, and I knew I'd never feel quite the same about myself again. But it had to be done. And it was. I reloaded the derringer, slipped it over his right thumb, then walked out, locking the freezer door behind me. The screams of pain had turned to rage. I glanced in the porthole. I assumed Rooke had tried to turn the pistol around in his hand so he could shoot me in the back. Because it lay between his bound feet. I left him there in that terrible room of his own making, left him without looking back.

When I got back to the ranch, the kids had gotten back from Vegas early, driving straight through once they realized I had sent them on a useless chore to get them out of the way for a few days. I had some idea how the night with Ty Rooke might go and I didn't want them involved. They wanted to know what had happened, but

I snapped at them, told them to shut up so harshly, they actually stayed quiet. And never brought it up again.

I needed a bar, but they were all closed, so I made the kids stand around the fire pit and drink with me until dawn as we ditched the gear I'd taken, the telephone uniform, and even the tires off the telephone van. Bob melted the derringer down with a welding torch. I didn't think anybody would want to investigate Ty Rooke's disappearance too hard. Particularly after the law found where he was hiding.

During that long night's aftermath, I discovered why CJ had been blessed with two names at birth, and managed to listen to the details of every arrest Bob had made during his time as an MP in Germany, but finally about dawn the kids ran down and drifted off to bed. I seemed to have been pouring the tequila into a hole inside me, a hole that I could not fill. Whatever sort of drunken relief I had been seeking refused to come. I took the Herradura bottle and a six-pack around front. I meant to sit on the porch and watch the sunrise, but I was drawn to the abandoned dairy barn. The flat sunlight scattered like tiny knives off the corrugated steel walls. I went inside, into the tin shadows to sit on the cot and drink. Sunlight shot through the bullet holes in the wall, shafts of light as solid as the rounds that had given them form. I had a dozen things to think about, but the memories of Molly filled my mind. I dug Tom Ben's worthless option out of my billfold, stared at it until the letters blurred in front of my eyes. Fucking greedy bastards. They had started it, and now I had to finish it. But right now all I had to do was hope that I'd be able to finish the tequila before it finished me.

CHAPTER SIXTEEN

EXCEPT FOR MY two-a-day workouts, which CJ refused to let me stop, and a procession of legal messengers, everything came to a halt for a week. When I had the strength, I sat on the front porch with my pocketknife, whittling a pile of thin cedar blades, sipping slow, tasteless beers, and watching the cloud shadows drift across the breaks of the Hill Country. Finally, after lunch one day just as I was finishing the ninth or tenth blade, the kids rebelled, stomped out on the porch to demand action.

"Okay, boss-man," CJ said sternly, "we can understand that you've been through some tough times, but quite frankly we're gettin' bored bein' paid for doin' nothin'."

"That's right," Bob agreed.

I checked the tips of the wooden blades with my thumb until I found one to my liking, then said, "Bob, you drive up to Killeen this afternoon, buy a couple of gillie suits for you guys. Pay cash. Cover your tracks. And CJ, I need aerial photographs of Travis Lee's place on the Gulf and a USGS topo map. When you get back, we'll get out the fiberglass tape and build a slightly larger cast for my arm. Cash. No tracks." They nodded and headed down the walk.

"And before you go," I added, "somebody hand me my cell phone."

I finally returned Sylvie Lomax's calls. She didn't want to take my call, but I badgered and threatened various functionaries until she came on the line, breathless and angry.

"Mr. Milodragovitch," she said stiffly, "I thought all our business was concluded."

"Except for two things, Mrs. Lomax. I want to make a final report, in person," I said, "and I want to meet with your husband, also in person."

"I'm afraid that such a meeting would be quite impossible," she said.

"Tell him that I've got the signed option for Tom Ben Wallingford's ranch," I said. "Maybe he'll be interested in that. And if you're interested in maintaining your life in the current manner, you better make it happen. I'll tear this shit down around your pretty little Cajun head." She started to say something, but I rode right over her. "Ten o'clock in the morning three days from now." I wanted the meeting before the onshore breeze kicked up. No wind to push the rifle rounds. "And let's meet on neutral ground. Travis Lee Wallingford's place on the Gulf. On the deck. I'll come alone and unarmed. You people can bring as many guns as you want. Just as long as you're there, your aunt, and his Aunt Alma. These are my last days here, lady, so this is your husband's only chance to deal. And your only chance to save your ass."

"But there's not enough time," she wailed.

"Make time," I said. Before I broke the connection, I overheard a burst of Cajun French that I assumed was directed at the fat woman in the wheelchair.

Travis Lee wasn't any more interested in the meeting than Sylvie Lomax had been. Until I dangled the promise to let him broker any deal that might come out of the meeting. When I got hold of Betty, she flatly refused to attend. I reminded her that this was her last chance to influence the future of Blue Creek. Then she reluctantly agreed. Cathy was harder to convince, but I knew enough about her involvement to force her to come.

After the kids took off on their chores, I took the Ladysmith and sacrificed one of Tom Ben's goats. I gave the goat to Maria to butcher, dug the .357 slug out of the rocky dirt. Once I had packaged the revolver and the slug, I called Gannon at the courthouse to ask him to meet me at the bar. He was reluctant, but I made him promise.

Once we had hunkered over our drinks at the far end of the bar, he stopped grousing long enough to ask, "What the hell do you want?"

I waited, staring into the depths of Blue Hollow. "I understand Ty Rooke is missing," I said slowly.

"You want to tell me how it is you know that, partner?" he said.

"Partner?" I said. "Is that your new boots talking?"

"Nobody knows outside the department," he said, blushing about his cowboy boots. "How the hell do you know?"

"You don't want to know," I said. "You search the house?"

Gannon looked around as if somebody might be listening in an empty bar in the middle of the afternoon. "It looks like somebody came in, tortured him, then took off with the body. My crime scene boys said nothing of value was missing from the house. I guess we're going to have to bring in the FBI."

"Hold off on that," I said. "Three days if you can work it. Then go back, check out the garage. There's a switch under the vise that unlocks the workbench. Pull it out. The pegboard will come with it," I said. "You'll find some stairs and some shit in the basement that will make you sick but it will nail down your job permanently and maybe even make you sheriff next election."

"So what do I owe you for this information?"

"Not much," I said. "You're one of the few people down here who never lied to me. But you could take care of this," I said, then handed him a package. "There's a Ladysmith .357 in here and a flattened round. Swap it for the one that killed Ty Rooke, fix the paperwork, and bring me the other piece."

"Not much?" he complained angrily. "Jesus, you're taking a chance."

"Right. But you'll do it," I said.

"Why should I?"

"Because it's the right thing to do," I said, raising my glass. "That has to be worth something to you."

"I hope this is goodbye," Gannon said, raising his drink.

"As soon as I have the piece in my hand," I said, "we can have that last drink, man."

"You're a son of a bitch," he said.

I sat at the bar, sipping slow beers and staring down into the sparkling water of Blue Creek as it streamed over the low water crossing in the park below. The afternoon shadows bleached the grass and the pale new leaves. Joggers wound through the paths. Winter seemed forever away. I intended to keep it away.

Gannon came back an hour later and handed me the package. He refused a drink, though, and refused to shake my hand. He was a cop, after all. After one more hard look, a sigh that came with an angry tilt of his thick jaw, he turned, and lurched out of my life. He still hadn't mastered cowboy boots.

Of course the last day had to be a perfect day. During the night before, battalions of storm cells moved through, resplendent with wind and lightning, but this morning, the Gulf was as gray and flat as a lead coin, the shallow swells gasping their last against the hard-packed sand. A breeze swept across the beach, dry enough to keep the humidity down, the air bearable. Great clumps of clouds passed overhead occasionally, providing snatches of shade.

Bob and CJ had been deployed since the night before. Their position wasn't perfect—we had to work the topo map and the aerial photographs by flashlight—but they were invisible, sight lines clear, buried in the dune grass down the beach from Travis Lee's house. I could only hope they wouldn't hesitate to pull the trigger when the time came.

I arrived at Travis Lee's thirty minutes early, but the four Lomax bodyguards were already arranged around the glass-enclosed deck. I came without weapons, except for Betty's revolver, which I carried by the open cylinder. I set it on a table by the door, so I was clean when the bodyguards searched me with both their hands and a metal detector. They took my weighted crutch away, but CJ had made the cast on my left arm heavier than usual and camouflaged it even further with a sling. The bodyguard with the puckered scars on his cheeks hit me in the nuts fairly hard when he searched my crotch. I tried not to give him the pleasure of grunting and bending over, but I couldn't manage it.

"You're getting older every minute, old man," he said, "and I think maybe you're about as old as you're going to get, you fuck with my boss. Where's the paper?"

"Believe me, man, I'd never fuck with your boss. She's too good a shot," I said as I flopped heavily into a redwood deck chair. He ignored my comment. "This is just business," I added. When Travis Lee stepped out of the back door, I saw a shadowy figure half-hidden, and I asked for a beer. "Something in a can," I added. The scar-faced bodyguard nodded in agreement. Travis Lee went back inside without a word.

"You're smart, old man," the bodyguard said, patting me on the shoulder like an obedient child. "Stay that way. You'll live longer." Then he took up his stance directly behind me, his coat open for easy access to the mini-Uzi hanging under his arm. His compatriots leaned against the glass wall windbreak, one in the middle, the others at the far corners of the deck.

Travis Lee, dressed in his lawyer suit and black boots, his golden belt buckle gleaming dully in the sunshine, joined me at the table as he handed me a can of Tecate. Travis had a stiff bourbon in a heavy crystal glass wrapped tightly in his hand. "You want to let me take a look at the option, son?" he said.

"Lomax sees it first," I said, then added, "But you can hold it." Then I slipped it out of the cast and handed it over. He took it, trying very hard not to look at it or smell it. "You know, a bartender once told me that when Mandy Rae came through town she fucked everybody from the governor to his pet bullfrog."

Travis Lee looked at me oddly, then glanced down at the folded, rumpled paper. "Where's the check, son? The check was never cashed." I slipped the check out of my cast and handed that to him. It had been in the envelope the lawyer had handed me at Tom Ben's probate hearing. Travis Lee laughed, waving the check and the option together. "Looks like a negotiable instrument," he said. "We can do some business this morning."

"But it's my business, Wallingford," I said as I jerked the option and the check out of his hands. "So I'll take those back please. Bring him to me."

Betty and Cathy showed up on time, which I hadn't expected. They sat down at the table by the door, their faces pale and stiff, their eyes hidden behind dark glasses, their mouths pressed into straight, tight lines. Betty touched the Ladysmith carefully with one finger as if the piece might be alive.

"What's this?" she said to me.

"Your ticket out of this mess," I said.

"The detective gathers the suspects," Cathy said with a sneer.

"Suspects is not the word I would have chosen," I said. "You ladies should have killed me while you had the chance. Because you're going to regret it now."

Cathy's answering smile was only vaguely human. "Maybe you'll pay more attention to who you fuck *now*," she said.

"You can count on that," I said.

At least Betty had the grace to look away.

A few moments later I heard the Lomax parade arrive and park under Travis Lee's house. The quiet rumble of the stretch limo, the whirr of the wheelchair, the murmurs of their voices—all of the sound loud and clear as it echoed off the glass walls. Sylvie walked beside the driver, who guided the old woman's electric wheelchair up the ramp. The old woman had one shawl draped over her shoulders, another over her useless legs. She stopped her chair at the table nearest to the end of the ramp, and Sylvie sat beside her. Once again both were dressed in black.

Hayden Lomax and his Aunt Alma followed them. Lomax was middle-aged but still as trim and with the same bouncing walk that he must have had on the courts of his youth. He had arrived in a polo shirt, chinos, and deck shoes. As if down for a party weekend. His curly hair was shot with gray, but his face was cherubic, pleasant, complete with a boyish grin that he couldn't seem to control. For all the world, I'll swear he looked like an innocent.

His Aunt Alma walking beside him was something else. She had the countenance of an axe murderer. She had to be in her seventies but she wasn't even slightly stooped with age. In fact, she looked as if she could still get right in your face and go to the basket. Or knock you to your knees and make you pray for forgiveness until they bled. Lomax obviously deferred to her, and not just because he had to look up to her. The old woman was at least six inches taller than he was, even with his bouncing, youthful gait. Another thing was obvious: The old woman despised Sylvie and the woman in the wheelchair. When she happened to glance their way, her lips pursed as if she had just eaten a persimmon. Or smelled something deeply corrupt. This verified the rumors Bob and I had picked up in the bars from people who had once worked for the Lomaxes.

The Lomax parade gathered at the two tables nearest the ramp. Travis Lee fawned over them as he provided drinks. I stayed where I was, scratching not so aimlessly at the inside of my cast.

"Mr. Lomax," Travis Lee boomed as he brought him over to my table, "I'd like you to meet my partner, Milo Milodragovitch."

Lomax acknowledged me with a nod and his involuntary grin. "Milodragovitch," he said.

"That's Mr. Milodragovitch," I said, suspecting that he had never heard my name in his life.

"Be nice," the bodyguard whispered behind me as he slapped me lightly on the head.

"I've never heard that name before," Lomax said in an oddly

high, piping voice, a voice that went with his silly grin. "What is it, Russian?"

"Irish, I think," I said. I was right. He didn't know who I was.

Travis Lee said, "Let's get down to business."

"First things first," I said. "Mr. Lomax, for reasons I won't go into, but I'm sure you'll understand shortly, it's imperative that this conversation be private, unrecorded. Believe me, sir, you're not going to want a record of this meeting. So if everybody will throw any electronic devices they're wearing or carrying over the fence, we can proceed privately." When he hesitated, I said, "What are you worried about, sir? You're not running for office, are you?" Aunt Alma chimed in loudly, "Forgive me, young man, but my nephew doesn't run for office, he owns the fools who bother."

Lomax had the decency to be embarrassed, so he gave an irritated wave to his men, who dumped their walkie-talkies and recorders without complaint. Lomax himself wasn't wired, but Wallingford was. He grumbled the loudest but quickly complied after Lomax snapped at him. Then he snapped again. Wallingford and the bodyguard stepped just out of earshot.

I leaned across the table, the option in my hand, and said very softly, "Mr. Lomax, after you look at this option, I want you to think long and hard before you say a word, and whatever you say, it's very important that you say it quietly. Very important."

"This is a copy," Lomax said quietly, confused.

"Read the words at the bottom of the document," I said.

He glanced down, then he sighed so deeply I thought he was going to faint. He grabbed his face as if to catch his infernal grin before it bled at the corners. "I knew it would come out someday," he whispered as two tiny tears formed at the corners of his merry eyes. "How the hell did you find out?" he said softly.

"Pretty much a string of coincidences," I admitted. "Your damned mother-in-law kept trying to shoot me."

"She's like that," he said.

"That's what I thought. An old boy has to watch out for a

woman scorned. She just threw a few rounds at me. She buried a stone in your heart."

Lomax just shook his head slowly.

"The trick now is for you to keep quiet," I said. "Your future depends on my silence, just as much as my future depends on your silence. I know you've used your offshore rigs to smuggle cocaine," I said, "and that you set Mandy Rae and Enos Walker up in business. You've probably got too much political clout for me to touch you with the cocaine thing. But I can fucking promise you, if you don't behave, I'll break your aunt's heart and shove the pieces up your ass."

"Yes, sir," he said, then shook my hand, a businessman all the way. He knew when he was beaten. His grin flashed on and off like a faulty neon sign. "Thank you," he said. "Thank you very much." The little bastard cared more about what his mad aunt thought of him than the chance that I could send him to prison. As if people like Lomax ever went to prison. "I didn't know," he said. "I swear to you I didn't know. I'll provide anything you want. Anything."

"Stop whining, put a cork in your greed, and whatever happens next, you clean it up. And you should get your aunt out of here because I can't control what happens next."

He nodded cheerfully, walked over to his aunt, escorted her to the driver, then bounced back to the table across from me, his grin wooden and lost. He sat down as if he was a very old man.

I stood up and said, "First, I want to report to Mrs. Lomax." Sylvie looked up startled, as if she had forgotten that she had hired me, then she turned to the old woman, who patted her on the arm. Sylvie didn't look comforted. She looked very young, confused, and afraid. "I don't know what the Molly McBride woman had of yours, ma'am, but whatever it was, it died with her in a fire at the Punky Creek Mine up in Montana, died with her and Enos Walker. So you don't have anything to worry about." I wasn't surprised that nobody was surprised. Except Lomax. He had heard about Punky Creek but not what it meant.

"And for public information, you people leave Tom Ben Wallingford's place alone," I said. "You don't need it." I had donated the ranch to the Texas A&M agricultural research center, designating its use, as Tom Ben had suggested, as a living laboratory to find more and better land-friendly ways to raise cattle. "Is it a deal?" Lomax held out his hand, but I ignored it this time.

He nodded slowly. He knew I had the mortal nuts on him, knew I wasn't bluffing.

"What happened?" Travis Lee wanted to know. "You boys make a deal?"

"Right," I said, "you old son of a bitch, we made a deal, but you're not part of it. By the way, your bald-headed prosecutor buddy is dead, locked in a freezer with the pieces of the women he and his brother killed." Travis Lee's face collapsed, hollow and aged. "And you might as well tell Sissy to come outside," I said. "She's part of this fucking mess, too." Travis Lee acted as if he hadn't heard me, but after a moment he walked stiffly over to the back door. A moment later the dark figure slipped silently out the back door. Sissy looked her age now, and terribly frightened that she wouldn't get any older. "Hi," I said. "If I were you, Sissy, I'd run for my life. Tomorrow Eldora Grace's family will know how you used her to fake your death, so somebody will connect you to it somehow."

"They didn't tell me," she wailed, then slumped into a chair.

"And you, old bastard," I said to Travis Lee. "You better run, too. I've bought up every piece of bad paper you've signed. The only thing you own now is your boots and your bullfrog belt buckle. The two of you have blackmailed the last penny you're ever going to get out of Betty." It hadn't taken too long digging through bank records to discover that Betty was broke, her money, I assumed, shoveled into the failed deals that her uncle, even after looting her trusts, had funded with blackmail. He wasn't just broke, he was about to sink. The IRS wasn't looking at me but at him. I had already started the paperwork to take the Lodge away from him. "I figure you planned it this way, you old fucker," I continued. "You thought that because Betty and I were the beneficiaries of Tom Ben's will, if I was killed with her piece, she would be convicted and couldn't benefit, and it would all kick back to you. You just hired the wrong help." The silence was louder than the rising south wind. The only sound, Sissy Duval's sobbing. I dug under my cast for the wooden blade.

"You fucking people were all there that night, when Mandy Rae Quarrels dropped the hammer on Dwayne Duval," I began to explain.

But the crippled old woman in the wheelchair interrupted with a grunt, then growled, her voice deep and ruined by the exploding chemicals of a heroin cooker. She nodded toward Betty, "It was her, there. Little Miss Priss. She'd be the fuckin' chick dropped that second hammer, 'cause ol' Dwayne wouldn't stop running his one-eyed snake up her dirt track," she cackled. "Little bitch loved it. Loved it so much she had to kill sweet Dwayne—just like she gunned down her little nigger boy toy that time before."

Betty's face was stunned to tears, and Cathy turned to clutch her shaking shoulders.

"Well, I guess that's how the cow ate the corn," I said to no one in particular, completely blindsided.

The crippled woman swept the shawl off her legs, cursed in Cajun French, and raised a stubby submachine pistol—a suppressed Mac-10—with her scarred hands. The first unaimed sweeping burst scattered everybody around the deck. Except for me and my Corsican keeper. In those arrested moments before the gunfire began, that long moment when nobody moves because nobody believes it's going to happen, I had slammed my shiv under the bodyguard's chin, six inches of sharp cedar. Which was almost a mistake. All I did was knock out his false teeth. Somebody else had shot the real ones out. But the limber dagger of Hill Country cedar bent when it hit his lower plate, then drove through his tongue into the back of his throat. He was too busy strangling on his blood to bother with me as I tried to tear his mini-Uzi off the shoulder strap.

The bodyguard at the far corner went for his piece, but the kids came through just as I had asked. *It's not a man,* I had told them over and over, *it's a target.* I had drilled it into their heads. Bob's round blew out the glass panel, then CJ's round sliced through the little guy's body armor and dropped him into a shapeless puddle. Then they took out the one in the middle of the deck the same way.

As I struggled to untangle the Uzi from the bodyguard's shoulder strap, the second burst from the wheelchair was more controlled. A burst sprayed at Lomax as he dove under the table. His thumb popped off, flying through the sunshine like a cocktail frank. The table where Betty and Cathy sat caught the burst thrown at them. Then rounds popped over my head and exploded the glass walls behind me.

Betty rose long enough to throw her empty piece at the woman in the wheelchair, which bought me a second. I slipped behind the bodyguard, catching a quick glimpse of Mandy Rae's ruined face. She looked as if I was the first target she had missed in her entire life. And now she'd missed me three times. Her glittering mad eyes said she wasn't about to miss again.

I got behind the thick chest of the dying bodyguard as the next burst thudded into his Kevlar vest. Amanda Rae Quarrels didn't get another chance. The bodyguard's Uzi was in my hands now. Two three-round bursts dead center into the thorax area. The first ones shattered the stamped metal of the submachine gun so badly that Mandy Rae might as well have been holding a live grenade to her chest. My other rounds punched through the bloody chest, banging into the metal back of the wheelchair, driving it backward. The chair gathered momentum slowly as it drifted down the wooden ramp. It paused, then rolled across the hard-packed sand into the flat waves of the Gulf. Where once again it paused, as if for effect, then tilted its shapeless burden into the gray water. The wild-ass country girl had cut her last caper.

With both his partners down, the other guard quickly threw his hands into the air in surrender. His boss was dead. He was two thousand miles from home. The rest of the crowd, trapped by lies and foolishness long past, rose slowly, shadowed by the passing clouds. They just stayed there, too, as I swept the Uzi barrel across the group and focused on Wallingford, who slithered toward the house, Sissy held in front of him like a shield. But when I locked the barrel on

Lomax, he just stared at me, his right hand clamped over the bleeding stump of his left thumb, staring without a flinch.

"You've never been closer to death, man, than you are this second," I said, then lowered the barrel.

"I know," he said, still not flinching. "Thanks."

"You fucking people were all there that night," I said to everybody else. "One of you cowards better have the fucking guts to get Dickie Oates out of prison . . ." I stopped. What could I threaten these people with that they hadn't already done to themselves? I raised the submachine gun at Lomax again. "Do it."

He nodded. I stopped long enough to empty the magazine into the sky—just about the only fun I had that day—then I tossed the ugly little weapon over the glass wall, and walked away.

As I passed Betty, she took off her glasses to look me angrily in the eyes. But it had no effect. She had crossed that final border where betrayal becomes a way of life. Off to that final country from which no one ever returns. The country of lies. I almost told her that if she had told me the truth from the beginning, everything would have been different. But it would have been a waste of time. Cathy looked at me, too, but her eyes were full of death.

When I walked past the former Amanda Rae Quarrels, the shallow waves had ruined her. Ribbons of blood mixed with swirls of black dye and soft drifts of moving sand. She could have been a dead sea creature or a living tar ball, she could have been coming or going. I tossed the crumpled option into the water, watched it unfold, watched my note wash off the paper.

When did you find out you had married your fifteen-year-old daughter?

Amanda Rae Quarrels might be dead but her revenge lived on. I hawked up something from the back of my throat, something that tasted like bear spit. But I kept it to myself.

A FINAL WORD

I F JUSTICE WERE TO BE DONE, I guess, they would all be in prison. But it didn't happen that way. As usual, the innocent suffer; the evil of greed lives on past all belief. Everything disappeared behind Hayden Lomax's rich influences. Nobody's in jail. And nobody's disappeared except for Sissy Duval. She had stashed enough of Betty's money to hide somewhere in Brazil. At least Richard Wylie Oates is out of prison. He's home, farming. The Herreras were delighted to agree to my terms to buy the bar. Richie and Renfro are running the Lodge for me, turning it into a world-class B&B, *the* place for same-sex marriages in that part of the world. Travis Lee is out of business, out of any kind of business, stuffed into a retirement home in Georgetown, living on my charity, which he probably hates as much as he does sitting in his own shit every day. They say nobody ever visits. They say he's dying. Slowly and painfully, I hope.

Afterward, the kids and I melted the rifles into scrap, cleaned up what we could, and burned the rest. They're married now. Bob is copping in Gunnison, Colorado. CJ is pregnant, going to college at Western to get a teaching degree. I gave the bride away at the wedding at the top of a summer ski slope in Telluride, then sent them on a honeymoon to Paris. The ten days didn't ruin them for middle-class American life, but it surely changed the way they looked at it. I wish I had gone along when they invited me. I've never been to Paris. With a bit more luck, Molly and I might have made it to the City of Lights.

These days I feel a bit more like a human being. Ever since the moment I donated all the money my ex-partner and I had stolen from the *contrabandistas* to the International Red Cross. I didn't realize that money had much meaning until I gave a bunch of it away. I also paid the taxes on my father's blighted inheritance, which still left me with enough clean money to behave badly, or at least as badly as an old man can afford, as long as I want.

I'm back in the bar business again, sort of. I bought a little place from a couple of aimless Brits within walking distance of the waterfront in Belize City, a warm, placid place rife with friendly strangers, run-down, colorful, and forgiving. I live in a hotel room. Another place that isn't mine. That's the way it has to be now. I've searched the country fairly thoroughly for another copy of the Shark of the Moon. Without success. Sometimes love works that way.

The grass widow, Sherry, told me that rumor says Betty and Cathy came to a parting of the ways. Betty shares her ranch with a religious woman now. Maybe she has found a religion herself, one that forgives pathological lying and murder. Cathy has taken her act to California. I don't know what to think about that. Or what to say. Sherry's divorced now and for a while she'd fly down and sleep with me. Until we realized that we were holding hands more than making love. Petey and Carver D have visited a couple of times from Boston. Petey's kicking ass at Harvard, which is a perfect revenge for a kid born to unreconstructed hippies in an alley in Austin. Carver D is happy, as funny sober as he was drunk, a gift I suspect I sorely lack. My ex-partner came down for a few days of bonefishing, but a hurricane was brewing, so we just had a few drinks, and a small conversation.

"Shit, man, you didn't come out too badly," he said. "The kids are happy, and the farm boy is riding his tractor."

I begged to differ. "Let's look at it this way, old buddy," I said.

"I discovered that the woman I loved had lied to me endlessly and unnecessarily, had murdered at least two men. For good reasons, perhaps, but murdered them nonetheless. My business partner turned out to be as crooked as a snake's asshole. I killed a cop and a district attorney, broke a fat woman's hand, beat the shit out of a one-armed man, and got the man I meant to keep out of prison killed. Shot a woman in a wheelchair. And God-fucking-dammit, I got Molly killed, too."

"You never could look on the bright side of things, could you, Milo?"

"The children of suicides seldom do, buddy," I said. "So leave it the fuck alone." We sat silent for a long time, then I relented. "The wind's calm as a nun's breath," I said, "but watch the swells. They've doubled in size the past hour. A big blow's a-coming."

He stood up, stretched like a man heading for his hotel, sighed, "Come see us this fall."

"I'm going to Paris," I lied, and he walked away without looking back.

It's done. This may not be my final country. I can still taste the bear in the back of my throat, bitter with the blood of the innocent, and somewhere in my old heart I can still remember the taste of love. Perhaps this is just a resting place. A warm place to drink cold beer. But wherever my final country is, my ashes will go back to Montana when I die. Maybe I've stopped looking for love. Maybe not. Maybe I will go to Paris. Who knows? But I'll sure as hell never go back to Texas again.